Ultima Skylar

By

Omayra Vélez

Second Edition

Copyright

Ultima Skylar
Copyright © 2021, Omayra Vélez, all rights reserved to include the cover design. No part of this book may wholly, or in part, in any form, by any electronic or mechanical means, including within information storage and retrieval systems, without permission in writing from the author be copied or reproduced. Exceptionally, reviewers may quote brief passages not exceeding 0.5% of the whole which may be pertinent to their reviews.

Library of Congress Cataloging-in-Publication Data

Names: Vélez, Omayra, author. Ultima Skylar/Omayra Vélez
Description: Florida: [2021]
Identifiers: ISBN 978-1-7364473-0-7 (paperback first edition),
ISBN 978-1-7364473-4-5 (paperback second edition),
ISBN 978-1-7364473-8-3 (hardback second edition),
ISBN 978-1-7364473-1-4 (eBooks)
Subjects: Tsestelago, Yakuta, and Behui Kingdoms (Imaginary Places)–Fiction. | Fantasy Fiction. | Romance fiction. | BISAC: FICTION / Fantasy / Romance | FICTION / Action & Adventure. | FICTION / Fantasy / Romance / Action / Adventure.
Classification: LCC TXu 2-249-203 Omayra Vélez Publisher
Second Edition LCC TX 9-056-088 Omayra Vélez Publisher

eBook ISBN 978-1-7364473-1-4

www.omayra-velez.com

Dedication

To Elsa Luciano, thank you for teaching me English and making sure I was ready for life.

Map of the Kingdom of Tsestelago

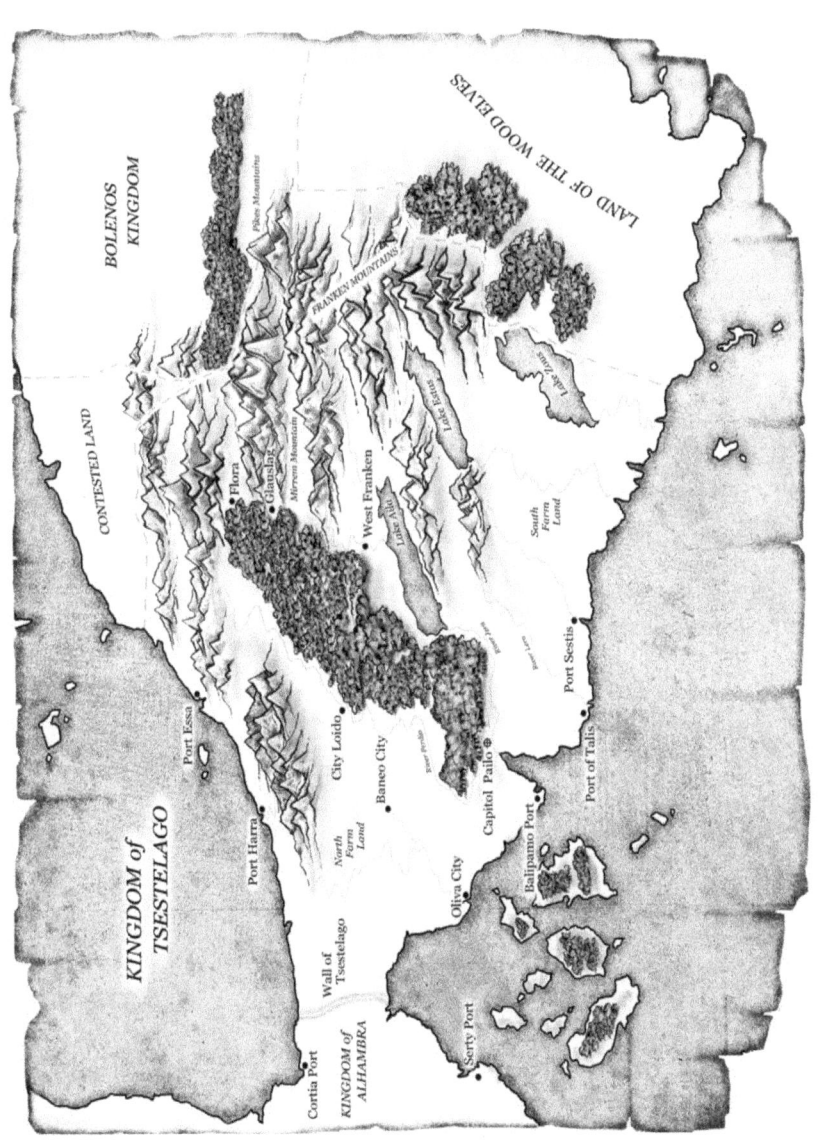

Table of Contents

ULTIMA SKYLAR	I
COPYRIGHT	II
DEDICATION	III
MAP OF THE KINGDOM OF TSESTELAGO	V
CHAPTER 1	3
This Can't Be Happening	
CHAPTER 2	13
Clients, Visitors, and Demons	
CHAPTER 3	21
The Broken Exotic	
CHAPTER 4	30
The Bachelor Party	
CHAPTER 5	46
The Party	
CHAPTER 6	62
The Fox Hunt	
CHAPTER 7	71
A Foreigner Came to Visit	
CHAPTER 8	80
One Dead, Two Free	
CHAPTER 9	88
Ultima's New Trade	
CHAPTER 10	98
One Fool	
CHAPTER 11	108
Take Away and Give Away	
CHAPTER 12	118
Masters and Helpers	
CHAPTER 13	128
A New Hightower	
CHAPTER 14	140
Training Session	
CHAPTER 15	148
You Can Be More	
CHAPTER 16	156
The Train Ride	
CHAPTER 17	168
Dinner and a Story	
CHAPTER 18	177

Wardrobe, Armor and a Lesson	
CHAPTER 19	186
On Our Way to War	
CHAPTER 20	196
The Battle at Pikes Mountain	
CHAPTER 21	211
The Days After the Battle	
CHAPTER 22	223
Unfaithful	
CHAPTER 23	235
On the Way Back to West Franken	
CHAPTER 24	250
Otto or Soren	
CHAPTER 25	263
Are We Riding Horses to Pailo?	
CHAPTER 26	272
Captives	
CHAPTER 27	282
The Boleños	
CHAPTER 28	293
When Men Talk, Women Roll Their Eyes	
CHAPTER 29	307
Evil in His Home	
CHAPTER 30	318
Mage Training	
CHAPTER 31	329
The Return to the Trade	
CHAPTER 32	339
Old Clients	
CHAPTER 33	351
When Persecuted, We Run	
CHAPTER 34	365
Wrong Assumptions	
CHAPTER 35	377
The Prince, Queen, and King	
CHAPTER 36	384
The Dead Sing	

"Never let your memories make you sad, let your memories make you wiser." Amparo Feal

CHAPTER 1

This Can't Be Happening

"Your Royal Highness, before we start, I need to make you aware of some rules. The first one is, the mask stays on until you shout in passion," said Exotic Ultima. Under her signature mask, her almond-shaped blue eyes twinkled; her mouth turned up slightly at the corners in a familiar smirk so characteristic of the woman. She looked upon Prince Marco as she would any other man or woman she had serviced through the years, with sarcasm.

"You do know I'm Prince Marco? I cannot believe you are giving me, the Crown Regent of Tsestelago, rules. A fine gift Abernathy has given me for my thirty-fifth birthday," said the swaying man, holding a glass of liquor—half-full—in one hand, the other hanging onto one post of the four-poster bed, trying not to fall. The large room held many antique pieces of furniture, and several tapestries depicting ancient wars hung on the walls.

"A million apologies, my Prince," said Ultima, gently moving her hair away from her face. "I'm considered the best Exotic in the entire kingdom. I've been a full Exotic for many years, and during all that time, the Trades Office has required me to say this. Maybe when you are King, things will change." Ultima smiled at the Prince Regent.

"Continue, Exotic, what are your rules?" said Marco, drinking even more liquor.

"The next rule is simple—please don't hit my face. My complexion must stay the same as when I arrived." Ultima took off her coat and laid it over a chair. That night she was dressed in a black bustier and a form-fitting skirt with a slit opened to her hip. She pulled a few laces from her bustier, revealing her cleavage. Prince Marco smiled, just like all others before him who liked what they saw. Ultima, a renowned Exotic, knew how to entice her clients.

"So, I'm beginning to see why everyone I know calls you the most beautiful and exquisitely trained Exotic in the entire Kingdom of Tsestelago," said Marco.

"Oh, thank you, my Prince! I'm surprised you haven't met me sooner."

"I'm the Prince Regent and have been a happily married man for many years. I don't have time to go looking for Exotics."

"Oh, I know tonight is a special occasion," said Ultima.

"Cheeky woman, you are only here because my best friend, the Duke of Abernathy, wanted to give me a special gift, so he got me you! I've been a little stressed with my duties. So, my friend wanted me to relax and enjoy my birthday."

"I'm honored to celebrate your birthday. It should be a national holiday, my Prince. That way all your loyal subjects could … celebrate with you," said Ultima, raising her arms in the air and swaying her hips closer to Prince Marco.

"Oh, you are delicate; I'm listening," said Prince Marco, reclining against the bedpost. Ultima inched closer, knowing what anticipation did to her clients. The cold room made the hair on her arms stand on edge, and her nipples perk up. Her golden earrings dangled and her matching rings made a slight noise every time she moved her fingers.

"I see our Prince likes to entertain his women in cold rooms," said Ultima, reaching him and laying her palms on his chest.

"I like what the cold air does to women." The prince wore a red and black smock and black pants. Ultima could tell the man was getting aroused.

"Next rule, if you turn your face from me, or I feel you don't like my touch, we are done and I will leave." Ultima took the prince's hand and walked with him to a chair close to an open window. The prince tried to touch her soft skin, but Ultima held his hands.

"I've never seen a woman of your color. You are so pale," said the Prince, pulling his hand from Ultima's hold and touching her arms with his fingertips.

"I take very little sun," said Ultima.

"You take very little sun. Why?" asked the Prince.

"I'm an Exotic slave. My work is mostly at night. I rarely entertain anyone during the day," said Ultima.

"Something so beautiful should never be caged." He went to hold her neck.

"Not yet, I'm not done with the rules." She kissed him and nuzzled him into the chair and stood away. She removed her skirt and stood in front of the prince, still in her tight, provocative inner clothing. The gasless lanterns stood on the bedside tables on either side of the bed. The golden brothel insignia adorning her arms glimmered in the light as she moved.

"The fourth rule is simple. Please, my Prince, don't hold or pull my collar. I enjoy having air in my lungs, and I must leave as I arrived here tonight. This—" as she pointed to her inner leg, "is my pain threshold." So saying, she moved her leg, the better to display her tattoo by the side of her groin, showing the level of pain she could endure.

She moved her leg back down, walked to the prince's side, and took off her bustier, letting it drop to the floor. Her breasts, now fully revealed, showed her Exotic mark on her left breast, which further defined the prostitute courtesan-tattoo on her right arm. She approached Prince Marco, took a chair, and sat in front of him, placing one of her legs over Prince Marco's leg. The prince kissed her, and Ultima took his hands and placed them over her breasts.

♦♦♦

As the pair kissed, starting a night of lustful desires, a dark figure dressed in a black leather suit entered stealthily via the open window. He stood in the shadows a second or two and looked at the beauty in the arms of the Regent of the Kingdom, then scurried over to the pair, grabbed the prince's dark-blond hair, pulled, and slit his throat from ear to ear. And that was the last kiss Prince Marco ever gave. His blue eyes opened wide, looked up, and saw the eyes of the one who killed him. Did he know the man with the knife? Only he knew, and he wasn't talking. If he knew the name of his murderer, he took the identity to his grave.

♦♦♦

Ultima's eyes sprang open and she started to scream, but her scream was muffled by a spray of blood. As the neck of Prince Marco was slit open, a fountain erupted, and the life-giving liquid drenched the Exotic woman of the night. Bathed with the blood of a royal man, she was baptized and anointed. Face stunned, mouth full of blood, eyes full of fear—she screamed.

"HELP, FIRE!" A slap of panic showed on the Exotic's face. The hooded man grabbed her neck with both his hands to silence her. She placed her hands under his grip and opened her hands wide to release his hold. Then, with open palm, punched him hard on his nose. He staggered back and touched his face with the back of his wrist.

"Bitch, you'll be dead in minutes. Sad that I must kill such a beautiful woman," said the man. His black leather made him seem like a panther ready to strike. She pushed the chair back, stood up, and tried to run. However, despite a little stumble, he lurched forward, grabbed her, and pushed her down to the floor. He kicked her leg in anger, breaking it. She spat out some blood that had splattered in her mouth and screamed in pain. He went to kick her in the stomach but missed, giving Ultima the opening to kick up into his groin with her uninjured leg.

He stumbled back.

"AAAAHHHHH, you bitch," shouted the assassin, grabbing his groin and doubling over in pain, giving her a moment to bellow as best she could with her naturally soprano voice.

"FIRE, FIRE! PLEASE, HELP US. THE PRINCE IS DEAD! FIRE. FIRE. HELP, COME HELP!" Xawata had trained her to scream *fire* if she ever found herself in a situation where the men were hurting her or using her in ways outside her trade license. Blood covered her face and chest, her hair matted with the red royal blood, but her mask was still in place. With her remaining uninjured leg, she kicked out again and connected with his knee, making him stumble, and then she squiggled and rolled behind a small table.

"Come out here," said the assassin, walking toward the Exotic.

"NO, FIRE, HELP!" shouted Ultima.

"You're going to die!" said the assassin.

The guards arrived, flinging open the door; the assassin looked once at the guards, then ran to the window leaving bloody footsteps in his wake. He turned to look back at the Exotic beauty and the guards.

"I'll get you," said the assassin in a ragged voice, pointing at Ultima, and jumped out the window, down into the river that ran below.

The man had worn a black face mask, and she had only been able to see the color of his eyes, brown, but she saw his trade-tattoo. The man had been a warrior. And she'd felt it: he had magic. He had shown no emotion when he jumped out the window. Just as those thoughts ran riot through her mind, Ultima collapsed on the floor, the traumatic events having sapped all her energy.

♦♦♦

In an instant, guards stormed the room. Ultima, naked from the waist up, very little covering her lady parts, lay on the rug, covered in royal blood, and heaved. Ultima survived, despite the broken leg and the excruciating pain that came with it. Tears followed. In the past, she'd had clients die on her while in bed in the middle of a passionate sexual moment. She had clients who had died after a night of quiet, lulling cuddling in their old age, but this was the cold-blooded slaying of a man.

They had seen the assassin jump out the window but regardless, the guards came at her, pulling her from the floor and manhandling her.

"You must have helped the killer assassinate our Prince," said one guard. Even in her dazed state, this seemed a little far-fetched to Ultima. She was a little woman of barely five feet nothing, and the prince was strong—five-foot-ten, a powerful man in the prime of his life, celebrating his thirty-fifth birthday. However, the guard who removed Ultima's mask saw the opportunity to touch and grope the famous Exotic Ultima Skylar—at least until the Commander of the Guards, Lord Baxter, arrived. Ultima's owner Xawata Faan ran into the chamber next and saw his most precious, expensive Exotic broken in the hands of a guard.

"What happened here?" asked Lord Baxter, a barely dressed, tall, black man. It was late at night, and by his smell and appearance, he too was enjoying one of Xawata's courtesans.

"The Prince is dead; we saw the assassin jump out the window. This Exotic is still alive. She must have helped the murderer," said one guard.

"Oh my, Ultima, my sweet darling, what happened? Where is your mask?" asked Xawata. He picked up Ultima's cloak, wrapped her in it and took her in his arms, not letting any more guards touch her. Upon realizing her leg was broken, he pulled up a chair and gently sat her down.

"A man came out of nowhere and slit his throat." Ultima's voice was barely audible. "Master, the man tried to kill me as well. He broke my leg. The guard took my mask off," said Ultima in a whisper. Her face turned pale, and her hurt expression made her look younger. She turned away and vomited what little she had left in her stomach.

"Lord Baxter, look at our Prince; this is horrible. There is too much blood here. I'm going to be sick, and my poor, broken Exotic needs care. She won't be able to work like this. What will my clients say? I must take my Exotic and get her a healer," said Xawata, pacing and waving his hands about every which way. The old man shuffled to the left, then back to the right, shaking his head and covering his eyes every time he walked toward where the prince's body lay.

"Xawata, I think you are more concerned about what this is going to do to your Exotic and the reputation of your business than the well-being of the nation," said Baxter.

"I'm just a merchant, not a soldier." Xawata took out a handkerchief and covered his mouth.

"Exotic Ultima, did you recognize the man that killed Prince Marco?" asked Commander Baxter.

"No, I only noticed what happened once the prince was already dead. We were kissing, and I had my eyes closed. Afterward, there was blood everywhere," said Ultima.

I can't tell them about the magic the man had. They will find out about my magic. How is this possible? He killed him in cold blood and so fast. Blood, so much blood ... I must hide. He may come back. My leg ... Ultima's thoughts rambled, repeating some scenes in her head over and over again, thinking of new ones.

"When you opened your eyes, did you see something, anything?"

"I can't remember much. I fought him," said Ultima, with her eyes closed.

"When you fought him, perhaps you saw his face then?" suggested the Commander.

"It happened so fast. The man's head was covered with a hood and his face with a cloth; when he first grabbed the prince, I opened my eyes in surprise and got a face full of blood, including in my eyes, but—when I fought him—his sleeve pulled up. I saw a little of his arm. He was a white man with brown eyes, and I think he had a warrior's tattoo with an added animal-related skill. That is all I remember, truly." Ultima's injured leg made her head swim and she almost lost consciousness several times.

"I feel faint," said Ultima, and she almost fell off her chair, but Xawata ran back to her and held her in place.

Xawata's servants hovered in the background, as they usually did when he let his Exotics service outside the brothel. And just as Xawata tried to prop her up, Orrun, one of Xawata's servants entered and took Ultima in his arms as if she was his baby. And another man entered the room at a run, his gray hair tossed in every direction, smelling like sex and whiskey. He, too, had been enjoying one of Xawata's courtesans, maybe. He pushed the guards out of his way and shouted.

"For all the gods in Yavos, Baxter, look at the Regent! This isn't possible! Has anyone told the King?" Archimage Saigai demanded as he entered the room. He carried on speaking to no one in particular but to the room in general, "No, no, this isn't possible. Today was his birthday. Princess Harriet will die when she finds out. Prince Marco—so much blood, I'm going to be sick!" He covered his mouth and mumbled from behind his hand, "This will kill his mother. And his wife is so young …"

"Saigai, we just got here. She was the Exotic in the room with him, and she witnessed the murder," said Commander Baxter.

"What? Did you interrogate her?" asked Saigai, standing with his hands on his hips.

"Yes, I asked all the questions, but one thing at a time. I'll send word to the King in a minute," said Baxter.

"Who did this? You must find who did this." Saigai looked at Ultima in Orrun's arms.

"Did she see his face? She must have helped the assassin. You're not going to let her go?" said Saigai, raising his thin arms and his voice.

"She is a well-known Exotic, and the assassin tried to kill her as well," said Commander Baxter, exasperated.

"My Lords, I must take my Exotic and provide her with proper care. She has great value to me. If you need to ask more questions, you know the location of my establishment. I'll take all my other girls, but I'll give you both an hour of services on another day. However, you must come to my establishment. You understand, I'm sure—I must protect my girls," said Xawata.

Ultima heard Archimage Saigai continue to argue with Baxter over letting her go as she was carried away. Ultima feared Xawata's reaction once they reached the brothel, but this wasn't her fault. She did her job, and all else was out of her control. As they left the castle, she lost consciousness once more, cradled in the arms of Orrun, Xawata's personal slave.

♦♦♦

The stench of rotten eggs and seagrass accompanied the wet, hooded man who walked through the gathering hall of the enormous castle. Darkness blanketed every corner of the room, lit only by a few candles mounted on tall candlesticks that stood on the polished floor, giving a flickering light. His black leather stuck to his slim body, and his boots left evidence of his every step. The glacial silence was interrupted by the echo of his footsteps. He walked with the stride of confidence and the precision of someone used to marching with a group.

"Hello, drifter! I know the prince is dead, but tell me what happened," said the man smoking a cigarette in the shadows. The wet man stood still in the middle of the hall.

"I carried out the hit as you paid me to do, but the woman with him wasn't a soft target as she was supposed to be. I thought you said she was an Exotic?"

"She is an Exotic," said the smoking man.

"This Exotic almost made me vomit my balls," said the assassin.

"I thought you were a fighter. We paid for her elimination," grumbled the man from the shadows.

"Yes, I know, but that Exotic had warrior skills. She knew how to fight. I got him, but before I could finish her, the guards entered. She lives," said the wet man.

"Did you blow your cover? Did she see your face?" Irritated, the man in the shadows threw his cigarette down in the middle of the hall.

"No, I kept my face covered the entire time," said the wet man, taking his gloves off.

"I heard she saw your trade-tattoo. You cut that loose end and do it soon. I already paid you for the job," said the smoking man.

"I know, but you lied. That Exotic was skilled." The wet man dropped his gloves on the floor and removed the top of his leather armor.

"And you are a professional assassin and warrior," he said by way of reprimand. "Now, you have two new targets," said the man in the shadows.

"Who?"

"Grand Duke of Hausman and Prince Soren are your next targets. We will give you instructions on who to target first. And don't forget about the Exotic woman, but wait a few weeks on the woman and make it seem like an accident," said the man in the shadows.

"I'll get started on the next two," said the wet man.

"You must write a full report of what happened with Prince Marco," whispered the man in the shadows.

"Stop. Before you go, you must pay for these new assignments. And I want to know who—" As the wet man was talking, he had been walking to where the man in the shadows was standing. Once he got to the place where the shadow man was hiding, he found no one. Only the stubs of several cigarettes remained.

CHAPTER 2

Clients, Visitors, and Demons

Xawata found it difficult to keep pace with his servant, Orrun, who strode quickly despite his carrying Ultima. They hurried back to Xawata's brothel and into Ultima's rooms, where he gently laid her on her bed. Although Ultima had woken in Orrun's arms on the way there, she only opened her eyes once she felt the delicious coolness of her own rooms. He called none other than the registered Healer Goren before leaving the castle, and the man appeared at the brothel soon after they arrived. Little Akina was in the room, and she helped take off what little clothing her mother Ultima had left.

A servant escorted Healer Goren to Ultima's room, where he worked on her injuries right away.

"Oh, my Exotic is so broken," said Xawata when he saw Ultima's naked body.

"I'll do the best I can, but she will be in pain for a few days, maybe weeks." As Healer Goren administered his magic to Ultima's leg, Ultima realized the man was caressing her leg and admiring the beauty he was healing.

"I'll leave some medicine for her to take at night to help her sleep," said Healer Goren.

"My steward will pay you in my office. Thank you, Healer Goren," said Xawata. He turned to his servant, "Orrun, escort the healer to my office."

Once the healer finished setting Ultima's leg and providing the healing she required, the man placed his things in his bag and left the room. Now alone, Xawata started to question his prized possession.

"Ultima, who bruised your body? Look at your stomach and your leg. Who bruised you, the prince or the assassin?" Xawata was standing by her fireplace.

"It was the assassin. The prince had barely touched me."

"Damn! I can't charge the Duke of Abernathy more for your injuries. You know I can't give you many days of rest. We must make-up what I lost tonight." He turned to Akina and his voice suddenly took on a childish note, "And you … you will make sure your momma does all she needs to do to get healthy fast. You hear me, young lady?" said Xawata. He turned back to Ultima, voice changing again to something more hateful, "And you, do what you can to help yourself heal faster. Use your magic but as always keep it hidden."

The old man left the room, and Akina stayed behind. Ultima felt sorry for her daughter and love of her heart, little Akina. Her obnoxious owner had ordered her to train the child, from the tender age of three, to be an Exotic. The girl was growing up to be appealing to the eye with her slight body, clear complexion, black hair, and her deep-green eyes.

However, little Akina and Ultima shared a secret. Ultima was an unregistered healer mage and Akina an unregistered arcane mage, a summoner, and illusionist. Mother and daughter kept each other's secrets.

"Momma, I hate Xawata. That man treats you poorly," said Akina.

"Love, please never say that outside this room or to anyone else," said Ultima, trying to stretch her back.

"You still need more healing than the meager care that man gave you. I hate I'm not a healer mage," said Akina.

"We all have our gifts, Akina. I wish I were an illusionist," said Ultima, caressing the girl's face.

"I don't know how to use my magic, Momma," said Akina.

"Not yet, but you will soon. I'll get you a teacher to give you lessons behind Xawata's back. There has to be a mage that would take me as payment for lessons for you and keep it a secret," said Ultima.

"Momma, I wish we could leave this place. Xawata is a mean master," said Akina.

"I know, love, but you must never say these words to anyone in this house. We are slaves, and this is where we live. Little by little, I've been selling all I get as gratuities and saving my coin. We just need to wait nine more years for me to become a Prime Exotic. Then I can make my own coin. Once I do, I'll have enough coin to buy you from Xawata, but for now you need to go and practice your dance," said Ultima, resting her head on her pillow.

"You look tired," said Akina.

"I want to sleep for eternity. Would it be too much to ask for one free night away from this place? I'm so tired of parties, balls, hunts, and gatherings. I don't know how much longer my body can take this level of work," said Ultima from her bed.

Akina had left the potion the healer gave her on top of the dresser. Ultima used her magic to make it levitate and come to her hand. The potion was supposed to help her go to sleep.

"I wish I could move objects at will," said Akina.

"You know I can only move small objects," said Ultima.

"It doesn't matter; it's a nice magic to have," said Akina, standing up and getting a glass of water for her mother.

♦♦♦

There was considerable unrest in the kingdom. The assassination of the kingdom's Regent, Prince Marco, had been a shock for the King's subjects. Prince Soren, the King's second son, fought with the kingdom's army on the battlefront. The late-Prince Regent's oldest son was an eleven-year-old boy, Prince Leer. He also had one young daughter named Princess Joy-Anna, twin to Leer, but they were both born powerful elemental mages.

King Trevino had lost the firmness of his muscles and the pep from his walk. His health had deteriorated in the last years, and he had passed most of the kingdom's running on to his son, Marco.

"Your Royal Highness, we sent word to Prince Soren to return to the capital immediately," said Archimage Saigai, smoking his cigarette.

"I don't want to leave my grandson, Prince Leer, as King of the Tsestelago Kingdom. He and his twin sister Joy-Anna are mages—and just children of eleven years. They are not suitable to rule," said King Trevino to his war council and commanders. His brown eyes settled on his commanders, but whether they saw any detail was unknown. There was an opaqueness that suggested otherwise. He had lacked energy for months, even though he was only in his early sixties.

"Abernathy, I know you said it was a bad idea to let Prince Soren command the fighting in our war with the Kingdom of Boleña. Now you have got your way. I can't do anything but call him back," said the King.

"The last we heard of Prince Soren's men was a week ago. Our sources said that the fighting has mostly been waged in the vicinity of the Pikes Mountains, in the northeast," said the Duke of Abernathy.

"Those mountains have been ours for over two hundred years; why these Boleños keep fighting for our land is a mystery," said Archimage Saigai.

"There have been problems communicating with the troops," said the Duke of Abernathy.

"Prince Soren is only nine minutes younger than Prince Marco, but he was not trained to rule a nation. Although they are twins, we trained Soren to command an army. My King, your son will need a lot of training," said the Duke of Horrel.

"Your son is a man of war, a powerful warrior, a leader of soldiers, but he isn't married and thus has no heirs, and he's not prepared to rule a kingdom. Maybe we should take Prince Leer and start training him to rule," said the Division Commander, General Cauldron.

"No, Leer is a mage. You know mages can't be kings. Soren must come back to the capital now. We will make him my Regent whether he likes it or not. He's a royal prince in the line of succession; I will not tolerate anyone speaking ill of my son," said the King.

"I sent the message the moment you made the request last night, my King," said Commander Baxter.

"For the last three hundred years, there has always been an Otarana King in Tsestelago. I will not allow one of these scheming nobles from any other kingdom to come and take our throne. I want the man who assassinated Marco captured alive; dead, only if there's no other option," said King Trevino.

"Your Majesty, the assassin left the Exotic alive, but she had very little information," Archimage Saigai said with his arms crossed.

"I don't care who she is. Baxter must make her talk. She has to know something," said the King.

"There is talk that the assassin could be part of a guild of mercenaries and pirates, based on the trade-tattoo the Exotic described," said Baxter.

"I suggest you call the dukes and maybe have them and a few of your commanders take a more active role in dealing with the people. They must have a stronger hold on the people. Fear always makes peasants talk," said Archimage Saigai.

"This is my kingdom, and we are going to follow my laws. In the meantime, you have the protection of Prince Leer and Princess Joy-Anna to ensure, until Prince Soren arrives from the northern lands. If they die, you die! Do you hear me?" said the King.

"Yes, my King," said Saigai, snuffing his cigarette in a nearby ashtray.

King Trevino stood up and stared down at Commander Baxter. "If Prince Soren never makes it back to Tsestelago or anything prevents Prince Leer or Princess Joy-Anna getting out of the nursery, I will make sure all the soldiers guarding them wish for death. I will have them all thrown in a pit of fire. And that is an order, Baxter," said the King, before storming out of his war room looking for his wife, Queen Elenore.

❖❖❖

Three days passed, and Ultima was still in pain despite the trickle of healing she kept self-administering to reduce the bruises on her stomach and broken leg. Healer Goren came to visit her one more time to give her a second session of healing magic. However, it was her mind that needed the most soothing and she couldn't rest. Each night she had nightmares of a man entering her room and attacking her. An older servant had placed a sofa in her bedroom for Orrun to sleep upon in her private room some nights, while Akina slept with Ultima in her bed. At least this enabled her to fall asleep.

Her leg was mending, but Xawata wouldn't give her much time to rest. Xawata said he would only give Ultima a week of free time to recuperate from her broken leg. After that time, he said she would have to work. She was nervous to return to work, as she expected to be assaulted at any moment. She feared that one of her clients would turn and slit her throat. She had to keep receiving clients, even with an injured leg. However, Healer Goren told Xawata she couldn't perform any services that required her to stand for another three weeks, and she couldn't dance for another three months.

Nevertheless, a day later, early in the morning, a young servant entered Ultima's room quietly.

"M'lady Ultima, please wake. Wake up. I'm sorry to interrupt your rest," said the young woman.

"What is it?" asked Ultima in a sleepy voice, lifting her head from her pillow.

"Why are you waking us so early?" said little Akina in her childlike voice.

"I'm sorry. Commander Baxter—the one that guards the King—he's here to talk to m'lady Ultima," said the servant.

"And this couldn't wait until the brothel was open for business tonight? Wretched man!" Ultima dropped her head back on her pillow.

"He is here now with a warrant," said the servant insistently.

"Fine, go down and tell Xawata and the commander I'll be down in thirty minutes." She nudged her daughter, "Akina, get up and get ready for your classes."

That morning, her mending leg had her in so much discomfort that Ultima asked Orrun to carry her to the receiving parlor. Xawata insisted she dress in expensive lace dresses he provided, but this early in the morning, she wore just a night shift and a robe. Besides, Commander Baxter had already seen her almost naked.

When she entered the room, Xawata was already in the parlor in his night robe, looking like a Palermo rooster with his white hair all up on end. Ultima was seated on a chair, while Xawata stood by her, caressing her neck, but holding a golden leash attached to her golden collar.

"Good morning, Commander Baxter. It's been four days since the prince's murder. What is so important that it couldn't wait for the business hours of the brothel?" asked Xawata.

"Commander, please forgive us, but we keep night hours," she spoke with a gentle and lovely voice. Her delicate manner gave no hint of emotion other than concern for her master.

"Well, the King requested a report, and this morning was the only time I had available. I need to report to the King within the next day," said the Commander, straightening his uniform. The man stood a foot taller than Xawata.

"Fine, ask your questions. We must return to our sleep. My beauty, Ultima, needs her rest." Xawata caressed Ultima's face, but he pulled hard on her leash, forcing her to sit up tall and back straight.

"Exotic Ultima, did you remember any other markings on the man? Did he talk or say anything?" The commander had a small notebook.

"The man was covered from head to toe in black leather. I only saw a little of his arm and his trade-tattoo. He talked. He said to me, 'Bitch, you will be dead in minutes.' I didn't recognize the voice. He isn't anyone that I had ever serviced. Do you have any other questions? I'm exceedingly tired," said Ultima, her hands trembling under a blanket she had brought with her.

"Thank you, Exotic Ultima, that will be all for now," said the Commander. He thanked Xawata and departed.

"Orrun, take Ultima to her room; she needs plenty of rest. Later, make sure she has a relaxing bath," said Xawata, and he left the parlor tossing Ultima's leash to Orrun.

Ultima just wanted to sleep for a month, but she had to work that night, and like Orrun, she was just a slave.

CHAPTER 3

The Broken Exotic

She sang on the night of the lovers
An Angel from the land of Yavos.
One look and I melted, you said "Hello"
I sighed, a laugh that remained in my mind
She came on the night of the lovers.

Your perfume consumed me,
My mind melted fully.
A pair of hands went to your neck and your breast
Two hills closed together, I wanted to caress
I wanted to touch that grass over the hills
She came to me on the night of the lovers.

In my dreams,
She came to me.
Soft hands touched
And they set me free
I felt alive, in bliss, and I melted.
One look, one touch, one kiss, neck scented.
I was lost to her, on the night of the lovers …

Ultima was singing a song from the old times. They were some of Ultima's favorites to sing. A man, her client, insisted on undressing her while she sang and played the lute, her heart wrapped up in the song. She was mostly undressed and the man now sat next to her on the sofa, his legs crossed and eyes closed, while he caressed her shapely leg, when she thought she saw a shadow move on the far side of the room near the curtain. Was it a man or a trick of the light in the night? *It's most likely a shadow thrown by the flickering lamp,* she thought, and she continued with her song, but she kept looking at the shadow that was taking the form of a man's silhouette, inching away from the window toward the table where he stood for a moment and waited. When she finished her song, her client stood up, and in silence took the lute from her hands and fully undressed her, unaware of the shadow in the corner that appeared to be watching them.

Ultima needed to speak out. She wanted to give a warning, but she couldn't say a word. Her voice had gone, body frozen, and her fear took over her mind. Her client kissed her and was beginning to mount her naked body, when the silhouette drew out a bow and arrow, aimed and fired in one motion, and hit the man. The arrow went through him and bit deep into her body as well. A pain like no other hit her in the chest.

"AAAHHH!" She woke up with a start and screamed. She had not seen the face of the man in her dream, only that it was a man.

Ultima sat up in her bed; her bed sheets were wet with sweat and her body was trembling. She stood up and on shaking legs, using a crutch the servant, Orrun, had made for her, she hobbled over to her bathroom and washed her face. Minutes later, she returned to her room; still, she added some wood to her fireplace with trembling hands. A dim light was beginning to enter through the windows, making her room fill with light ever so slowly, which gave Ultima peace. She had slept for only two hours. Xawata had scheduled three clients for her the previous night, and they robbed her of every ounce of energy. The bastard of a man. Xawata's greed, compared only to his gluttony. Limping a little with her crutch, Ultima returned to her bed after she closed the curtains completely. She needed to return to sleep.

Xawata had made her work four days the last week and take at least three clients, and that evening she had to sing for two men. Her wretched master owned over thirty slaves, and he worked them until they died, still in his possession. Even his Exotics had to work more than an average Exotic. Ultima reached her bed and laid back, adjusting her collar; the bothersome cold metal got in the way on her pillow. She tossed and turned, but finally she fell asleep.

Later, during her evening meal, Ultima was sitting with Akina. Her nightmare was still clear in her memory, and she knew she had to tell it to someone.

"Momma, it was only a nightmare. Do you want me to ask Orrun to put you in his schedule and come and give you a massage?" asked Akina.

"Yes, thank you, Akina love, that would be lovely." And Ultima kissed her little Akina on the top of her head.

❖❖❖

A few days later, Ultima fully woke an hour before the noon meal. She took a bath, and afterward she needed to spend some time with her daughter and student, Akina, the only young girl in the brothel being trained by Ultima to be an Exotic. Xawata had allowed Ultima to keep the babe, but had made Ultima start training her daughter when Akina was just three years old.

Ultima walked slowly through the halls until she reached the dance floor, where she found her beloved daughter. Her long black hair was all a mess. It was clear she had finished a dance lesson. Akina could sing like the birds.

The girl was now eleven, and Xawata had pre-sold her virginity to a nobleman on a promise. He was waiting at least six more months for her twelfth birthday and for her courses to start. Technically it was illegal to sell a child that young. To abide by the law, Xawata should wait for Akina to turn fourteen, take her to the Trades Office, and give her both the official prostitute-tattoo and the first initial mark of an Exotic on her breast and wrist. On the other hand, Xawata did not want to break his precious doll and secretly did not want to upset Ultima for fear she may lose her edge as a singer. The Marquis of Brindle had offered Xawata one hundred *gold* for Akina. So, the greedy animal, Xawata, collected the gold coins, but insisted they wait for Akina to turn twelve *and* have her courses for at least six months.

Ultima, however, was aware of the end timeline as she reached the dance floor where young Akina passed her morning.

"Akina, come here to me," demanded Ultima. Her daughter was in a corner crying, while the three other girls surrounded her. Akina's flushed skin, red from exertion after an obviously full morning of training, made her seem younger than her eleven years. They clearly had been practicing an intricate dance Master Lucy had undoubtedly choreographed for their training.

"All of you girls, go to your rooms and get ready for your history lesson," said Dance Master Lucy.

"Are you training Akina the rest of the day?" asked the dance teacher. Like all the other teachers in the house, the dance teacher knew what was to happen to Akina.

"Yes, Master Lucy. It is great to see you, by the way. I'll take it from here." Ultima walked to Akina's side. The young mage tried to create the illusion of happiness, but Ultima knew when Akina was using her magic, trying to deceive. So, Ultima spoke to Akina with tough love, but decided not to scold her for trying the deception.

"You must stand up, and stop using your glamour magic with me this very moment, young lady," said Ultima in a loving but stern voice. Akina looked up, cleaned her face, and stood in front of her Exotic mother.

"Yes, Momma," said Akina. At eleven, she was just a scared young girl, and Ultima understood her. Akina looked down at her feet, sighed, and sniffled a little. Ultima could see her reddened face, and she knew Akina's thoughts were on her impending initiation. Like all the other girls in the house, she knew who Exotic Ultima was and what she did. Akina knew her mother and master well.

"Follow me!"

Akina followed her mother to a nearby tall mahogany table with three tall chairs.

"Now, you must listen. You see this golden collar I have around my neck?" Ultima held her collar, looking directly into the girl's eyes. Akina's almond-shaped, deep-green eyes were still full of tears.

"Yes, Momma," Akina sniffled a little.

"It is a collar, just like the one you have around your neck. Your collar may be bronze, and they made mine of gold, but they are both collars. We are both slaves. Listen to me because I will never repeat these words. What Xawata has prepared for you isn't your fault, nor has it anything to do with your worth as a human or a woman. It has to do with his greed. Do you understand?"

Akina nodded.

"We are slaves. You and me both, and we do what our owner tells us to do. Xawata has sold your body, but he can't touch your soul. What will happen is that a man will touch you and kiss you, and by orders of Xawata, you must let him. However, that doesn't mean that you, Akina, are bad or that your soul will be lost in the event. Your mind is more powerful than any man alive. You will fight in your head; do you hear me?"

Akina nodded again, but Ultima could tell she was a little unsure.

"The way you fight is by telling yourself that *you decide* the man doesn't own your mind. You must choose to fight. You must repeat to yourself, over and over in your head, that Xawata doesn't own your soul. If you do that, you will be the best Exotic in the world. You will be better than even me. You are my daughter: my Akina, the student of the best Exotic in the entire Kingdom of Tsestelago. Do you understand me?" said Ultima, holding Akina's chin. And the child nodded, this time more confidently.

"Stay calm and don't cry. Let's go; we must work on your Yakutan language skills." Ultima stood up, hugged Akina, and took her by the hand as they left the room together.

They walked through the teaching halls of the brothel, looking for an empty classroom.

"Stupid vazey, go pick up those books," said a teacher, hitting the child's arm in the hallway as Ultima passed by, still holding Akina by the hand. The teacher stood up and let Ultima pass, showing her respect to the Exotic, but continued hitting the child. Ultima stopped in front of the woman while Akina lowered herself to the floor and helped the child pick up the books.

Ultima looked forward, but avoided making eye-contact with the woman, and she said: "That child is being prepared to be an Exotic. She is neither stupid, dirty, nor worthy of mistreatment. If you want respect, you must give respect first. If you value your job, I hope I won't hear that you are mistreating a child again." Ultima turned her head, looked straight at the woman, and smiled. She took hold of Akina's hand again and continued walking.

♦♦♦

Two weeks later, after Ultima's secret self-ministrations of healing, she had nearly fully healed her leg. She could stand and even walk without the walking stick, but Akina begged her mother to be careful and not dance or run. If she ended up hurting herself further, Xawata would take his anger out on the servants. Ultima promised she would be cautious.

On Ultima's day off, she took Akina shopping for new dancing shoes and some daytime dresses. Ultima always spent a little of whatever coin she had on Akina. Xawata would not give her a salary, but Ultima's clients would leave her gratuities and gifts and Xawata let her keep those. So, she was a wealthy slave. She would never have enough to buy her freedom, but she had all the other things she ever wanted in life.

"Akina, you are growing faster than the weeds. I just bought you a pair of shoes four months ago, and you need new ones already!" Ultima said with a smile.

"Master Lucy said that as long as I gain little weight, growing taller will not stop me from becoming a good dancer," said Akina as they crossed the street to reach the cobbler's store.

"She is right. Slimmer dancers have an easier time doing the routines, and they look elegant. You must listen to your dance teacher. She will show you how to be the best dancer in the kingdom. However, I'm your mother. So, you must listen to me first. I want you to eat and grow strong. We can't have you getting sick because you're not eating. I've been teaching you to be an Exotic since you were a little girl. I'm going to do everything needed until I can buy you from Xawata, but that may take some time. I didn't find out I was a healer mage until the day Xawata was having me fixed. I have never had the opportunity to learn how to use my magic. You are going to have to work as an Exotic for some years. I want you to be free and go to the mages' academy, but for now, that is an impossibility. I'll figure a way out for you. I will fight for you to the end of my days, my heart," said Ultima.

By midafternoon, they had already finished their business in the cobbler's and seamstress's stores. Ultima wanted to buy some books on magic, so she went to visit Audrey's Books and Papers.

When they arrived, a distinguished young man with light-brown hair and hazel eyes was standing by the store's entrance. When he saw Ultima and Akina walking toward the store, he said, "Your child looks just like my mother, but with black hair. She is beautiful."

"Thank you," said Akina.

"Excuse us, my Lord," said Ultima, and the man opened the door to the store.

"Thank you," said both Akina and Ultima in unison.

They entered the store. Ultima thought nothing of the man's remarks, and she went to look for books on magic, while Akina looked through notebooks and sets of ink and pens. Ultima was determined to have her daughter learn some magic, without Xawata discovering their secret. Ultima tried to hurry; they were supposed to be back at the house for the evening meal.

As she looked through the magic section, she saw the man perusing through books in the same aisle, by the selection of magic books. She made a point to never stare at anyone when she was out of the house as it could so easily be misconstrued. Her golden collar let everyone know she was a special slave, one with status. Xawata had given her permission to purchase goods in many stores around the city, so the owners would sell to her without Xawata or a servant present.

On this occasion, she could not help staring at the man from a distance. Ultima found the man striking. His interest in books attracted her attention. She loved learned men. He was reading one book and then looking at another.

She kept looking; he turned; she looked some more. He wasn't your typical man of books. This man had the body of a warrior. He looked unlike anyone she had ever seen in her life, and she had seen many men. She tried not to stare. He wore a hat, but it looked like he had short, light-brown hair under his hat. The man's tailored suit was certainly out of the ordinary, and he had a hat to match. Ultima realized the man had to be a foreigner.

The man found a book in the magic section and added it to three others he already held in his arms. He walked to the front of the store, paid for his books, and left. Ultima followed him with her eyes, but she stayed hidden in the row of books. The sight of the handsome man perplexed her until she heard a familiar voice from the opposite side of the row of bookshelves, it was the voice of a man she would never forget.

"You are one beautiful woman," said the man. Ultima felt as if someone had dropped snow down her spine. She would never forget that voice. Those were the same words the assassin had said to her. The killer was in the store, on the other side of the bookshelf.

Oh no, what if he sees me, what if he follows me? Where is Akina? Ultima's thoughts ran rapidly through her brain. She didn't have time to think; she just reacted. She rushed to the end of the aisle and tried to see where the voice had come from. Ultima had to know the face of the man who killed the prince. She was in turmoil; she didn't want to know, but she had to know.

Ultima tilted her hat to cover her face, and tried to look. There was one man and a woman. The woman was looking in her direction, and the man had his back to her as he talked to the young woman. She looked familiar.

Ultima tried to hide behind another bookshelf, horizontal to the aisle, but the man walked away with the woman obscuring the view. All she could see was that the man dressed as a gentleman, and he carried a cane. Ultima couldn't recognize the man from the back. He had dark hair cut short at the back, but she couldn't see his face. The woman was young, but too far to see who she was.

The man and woman left the store, and Ultima's clammy hands shook. The assassin had been but a few meters from her. She stayed, looking at them leaving the store when a hand grabbed her arm. Ultima jumped, and the books she was holding dropped on her foot.

"Ah, ouch, oh my stars. Akina, you gave me a fright." Ultima jumped and held on to Akina's arm.

"Are you well? You look pale," said Akina.

"Yes, I'm fine. Let's pay for your things. We must get to the house." Ultima paid for her book and Akina's things, and they left. When they stepped out of the store, Ultima looked around for the young woman, but they were gone. So, Ultima called for a carriage to drive them back to the brothel, thinking on the day her daughter was conceived.

CHAPTER 4

The Bachelor Party

Twelve years prior, when Ultima was only nineteen, it was the night of the Duke of Greenwood's bachelor party. Ultima walked into the ballroom, and its splendor caught her breath. She had never been in a place so elegant and magnificent. She enjoyed this part of her trade. The lavish luxury of her surroundings was like a lather of fun. Xawata didn't let her entertain outside the brothel often. However, Ultima would soon be an Exotic—currently in the last stages of her training. Her teacher tested her constantly, and this party was her final exam. Ultima knew her fate well. She was to be an Exotic slave for life, but she cared little. She would be immersed in luxury.

    Ultima walked into the ballroom, admiring everything in her path. She noticed a magnificent crystal chandelier spiraling down from the arched pale-blue and white ceiling. It made the room seem imposing by illuminating the glimmering peach and light-gray walls. The floor was so polished it reminded her of an ice-covered street. Paintings of men and women of times past, displayed in their best clothing, and sceneries of pastures and country scenes covered the ballroom walls. There were statues in a corner here and there, and the cathedral ceiling, with its lovely gold crown moldings, gave an air of grandeur.

Oh, this place wasn't just any manor—this was the home of the nephew of King Trevino Otarana. The duke was the son of King Trevino's only sister, and the duke had finally found a bride. He was getting married in a week. He had invited many of his friends to a party at his manor to say goodbye to his singlehood.

There was a five-piece ensemble that provided music for dancing. Ultima was there to sing and dance in a group play. And she had done her part in the first hour of the party. She walked around the rooms, picking at the different pastries on the serving tables. It wasn't every day she could eat chocolate-covered strawberries.

Men talked to her and asked her to dance, which she enjoyed as much as engaging in interesting conversations with them. Ultima took a moment to rest from the dance floor and walk around the manor. She noticed card games going on in some rooms; in others, Exotics sang the favorite songs of the men in attendance. Servants walked about with flutes of champagne, one of which she accepted. Xawata allowed her only the one alcoholic beverage per party.

The top Exotic dancer and singer of the group was Exotic Leliana, Ultima's teacher and chaperone. Ultima thought Leliana was so beautiful with her red hair and oval-shaped face. It was Leliana who offered exclusive entertainment to the groom, while Ultima was one of many entertainers of the night. Xawata had sent three of his most famous dancers and three singers, besides four other Exotics.

In the last weeks, Ultima's life had moved from plays to recitals. She knew the whole thing was part of a well-orchestrated social construct to keep the elite entertained. Her trade was her life. It wasn't an act. Nothing was fake; it was all real. For Ultima, her appearance was vital to her success, and at the party, her clothing said who and what she was. Ultima knew she represented wealth, education, and sensuality. The manner in which Ultima behaved and spoke communicated to others which brothel she came from and the quality of her education. So, Ultima used her hard-earned knowledge to show all, especially to Leliana, she was ready to get her full license as an Exotic.

Ultima talked to the many men who approached her, and as she sauntered around, she kept control of herself and the situation. She stayed aloof, yet a little sexy, playful, and confident. Ultima kept her distance, and ensured her half-mask covering the upper part of her face never came off, adding to her mystery.

The night progressed, the men got drunk, and things changed. Some left, and for those who remained, the party moved to a smaller room. Ultima knew almost all the men at the party. Her teacher had introduced them to her over the years.

She walked into a room where Leliana was whispering something saucy into the groom's ear by the look on his face. That's when Ultima saw him—a young man playing cards and having fun with his friends. He looked up, and she noticed his eyes, deep-green eyes. Those eyes mesmerized her, but he quickly looked away.

The man had light-brown hair and a slim body, which reminded her of the strong dancers that helped her practice her routines. He had his shirt sleeves rolled up to his mid-forearm, and she noticed his lightning battlemage trade-tattoo. He appeared to be in his twenties. Ultima's hairdresser had collected her black hair in a cascade of curls that fell gracefully down her back. She looked down at her dress. A bright red gown, tight across her body and open at her back, exposing her upper breasts and revealing the first marks of the Exotic-tattoo. She looked the part, but he hadn't spared more than a moment's glance to look at her. The young man kept winning at his game of cards until he eventually stopped playing.

"That's it. I'm taking my winnings," said the handsome young man.

"What? Won't you let me win back some of what I lost?" said the Duke of Greenwood, son of the king's sister, Princess Marguerite.

"If we don't stop, I'm going to win your dukedom," joked the young man.

"Henry, you better cut your losses. This young man has the luck of the Lady of the Lakes," said the Duke of Abernathy. He too held the room's feminine attention with his devil-may-care appearance, light-brown hair, cut short at the back and left a bit longer in the front. One arm circled the courtesan who sat on his lap, the other held a drink which he moved a little vigorously, splashing it about the place as he talked.

"Ha, ha, ha, ha, my dear nephew, I agree with Noah. Cut your losses and run, son," said the groom's uncle, slurring his words a little. He was the Grand Duke of Hausman, younger brother to the King of Tsestelago.

"How about this, let's play one more game; if you win, you get this beauty for the entire night. I surely can afford her. She isn't one of the top Exotics, but all the entertainers here are Xawata's. So, she's bound to give you great service." Ultima was standing next to the groom, gawking at the young man when the duke took Ultima by the arm and showed her to his opponent.

"Oh, she's a pretty one. Come on, do it; one more game. In your boots, I'd do it," said Lord Thomas, the youngest son of the Duke of Hausman.

"If I win, I get all my winnings back and your new Takapian stallion. How's that, my friend? One more game, please!" said the young Duke of Greenwood. The young man looked at Ultima from head to toe, and he smiled at her.

"She is pretty. Fine, set up the game," said the young man in a pleasant voice.

Exotic Leliana approached Ultima quietly and whispered, "Ultima, you came here to sing and dance, not to give any sexual services to anyone, but in this case, if the Lord wins, I'll permit you. I'll charge the duke for any services you give. Remember to do only what is in your trade license, and if he forces you to do anything outside your trade limitations, you must let me know right away."

Ultima nodded as she stood next to Leliana, while the men continued playing their card game. Ultima knew how to play many different card games, but this time she lost track of who held what, and what was happening in the game. She was the price, for intimacy with the one person she was attracted to in the room.

What if he wins the game? That would be lovely. Ultima didn't want to think about it. She wanted to believe that maybe he would like her. Perhaps he would come to visit her at the brothel, and they would in time have some type of romance, like many of the Exotics had. Or if he didn't like women, he might simply get to know her and they would have a friendship.

And suddenly, AHHHHH, laughter and an uproar of shouts and congratulations. The young man won the card game.

"What? You can't win six games in a row! If I didn't know any better, I'd say you cheated," said the groom, laughing and standing up from the card table, giving his opponent a hug instead.

"Well, have fun with your young woman. Leliana, where are you? Tell Xawata to charge me for a full night with her. Enjoy your time with this beauty," said the Duke.

"A Xawata beauty, this should be interesting," said the young man, and he took Ultima by the hand. They left the card game room, and he took her upstairs to a second-floor bedroom.

✦✦✦

It happened. The handsome man had won her time. She was ready to entertain the man, and as a bonus, he was one she liked. Her hands shook. She had entertained many men before, but this time, her heart pounded fast and hard; he was so handsome.

Ultima followed the winner of the card game in a daze. When they reached his room, he opened the door and let her enter first.

"So, you are my prize for the night. It's not every day I see a woman with black hair and blue eyes. And your complexion is so creamy. You are unique," said the young man. He moved over to the fireplace and poked at the fire.

"Thank you," said Ultima.

"Let me see your arm. I want to see all your skills," said the young man in a charming accent. Ultima lifted her right arm, the better to display her trade-tattoos to him. No man had ever asked her to show them her right arm. He walked back to her and gently took her arm.

"I'm not originally from the Kingdom of Tsestelago, so if the trade-tattoos work the same way as in Yakuta, all these skills rising from your wrist to halfway up your upper arm tell me that you must be of the highest echelon, no ordinary prostitute. An Exotic, for sure—I'm not surprised."

"Not quite, my Lord," said Ultima, "I've yet to pass my final test, but I do have all the necessary skills as you can see."

"Yes." He continued examining her arm. "If I'm not mistaken, I see here you can speak Yakutan! Good, that is my language. I will only speak Yakutan from here on," said the young man. With a gentle tug on her hand, he urged Ultima to sit next to him on the sofa that faced the fireplace.

"Do you smoke? Would you care for a cigarette?" asked the young man.

"No, thank you," said Ultima, feeling a little less nervous. *He's so handsome. I wonder how well he kisses.*

"Good! I love women with black hair." He said, touching Ultima's curls. "Do you know any Yakutan Songs? I want you to sing for me."

"I will do whatever you ask of me that is within my trade license. However, there are a few rules I need to make you aware of before we start," said Ultima with more confidence. *He is so attractive, I want to touch him,* thought Ultima.

"Oh yes, the rules, I know them: don't hit your face, don't ask for anything that isn't within your trade, and I only have whatever hours that were paid. I know the rules," said the young man.

"And my mask stays on the entire time until I make you scream in passion," said Ultima.

"Oh! Interesting," said the young man.

"House policy."

"So, you are just letting me know of the policy?" asked the young man.

"I'm just doing my job, my Lord," said Ultima.

"Do you know how to play *Take the Castle*?" asked the young man.

"Yes, I love that game," said Ultima, surprised he asked her about the game.

"I have a board for the game in my bag. I want to play." He stood up and went to rummage in a bag. He took the board out and set the game on a small table by the window. They played a game, and Ultima let him win.

"You let me win!" he said, all upset.

"Did I do anything to upset you?" Ultima frowned.

"I don't want you to let me win. I want you to strategize and play to win. I want a challenge. Let's try again." And he set up the board game again, and this time, the game took longer. An hour later, Ultima won the game.

"Nicely played! I didn't see those last moves coming. You are brilliant." He sat back, crossed his arms and legs, and smiled.

"Thank you. Would you care to play another game, or maybe you prefer to dance?" said Ultima.

"I'm thirsty. I'm getting some wine. Are you thirsty? Perhaps you'd care for some wine yourself or something else to drink, maybe a port?" He stood up and went to serve himself a glass of wine.

"You should have asked me to serve your wine," said Ultima.

"Why? I have two good hands. I can get it myself. We have here white and red wine from Alhambra, some hard liquor, a juice of some sort, and water. Which would you prefer?" He was looking around the drinks table.

Ultima stood up and went to get her drink. "Water for me, thank you," she said. And he poured her a glass and gave it to her. He stood near her and inhaled deeply.

"I love the way you smell. It reminds me of a meadow full of lavender," he said, looking at her and smiling. He returned to the table where they had the board game. The young man sat and removed his boots.

"I need to get new boots. I traveled from Alhambra to be here at this wedding, and I'm tired. Your trade-tattoo indicates you can sing." He reclined on the sofa, relaxing, with one arm trailed along the back of it.

"I've been a singer my entire life. I can't remember a time where I wasn't singing," said Ultima as she sat on the sofa next to him.

"Do you know any songs from Yakuta?" asked the young man.

Ultima sang an old Yakutan song. She sang one song and then another song and then another. At the end of the third song, he stood up and offered her his hand.

"Let's dance," he said. There was music coming from the first floor. He took Ultima in his arms, and they danced to the tune of the distant music. As they danced, the young man hummed the song's melody, and Ultima joined in to sing the words of the song. At the end of the song, they stopped dancing; he took a small step back, a little away from her.

"May I kiss you?" he asked.

"Why are you asking?" Ultima couldn't understand the man. *Why does he behave as if I'm a woman to be courted?*

"If you don't want me to kiss you, I'll not do it. We can spend the night talking and playing games," said the young man.

Ultima frowned. "I don't understand."

"Simple, I only kiss women that want to kiss me," said the young man. Ultima opened her mouth, and it took her a minute to comprehend. She looked around and then at him and his green eyes.

"Yes," she whispered.

He kissed her.

He is kissing me—I'm not kissing him! This is sublime. He certainly knows how to kiss properly. Not invasive; not biting me. No rough beard or mustache. I don't have to do anything but enjoy his kisses. This is nice.

He broke the kiss, still holding Ultima in his arms.

No, no, no, no, don't stop the kiss.

"I want to touch you," said the young man.

"Yes, touch me," she said, smiling at him.

He pulled a few strings, and the top of her dress fell to her hips. She stood half naked, held in the arms of the first man she was truly attracted to. He was touching her arms and the roundness of her breast. He kissed Ultima again, separated from her, and took off his shirt.

Ultima walked over to the bed with a slow and sexy walk. He took off his pants.

Still standing, she turned to watch him. *Yes! I like what I see. It will be nice to please him. Oh, his body is so well proportioned. He has the typical golden, red, and white lightning veins, beautiful.* Ultima's thoughts were all about the man she was about to service.

He walked over to Ultima, took her in his arms and touched her face.

"You are one beautiful courtesan, and so young. How old are you?" he asked.

"I'm nineteen," said Ultima.

He stroked her breast, just over her tattoo. "I see the first marking of an Exotic. If you are not a full Exotic yet, then what are you?" said the young man, pulling a little away from her.

"Please, don't turn me away. If Exotics were a mere trade, I would be a journeyman. I've worked hard to get where I am now. I need to stay, else my master will take my golden collar from me and demote me," said Ultima, holding on to his arm.

"Golden collar? You are a slave, Exotic?" he demanded.

"Yes, I've been a slave my entire life; being an Exotic is a great honor for me," said Ultima. The young man took a deep breath, lowered his arms and stepped away.

"I see you have a golden necklace, but it doesn't look like a collar."

"My master thought it would look better with my dress. Don't you desire me?" asked Ultima.

"I only consort with free Exotics. Slave Exotics are the same as sex slaves, only for rich men. We don't have slaves in my kingdom. It isn't your fault. Get dressed and go. You have no fault in this," said the young man. He stepped back, put on his pants, and sat on the sofa. The man took a deep breath, stretched the back of his neck, and closed his eyes.

He told me to go. Ultima didn't know what to do. This man wasn't what she was used to, and that piqued her curiosity. She thought his body was gorgeous. Ultima wanted to touch every single one of his blue lighting markings on his body. He did things differently, and that was so sexy. She wanted to taste his kiss again.

Ultima looked at the man, and she noticed he had the start of an erection. He wanted her. And in the middle of it all, she wanted him; he aroused her, so she listened to her body. Ultima went to sit next to him and touched his leg.

"My Lord, I may be a slave, but I'm also a woman, and I wish to stay. I like you. I said I wanted you to kiss me, and I meant it. I said I wanted you to touch me, and it wasn't a lie. Will you let me stay? If you truly don't want to touch me, then we can play games or converse if you like," said Ultima.

"Slaves have no choices," said the young man. Ultima looked at his body, gave him a half-smile.

"My master will get paid whether I go or stay. You told me to leave, but I want to stay. That is my choice," said Ultima.

"That is your master talking. You are beautiful, and it would be easy for me to take you, but your master has taken your will from this event. Your master will get paid for your work, and you will get nothing. You didn't choose me or my touch. You didn't choose this life. Go!" said the young man. Ultima looked at him. Never in her life had anyone treated her this way.

"You gave me a choice. I could have played games all night with you, but I let you touch me. I'm choosing to stay. In this moment, I'm a woman, fully knowing what I want, and I want to stay. Why don't we play another game of *Take the Castle*? I want to play a game," said Ultima with a smile.

"Alright, let's play, but don't let me win." He said with a smile. Ultima raised the top of her dress, but she didn't tie the bindings.

"Fine, but this time, let's play for a wager. If you win, what would you like me to do?"

"I should like for you to sing, but in Palermo this time." He said, stretching his back.

"Deal, and if I win, I want a kiss. I like your kisses," said Ultima.

"Ha, ha, ha, you are relentless. Fine, I enjoy kissing you as well," said the young man. And they played a new game. After a while of playing, Ultima won again.

"Nicely played." He smiled.

"Thank you; you make it hard for me to win." She stood from her chair and went to get a drink.

"Will you have another glass of wine?" asked Ultima.

"No, thank you."

She noticed he was watching her every move.

Ultima returned to him and reclined on the table in front of him with a glass of wine in her hand. She took a sip.

He leaned forward and kissed Ultima, and she kissed him back.

"Would you like to play another game?" said Ultima in her sexiest voice. She wanted him. Never in her life had Ultima wanted a man as bad as she wanted him at that moment. It was all about sex. And she was going to have it.

He kissed her again.

"I want you. I would do this for free," said Ultima, and he took her dress off.

Lifting her in his arms, he took her to bed. Ultima had the best time of her young life.

Sometime later, the young man shouted in passion, and he removed Ultima's mask.

"You are exquisite," he said, kissing her, and they both fell asleep.

❖❖❖

<u>Four and a half months later</u>

"Ultima, what have you done?" asked Exotic Leliana. The woman was pacing from one side of the room to the other. Her long skirts made a swooshing sound as she walked over the hardwood floor.

"I didn't know what was happening. You fixed me when I was twelve." Hands shaking, fingers feeling like a million pins were prickling them. Sweat flowing down her spine, Ultima shuddered. "Xawata will come to your room soon," said Leliana. And a few minutes later, there was the sound of footsteps outside her door.

Thump, thump, thump. Xawata opened the door, and he entered—as tall as he was ugly.

"Four months, four months!" shouted Xawata. "Why did you wait so long to tell us? And the most important question: 'How in hell did this happen?' WE. HAD. HER. FIXED! Leliana, she is your student. Didn't you teach her how to prevent this from happening?" Xawata's blue eyes bulged out of his sockets.

"Ultima, do you have anything to say about this?" asked Leliana.

"I thought I was fixed. I never had to worry before. And now, it just never crossed my mind that I was with child," said Ultima.

"What I don't understand is how the maids didn't notice she wasn't bleeding for the last four months? This is a conspiracy against me," said Xawata.

"That's just it. I was bleeding. So, I noticed nothing until this last month that I didn't bleed at all," said Ultima.

"How do we know we can't get rid of the thing? There's got to be a way. It can't be four months," said Xawata.

"We had a healer brought here to get it removed, but she was the one that told us it was more than four months and removing it would kill Ultima. The child is too large. Look at her; she is showing," said Leliana.

"I'm sorry!" said Ultima, lowering her head. Eyes watering.

"You're sorry! Ha, this is unheard of, an Exotic mother," shouted Xawata.

"She must have the child; there is no other way now," said Leliana.

"Fine, but she will still work as a singer and entertainer. We will hide the pregnancy. She will teach history, numbers, and languages to the Exotic girls in training. She will serve as a servant if needed. As soon as the child is born, I want her to start a regimen of exercise to regain her body shape," said Xawata.

"What will happen to the child?" asked Leliana.

Ultima's head snapped up, eyes wide open, still full of tears and now with a runny nose too; she looked at Xawata.

"Let me keep it. I'll work hard for you. It will not be in your way," said Ultima, with tears rolling down her face. Xawata looked at Ultima, and the old man smiled. He said nothing for a few minutes.

"Fine—but the child will stay as my slave. Do you know who's the father?" asked Xawata.

Although Ultima knew his face, she had never found out the name of the man she serviced at the Duke of Greenwood's bachelor party.

"No," said Ultima.

"What will this do to her status as an Exotic?" asked Leliana.

"She can continue to move up depending on how fast she can get back to receiving clients. I've spent a lot of coin on this one," said Xawata.

"We can do this if we make her exclusive enough to keep her away from the rough ones until her body is ready to take on the challenge. Giving birth will raise her level of pain tolerance to a higher threshold, which will be a good thing for you," said Leliana.

"I want her fixed again once this bastard child is born," said Xawata.

"I think her magic got in the way, that is probably the reason she was able to conceive the child. She is a healer. Her body just might heal itself," said Leliana, looking from Ultima to Xawata.

"This is all I need, an Exotic that can't stay fixed. Teach Ultima to prevent getting with child, now that we suspect she can't stay fixed." said Xawata.

"I'll teach her all she needs to know, so that this will never happen again. I'll also get her on a special schedule," said Leliana. And Xawata left the room, slamming the door on his way out. Leliana rubbed the back of her neck and looked at Ultima with disgust.

"It is a miracle he didn't have you killed. He just loves his coin too much. Fortunately for you, he's invested way too much coin in your education by now. You owe him your life and the life of your child, so make the best of it," said Exotic Leliana, leaving the room.

Ultima stayed in her room, smiling. Her scheme had worked. She kept her child. She remembered the night at the bachelor party. When their time was over, she fell asleep to wake only when Leliana came to get her in the early hours of the morning. She hoped she could see him again, but that was highly unlikely since he had mentioned he would return to Yakuta after the duke's wedding. And it wasn't until she returned to the brothel that she bathed and cleaned the evidence of her union with the handsome man.

He was the only one with whom she had had sex for two months before the party, and she had not sexually entertained anyone for six weeks after the party. So, when two weeks after the party had passed and she missed her courses, then another week went by and she still had not had her courses, she knew she was with child. Ultima could feel it and she knew exactly who the father was.

She never expected to conceive; she was always so very careful. However, when she did find out, and the evidence was ever present, the shock made her panic. Panic made her anxious. And anxiety made her run out to the backyard of the brothel. She needed air.

"What will happen to me?" said Ultima to herself while standing next to a tall tree. Pregnant slaves were treated poorly. And an Exotic with a child would indeed be reason enough to make Xawata beat her. Xawata had spent loads of gold on her education. She wanted love and a family, but those were dreams.

In the brothel, she had no one to love her. Instead, she needed to be the top Exotic. She wanted to be the best. She wanted her full Exotic license. That way, no one in the house would treat her poorly ever again. Exotics were not mothers. Here, she had no choice.

After an hour of crying, she took a deep breath and went to tell Leliana. She stepped away from the tree, walked back to the big house, and entered through the back door. On her way to Leliana's room, she passed the servants' rooms, where she encountered a commotion. The housekeeper and a maid were running in and out of one of the servant's rooms. She heard the voice of a woman repeatedly saying. "Breathe, you must breathe." Followed by a moan and a muffled scream. Ultima's curiosity piqued. She had to look.

"What is happening in there?" she asked a servant who came out of the room.

"Mila is having her baby," said the young servant, leaving the door to the room open. Ultima looked in the room and the young girl, who couldn't have been older than sixteen, lay on her small bed. Her sweaty hair up in a bun and the color of her skin looked pale, just like Ultima's. The housekeeper entered the room and saw Ultima standing at the threshold of the door.

"Ultima, you must leave," said the woman.

"No, I want to see. How can I help?" asked Ultima.

"Here, take these and place the cool rag over Mila's brow." The housekeeper gave Ultima a basin with cold water and a rag. Ultima did what she was told. The girl screamed and moaned and after many hours, the girl gave birth. It was a boy. Ultima got to see a child being born and the joy of the girl with her child. A few minutes later, the girl was nursing her boy, and Ultima watched. And then the young mother sang a lullaby to her baby boy.

Ultima stayed there, watching. A few minutes later, she congratulated the girl and walked to her room. She had witnessed a living miracle.

Ultima had a chance to have what society denied to all Exotics like her. She had the once-in-a-lifetime opportunity to have a family. Once again, she had a choice. At the bachelor party, the young man she serviced gave her a choice. She made her choice and she was happy with it. And now she had a choice again. She could keep quiet, fool everyone for a few months, and have her child. The problem would be figuring out a way to keep her child, but she would think about that later. So, she chose her child, and she kept quiet.

In her room, she cried some more, scared of the choice she had made. After a while, she looked at herself in the mirror and smiled.

Ultima did her best to hide her secret from her slave master. That night and for the next four days she ate her meats seared only, to collect the blood and keep her miracle alive. She did it again in the second month and the third; long enough until she couldn't keep her secret quiet any longer. Ultima wanted what free women had—a family.

Who was the man that fathered her child? She didn't know his name, but she would never forget his face and his green eyes. One thing she knew, she was happy with the gift he had given her.

CHAPTER 5

The Party

Xawata had Ultima's schedule set for the year for all the significant social events. There were even events Xawata had booked for her two years in advance. And then there were events where Xawata's clients paid extra just to have Ultima as an escort. As had just happened. Ultima was to be the escort to Gregor Camp, the ambassador from Palermo to Alhambra, but who had come to the city for the engagement ball of Lady Nancy Otarana, the daughter of Prince Robert Otarana, the Grand Duke of Hausman, to the Earl of Portmore, Lord James Tanning.

Ultima wore an elegant dark-green dress with red accents. Her long, black hair was taken up into an intricate design, with curls artfully draped down around her face and neck. She wore a unique gold necklace inlaid with rubies and diamonds. The ambassador was waiting for her at his hotel where Ultima found him, and where the two climbed into his carriage for the short journey to the event.

The ladies of nobility and wealth made the parties a little uncomfortable for Ultima, as they all knew her to be an entertainer. They accepted that Exotics were a part of polite society, but she was an expensive source of entertainment for someone, and thus she was adored by many, embraced by some, and only tolerated by others.

When Ultima and the ambassador arrived at the Duke of Hausman's manor, he couldn't contain his awe.

The Ambassador gasped. "This isn't a manor—this is a palace!"

"Well, this used to be a castle at one point. The Otarana family stonemasons transformed it into the largest manor in the capital. It has a rich history. This manor has been part of the royal family's properties for centuries. The title *Grand Duke of Hausman* doesn't get handed down from father to son, rather it is a title given to the living brother of the king. The king passes the title and the manor to his brother once the king has adult heirs of his own and the current Grand Duke has passed. I'm assuming this is the first time you have visited the Grand Duke's manor?" asked Ultima, as she adjusted her gloves.

"Yes, this is my first time. I have heard stories, but this is a beautiful piece of architecture. We have nothing like this in Palermo," said the Ambassador.

"If the outside impresses you, wait until you see the inside. It is breathtaking," said Ultima. And the horseless carriage pulled up at the front of the property.

"I'm ready, are you?" said the Ambassador, extending his hand to Ultima. They exited the horseless carriage and made their way to the entrance of the manor. When they reached the main hall, the butler introduced them to the host at the door who ceremoniously announced their names to those already in the room.

Most of Ultima's regular clients were in attendance at the engagement party. They looked at her, and many saluted their favorite Exotic. The wives of the men gave her nasty looks, but she didn't care. Ultima was a well-known Exotic. She was the best in the kingdom, and they all knew it.

The ambassador and Ultima spent the night talking to the members of the court, and when it was time to move to the dining room, he offered her his arm and escorted her .

Dinner finished, and as the night continued, the dancing started. Ultima was talking to Lady Balmer, one of her favorite clients. The older woman loved to hear Ultima sing, so once per month she would pay to listen to her sing. She was enjoying her conversation with Lady Balmer until Ultima saw the most handsome man walking toward her, and her attention centered on him. The man who approached her was the one she had seen at the bookstore. She smiled; no man had ever before affected her like the attractive man reading the books at the bookstore.

"May I have this dance?" asked the man. Ultima tried to remember if she had ever met him. Oh yes, she remembered him. Twelve years ago, at the bachelor party of the Duke of Greenwood. He was the same young man that had won the card game and thereby, the right to be with her for the night, but she never knew his name. What was his name? He had changed. His body was more muscular, and his tight haircut made him look menacing. He now had a scar on the side of his head. The scar gave Ultima the impression this man wasn't one to be trifled with or made angry.

However, to Ultima, that scar made him look so sexy. He wasn't an overly tall man compared to others in the room, maybe a little above five feet, ten inches. She only reached to well below his chin, even with her high heels, but his broad chest and muscular arms made her think of a warrior. His sweet smile and his dark-green eyes looked at her with a twinkle she had only seen in young children.

Oh, this is definitely the man from the bachelor party. Those green eyes, I'll never forget those eyes. He is the mage I serviced at that party twelve years ago! I can feel his magic. He's still so handsome! thought Ultima.

"Yes, a dance!" said Ultima. It was a soft three-step dance, nothing fancy. He took her by the hand and escorted her to the dance floor, and the music began.

"And what may I call you? I know most, if not all, of the people in this room, but I don't know you or your name," said Ultima walking toward the dance floor.

"I'm Lord Otto Hightower."

"Oh, you are from Yakuta. You have a charming accent," said Ultima.

"Thank you! Yes, I'm from Yakuta," said Lord Otto.

"What brings you here?" asked Ultima.

"Business, mostly, and this celebration," said Otto.

"Well, Lord Otto, if you haven't been welcomed yet to our capital, then welcome to Pailo," said Ultima, fully knowing the man had been to Pailo at least once before.

"Thank you, but I have been in Pailo for well over a week. However, things look a lot different since the last time I was here," said Lord Otto.

"When was the last time you were in Pailo?" asked Ultima.

"It was twelve years ago. It was for an engagement and a wedding, same as this time," said Lord Otto.

"Oh, a wedding. Could that have been the Duke of Greenwood's wedding?"

"Yes, it was. My family and the duke have ties that run generations, but how did you know?"

"A guess, that was the wedding of the year, twelve years ago. However, many things have changed in twelve years," said Ultima.

"Yes, many things. You have my name, my rank in the family, and where I'm from, but I don't even know your name."

"Huh, it is hard to believe that none of your friends have told you who I am."

"I don't have many friends in this part of the world. So, who are you?" asked Otto.

"I, I am Ultima Skylar." Ultima looked directly into the man's eyes when she told him her name.

"Well, that is your name, Ultima Skylar, but it doesn't tell me who you are," said Lord Otto.

"My name is who I am," said Ultima.

"Your name is who you are? That is enigmatic," said Lord Otto.

"Darling, haven't you looked at my right wrist and left breast?" asked Ultima. Lord Otto looked at her arm and breast, and his smile faded away.

"Oh, an Exotic!"

Ultima chuckled, "Don't tell me you didn't notice. My exotic mark on my breast is for all to see."

"I wasn't looking at your breast. I was looking at your eyes and your face. You look very familiar. It's not every day I see a woman with black hair, blue eyes, and your color skin. I think I've seen you before. I *know* I've seen you before," said Lord Otto.

"Maybe at Duke of Greenwood's bachelor party," said Ultima.

"You were the courtesan I won for the night!" said Lord Otto.

"Small world, huh," Ultima gave him half a smile.

"You have the hair and eyes of a person from Albria," said Otto.

"You are the first person to make the comparison," said Ultima.

"Maybe because not everyone visits Albria," said Otto.

"Maybe," said Ultima, looking away from him.

"So, Exotic Ultima Skylar, why didn't you give me your trade title when you introduced yourself?" said Lord Otto.

"Because I never had to do it before. And it was a little fun," said Ultima.

"Are you alone at this party or with a client?" asked Otto.

"I'm with a client. It is hard to believe you have never heard of me," said Ultima.

"I don't have many friends, and with the ones I have, we don't talk about Exotics," said Lord Otto.

"Huh, interesting. So how long are you going to stay in Pailo?" asked Ultima.

"A few months, maybe. Why do you ask?"

"Maybe, you might want to visit me; I would love to listen to your stories about Yakuta," said Ultima.

"I don't think our paths will cross again," said Lord Otto, disappointing Ultima with his response.

"I have a variety of skills. I don't need to service you in any physical way if you are now interested in men," said Ultima.

Lord Otto laughed at that, "No, I very much like women. I just stopped frequenting brothels."

"Oh, you are married!" said Ultima.

"No, no, I'm not married. I just make it a point not to frequent brothels, and if I remember correctly from the last time we were together, you are a slave, and I never visit slave Exotics, remember?" said Lord Otto. Ultima smiled, and then frowned. His response was upsetting. The music slowed to a lull.

"Well, Exotic Ultima Skylar, it was my pleasure to have formally met you after twelve years." When the dance music finished; he gave her a bow. She curtsied, and they went their separate ways.

It was interesting to have danced with the man that she had serviced twelve years ago. The man who didn't even remember her at first. She had been wearing her mask at that bachelor party, and he only took the mask off at the end of their encounter. He had the most beautiful dark-green eyes she had ever seen in a man. Ultima looked back and saw Lord Otto walking to the card game rooms' direction, and he didn't even give her a second look.

After that one dance, she turned down all requests for dancing any vigorous dances; her leg bothered her, and she had to stay on her feet until past midnight. An ensemble of a piano, violins, viola, cellos, flute, and oboe played in the corner, and the guests danced the night away.

Ultima wondered who exactly Lord Otto Hightower was. A man that didn't know the famous Ultima Skylar until she pointed out her tattoos was a real enigma. She walked around the manor looking to see if she could spot where the intriguing man had gone rather than have a second dance with her. She passed by several rooms with card games and a separate large room where she could see some of her dancer friends performing a play.

Ultima walked around as her client, the ambassador, talked business with other nobles and officials. She loved to walk around the Hausman manor; it was the most extravagant in the capital. Then she noticed Lord Otto in the front hall, taking his hat and coat with two other men. *They are leaving before the engagement announcement! That's odd.* However, Ultima learned long before that the aristocracy was a strange bunch, and all she had to do was keep them entertained.

Ultima had wanted to talk to Lord Otto one more time. She was sure the man was lying. He must have known about her, and for a man that handsome to not frequent brothels—he must have a mistress then. The night continued. Until Ultima got hot, and she needed some fresh air. She went to stand outside on a balcony by herself, taking a few moments of breeze, when she felt a tap on her shoulder. Ultima turned.

"Commander Baxter how are you doing tonight?" said Ultima.

"I'm doing well. How about you, Exotic Ultima? I see you are well recovered from your leg injury," said the Commander.

"I'm well, thank you. My leg has mended nicely, all thanks to the ministrations of Healer Goren. Have you heard of him? He serves the King," said Ultima.

"Oh, I'm sure, Xawata gets the best care coin can buy for you," said the Commander.

"Are you enjoying the party?" asked Ultima.

"I'm not much for the entertainments of nobles. Would you like a cigarette?" asked the Commander, lighting his cigarette and offering one to Ultima.

"Yes, thank you. I distinctly remember you enjoying a highly trained courtesan. That is one of the high society's entertainments, isn't it?" said Ultima, letting Commander Baxter light her cigarette.

"A man can enjoy a woman's touch. Tell me, can you still not remember anything else of the night of the assassination?" asked the Commander.

"As I've told you before, the man had his face covered. All I can remember is that the man had brown eyes, he was white, and his trade was a warrior. I will never forget that night. His voice comes back in my nightmares and haunts me at night." Ultima noticed the man's mannerisms, like those of any of the men who desired her, but she couldn't read him. Her harmonizer magic didn't help her with this man. She looked inside the hall and found the ambassador had entered the dancing hall. She snuffed her cigarette and fixed her hair a little.

"I must return. It was nice talking to you, Commander." And Ultima returned to the dancing hall and went to stand next to the ambassador.

"Exotic Ultima, I wondered who had the pleasure of your company tonight," said the Duke of Horrel from behind her. Ultima disliked the duke. He had an evil disposition. Every time she was around him, she wanted to argue with him. His petulant personality irked her. He was odious to her.

"Hello, Your Grace; I'm here with Ambassador Gregor Camp from Palermo. Ambassador Camp, this is His Grace, the Duke of Horrel," said Ultima. The ambassador turned and made a slight bow to the duke. The men talked and exchanged pleasantries, while Ultima stayed by the side of the ambassador. She was used to being the intermediary in the introductions between men. It was interesting how many men she had introduced to each other and had helped make business contacts.

A few minutes later, quiet was called for, and the Grand Duke announced the engagement of his only daughter, Lady Nancy, to Lord James Tanning, the Earl of Portmore, observing the proper congratulatory customs. The groom's mother made the congratulatory speech for the Tanning family and thanked all by the end. And when the formalities concluded, a dance commemorated the event. However, once most of his peers had congratulated the Grand Duke, and the duke was talking to one of Ultima's clients, she approached him to give her congratulations in person. The Grand Duke wasn't one of her regular clients. He visited her once every six months to dance with her or hear her sing. The man was kind to her.

"Your Grace, that was a lovely speech. It must be a great joy to see your daughter make such a harmonious match," said Ultima, curtsying to the man.

"Exotic Ultima, you are a welcome sight. Yes, yes, I'm pleased. My daughter found someone she likes and with whom I can trust. Although I wanted a duke or a marquis for Nancy, but the Earl of Portmore is enamored with her. My wife thinks that is a good thing to have. James, come here son, I want to introduce you to the jewel of our capital," said the Grand Duke of Hausman.

"Oh now, your wife will have a word with you if she hears you. Let's hope she's not around," said Ultima. The Earl of Portmore came to where the duke and Ultima were standing.

"James, I don't know if you have made her acquaintance yet, but this is Ultima Skylar. The best singer and dancer and most beautiful Exotic in our capital," said the Duke, kissing Ultima's hand. The Earl bowed his head, and Ultima curtsied deeply in return.

"Enchanted," said the man in a raspy voice.

"What is wrong, James?" said the Duke.

"I think I'm coming down with something; will you excuse me," said the Earl, coughing into his hand.

"He is a good man, but a bit frail. I'll be surprised if they ever give me grandchildren," said the Duke of Hausman.

"He seems fit and strong," said Ultima, although she could feel the man was a mage and he gave her a bad feeling.

"James comes from a family of rakes. There are rumors that his father had more illegitimate children than he had properties, and the man was exceedingly wealthy," said the Duke.

"Since you have agreed to the marriage, the man must be better than his father," said Ultima.

"He doesn't have the reputation, himself. We know little about him since he spent much of his time with his mother's family in Alhambra. He just came to the capital a year ago, when his father and two eldest brothers died. He took on the title, and I have it upon good faith that he's been an excellent Lord to his people," said the Duke.

"In all that time, I have never seen him in Xawata's," said Ultima.

"Enough of that. Will you dance with me?" said the man, drinking the last of his port. Ultima heard when they announced the next dance, it would be a slow one, and would not be an intricate dance that might challenge her leg, so she agreed.

The Grand Duke escorted her to the dance floor, and the music began. They danced, and Ultima was thankful her earlier decision had been to refrain from dancing, following her dance with Lord Otto. Her leg was aching.

"Do you know Lord Otto Hightower?" asked Ultima.

"Oh yes, he is the third son of my good friend, Lord Gareth Hightower, the Duke of Vurthas, from Yakuta. Why are you asking?" The duke turned his head and looked at Ultima with inquisitive eyes.

"I met him today. I was just wondering why I have never met him before at any other party," said Ultima.

"The family only socializes with a particular group of people in Tsestelago. When they come here, it is usually for business, and they leave soon after. I doubt you will ever see any of them in any other gatherings," said the Duke of Hausman.

After that brief exchange, the duke talked little. The thought of not seeing Lord Otto again made her heart skip a beat, that was so unlike her. Why would she care if she saw the man again? She wiped the thought from her mind by trying to concentrate on not letting her aching leg take over. As she danced, she noticed a shadowy figure on the balcony of the hall. A man moved from the corner pillar, toward the banister, and he had a weapon.

The shot was as unexpected as a sneeze. Ultima saw the arrow coming her way. She pushed the Grand Duke to the side and onto the floor. She fell with the Grand Duke, and the arrow hit a nearby dancer's leg.

Screams from the women and shouts of orders from the men led to mayhem. From the floor, Ultima could see the other dancers scurry away and servants running both toward the Grand Duke and up to the balcony. The shadowed man ran along the length of the balcony and disappeared behind some curtains blocking her view. He left as fast as he had appeared.

The Duke helped Ultima stand, and they ran to a corner of the great hall. Ultima's heart pounded fast. At the start, her legs felt as heavy as two boulders. She had to run, but she could barely move. She forced herself to one step and then another, moving past many guests who were also running for safety but in all directions, and then the pair heard the Duke's wife scream from another direction.

"Take Ultima to my study and wait for me there," said the Duke to two of his servants. The duke had the two servants escort Ultima to safety, while he went to secure his family. The hunt for the would-be assassin began. Commander Baxter, who had been dancing, called over a servant. He tried to calm everyone down and stop them from stampeding and trampling over other fallen guests. Ultima ran along the hallways with her escort and entered the Duke of Hausman's study. She ran to the window where she could see the people as they ran out of the manor, leaving coats and even shoes behind. The two servants stayed with her.

Thump, crash, pump. There were noises of things breaking outside the room, and of doors opening and being slammed shut. She ran to the door and tried to listen. There were footsteps, and another door slammed.

"Help me place the larger of the desks in front of the door." Ultima and the two servants tried to push the heavy oak piece of furniture in front of the door, but the big thing wouldn't budge. As they pushed on the desk, Ultima heard footsteps running outside.

"Push, we must push this thing in front of the door now." Moisture covered Ultima's brow and sweat trickled down her spine. "Push, harder." The men put all their weight onto it. They pushed hard, but still Ultima had to use a little of her telekinetic magic to help make the desk move.

SLAM, a door made a horrid noise. Droplets of sweat dripped into her eyes, but then the desk moved slowly, and they placed it in front of the door, enough to cover the doorknob.

Rack, rack, thump. Someone tried to open the door. It hit the desk. They opened and closed and slammed the door, but the heavy desk stood firm. Whoever was on the other side stopped trying to open the door. The sounds of leaving footsteps on the marble floor made Ultima's ears ring. After a few seconds, Ultima became aware her breaths were increasing, and she could no longer control it.

"I need to calm down," said Ultima. She laid on the sofa and closed her eyes. "This can't be happening to me." She counted all the men she had ever slept with, within her mind, to keep herself from fainting.

✦✦✦

After several hours of a pursuit for the perpetrator, someone was pushing the door again. Ultima got up from the sofa.

"Open the door; this is the Duke. Open the door to my study," the Grand Duke shouted.

Ultima helped the servants push and shove the heavy furniture with her magic and let in their master.

"Ultima how are you doing?" inquired the Grand Duke.

"I'm sorry we moved your furniture, but someone was trying to get in. It scared me," said Ultima.

"It was me, darling Ultima. The servants and I were looking in the rooms for guests to bring them outside," said Lord Thomas, the Duke's second son. The Earl of Portmore, Lord James walked into the study a few minutes later.

"I'm sorry." When Ultima saw her reflection in the bookcase's glass, it showed a ghostly pale face and dry lips looking back at her.

"No need to apologize. I owe you my life," said the Grand Duke.

"Did you catch the man?" Ultima asked Lord James.

"No, but we are still looking. My fiancé and the family are all safe and secured, but I want guards keeping watch at the manor," said the Earl of Portmore, breathless and coughing.

Once his son and the Earl of Portmore left, the Grand Duke ordered a drink for himself and tea for Ultima. The servants left in a hurry, and ten minutes later, as Ultima was drinking her tea, Commander Baxter knocked and entered the room.

"Exotic Ultima are you hurt?" asked Commander Baxter.

"No, I'm just shaken and nervous. What happened? Did you catch the man that tried to kill the Grand Duke?" Ultima's words came out with a pause and less grace than she would have wanted.

"We found no trace of the man. Did you see the man trying to kill you?" asked the Commander.

"No, but he wasn't trying to kill me. He was aiming for the Grand Duke's back." Ultima couldn't get her icy hands warm, even though she was sitting near the fireplace.

"My dear Ultima, you were in my arms, tight to my chest. If that arrow had hit my back, it would have gone through me and hit you as well. Arrows go through a human body, and that arrow was long enough to hit us both," said the Grand Duke, whiskey glass in hand.

"It was serendipitous that you pushed the Grand Duke out of the way," said a bear of a man from the door. The man entered the room as the commander and Ultima were talking.

❖❖❖

"Hello, I'm Marshal Paul Donnelly. I'll be investigating the attempted murder of the Grand Duke. One of your guests alerted me," said Marshal Donnelly, standing tall and intimidating. The man wore a long leather coat, over a navy-blue tailored suit. His neatly combed dark-brown hair made him look handsome, but his body, as a boulder of a man, made him seem menacing.

"I'm the commander of the castle guards. I'll be taking charge of the investigation," said Commander Baxter, but his petulant attitude quickly deflated with the marshal's response.

"That may be the case. However, your commission is to guard our King, secure his safety, and control the soldiers and the castle. This assassination attempt is a civil offense and falls outside your jurisdiction. It is a case for the Marshal's Office and therefore solely under my authority.

"I represent the King's Law of the land, and I intend to conduct my investigation to the fullest capacity as decreed by the King himself." That said, the man walked into the room and directly over to the window to look outside.

"Exotic Ultima, this is the second time you have survived an assassination attempt. It wasn't until recently that the commander's people made my office privy to the fact that you were present at Prince Marco's assassination. I'll be paying you a visit in a day or two to talk about the prince. However, for now, did you see the man that tried to kill you?" asked Marshal Donnelly.

"No, the man was in the shadows. I didn't see his face. I'm sorry." Ultima took a deep breath, and allowed her hands to relax by the sides of her body. After a few more questions, the ambassador from Palermo returned to his hotel. They took Ultima home in the marshal's carriage.

When Ultima entered the brothel and Xawata found out what happened at the party, Ultima could tell he was angry but he said nothing to her. In her room, thinking of the day's event, Ultima shuddered. What if the assassin was really trying to kill her? What if he came to Xawata's and finished her in her sleep? Her hands shook, and she had to fight to breathe. She had never suffered from anxiety. She was a level-headed woman. Sleep, she needed to sleep; sleep was the best equalizer, but what if that man came while she was sleeping?

"Tomorrow is going to be a fresh new day, and with it will come the possibility of something good happening, like Xawata dying in his sleep," said Ultima.

She went to clean her face of her make-up and wash her body with a cloth before going to bed. *Thank the good gods of Yavos,* she thought, Orrun was in her room, ready to sleep on the sofa and protect her.

♦♦♦

The next day following the assassination attempt on the Grand Duke of Hausman, late in the afternoon, a young maid came to Ultima's room and told her Xawata expected her in the receiving parlor.

"Why? We are not open yet. I'm not ready to receive my clients, and my first client will not arrive until later tonight," said Ultima.

"It is the city marshal, m'lady," said the young maid.

Marshal Donnelly had presented himself at Xawata's brothel one hour before the brothel was to open its doors for business.

Xawata met Ultima at the top of the stairs and walked her down to the receiving parlor where Marshal Donnelly was sitting on a chair, waiting for them.

"I'm going to charge you people for my Exotic's time," said Xawata.

"You can try, but I have a warrant to talk to your Exotic," said Donnelly.

"You are here about the Grand Duke's assassination attempt, aren't you?" said Xawata.

"Yes, I told your Exotic last night I'd be here today, soonest."

"Fine, you can talk to her, but only for a few minutes. She must work tonight," said Xawata, sitting on a chair facing the lawman and looking at him with contempt.

"What can I do for you, Marshal Donnelly? As you can see, I'm not ready to receive my clients, so you must be brief," said Ultima. She was in a robe and kept her black hair tied back, behind her head and away from her face.

"I'm just here to ask a few questions. Do you mind if I smoke?" asked the man.

"I don't mind," said Ultima.

"When the attempt happened, where exactly on the balcony was the shadow standing?"

"He was to the left of the grand hall looking down from the long veranda of the second floor," Ultima tried to remember the event, but it had all happened so fast.

"How long from the moment you saw the shadow to the moment the assailant shot his arrow?"

"Not long, a few seconds. At first, I thought it was a reflection from a coat of armor. When the shadow moved, I realized it was a person." Ultima crossed her arms, and her icy hands hugged her body which had started to tremble once more.

"Do you have any more questions to ask my Exotic?" Xawata sat cross-legged, with a hand rubbing over his eyes and face.

"No, I think I have enough for now. Exotic Ultima, if you remember anything in the next few days, please contact me. We have an assassin on the loose, and after the assassination of our Prince Regent we must take all precautions." The man snuffed his cigarette in a porcelain ashtray and left the parlor. When the marshal had left the house, Xawata got up and went to stand in front of his Exotic.

"Ultima, I better not find you involved in any illegal schemes or find that one of your clients has lured you into doing crazy, stupid things. Listen to me and heed me well. Before I lose this brothel, I'll have you killed," said Xawata, and he left the parlor in a hurry.

Ultima stayed behind, ears ringing. And now, her fear of a man entering through her window came back to haunt her during the day. She left to get herself ready for the night, still trying to remember anything that could help catch the assassin.

CHAPTER 6

The Fox Hunt

Xawata had sold Ultima's time a year in advance to the Countess of Kellin for the annual King's Fox Hunt. For the last four years, every person who had gone to the hunt with Ultima had won the hunt. The countess enjoyed the company of women, and as long as she didn't look for another man, the Earl of Kellin would satisfy his wife's every desire.

Xawata had Ultima's riding suit made to perfection. Her seamstress would make sure her suit protected her on the hunt. She had the best that coin could buy.

The day of the hunt was three days after the engagement party of the Grand Duke of Hausman's daughter. On the day of the hunt, the countess sent a carriage for Ultima. She was to be at the hunt site well after everybody else arrived. The countess wanted to show off her friend, the Exotic Ultima. The most prominent earls, dukes, marquises, and viscounts were all expected to appear at the hunt. After the prince's death, they expected the King to disallow the annual event to run. Instead, this year there were extra guards with additional security measures to ensure the foxhunt could take place.

"Hello, Exotic Ultima; it is lovely to see you looking so beautiful," said the Countess of Kellin. The countess was an older woman who retained her beauty, by tooth and nail. She dyed her hair to hide the gray growing faster as time went by, and she wore the latest trends. Her small blue eyes were always looking for other people's faults, but she had much influence in the palace court, so people tolerated her and even feared her tongue.

"It is my pleasure to see you as well, Countess. It has been too long since you requested my time. I believe the last time we saw each other was two years ago. I was wondering if you had forgotten me," said Ultima, putting on her riding gloves. Her round, dark glasses covered the red rims around her blue eyes. Xawata made her work the previous night, and she had had little sleep.

"Oh no, how could I forget Exotic Ultima Skylar, the most beautiful Exotic in the entire capital?" said the Countess.

"Oh, you flatter me," said Ultima.

"Let's go, my dear; I want us to be the talk of everyone at the fox hunt," said the Countess.

"Which of your horses are you riding this year?" asked Ultima as they walked to the meeting area.

"I'm riding The Twisted Harp, my newest addition. I bought her from Lord Koutsu. The best horse trainer in the entire Alhambra Kingdom. You will ride Hot Summer's Day. He is a gelding that my husband loves to ride," said the Countess. When Ultima saw the horses, happiness brought a shine to her eyes. She saw the palomino she was to ride in today's hunt and her heart leaped.

"Oh, he is gorgeous," said Ultima as she touched Hot Summer's Day's soft mane. The horse was pure grace.

"I knew you were going to like him," said the Countess.

This year the fox hunt was taking place at the King's summer property. The summit above the summer castle was over a thousand acres of unbroken woods and valleys outside the capital. The King had all his hounds ready to start the hunt. They released a red fox, waited ten minutes, and then they released the hounds. The horn sounded and all attending the hunt chased after the dogs. Ultima rode astride. That way, she could ride faster and more comfortably, and more importantly as far as Xawata was concerned, she was less likely to fall off and get injured. The hounds barked, and the group of riders kept going after them, weapons in hand.

The Countess of Kellin rode beside her, and after thirty minutes of the hunt, Commander Baxter caught up and rode next to them.

"Have any of you ladies seen the hounds? I can hear them but not see them," said Commander Baxter.

"We have been following the Duke of Hausman's hounds, but I think we took a wrong turn," said the Countess.

They slowed down when they found a stream.

"I think I can see the fox. Look, it's hiding inside a hollowed tree." She took her rifle and pointed, but then there was a loud *bam* that came from the distance.

Commander Baxter, Ultima, and the countess looked around.

"It sounds like someone has found the fox," said Commander Baxter. What Ultima thought was a fox was a log wedged inside the hollowed log. They rode on, evaded a cluster of trees, and reached a sloped area that led down to a dry stream; they had to slow down to cross. There was another shot, but this time it was nearby. Ultima's horse bucked, and she almost fell but held on. Commander Baxter on the other hand, who was right next to Ultima, fell from his horse.

Ultima and Countess Kellin dismounted their horses and went to help Baxter.

Bam, bam! She heard two more shots near them, but Ultima kept her head low. She crawled slowly to Commander Baxter's side. The man was bleeding profusely.

"The commander's been shot," shouted Ultima.

"Do something," ordered the Countess. Ultima looked around and then at Baxter.

"What do you want me to do?" asked Ultima.

"You are the Exotic. You help him. Do it now," said the Countess. Ultima's hands shook. She kept looking around. She took her inner shirt, tore a long, thin piece of material, and pushed the material inside the hole from the bullet with her pinky finger.

"What are you doing?" asked Countess Kellin.

"You ordered me to do something. This should help stop the bleeding until someone comes to help us," said Ultima.

Ultima hesitated. She could take away his pain. She knew that much, but she couldn't reveal her magic at any price.

"UHHH," moaned Commander Baxter.

"He is in so much pain," said the Countess. Ultima placed her hands on Commander Baxter's arm. She didn't heal his injury. She only took his pain away.

"Commander Baxter, please wake," said Ultima, but the man didn't respond. There were two more shots. The countess screamed, and the horses reared and galloped away. The countess kept calling until a group of riders came to where they were.

"Riders," shouted the Countess.

"Who are they?" asked Ultima.

"Oh, thank our lucky stars. It's the Duke of Hausman, Lord Meedo, Lord Thomas, and another gentleman I don't know," said Countess Kellin.

"Go get help," ordered the Duke to his son, Thomas.

"What happened? Was he in the middle of a shot from someone else?" asked Lord Meedo. The man was immense, as tall as he was portly.

"I don't think so. No one came to help us or called the shot," said Ultima. The unconscious Commander Baxter laid on the ground, face down. The shot to his back had exited through the side of his body.

Ultima looked up. The other Lord turned out to be Lord Otto Hightower. He wore a Yakutan hat that made him look so sexy, but Ultima could see a look of concern under the rim. She recognized Lord Otto right away. He dismounted and lowered himself to where Ultima was kneeling. She was still holding the piece of dress in the bullet hole in the commander's back. When Lord Meedo took over assisting the commander, Lord Otto helped Ultima stand. Ultima stood and moved away from the commander, but when Ultima touched Lord Otto's hand, she felt it. The man was angry. Those dark-green eyes looked back at her, and his soft smile made her want to touch him.

"Are you hurt?" asked Lord Otto.

"No, I'm not hurt," said Ultima.

"You have blood all over your hands. Here's a cloth. Let me pour some water in your hands," said Lord Otto. Ultima cleaned her hands.

"Try to drink some water." Lord Otto gave her some water from another pouch he carried. She drank and gave the water pouch back.

"Thank you for your help, Lord Otto," said Ultima.

"You are welcome, Exotic Ultima." He smiled and went to help the others move the commander.

She would never forget those eyes.

When a group of men came to take the commander and escort Ultima and the countess back to the stables, the Duke of Hausman accompanied them, but Lord Otto disappeared.

The hunt halted. Someone called a healer for the commander and another for the Countess of Kellin to allay her distress.

"There is too much commotion. It is best for you to return to your home," said the Duke of Hausman. So, Ultima went back to the brothel, accompanied by Lord Meedo.

◆◆◆

"What did you do? The Countess of Kellin said you did something to stop Commander Baxter's pain, and they all said the commander was too quiet for the injury he had when they arrived. Everyone knows you did something. What did you do?" demanded Xawata. "I swear, I'll take my anger out on Akina if you don't start telling me the truth."

"No, don't. I'll tell you. I only took his pain away. I didn't do anything else. I swear," said Ultima.

Xawata paced Ultima's room, muttering to himself. "'Only took his pain away,' she says. What does that mean? Did you use your healing magic? Did anyone see you use your magic? I swear if anyone suspects you are a mage, I will kill Akina." On and on he muttered as he paced back and forth. Then he stopped and looked at Ultima, and pointed his long, bony finger at her. "You will not see any clients outside of the house for the next six months," he shouted, spittle flying everywhere. Abruptly he turned and left Ultima alone in her room.

Later that same day, Marshal Donnelly came to the brothel asking to talk to Ultima.

Marshal Donnelly's dark-brown hair matched the color of his coat. When he saw Ultima entering the receiving parlor, his eyebrow lifted a little. She had changed into a day dress, and her face was rosy with the sun of the day. Xawata wasn't present, and the marshal was alone with Ultima.

"Exotic Ultima, here you are again in the middle of another assassination. I'm believing that maybe you have something to do with the events, or the assassin is trying to get to you," said Marshal Donnelly.

"What do you mean, another assassination?" said Ultima.

"The commander didn't survive his wounds. The healer got to him too late," said Mr. Donnelly.

"Oh no, that is horrible, but I have nothing to do with this, I assure you," said Ultima, sitting on a cushioned chair in the receiving parlor on the first floor.

"Did you see anyone?" asked the man.

"No, I was looking for the fox. The hounds were near, and we kept moving until we reached a downward path of the stream," said Ultima.

"You happened to be at all these assassination attempts and each time when ask, you respond, 'I saw nothing.' Are you hiding something? I'm starting to believe you have something to do with these occurrences," said the Marshal.

"It's not my fault these men have been targeted and I *happen to be* there. I go to many, if not all, high society events," said Ultima.

"Have you given some thought to the possibility that maybe the assassin is actually trying to kill my Exotic?" Xawata was at the entrance of the parlor, dressed in his favorite dark-blue, pinstriped suit.

"All these events are causing me great distress," said Ultima.

"Ultima, the conversation is over. Go and get some rest. You are not working tonight," said Xawata. Ultima stood up and prepared to leave.

"I'm not done questioning her," said the Marshal.

"Yes, you are. And next time you want to talk to any of my slaves, I must insist on being present," said Xawata, and Ultima left the parlor to return to her room.

She entered her rooms and undressed, preparing to bathe. She ran herself a bath and sank into the welcoming water, sighing. Ultima wanted to stay in the water forever, but she knew life would never be easy for her.

❖❖❖

In the third week of the month, on the fourth night of the week, Ultima sat by the vanity in the orange room, waiting for her recurring client, the Duke of Horrel. The orange room was Horrel's favorite room. She hated the fourth night of the the third week of every third month—Horrel's night. Ultima's mind would need to find a place to keep her sanity. She had never visited any other place outside Pailo, but she had read of the mountains, the rivers, the valleys, and deserts. She wanted silence, but she knew all she was going to get were screams. Horrel arrived, and so did the three young prostitutes he requested. They were all younger than fifteen. The man loved little girls; the younger, the better.

All four women wore black. Ultima's form-fitting dress had a slit that opened high to her hip.

"Exotic Ultima, my favorite expert in love. You three little things stand back by the wall. Tonight, I want to start with you, Ultima," said the man. The three young girls stood by the wall, looking scared.

"Hello Duke Horrel, I see you requested dinner. Will you have me sing while you eat?" said Ultima. Her hate was well hidden, but contempt covered her heart every moment she had to share a room with Horrel.

"Not yet; I want you to eat with me." The black tobacco stains between his teeth made Ultima want to gag. She had to control herself, no gagging reflex on the job. Ultima sat across from the man.

"No, I want you to sit to the left of me," said the Duke. Ultima stood up from her vanity, walked with unhurried steps, and sat next to the duke. The duke ate with one hand and rubbed Ultima's leg with the other. He drank scotch and ate a small morsel at a time.

Eat faster and get drunk. The faster you eat and get drunk, the faster we are done with you. Ultima's thoughts were all hers.

"My Lord, I hear you are making quite a stir in the House of Lords. I must congratulate you on your selection for the overseer of the Slave-Trade taxation," said Ultima, taking a little mouthful of her food, trying not to look at the man directly.

"Oh, thank you. It was overdue. I've been working with the Trades Office for many years. Sing my beauty." And the man's hand kept caressing Ultima's leg, reaching down almost to her knee and up again as high as her groin.

In the middle of the night with a full moon, the Alhambra desert feels hot. The heat comes up from the sand, but the air cools everything. Ultima kept reciting facts to herself, her thoughts needed to keep her mind from collapsing.

Ultima sang. She knew Horrel's favorite songs. The man moved his hand up and down her leg until his nails scratched her leg. She stopped singing, and her hand stopped his hand.

"I must stay as I came to you, house rules," said Ultima. The man laughed. "I paid for pain."

"Remember, you can't damage my skin and cause an open wound," said Ultima with a half-smile. The man pushed her hand away, and he stood up.

"Stand up Exotic," shouted the Duke. Ultima stood up, and his hand went up between her legs. He inflicted pain. Ultima didn't flinch. She was used to feeling pain.

"You three come and follow my lead," said the Duke. With his hand inside Ultima, he pushed her to the bed.

"You three undress the Exotic." The girls undressed Ultima and Horrel …

In the Alhambra, deserts are where the Desert Dwellers live, and they raise and train the flying feathered dragons called minokawas. Maybe one day I will get to see a minokawa.

Ultima's mind went to a safe place, while Horrel had his type of fun with her body.

❖❖❖

Two hours later, Ultima lay bent over in pain, and two of the three little girls lay next to her, bruised beyond recognition. The three lay, breathing hard, with silent tears coursing down their faces. The third little girl lay on the floor near the bed, in a fetal position, crying. Horrel got up from the large four-posted bed. He walked over to the large chair in the room's corner where he had lain his clothes, and he dressed slowly. When he finished dressing, he went to the crying girl on the floor. He squatted down and took a red curl and pulled it.

"Stop crying!" said Horrel, but the girl couldn't stop.

"I said: Stop. Crying!" shouted Horrel, but the girl just covered her freckled face with her bruised hands. Horrel stood up. He looked down at the girl and kicked her body until she stopped crying. Horrel smiled. He turned to look at Ultima.

"I had fun. I'll see you in three months, Ultima," said the Duke of Horrel, and he walked out of the orange room.

CHAPTER 7

A Foreigner Came to Visit

A week after Horrel's last visit to Ultima, a man walked into Xawata's brothel in the late hours of the morning. The white-haired man walked tall and straight. In one hand, a cane, and his other hand in his coat pocket. He asked to talk to the owner, Xawata Faan. The man dressed and walked like a noble accustomed to being obeyed.

Xawata met the man in his office and showed him the best hospitality of the house.

"Hello! What can I do for you?" said Xawata.

"Hello, I'm Lord Gareth Logan Caleb Otto Hightower, the Duke of Vurthas from the Kingdom of Yakuta. I'm here in the kingdom for business and want some company," said the man.

"I'm sorry, Your Grace; no one told me to expect a high-ranking noble," said Xawata, standing up and giving a slight bow to the man. A second man entered the office after the duke.

"Lord Hightower, didn't I tell you this place was the best?" said the old Marquis of Carlton with a broad smile.

The man's salt-and-pepper goatee matched the hair on the sides of his head.

"Marquis of Carlton, it's been months since your last visit," said Xawata.

"I've been away from the city, but as soon as I came back, I knew I had to bring my old friend Lord Gareth Hightower, the Duke of Vurthas, to your establishment for some fun," said Carlton.

"I hear you have the best brothel in the entire capital," said the Duke of Vurthas.

"You shouldn't be listening to lies. Mine is the best brothel in the entire Kingdom of Tsestelago! Could I interest you both in a port? Something else?" Xawata stood behind the desk.

"Yes, whiskey," said the Duke of Vurthas.

"How about you, my Lord?" asked Xawata.

"Whiskey is fine for me as well," said the Marquis of Carlton, standing by the fireplace.

"My Lords, please sit and be comfortable," said Xawata. And the duke and marquis sat on chairs in front of Xawata's desk.

"Orrun, get us the best whiskey we have in the house."

The servant left the three men alone in the study, and returned in a few minutes to serve the liquor, then left again.

"This whiskey comes from Yakuta," said the Duke.

"Yes, it's G&G whiskey; I spare no expense. So, what will be your pleasure? I have three Exotics to choose from and many courtesans."

"I'm here to buy the time of your Exotic Ultima, but I want her for the entire night."

Xawata raised an eyebrow, and a wicked smile came to his face. He almost had a heart attack thinking of all the coin he would make in that one night alone. Only a few men could afford to purchase his greatest possession, Ultima, for an entire night. All considered Ultima's fee per hour to be extravagant.

"I was told your Exotic was the best in the entire kingdom, and even the world. I seriously doubt it, for we have several beauties in Yakuta, but I had to find out for myself," said the Duke.

Xawata's greed made him salivate over the words of the man.

"My Ultima is a beauty and exceedingly well educated. Her fee for an hour starts at ten gold coins for conversation, and her fee increases depending on what you want. If you want her time during the day, she can be yours for twenty-eight gold and ten silver coins for three hours, but no physical contact. If you want something more intimate, there is an extra fee. An entire night will be one hundred and fifty gold coin pieces. The night starts at eight o'clock, and is up two hours before dawn. If you want to lie with her, it will be an extra fifty gold pieces for one lay." Xawata knew that the most Ultima would make in a night was twenty or maybe thirty-five coins of gold, for he would only sell her to two or three men per night. Some nights she would only sing in a concert, and for that, he would charge five silver per person who entered the salon, but in total he had to make more than ten gold pieces before he would let her sing.

The duke took a few minutes to think. He looked at Xawata, then stood from his chair, extended his hand to the man and said, "Agreed!"

Xawata drafted the contract to let Ultima be with the man for one full night.

"Before I sign your document, I would like you to sign my document," said the Duke.

"I've never signed any documents without my man of business present," said Xawata.

"Mr. Xawata, this document simply says you will not stop him from keeping the Exotic for the entire night. We know you have the reputation of kicking new clients out of your establishment if you even *think* the person's hurting the girls. We don't want any problems saying that the Duke is infringing on your rights," said the Marquis of Carlton.

"I must protect my property. These Exotics mean coin for me," said Xawata, standing from his chair.

"I know I'm a new client," said the Duke of Vurthas.

"Xawata, my friend, we know you don't do it regularly, but you have done it often enough to have a reputation in Pailo. Go ahead—read the document. It has only ten pages. It also says you will never use the purchase of the Exotic as blackmail against the Duke of Vurthas. There is a part that says you will never use this transaction as a form of a gain in the Assembly of Dukes. It also says that you will tell no one that the duke ever visited your establishment. If you do, you will pay the duke a fee," said the Marquis of Carlton.

"This establishment is the best in the kingdom. And I'm a reputable owner," said Xawata.

"Then we understand each other, Mr. Xawata. This document is just to protect me and my investment. After all, we are talking about one hundred and fifty coins of gold. I assure you; I will not harm your Exotic in any way or ask her to do anything that isn't in her trade license. However, I also have a reputation to take care of, and I'm an old, married man. I need to protect what is mine, and I have a business to safeguard," said the Duke of Vurthas.

Xawata looked from one man to the other. The ten pages in his hands had the ducal seal and even the city seal, so this was an official document. The duke took a large bag of coins, and he poured the contents over Xawata's desk.

"I'm ready to pay now, but you must be discreet about me being here, and my document must be signed. I don't want anyone knowing I visited your establishment," said the Duke. Xawata's eyes went down to the gold and up at the duke. The man rummaged around his desk until he found a pen, and he signed the document without even reading it. The Duke of Vurthas followed his signature, and the Marquis of Carlton signed last. The greedy, conniving scoundrel Xawata took the bags of coin, counted them, and placed them in a drawer.

"No problem, I'll log the gold entry as an Ultima business transaction and nothing else. Will you be bedding my Exotic because that is an extra fee," said Xawata.

"No, I will not be bedding the woman. Thank you, Mr. Faan. I'll be here by 7:55 PM, and I want to have dinner with her. I want her to sing and dance for me tonight." The duke placed the contract in his coat pocket and left.

♦♦♦

Xawata instructed Ultima and all the women working for her to arrange everything for the duke's visit that night. After all, Xawata had sold her time for an entire night and he wanted to ensure his reputation was maintained.

For Ultima, it was just another client. She carried out her daily beauty routine and dressed in her finest. She waited for her client, fixing her hair a little here and there. Her form-fitting black dress had a slit that opened high up her thigh, and she was sitting in front of the vanity in her working room. She tried to smile, but today no smile came to her. She put on her mask, and her revealing black dress left enough of her breast exposed to show her mark of the Exotic.

Ultima decorated the room in which she worked to her own preferences; her taste was delightful. She decorated the room in a soft, creamy light green and pale blue with red accents around the coverings. She had placed a large sofa in front of the fireplace, and the room had a generous space for dancing. In addition, the room held a dinner table, arranged for two, and several smaller tables with various table games set up. There were paintings and sculptures, making the room elegant. Ultima had chosen a majestic bed and situated it in an adjacent room, next to which there was a bathroom with a tub large enough to fit four people.

The man knocked and entered the room, and paused as he took in all that he could see, a little woman with long, black hair and blue eyes, sitting in front of a mirror. She quickly lowered her half-mask into place, turned from the mirror, and looked up at him and smiled.

"Please, enter Your Grace; I've been expecting you," said Ultima, standing up as the man entered the room. She gave him a curtsy.

The duke was a strong and distinguished man who looked to be in his sixties. He entered the room and walked to the dinner table. He was a head taller than Ultima, even with her high heels.

"You are a good-looking woman," said the Duke.

"Thank you, Your Grace. And you are very dashing and handsome yourself. However, before we start, I must tell you that there are some rules for the night," said Ultima, in her sultry voice.

"Rules? I paid a sizable sum of coin for you. I'm not interested in rules, young lady. I'm not planning to touch you tonight. Come sit, let's have dinner. I'm famished, and I wish to speak in my native tongue, Yakutan. You can speak Yakutan?" asked the Duke.

"Yes, of course," said Ultima, in perfect Yakutan, as she walked over to the dinner table. "However, you must be aware of at least four very important things," said Ultima.

"Fine, what are those important things?"

"First, please don't hit my face. I must keep my face flawless. Second, please don't pull me by my collar. I like air in my lungs. The third, I will need some moments of rest in between your services throughout the night. And the last, if you want to bed me, you must let me know now. I was told that was not in your contract." Ultima arranged the napkin on her lap and looked at the man with a soft smile.

"Fair enough; I hear you are an excellent dancer. I may ask you to dance with me if there is any music. I do want to hear you sing, and I have many questions for you."

"Which topic, Your Grace? I'm well versed in several, but not everything," said Ultima.

"Oh, I know my questions are in your line of expertise. You can have all the rest you want and need. I will leave after you satisfy my curiosity, but don't fear, it will be well before two hours before dawn. I need my beauty sleep," said the older man with a chuckle—Ultima smiled below her mask.

"Well, fine, Your Grace, it's your night. I'll do what you ask of me," said Ultima.

"Very well, do you have any servants around that can assure us protection if any *undesirable* person tries to enter?

I hear your kingdom just had an assassination attempt on the Duke of Hausman," said the Duke. In response, Ultima lifted a hand and pointed at the nearby servant, Orrun, standing in a corner, silently watching.

"He is our servant and guard for the night. He is also the one that calls the time, but don't worry, he will not interfere with us. He will leave and watch through a hidden window and will only enter if we need his assistance, or you break any of the four rules."

The old duke laughed.

"You are a cheeky girl. I want to see your face; there is no need for your mask with me." Ultima took off her mask and looked directly at the man, eye to eye.

"You are more beautiful than my friends mentioned," said the Duke.

"Thank you."

The duke sat at the table and asked for wine. Ultima rang a little bell and out from a corner, two servants appeared with food and drink. With that, a night of singing and conversation started.

❖❖❖

The night went on, and three hours before dawn, Ultima left the room where the duke slept soundly. The duke never touched her other than to dance. Like he had said, they talked, they danced, and she sang.

The servant, Orrun, followed Ultima to her room, just as he was accustomed to doing every night after Ultima entertained late at night. When Ultima entered her room, she asked Orrun to look around. Her fear of having someone hiding in her room was with her every night. When Ultima entered her room, it was refreshingly cool, just the way she liked it. She walked to her night table and removed the top of her dress when she noticed Akina. It did not surprise Ultima to see young Akina sleeping in her bed. The young girl loved to sleep with her mother.

"Orrun, wait! Please pick up Akina and carry her to her bedroom. She must get used to sleeping by herself. I don't need her with me tonight." Ultima stretched her back and sat next to Akina, and she caressed her head and face with all the love she could give, to the only person she had ever cared for in life.

"It is your fault, darling. You were the one that let her sleep with you since you gave birth to her. When she turned seven, I told you it was time for you to stop the coddling. You never stopped; I told you this was going to happen." Orrun placed his hands on his hips and smiled at his mistress.

"I know you did, but it is too sad; she will soon be working. I know I coddled her, but she is my daughter. And Xawata is so horrible to her." Ultima kissed little Akina's cheek and let Orrun lift her out of the bed.

"I remember he wanted to be present when he ordered you fixed the second time," said Orrun.

"He wasn't there; he got squeamish. That man is a piece of work. Take her to her bed. You were right. I coddle her too much. She needs to learn to be a woman." Ultima's sad words tasted bitter.

Orrun picked sleeping Akina up from Ultima's bed and took the girl to her room. Ultima went to clean her body with a wet cloth and then went to bed.

"I want to sleep forever," said Ultima as she closed her eyes.

❖❖❖

Two days later, Ultima had worked the previous evening, with a client who had stayed late into the night. It was the Earl of Furlong. Ultima had only had two hours of sleep when screams awoke her. Ultima shot out of bed and went running toward the source of the commotion. The screams were coming from Xawata's rooms. Ultima ran barefoot, wearing only her sheer night shift.

Ultima encountered several of the servants standing by the open door to Xawata's bedroom. When she arrived, all the servants let her enter. After all, Ultima was the top Exotic in the brothel. Xawata laid on his back with his eyes open, but with a glare of death.

"Lola, what happened?" Ultima spoke to Xawata's personal favorite Exotic.

"I woke to use the bathroom and I found him as you see him." Xawata's stiff body made no one cry. There was only one show of emotion, pleasant surprise. This was the occurrence of a lifetime. Xawata, her one master, went to live in hell.

"Call a healer, the trade officials, and a lawman. We also need to call his man of business," said Ultima to a nearby servant.

"What will happen now?" asked one prostitute, standing by the door.

"Who will inherit the brothel?" asked a half-naked courtesan standing by the bed.

"Ultima! What will happen to all the servants that work here? And what about the slaves?" asked Orrun, passing his big trembling hands back and forth over his curly hair.

"Why do you all ask me? He never talked to me about his private affairs. I know little about these types of things. Xawata didn't give me much education on the law of the land." However, despite her protestations, she knew she was happy for the first time in her life.

The healer, a mortician, and a lawman came to the brothel within minutes of being called. The trade officials came much later in the day of Xawata's death, with the man of business and the lawyers following closely behind.

CHAPTER 8

One Dead, Two Free

Everyone in the brothel was either in mourning, celebrating, or scared for their lives. Two days after the death of Xawata, there was a big commotion that woke Ultima early in the morning. She could hear the noise from her room as Orrun entered without knocking. She woke from a dream she couldn't remember.

"Ultima, Ultima darling, you must wake. The entire brothel is in an uproar. You must dress and go down to Xawata's office. And you must do it fast," said Orrun.

"Why must things happen so early in the morning? What is going on? I just went to bed, maybe four hours ago. I've been taking care of running the brothel, and I'm exhausted." She was dizzy from lack of sleep, then annoyed by the lack of respect for her status as the top Exotic in the house.

"Sweetheart, I know, I'm sorry I woke you like this, but I have bad news. I think we have the new owner in the house. You must get up and meet him downstairs. As the top Exotic, it is your duty," said Orrun.

Ultima took her time getting dressed. She couldn't care less who was at the brothel. If it was the new owner, that meant a new creep in her life, and she wasn't inclined to hurry. The new owner may want to spend a few days with her. Or maybe he might just leave her alone. In the end, why worry? She was a slave.

When she reached the office, an open door greeted her. She entered a brightly lit room. Ultima had never seen this room with so much light. Xawata always kept his office lit only with candles or lanterns. It was always dark and dreary. However, on this day, the curtains had been drawn back all the way, and someone had opened the windows. A ray of light entered through the corner window, and it hit the old desk, illuminating specks of dust floating about the office.

When Ultima entered, she first noticed Mr. Walter Fuller, Xawata's man of business. He was her client once per year, but the little pervert preferred young little girls, and for her to hit him. The sight of him gave Ultima a stomach ache. Then she saw big ears, Mr. Earnest Dawdled, Xawata's lawyer. A very young trade official with a long face was sitting on a small stool by an even smaller table, but there stood the Duke of Horrel. *What is he doing here? So early—it's not his day?*

"Hello, gentlemen, you summoned me, so, I'm here. But I have work tonight. I'd appreciate it greatly if we can finish here in less than thirty minutes," said Ultima.

"Hello Ultima, you are gorgeous as always," said Mr. Fuller.

"Mr. Fuller, do we have an heir? The staff needs to know what will happen next," said Ultima.

"You don't need to worry about an heir. You all have a new owner. The Duke of Horrel was Xawata's business partner, and now he keeps the business," said Mr. Fuller.

Ultima's world turned upside-down. She had a new owner, and this owner was worse than Xawata. She had not supposed that could ever be possible. Her ears rang, and she wanted to faint, but her Exotic training took over her body. She raised one eyebrow as the only evidence that the news registered with her. Horrel's greed equaled that of Xawata, but his sadistic ways were sure to make all their lives miserable.

"My new, most prized possession, Exotic Ultima. I think for the next few months, you will only serve me," said the Duke of Horrel. His blue eyes looked at Ultima from her head to her toes. He walked over to her, grabbed one of her breasts, and squeezed it. Ultima wanted to whimper; the man had no pity.

"So, will I be working for others? Will I be staying here, or will you be moving me? What about my taxes?" Ultima asked all the questions in a hurry and with shaking hands hidden in her skirt's pockets.

"Oh yeah, I'll keep you for myself for a few months. You will stay here and needn't worry about your taxes." Ultima could see Horrel's stained teeth, and again the gag reflex made her dizzy. It was good she hadn't broken her fast.

Then, as if out of nowhere, "Good morning to all. Gentlemen, oh, hello Duke Horrel, the man of the hour. I heard you are the new owner of Xawata's Brothel. I'm happy you are all here." It was the Duke of Vurthas at the door, with the Marquis of Carlton, plus two other men who accompanied them. He filled the brothel's door with his imposing personality.

"It has been a long time, Carlton. We are not open for business. What are you doing here, Gareth?" asked the Duke of Horrel.

"I came to pick up my property," said Lord Gareth Hightower, the Duke of Vurthas.

"What property are you talking about?" asked Mr. Fuller. "I was Xawata's man of business and there was never any talk of selling any of the brothel's assets."

One of the men who had come with the Duke of Vurthas reached into his coat pocket and extracted a large envelope. Mr. Fuller took the envelope, read, and passed the papers to Xawata's lawyer, Mr. Dawdled.

"He came to get his Exotic Ultima Skylar," said Mr. Dawdled to all in the room.

"What did you say?" shouted the Duke of Horrel. He actually growled like an animal and bared his stained teeth.

"Xawata Faan sold the Exotic, Ultima Skylar, for one hundred and fifty gold coins two days ago, to the Duke of Vurthas. I personally witnessed when Xawata signed the document," said the Marquis of Carlton.

The second man who accompanied the Duke of Vurthas and the Marquis of Carlton ducked under the doorway lintel and stepped forward, by far the tallest man in the room. "Hello, I'm Mr. John Sheldon, the Duke of Vurthas's lawyer. I took the document the same day and had it registered with the city clerk."

"This can't be a legally binding document. It was done but two days ago. Did Xawata have an entry in his ledgers?" asked Horrel.

"There is an entry of one hundred and fifty gold coins, but it only says, 'Ultima business transaction'."

"You are not taking my top Exotic," said Horrel.

"She is mine now, and I'm not selling her," said the Duke of Vurthas, as he walked over to Ultima.

"Hello, Ultima, go order the servant to get your things. If I understand the law fully, I own you with all personal property," said the Duke.

"The Duke has the original document signed by Xawata. Apparently, all the coin has been exchanged, and there was a witness to the signature. The contract appears legal," said Mr. Dawdled. The lawyers, businessmen, and trade officials couldn't deny the document. The Duke of Horrel was beside himself. He had lost Ultima. The contract had to be served.

"No, I'll fight this; I want my Exotic," said Horrel, and he left the room in a hurry.

Ultima moved to the side and gave orders to one servant.

"Pack all my things and do it quickly. And bring Akina to me, hurry," ordered Ultima. She knew Akina was leaving her bedroom to go to her morning classes.

She went back to stand in front of her new owner.

"Ultima, we meet again, but this time it's under different circumstances," said the Duke.

"Hello, Your Grace. Will I be staying here a day or two to collect all my things?" That was all Ultima could think to say; her mind was in a whirl.

"No, you will leave with me today," said the Duke.

"Very well, but Your Grace, there is one thing you must know. I have a daughter. I ask for your clemency. Could you buy my daughter? I will work harder for you. I'll take four clients per night and even learn to tolerate a higher level of pain endurance for her. Your Grace, the child will not be in your way. Please let me take my daughter with me. Xawata had her attached to my contract and pre-registered her as my Exotic student. Please, sir, consider taking my Akina with us. She is a brilliant girl and will serve you well," said Ultima with pleading eyes.

"Explain?" asked the Duke of Vurthas to his lawyers, with a slight smile.

"Your Grace, according to the trade's rules, the student is attached to the Exotic teacher, under the umbrella of Xawata's slaves. The child must stay with her teacher until the student becomes an Exotic, and then 90% of her revenue will belong to Xawata, and 10% belongs to the Exotic teacher. The student can't be separated from the teacher until her training is complete. It is a complicated law," said Mr. Sheldon.

"So, what does it mean?" asked the Duke.

"You need to pay for her value as of now. If you don't wish to take the student, she will be turned into a common prostitute, and her Exotic training will be terminated," said the trade official with the long face who had been listening intently to the conversation.

"Your Grace, I've been training her since she was a young child of three, and she will be a great Exotic in the kingdom. She will make you much gold. Although, for now she is too young to have the prostitute-tattoo, much less the Exotic-tattoo. Thus, you can change her trade if you like. She is adept in many areas of arts and academics. With her education, she can serve you in several ways. She is even fluent in Yakutan and Palermo. Sir, I will take on any extra skill you wish to add in payment for my daughter. Bring Akina to me," ordered Ultima to the servant standing in a corner. Akina had been waiting outside the office.

When called, Akina entered the room and saw Ultima with all the men in the office; she said, "Good morning, Gentlemen, and Master Ultima." With great poise, well beyond her years, she walked sedately to stand next to her mother.

Akina was in her dancing uniform, with her black hair tied in a bun on the back of her head. Akina looked like what she was, a child of eleven.

"Your Grace, this is my Akina." Ultima held Akina's hand. The duke looked at the child and then at Ultima.

"She looks just like my wife, but with black hair. She even has my wife and son's same color eyes, deep, dark-green eyes," said the Duke.

One of the trades officials started to speak, drawing the duke's attention. "If you take the child, will you register her as a slave?" asked the younger man. "Apparently, according to Xawata's documents, he had the child registered as Exotic Ultima's daughter and Exotic student. Akina will be twelve in eight months. She has the slave collar, but not the tattoo. If you give her the slave-tattoo, it will lock her trade." The trades official had his tattoo-making paraphernalia ready to mark Akina.

"Who is her father?" asked the Duke.

"Xawata had Akina registered as a slave child born to his slave Exotic. The child's birth certificate states the child's mother is Ultima Leighton Skylar but no father, and Xawata has no other entry in his log for a father. Xawata entered the child in the city registry as the product of a prostitute's work. Xawata had the child attached to Exotic Ultima's contract. If Exotic Ultima ever left the brothel, she would never see the child again. He was a crafty man. He locked Exotic Ultima into his possession, valid even after her slave contract expires on her fortieth birthday," said the long-faced trades official.

"I'll take the student. However, I want to register her as free," said the Duke, but Ultima interrupted.

"Your Grace, can she then come with me and not have to complete her Exotic training?" asked Ultima.

"You will leave this place with me as my slave, but I will register the child as free and your daughter. I will not give her a trade for now," said the Duke to Ultima. Ultima smiled, and Akina stood close to her mother, holding her hand tight.

"Momma, will this mean I can now show my magic in public and not be afraid of being found out?" whispered Akina into Ultima's ear.

"Did I hear right? She's a mage?" asked the Duke.

"Yes, Your Grace, Akina is a mage," said Ultima, and Akina hid behind her mother.

"Come here, little Akina," said the Duke. And Akina came out from behind Ultima's skirts.

"Yes, Your Grace!" Akina looked at him without flinching.

"What kind of mage are you?" asked the Duke. Akina looked at her mother, and Ultima nudged her.

"I'm an arcane mage," said Akina.

"My son Caleb is an arcane mage. He is going to love having you around," said the Duke, giving Akina a smile.

"My sweet girl, I guess this means you can show your magic in public and not worry about anything," said Ultima, and Akina did a little jump for joy but regained her composure quickly.

"I'm sorry." Akina lowered her head in apology, but she smiled at the duke, and the duke returned her smile.

The Duke of Vurthas paid the fee for the child to Xawata's man of business and kept the little girl Akina registered as free, daughter to Exotic Ultima. When the duke signed all the transfer documents, he removed the collar from Akina's neck and bestowed a kiss on the top of her head.

"You are free, little girl," said the Duke. To which, Akina gave the duke another even greater smile than before.

"Thank you, Your Grace," said Akina. "Momma, look, I don't have a collar anymore." Her eyes shining, she smiled at every one in the room.

"I see you, my sweet girl," said Ultima.

The trades officials attached a leash to Ultima's golden collar and gave it to the Duke of Vurthas.

"You will never be bound by that," said the duke, and immediately released Ultima from the leash. He left with Ultima and Akina walking in front of him.

"Where are we going, Momma?" asked Akina.

"Hopefully to a better place, my heart," said Ultima.

CHAPTER 9

Ultima's New Trade

The ride to the Duke of Vurthas's manor passed quietly. Ultima rode in the horseless carriage with the Duke and Akina, while the Marquis of Carlton and the two other men left separately. Ultima wondered what her life was going to be like in the house of this enigmatic duke. How did he get Xawata to sell her? She was the ruby in Xawata's crown, and all in the capital knew it. It was incredible that this man had that level of influence.

As the horseless carriage made a turn and entered the section of the city with the old manors, the one word that came to Ultima's mind was opulence. They entered through a wide, double gate, where ivy and ferns grew over the old stone of the property's surrounding wall. A winding stone-paved road led to the colossal structure. The mansion had a sense of arrogance. If a building ever had a feeling, this was what came to Ultima's mind. To Ultima, the manor was *arrogant*.

Along the road, two rows of old oak trees stood as soldiers, with branches and leaves moving gently with the cool autumn wind, waving hello to Ultima. She had visited many manors, castles, abbeys, hotels, but not this place. This manor was different; it was as if it had a spell over it, and Ultima could actually feel where the spell started as they rode onto the manor's property.

"This place has a magic spell," whispered Akina to Ultima.

"I know," whispered Ultima back at her daughter, and they looked at the duke. The man was reading a newspaper as the carriage moved along. When they reached the front of the manor, there was a semi-circular entrance. In the middle stood a delicate marble fountain with a statue of a goddess of old, with two elven children standing by her sides, and fairies sitting by her feet offering her fruit. The clear water emanating from the statue's hands created a pleasant gurgling sound that made a lovely backdrop, and the bright green of the gardens gave Ultima hope.

The Duke stepped out of the carriage, giving his hand to help Ultima descend. She looked up at the three-story-high mansion, with towers to the right and to the left sides of the house. Its dark-wood front door stood out well from the background of whitewashed stones that made up the walls. Birds sang and Ultima looked back to see many colored birds fly over the lawn and grounds. As they approached the house, Ultima worried that she might have to deal with a wife, sons, and daughters. This would be a hard life, if that was the situation.

"Come Ultima, this is your new home. I hope you like it here." Two servants were waiting for them by the entrance.

The Duke paused on the steps leading to the entrance and introduced Ultima and Akina to the pair. "Mr. Dobson, Mrs. Taneda, these are Miss Ultima and her daughter, little Miss Akina. They will live here with us. Mrs. Taneda, please, take little Akina and give her something to eat and drink, then bring her back to us." Mrs. Taneda curtsied, took Akina by the hand, and whisked her away.

"Your Grace, according to the Trades Office laws, if a man purchases an Exotic, he has to house her separately from his family. If I live here with your family, will I have any problems with your wife?" asked Ultima.

"My wife, Nívea, is in Yakuta. And don't you worry, young woman, all will be fine," said the Duke.

Ultima thought the place looked arrogant on the outside, and when she entered, the inside of the house said *opulence*. There was a crystal chandelier hanging in the main entrance of the manor. The décor was dark wood, white walls, and various shades of gray, silver, and light-green accents. The furnishings were of sturdy wood, large, and carved in beautiful angular lines. The manor was a manly place. As she walked through the different rooms, it was the same, a large space with large furniture. Until the duke escorted her to a parlor decorated in white, beige, and soft pink. This one room was clearly a feminine room.

"Ultima, please wait here. A servant will come and get you in a few minutes," said the Duke, and he left Ultima in the pink parlor. Ultima went to look out the window and, as she guessed, the manor had a vast, well-kept lawn. However, she did not have the time to marvel at all the riches around her. This was the time she had to think and analyze her situation.

I wonder if the duke had Xawata assassinated. She didn't have enough time to ponder on the *what ifs*, when a servant came and asked her to follow him. The servant escorted her to the duke's study, where an opened door greeted her, so she lightly knocked and entered. There were two trades officials waiting with the duke. As Ultima was expecting, it was another large room with large furniture, but this one had books covering the walls from floor to ceiling in built-in shelves. Then Akina entered the room and came to stand next to Ultima.

"Ultima, I'm going to change your trade-tattoo," said the Duke of Vurthas. Ultima's head snapped up. Was it right, what she was hearing?

"Your Grace, I don't think you understand the nature of my trade. Exotics will be Exotics all our lives. There is no other trade for us. There is no escaping my trade," said

Ultima. Akina held her mother's hand and tried to hide behind her.

"There is a way out for you. I need you to be free of your trade," said the Duke. He walked over to Ultima and took her hand.

"I don't understand," said Ultima.

"In Alhambra, a Marquis bought an Exotic as his wife. He had gotten her with child, and he later married her and made her his marchioness," said the Duke.

"But I'm not with child," said Ultima.

"Oh, but you already have a child—Akina. I'm arranging for my son to recognize Akina as his daughter and marry you. We are going to make you a Lady. I already own you as an Exotic, but I need you to walk around the country and society freely. Being an Exotic brings restrictions we don't need," said the Duke.

"Your Grace, Exotics don't marry. We have contracts and a trade that is for life," said Ultima.

"The only reason Exotics don't marry is because they owe their masters exorbitant amounts of coin for their education, and they have to work to pay for that education. In your case, I paid for your education when I bought you. And I'm the one arranging the union. I'm having my third son Otto marry you and get you out of your trade," said the Duke, pointing at a young man Ultima hadn't noticed when she entered the room. He had been standing in the shadows, but now stepped forward.

His son was holding a glass of liquor and had a concerned look on his face.

"This is my son Lord Otto Archer Fernand Milo Hightower," said the Duke. It was Lord Otto Hightower from the party and the hunt.

"Yes, we've met. I first met him twelve years ago and then again at Lady Nancy Otarana's engagement party," said Ultima.

"Well, great, you already know each other," said the Duke. The trade officials said nothing. They sat with their papers and logs, waiting for the people to make-up their minds. The duke paid the transfer for Ultima from slave to wife.

"Son, come and mark your new wife," said the Duke. Lord Otto had his arms crossed, but when his father called, he walked with strident steps toward Ultima. He stood in front of her and gazed at her from head to toe. Once more, he said nothing.

Ultima's eyes were opened wide. This was the man that danced with her at Duke Hausman's manor and helped her on the hunt. The handsome lord with the scar on his face who had been riding with the Duke of Hausman, was here and was apparently to be her husband! The green eyes she would never forget and were the same color as her Akina's. She wasn't expecting this turn of events.

She had never expected to be anything else besides an Exotic. She had worked all her life. She had done the job of a prostitute, and now this noble was marrying her to his third son. Why? What was happening?

Lord Otto went to the table, picked up the brand, and without looking at Ultima's face again, he gently placed the mark on her arm over the prostitute-tattoo, but even then, the action caused pain.

"Ah," screamed Ultima as the hot brand burned her skin, her legs buckled. It was a pain more of fear than the sensation. Here, she was in a new place. She had been a slave to Xawata and with the pain came the memories of the many men and women who had bought her time. She could see each of them in a rapid succession. Now she was going to be the slave of one man; she was a wife-slave this time. Lord Otto looked at her, eyes full of pain and resignation. And then his green eyes went to her Exotic mark.

"You must erase her Exotic mark also," said the Duke.

"Where is the key to her collar?" asked Otto.

Ultima hunched over, holding her arm. The duke gave Otto the key; he raised Ultima's head and removed Ultima's collar.

"You are free," said Otto.

Free? Ultima gasped and jumped a little when the golden collar came off her neck. In all her life she had only been without a collar for brief moments when Xawata was exchanging a golden collar for one with jewels or back to her regular collar, but she had never been without some type of a collar. The moment the collar came off, a breeze came and all the hairs on the back of her neck stood on end. She was free of the collar, but even though Otto said she was free, she didn't feel any different.

"I'll be as gentle as I can be, but there is another brand," said Lord Otto, looking at Ultima. She was looking at the golden collar on the table, and she lifted her head at the sound of his voice. In both fear and pain, she nodded.

Lord Otto again gently placed the mark over the Exotic mark on her left breast, but this time she muffled her scream with her hand over her mouth. A few tears fell, and her world spun precariously. Akina, who had been behind her back, held her and stopped her from falling. The servant who had brought Akina to the room provided Ultima with a balm to help alleviate her pain.

"Fine, now register Akina as my son's daughter and we will have the Jonellen priest officiate the wedding," said the Duke.

"Father, won't you give her time to rest?" asked Otto, with a frown.

"No, I need her protected. You two will marry today. The ceremony will begin now," said the Duke, and his word was law. The trade officer registered Akina as Ultima and Otto Hightower's daughter. The priest, who had been standing behind the trade officers, walked forward and conducted the ceremony. Lord Otto and the terrified Ultima married that day, ending the afternoon with Ultima being given a new, small tattoo on her left wrist. She was now a Lady in the Ducal House of Vurthas. Akina too sported a tiny new tattoo on her left arm, making her a Hightower.

❖❖❖

They had given Ultima a sizable room, and she had been resting after her rushed wedding. Her room, like all the other rooms she had been in the manor, was large, with large furniture, but they decorated this one room in baby-blue and dove-gray, but it had few furnishings. It was as if they furnished the house for giant people. Ultima tried sitting on a chair by the dining table in her room, but if she sat with her back touching the back of the chair, her feet dangled like a child's and if she sat with her feet on the floor, she was perched on the edge of the chair uncomfortably.

Ultima took a nap. She had slept only a few hours the previous night. While she was sleeping, the maids brought her belongings to the room. When she woke, she was amazed, and slightly disturbed, to find all her belongings either hanging in the wardrobe or folded neatly in the drawers. Someone must have silently unpacked her cases while she slept. It was almost time for dinner, so she changed into an elegant evening dress. She walked down the stairs to the main floor and to the reception room outside the dining room, where the men were waiting for her. She went to stand by the fireplace, away from the men, and she waited.

"My daughter, Ultima, you are not a slave anymore. Come. Tonight, we will dine with my eldest son, the Marquis of Pharlen, Lord He'nico Benicio Korn Alonso Hightower, and with my second son, Lord Caleb Marino Hawk Jaren and of course, your husband, Otto," said the Duke.

"Since we have so formally been introduced, what is your full name?" asked Lord He'nico.

"I am Ultima Leighton Skylar."

The Duke stood up from his chair and said, "No, you are Lady Ultima Leighton Hightower now. We are to have dinner together and use this time to get to know each other."

The Duke offered Ultima his arm, and they entered the dining room together.

"You are now family, my darling. Sit by the side of your husband," said the Duke, pointing at the chair to the left of Otto, with Caleb on her right near the head of the table, where the duke went to sit. He'nico sat opposite to the duke's right—an honorable position.

The duke called for dinner to start, and they ate. They talk about trivialities, and none of the men directed the conversation at Ultima. She ate and listened. They had trained her to listen. When desserts came, the duke turned to her and asked her opinion.

"You must be questioning why I purchased you and then arranged for you to marry my son?" said the Duke.

"Yes, Your Grace, I'm wondering exactly those questions," said Ultima.

"It is simple. I think you can recognize Prince Marco's killer." The duke was looking at Ultima as if trying to figure her out.

"I already told you, I didn't see the man's face," said Ultima.

"No. but you heard his voice. You felt his touch, you know the way he smells. There is more than the sense of sight," said the Duke.

"I don't know what you think, but I'm not psychic," said Ultima.

"Yes, but you told me you would never forget the voice of the assassin. I'm counting on you to recognize the killer's voice. And, I have a feeling the bullet that lodged in the commander was meant for you," said the Duke.

"I'm a singer and a dancer; those are my major skills. I'm also a polyglot and have other attributes and training designed for the pleasure of men, but I'm just an Exotic." She looked at the men, unintimidated.

"Ultima, we have abolished slavery in Yakuta. Thus, I broke Yakuta's law by purchasing you. However, I used a loophole when I married you to my son. I gifted you your freedom. You don't have to help us if you don't want to. You don't have to do anything. Now your skills will be useful to you, to use as you will. But I do request that you help me and my family catch your former Regent's killer. I would appreciate it if you chose to be a part of that," said the Duke.

"We are only asking that if you recognize the man who killed Marco, you tell us," said He'nico.

"That is simple," said Ultima.

"You are a Lady in the House of Vurthas, and that comes with certain responsibilities," said Caleb.

"What is my job—my duties?" asked Ultima.

"You have no job. There isn't an actual trade for you to do," said Otto.

"Changing the subject, a little. You should know, we are all mages, and we can help catch the assassin," said Caleb.

"Are you using me as bait?" asked Ultima.

"No, but you are the only one who can identify the assassin," said the Duke.

"We recall you said the assassin threatened you and said he would be after you, so all we have to do is … not leave you alone and we will catch him," said Caleb with a big smile. The wretched man had gorgeous hazel eyes. Caleb was pure charisma.

"I don't know what you think Exotics can do, but I'm not an expert on everything. I need to be around people to see if I can identify the killer. And you forget this killer had a trade-tattoo. He isn't a nobleman. Nobles don't have trade-tattoos. I don't service the common folk." Ultima was looking from one man to another.

"My dear, I already told you, you are not an Exotic anymore. I made you the wife of one of my sons to protect you. This way, all will think you are going to concentrate on being a wife and enjoying being a free woman. I'm hoping the assassin will not come after you on my property, but if he does, we will be ready to catch him. When we are among polite society, we will stay with you," said the Duke.

"That is supposed to reassure me, how?" said Ultima.

"I and all my sons are well-trained, high-ranking mages. As for the assassin's rank in society, we can never be too careful. My sons and I are noblemen, but we each have a trade-tattoo. We are mages, and thus we have tattoos signifying our magic skills. You don't know if the man was a common warrior, or a battlemage. They have the warrior-tattoo with an extension of mage. Knights at the service of the King have tattoos, and most of them are also noblemen," said the Duke.

"This can't be happening. Now, I'm bait," said Ultima, placing her spoon down.

"You'll get used to us," chuckled He'nico. "Your Exotic training will help you with our wicked sense of humor, or lack thereof, and for whatever else life may throw your way as a Hightower in the House of Vurthas."

"This assassin can't frequent our circles. I tell you, he has a trade. He was a warrior. He is a commoner, or at most a gentleman with means," said Ultima.

"Don't you worry. I have a theory about the assassination I must test first," said the Duke.

"What you need to do is simple. All you must do is listen and if you hear or feel the same vibrations as those you felt when you were in the room with the assassin, just let us know," said Lord He'nico.

"I will not promise you anything. It all sounds crazy to me, but I'll try," said Ultima.

"That is all we ask from you, to try," said He'nico.

"When I first saw you, I said to myself, something so beautiful should not be in a cage. And when I saw little Akina, I knew you both needed to be out of Xawata's house," said the Duke of Vurthas.

"Thank you for getting us out. We certainly would not have fared well with the Duke of Horrel," said Ultima.

"Why do you say that?" asked Caleb.

"In the past, when he visited the brothel, none of the girls liked to service him, including me," said Ultima.

"Why?" asked He'nico.

"He is a sadistic man," said Ultima, sipping her wine.

Ultima noticed that Otto said little during the entire conversation.

CHAPTER 10

One Fool

All the Hightower men had light-brown hair, except for the duke. His hair was almost white. The old man could charm his way into a house full of snakes and come out alive. Otto was the only one who kept his hair cut short. Even the Duke of Vurthas wore his hair long at the back. They talked late into the evening about many topics, and Ultima was glad she knew Yakutan. The men were happily surprised to learn that Ultima was so fluent in the language and had such a wide range of knowledge of Yakutan society and culture.

    Later in her room, Ultima was pondering on all she had learned at dinner. When she woke that morning, she had been a slave, but by that evening she was raised to being a Lady and a wife. Now, she was part of a family who, with some unknown others, conspired to protect—what? She wasn't quite sure. She didn't know what her role was in all their machinations. She was married to a man who obviously didn't want her, or so she thought, who could make her life a misery if he so chose.

She actually wanted her old life back. She knew her role, and what she was required to do in her trade and home. Despite being a slave, she had been the master of her own trade. Now, all this was new. Before, she had it all planned out. She was a thirty-one-year-old Exotic. As soon as she celebrated her fortieth birthday, she would be promoted to being a Prime Exotic in Xawata's brothel. She could earn wages and have a say on which clients she would service. She had a schedule, and then the stupid Prince Regent had to be assassinated in her arms. Now she didn't know what to expect. This was an unknown family and situation.

She got ready for the night. Surely her new husband would want to bed the most famous Exotic of the entire Tsestelago Kingdom. She finished preparing. She had bathed before dinner and removed all her body hair. After dinner she took a second quick bath in oils and applied several lotions to her skin. She had cleansed every crevice of her body and made sure her entire body smelled perfect, and she loosened her hair, letting it fall down her back, but in a style that was both artful and seductive. And she waited for her husband.

It was past midnight, but the man had not yet made it to her room, so she went to bed. It was the first time in many days she had the luxury of going to sleep early at night. He could wake her if he ever came to her room. She was tired and fell asleep as soon as her head touched the pillow.

She woke a little before dawn with something freezing by her side. It was Akina. The child found her way to her bed, the same way she had always done since she was little. However, tonight, Ultima figured the child must be afraid. This was a new place and a new life. And now she would have to think of a trade for Akina. Her daughter was shivering on top of the covers so she pulled them out from under her, situated her next to her pillow, and covered Akina with her blankets. And Ultima went back to sleep.

♦♦♦

Early the next morning, Akina awoke, warm and peaceful next to her mother. She often slept with her mother when she couldn't sleep. The housekeeper, Mrs. Taneda, had given her a room on the third floor of the house. She called it the nursery of the manor. Why would the woman place her in a nursery? Akina did not know. She had been training to be an Exotic since she was three years old, and had knowledge far beyond her years of things that most women would not know until they were much older, maybe only on the day before their wedding, and some they would never know.

At Xawata's, she had to share her room with three other girls, and they were her friends, but at the manor, in the nursery, Akina had a room all to herself. When she had been with her friends, they had done many things together, but here she was alone. Last night, her room was scary. The room filled with little beings that came from the nearby forest. And the beings talked to her. Never in her life had she ever been surrounded by forest beings—she had lived entirely in the city.

Often at Xawata's, Akina would leave her room late after midnight and go to her mother's room. It was usually safe to go to her mother's room well after midnight. By that time, her mother had finished working and she could go to sleep next to her momma.

And now it was morning. Through slitted eyes, she noticed the maid enter her mother's room, bringing tea. The previous day, Akina had been snooping around the manor when she found the kitchen. She overheard Mrs. Taneda asking which of the senior maids wanted the job of Lady's maid to her mother. No one had wanted the job when they found out Ultima was an Exotic. When Mrs. Taneda asked the younger girls, one stepped forward, and was promptly rewarded with eight silver pieces more per month. It saddened Akina that no one wanted to serve her mother, but that happened often to Exotics, and she knew that was part of being a prostitute.

When the maid entered the room, Akina noticed the maid stopped walking and stared at them. The curtains were closed, and the room was dark and cool. Akina rubbed her eyes, adjusting to the light until she could see fine. She watched the maid walk around the room a little more, and again stood still for a few moments. Akina wondered what the maid was doing, what she was thinking. The maid had entered the room as quietly as she could, and had left the tea on a table, and then she seemed to disappear slightly into the shadows by the wall.

Akina sat up in bed, stretched her back, and then jumped out of bed and ran to the window. She opened the curtains with enthusiasm, just as might be expected from a young girl who had never had a childhood. She ran back to her mother and shook her awake.

"Wake Momma, wake! It's morning and we are free. You are free. It's a new day. We are not slaves anymore. I'm so happy. Look! I don't have a collar anymore." Akina danced and twirled in the room, and the maid stood watching, mouth slightly agape, as Akina twirled around the room, having a joyful attack of dancing in celebration.

"Akina love, please close the curtains. I'm happy for both of us, but this is the first time in ages I've been permitted to sleep an entire night without any interruptions. Let me wake slowly. Please, love," said Ultima, covering her eyes with her arm. During all this time, the maid continued to stand still by the wall, apparently (it seemed to Akina) not knowing what to do. Akina closed the curtains as her mother ordered her to do.

"Come and talk to me," said Akina, and she ran to where the maid was standing.

"My name is Akina. What's your name?" Akina asked the maid, holding her hand and pulling her to the sofa. She sat next to the maid and continued to hold the girl's hand.

"What are your chores? I'll help you with your chores if you help me with mine. I don't know what mine are yet. My mother hasn't given me any. My mother and I were slaves and now we are free," said Akina, pointing at Ultima.

"She's the most beautiful woman in the world. Xawata made Momma train me to be like her since I was three; no, it was two. I was going to be the best Exotic in the entire kingdom just like she is, or was, but now I'm free, just like her. I don't have to be an Exotic anymore. What's your trade?" Akina took the maid's arm and looked.

"Oh, look at your arm! That is a freshly made tattoo. You are a Lady's maid. Wow, that is an important trade in the house. I don't know what my mother will make of me now. I'm so happy." Akina's exuberance and happiness overflowed, but the maid looked creeped out by it. Akina smiled at the maid, and jumped up, pulling the maid with her, and twirled them both around. Finally, she stood still and looked at the young woman, waiting for a response.

"My name is Mariza. I have never met anyone trained to be an Exotic," said Mariza, looking surprised at all the information she received.

"Well, now, you've met me. I'm so happy to be free. I hope Momma will let me work in the kitchen, or with you. I like you," said Akina, running to Ultima, shaking her, trying to wake her.

"Momma, please wake up; I need to know what I'll be doing today." Akina's black hair was all in a tangle.

"You are not going to let me sleep any more, are you? Fine, I'm up. Where's my tea?" Ultima rose from her bed, revealing a well-developed woman in a total state of undress. Ultima slept naked. Mariza's cheeks burned.

"My Lady, I'm Mariza. Your Lady's maid. Will you be breaking your fast in bed or going down and joining the Duke and your husband?"

"Be a dear and get me my robe. It's at the foot of the bed. At what time do the lords break their fast?" asked Ultima.

"In another hour, my Lady. What is your morning routine?" Mariza did not to look directly at Ultima. The Exotic woman's robe left little to the imagination. Mariza acted like she had never seen someone sleep with anything other than a cotton nightgown.

"Thank you Mariza, I'm used to doing things myself in the mornings, but it would be nice to have you help me with Akina. I want Akina to comb her hair, get dressed, and break her fast in the kitchen. She is then to come back to me. Can you help me with that? I don't need to take a bath, so I won't be needing your help this morning with my own personal preparations. Please come back with Akina as soon as she finishes breaking her fast. She is used to having lessons in the mornings, but since there are no teachers here, I'll be her teacher," said Ultima, getting out of her bed and finding a dress and some undergarments.

"Yes, m'Lady," said Mariza.

"Akina is my daughter, and she is only eleven, so she needs a governess. Please ask Mrs. Taneda to come and see me later." Ultima walked to the table to get her tea.

"Eleven? And she was training to be an Exotic since she was three? I'm sorry, m'Lady." The maid's already rosy cheeks turned even redder.

"Mariza, it's not a very well-known fact, but some Exotics, especially the slave Exotics, train at a very young age. In reality, I started teaching Akina lessons in languages from the moment she started talking at two years old." Ultima didn't move away from the table or get angry with Mariza. Ultima always spoke with a gentle voice and soft words. Akina was proud of her mother.

"Why so young? What is there to learn, for a—" Mariza caught her words.

"For a prostitute?" Ultima smiled at Mariza. "It's true if that was all we were, but Exotics are not simple prostitutes. We are entertainers, academics, musicians, linguists, dancers, singers, and yes, we are also experts in the art of sensuality. I can pass as a lady, even a queen, or a humble servant if that is required of me. I can ride horses and fire a multitude of weapons.

"I'm even trained to fight with a sword. Akina here is fluent in four languages, can sing and dance as a professional and is an adept rider. Now, go take Akina and get her some food and come back later. Go, I must get ready," said Ultima and Mariza left, holding Akina by the hand. Akina liked Mariza.

❖❖❖

For Ultima, it was divine to wake up in a large room full of light. To open her eyes and know she hadn't needed to work the previous night, nor would she have to work the next night. Her room was gorgeous, with polished hardwood floors, covered here and there by exquisite rugs. The room had small stars painted on the ceiling and the walls were covered in a lovely light-blue wallpaper. After Akina left her room with Mariza, Ultima had some tea. She took her dark glasses with her and went over to her window where the curtains had been partially drawn by Akina earlier. Now, she flung them wide open, and leaned out into a sunshine-filled morning. Below there was a well-kept garden with beautiful trees and marble benches placed opposite each other. She rarely got to enjoy this part of the day, unless a client asked Xawata for her services early in the morning, but that rarely happened.

Ultima withdrew from her window and went back into her room. She combed her hair and changed into clean clothing. The previous night she had bathed and her husband hadn't visited her, so she still felt clean.

An hour later, Ultima entered the dining room, where the duke and his sons were breaking their fast and reading the newspapers.

"Good morning, Your Grace, my Lords," said Ultima as she entered the breakfast room. She wore a simple dark-green skirt with a paler green blouse that made her look young and bright.

Sunlight entered the room from the window in the corner, shining throughout the room. Otto, the man who was now her husband was sitting to the left of his father, arms crossed and a frown on his face.

"Good morning," said the men, and they all stood when she entered the room.

"Come, sit next to me," said the old duke, standing and walking to the door to escort Ultima to the table.

"The news of your nuptials appeared in all the newspapers. The next thing we must do is organize a ball to celebrate the wedding," said the Duke.

"I'm not sure a party will be good," said Ultima.

"Why not? It would be a great way to introduce you as part of the family," said Caleb.

"How do you like the house? Is it all to your liking? Are you well-tended by the Lady's maid my housekeeper chose for you?" asked the Duke.

"Although the decorations are quite masculine, the manor is stunning. Your servants have treated us well. Thank you." Ultima sat, and the butler served her tea, toasts, and a portion of eggs.

"You are an intelligent woman. I can see you have questions for me," said the Duke.

"I'd like to understand how you got Xawata to sell me to you. It is a mystery to me," said Ultima.

"And it will stay a mystery," said the Duke, softening his response with a wink and a smile. "So, you were an Exotic with a vast range of knowledge and skills. Xawata had you attending the royal hunts. At what age did Xawata provide your weapons training and horse-riding lessons?" asked the Duke.

"I was in my teen years when I learned to ride a horse and in my early twenties when I learned to shoot," said Ultima.

"That old Mr. Faan had an eye for business," said He'nico.

"Xawata was one of those men that would do almost anything for coin. He catered to my clients' requests. His greed was boundless," said Ultima.

When Ultima and the Duke talked about her clients, Ultima noticed Lord Otto's brow furrow, and he stood up and went to get himself more tea from the credenza.

"Your skills will help you when the time comes and we go hunting for the assassin. We will keep you close," said He'nico.

"I must thank you for giving my daughter her freedom," said Ultima.

"You are welcome," said the Duke.

"Why didn't you let me stay an Exotic?" asked Ultima.

"We can't have you working as an Exotic. As a free noble woman, it will be easier for you to move about the kingdom. If we had kept you as an Exotic, you would have had to register in every city we visit and even stay at brothels. And even if you were a free Exotic, the trade would still have bound you. I want to keep you safe in our dealings. I also didn't want anyone trying to buy your time or get you into trouble," said the Duke.

"Well, Exotics have our limits, but I'll try to help you as best as I can," said Ultima.

"We also know of your magic. I know you are an unregistered mage. You have a rare gift. Not every day I get to meet a genuine gifted mage healer. And you are also a harmonizer; that much I know is true," said Lord Gareth.

Chuckling, she admitted, "To be honest, the greatest magic I have is making people happy with my singing." Ultima smiled and sipped her tea.

She *was* a healer and a harmonizer. She'd found out she had healing magic when she was twelve—the day the midwife was supposed to *fix* her friend. Her healer magic kicked in without thought or plan. She saw her little friend so hurt she touched her and she repaired the damage the midwife had done. By the next morning she just knew everything had been healed. Leliana had known of her magic and ever since that time, Xawata had forced her to hide it. At first, she was scared of the repercussions of having healed her friend. Xawata was angry with her. However, later she was more fearful of the consequences of using her magic and Xawata finding out and thus losing her daughter. As Xawata had threatened he would kill Akina if anyone found out she was a mage. The trade officers would have had her sent to one of the academies to learn control of her magic and serve the King.

"I'm an elenchus. I know falsehoods. Remember what I said yesterday, I don't like lies," said the Duke. Ultima looked at the man directly, nodded and smiled again.

"I'm a healer, and a harmonizer, and I can move small objects with my mind, but my only training is what I've learned by reading books and asking questions of other healers. Xawata knew and he hid my magic. He never made me register," said Ultima.

"I figured that much," said the Duke, "either he didn't know, or he knew, but didn't want to lose you."

"I felt your magic, but I thought you were a water mage," said Ultima.

"Yes, I control water as well. Now, let's eat," said the Duke.

CHAPTER 11

Take Away and Give Away

Later that day, Ultima was sitting in a parlor knitting a pair of socks for Akina when a maid came looking for her. The Duke of Vurthas had called her to his office. Ultima left her knitting behind to respond to the summons. When she entered the study, Marshal Donnelly was in the office waiting for her, with the duke and Otto.

"Hello, Lady Ultima! I read in the newspaper that Lord Otto Hightower married you yesterday. I guess congratulations are in order," said the man. Marshal Donnelly wore a tailored suit and designer shoes. His dark-brown eyes locked onto Ultima.

"Thank you, Marshal Donnelly. I'm assuming it is not your primary reason to be here, to congratulate me on my nuptials," said Ultima.

"I'm afraid not; I'm here on official matters," said the man.

"Do any of you mind if I smoke?" asked the Marshal.

"No, I don't mind, I'll have one as well," said the Duke.

"Would you like a cigarette, Lady Ultima?" asked Marshal Donnelly.

"No, thank you." Ultima just wanted the man to get to the point. Marshal Donnelly lit up his cigarette and placed it in an ashtray.

"Lady Ultima, I have a warrant to talk to you about Xawata Faan's death," said the Marshal.

"Why? Xawata died in bed with Lola, one of the other Exotics at the brothel. He didn't die in my bed," said Ultima.

"The healers found traces of poison in Xawata. In fact, more than traces, he had large amounts of hallucinogens and a male enhancement potion in his body. Do you have any idea of where Mr. Faan could have got these types of potions?" asked Marshal Donnelly.

"No, I was his slave. He and I had no relationship other than master and slave," said Ultima.

"Where were you the night Xawata Faan died? What do you remember of the night?" asked Mr. Donnelly.

"I was working in my assigned room in the brothel. I had three clients that night. My last client was the Earl of Furlong. He stayed until very late, after which I had gone to my private rooms. I had only been asleep in my own bed two, maybe three hours, when I heard Lola scream. I got up and followed the screams to Xawata's room where I found Lola there with him, he was already dead. Lola spent the night with him and as far as we all knew, he died in his sleep," said Ultima. In the edge of her vision, she noticed Otto's expression turn to anger in the corner.

"When you arrived at Xawata's room, did you notice anything different?" asked Marshal Donnelly.

"I'm sorry, Marshal Donnelly, but I had never visited Xawata's room previously. He never partook of my services. He said it was bad luck for him to ever touch me. That morning was the first time I was ever in Xawata's room," said Ultima.

"Did you notice anything on the night table like bottles of pills or vials?" asked Marshal Donnelly.

"I remember nothing else."

"Do you have anything else to say?"

"All I can recall is that I gave out instructions for a healer and his man of business to come to the house," said Ultima.

"Why are you asking her these questions?" asked the Duke of Vurthas.

"I'm asking everyone questions. It is serendipitous that Your Grace bought the Exotic Ultima and waited until Xawata was dead to come get your property," said Marshal Donnelly.

"If you read the contract, it says that Xawata was to relinquish Ultima when she fulfilled her remaining open contracts. Xawata and I had a spoken agreement between gentlemen that I would give Xawata time to finish honoring any outstanding paid contracts on Ultima's time. When he died, I saw no need to wait," said the Duke, smoking his cigarette.

"I think you are done talking to my wife. Ultima go, you are done here," said Otto.

"I have more questions," said Marshal Donnelly.

"No, my wife has answered enough questions. Come, Ultima, let's go." And Otto took Ultima by the hand and escorted her out of the office. They walked back to the parlor where Ultima had been knitting.

"I spoke the truth. Xawata never talked to me other than to give me orders. I was his slave. I wasn't with him the night he died. You must believe me," said Ultima, holding Otto's arm.

"I believe you. You are free now." Otto removed Ultima's hand from his arm, turned, and walked away, leaving her alone in the parlor.

❖❖❖

Two months passed, and Ultima had found the manor to be full of beautiful, comfy places to explore. She and Akina had established a simple routine. She would train Akina in Yakutan and Palermo language skills in the early morning, shortly after she broke her fast. Afterward, Ultima would send Akina to learn history, art, numbers, and science with tutors. The duke hired the tutors to teach Akina. Following Akina's language lessons, Ultima would take a book and walk through the gardens, finding a spot she liked to read. It was late fall, but the sun shined brightly, and the sky had not one cloud.

She had rarely had the chance to be out in the sunshine in the morning, but now that she was free, it was her favorite thing to do. This morning she had a book on magic. She walked to the gazebo in the back gardens and sat to read. The coldness of the morning encouraged her to take a sweater with her, as well as her dark, rounded glasses, and her gloves. She had been reading for an hour when her maid, Mariza, approached.

"Little Lady Akina finished her history lesson. Her art tutor sent word she's not coming today. Will you be teaching her dance today?" Mariza had brought tea with her to the gazebo. The servant placed the tray with the tea paraphernalia on a table next to Ultima, who lowered her book to her lap, took the cup, and drank her tea while deciding what to arrange for Akina's lessons. She stood up to return the tray to Mariza who had been standing by the entrance of the gazebo. Just as Ultima stood, there was a loud crack, and a bullet hit the post of the gazebo. Ultima grabbed Mariza by the arm and made them both drop to the floor of the flimsy structure.

"AAAAAH ... AAAAAH!" Mariza's banshee screams hurt Ultima's ears. There was another shot, then two large servants came running, brandishing weapons.

"AAAAAH. AAAAAH" Mariza kept screaming and Ultima's body shook. At first, all she saw was her tea cup lying broken nearby. Then she saw men run past the gazebo and all four Lords Hightower came running from the side of the house with weapons in hand. The dogs were released. Many other servants ran past, sprinting to the tree line in the distance. One servant came and took Mariza away, as she continued muttering, "They shot us, we are dead."

"Are you hurt?" shouted the Duke of Vurthas, as he ran toward Ultima.

"Hurry and catch the man. I want him alive," ordered Otto to the servants running ahead. Lords He'nico and Caleb followed, running behind the servants. Lord Otto reached where Ultima was sitting, followed closely by his father.

A cold sweat broke out over Ultima's entire body, and her body jittered when Otto took her by her arm. She jerked and tried to move away from Otto in a sudden rush of energy.

"Calm down, it's Otto. Look at me," said Otto, as Ultima kept looking toward the tree line.

"Look at me," said Otto, and Ultima looked at the man. Fear all over her face. Sweat covered her brow and with trembling hands she tried to keep Otto away from her.

"Where is he? He shot us," said Ultima.

"Are you hurt?" asked Otto again.

"No." Ultima looked at her dirty hands. Her book lay tossed near the teacup.

"I'm—I'm ..." Ultima closed her eyes, full of tears.

"Come, let's get you inside the house," said Otto, as the duke brought two more servants with him. Otto helped Ultima stand, and they walked together to the house. Once inside, Otto sat next to Ultima on a sofa and the duke went to look out the parlor's double door. Mrs. Taneda stood by wringing her hands, clearly anxious and at a loss as to what to do.

"Your Grace, I'll order a healer to come. In case Lady Ultima was hurt," said Mrs. Taneda.

"Good thinking. Now go and get the lady some tea and find Mr. Dobson," said the Duke.

"Mr. Dobson is with Lord He'nico, giving chase to the wretched man that tried to hurt Lady Ultima," said Mrs. Taneda.

"Fine. When he comes back, tell him I want to see him. Now go get us our tea," said the Duke.

"Yes, Your Grace."

"Did you see who shot at you?" asked Otto, kneeling in front of Ultima and holding her hands.

"No," said Ultima.

"Father, this has to be the same assassin that killed Prince Marco. Who else would want her dead?" said Otto, standing up and walking over to the door to look out.

"We were right to figure this would happen," said the Duke.

"Since he was able to enter Prince Marco's room in the royal palace, I bet there are few places to which this man couldn't gain entrance," said Ultima. Her sarcasm came as easily as one of the old songs she liked to sing.

"Yes, Ultima, but here we have several mages around the property," said the Duke, distractedly, but all his attention was on He'nico when he entered the room with two rifles in his hands. Ultima stood up and looked out through the floor-to-ceiling windows.

"Did you catch him?" asked the Duke.

"No, he ran away. I found this rifle by the tree line. He must have dropped it and ran. I could see him running, but then it was as if he disappeared into thin air. Even the dogs lost his scent," said He'nico. Like Otto's, his green eyes darkened in rage; the man placed his weapon on a nearby table.

Then Caleb walked in behind him, also with a weapon in his hands. "We found a few footprints and then nothing. I saw the shadow of a man, but then he disappeared. This man must be working with a mage and have some new type of magic. No one can just disappear."

"Your Grace," Ultima interrupted, "one thing I didn't tell the commander or the marshal about the assassin was that the man is a mage. He had a warrior's trade-tattoo, but he also had an extension tattoo I couldn't see. I *felt* his magic, but I don't know the type," said Ultima.

"And why did you omit that vital information?" said He'nico. Otto caught Ultima when her legs buckled. He carried her back to the sofa and lay her down.

"He'nico, relax," said the Duke.

"Lord He'nico, I was a slave. I had no other choice. I had hidden my magic out of fear. You can't imagine the trouble I would have been in if Xawata discovered I let anyone know of my magic, or worse, if the Trades Office discovered I was an unregistered mage. Xawata threatened to kill Akina if anyone found out I was a mage," Ultima looked from one man to the other.

"That is excellent information. Ultima, go rest. That assassin will not get access to the manor ever again. We will keep you safe," said the Duke.

"How are you going to do that? Keep me safe, I mean. He already entered the manor's gardens; he entered the palace," demanded Ultima in her anger. She stood up and looked for a cigarette. She lit one up with shaking hands and started pacing.

"You need to learn to trust us. We will protect you," said Otto.

"I trust no one," said Ultima as she turned around and sat on a chair.

"My dear sister-in-law, I have magic just like my brothers, and I will place magic wards around the manor. Everyone entering the manor will have to do so through the front gate. If not, for those entering any other way, the ward will cancel their magic. As for us, I'll ensure our magic still works on the premises," said Caleb.

"And do you think that will work? The palace has several wards around the outside and inside, but the man entered despite those wards," said Ultima.

"Yes, you are correct. That is why I think the assassination was an inside job. There must be someone in the palace that helped the assassin bypass the magic protecting the royal family. Here we don't have that problem, and we must ensure you are never alone. Rest and know we will be here to protect you," said the Duke.

Still shaking, Ultima left the parlor accompanied by a servant.

❖❖❖

Once Ultima was out of earshot, the men got together.

"Father, if the assassination of the Regent was an inside job, then House Trevino has a traitor or a spy," said He'nico.

"Maybe both! King Petro wants power, and he's been destabilizing the region for years," said Otto.

"It is an idea I've been thinking about for a while. Trust me when I tell you the palace wasn't as secure as you would think, if this man could reach the prince," said the Duke.

"When are we going to meet with the King? We have been in Tsestelago for over three months," said Caleb.

"We will meet this week, but for now, we will raise the wards and post more guards around the manor," said the Duke.

"I wonder why she wasn't targeted when she was at Xawata's brothel!" said Otto.

"Maybe he tried and wasn't successful. I know old Xawata had a spell put on that building. I could feel it the moment I entered. What it did exactly, I don't know. He probably also had wards around his property, not just the building. I also noticed Xawata had bouncers at every door. Moreover, that place had many servants and caretakers. And we don't really know if those two attempted assassinations, when Ultima was present, were targeted at her. Let's get this property protected," said the Duke. The men left the parlor, talking among themselves.

◆◆◆

Two days later, Akina was playing with her dolls in the garden, near the stables. She had told her momma that it felt a little childish when she first found them in the nursery, but soon realized that even when she was alone, her doll-friends could keep her company. The family wouldn't let her be by herself entirely, so she had to play where there were servants who could keep an eye on her. Caleb watched her from afar.

She had her dolls all wrapped in little blankets and Akina was making believe she was changing the swaddling cloth for one of the dolls. What surprised Caleb was that Akina was talking to a little forest sprite who would never have stepped out of the forest by his own choice. She was smiling and playing like any little girl would.

He could see she had summoned the little sprite from the forest to come out and play. This child was powerful. She could use her arcane magic by instinct. He had to talk to the little one.

"Hello, little Akina. What are you doing, inviting that little sprite out of his forest?" asked Caleb. Akina lowered her head and looked at the sprite.

The little sprite smiled. "She is happy. When she called, I wanted to come and play," said the little sprite.

"Well, thank you for playing with my niece. Now, go back to your mother, young sprite. I'll keep her company," said Caleb.

"Bye, Akina," said the young sprite.

"Bye, Giroby," said Akina.

"Akina, you got him to give you his name?" asked Caleb.

"Yes, we played for a while. I asked his name, and he gave it to me. Why?" asked Akina.

"Darling, for an arcane mage, once you know the name of a forest-, fire-, water-, or air-being, that being is bound to help you for life," said Caleb. "You are a powerful arcane mage. No being will give you their name willingly," said Caleb.

"Oh, I didn't know," said Akina.

"Now it is your responsibility to keep your friend's name a secret and not tell it to any other arcane mage. And when you call him for help, you must do it in a special language that will be just for you, that no one else will understand. However, all that is magic you will learn later at the academy."

"That is awesome," said Akina, holding her dolls.

"Well, well, little niece, what do you have here? How many dolls do you have?" asked Caleb, trying to lighten the conversation.

"When I was living in Xawata's brothel, I only had one little doll Momma bought me and I had to hide it. I could only play with it in Momma's room," said Akina.

"Why only one doll?" asked Caleb.

"Xawata said dolls were for free children and I was a slave, but Momma said I was her baby girl and I could play with dolls as long as I kept it a secret," said Akina.

"Oh, but I see you have three dolls here," said Caleb.

"Grandfather, the Duke, gave me two new dolls, so now I have three," said Akina, showing Caleb her two new dolls.

"They are beautiful."

"Thank you, my Lord," said Akina.

"You can call me Uncle Caleb."

"Really? I now have a grandfather and an uncle," said Akina, with a smile.

"In reality, you have five uncles and two aunts," said Caleb.

"That is awesome," said Akina, again. It seemed to be her favorite expression of late. "I have a big family now. It used to be just me and my momma. I'm glad Momma married Lord Otto."

"You and I are the arcane mages of this family," said Caleb.

"Momma said she would find a mage to teach me and see if he would accept her services in exchange for payment. Will you teach me, but not use her as payment?" asked Akina.

Her uncle laughed aloud at that, "Little one, I think your father would end up furious with me if I accepted that form of payment from your mother. I will teach you what I can for free. Come, let's play with your dolls and use them to do some magic at the same time. Would you like that?" asked Caleb.

"I'd like that very much," said Akina.

So, the child and Caleb played outside, and they practiced some arcane magic for the rest of the afternoon.

CHAPTER 12

Masters and Helpers

The day came when the Duke had his audience with the King. He had arranged the visit for a date three months prior, but the King had been busy with the burial ceremonies of his son, chamber of commerce meetings, the war council's machinations, and more. The Hightowers believed the King delayed and postponed the audience many times on purpose.

    The duke rode to the royal palace with his sons, He'nico and Otto, while Caleb stayed behind to protect Ultima. The palace stood in the middle of the capital city of Pailo. The red walls surrounding the palace opened to the north and the south, and all the buildings that comprised the palace had towers that reached much higher than the outer walls.

    The gate keepers let the duke's horseless carriage ride through the northern entrance, and they made their way to the front entrance of the palace. Once there, the duke and his sons started to walk rapidly, with a sense of urgency as they always did, but had to slow down to the pace of the servants, which aggravated the duke.

The King received them in his private study. The expansive room was full of books, with a large table and a fireplace in the corner. The curtains and the decorations were gold and maroon, the colors of House Trevino. There were basins of water in each corner of the room and a painting of the King's father hung on a side wall. After the duke and his sons bowed and gave the King his due respect, the two men hugged tightly.

"It is good to see you, Gareth," said the King, stepping back, and then repeated the hug with Otto and He'nico. The King was dressed in his usual black pants and fitted coat, but his shoulders had begun to hunch over, and he needed a cane to stand.

"It is good to see you, old friend," said the Duke of Vurthas.

"Who're you calling old?" said the King with a smile.

"Oh, don't start. You know I'm three months younger than you," said the Duke, and both men laughed.

"Sit, Gareth. Bring us tea, call Saigai and Healer Goren, and I don't want to be disturbed," said the King to his servants. The men sat around the large central table.

"I'm sorry for your loss. My godson, Prince Marco, was a good man," said the Duke.

"I can't believe my son is dead. What angers me the most is that the assassin is still walking the streets," said the King.

"I can understand. How is Princess Harriet?" asked the Duke.

"She is most distraught. She and Marco only had Leer and Joy-Anna as heirs. Now the twins are her only reminder of Marco, and those two little ones will grow up without a father. They are attending the Gayton Academy. She is distraught and grieving, or so my wife tells me." King Trevino sat back in his chair.

"Could Marco's son or daughter claim the kingdom?"

"No, they are both mages. Neither one can rule Tsestelago. Our society bound them to be archimages of the crown. It is good I have one other son. Soren will rule. On the other hand, if he can't rule, then my brother Robert or my sister will have the throne," said the King.

"Do you know the whereabouts of my other godson, Soren? Has he returned to the city?" asked the Duke.

"No, I sent for him, but have received no answer. His regiment went to fight up in the Pikes Mountain region, to the northeast, but they have sent no answers back confirming receipt of my orders," said the King.

The servants entered with the tea he had ordered, and conversation paused as they busied themselves with the distribution.

"You know Jadro has found a place in the Court of Alhambra?" said the Duke of Vurthas.

"I know. It is distressing to know, but I'm confident I have nothing to worry about," said Trevino.

"My King, did you call for us?" Archimage Saigai and Healer Goren entered the room together.

"Archimage Saigai, and Healer Goren, come. I want you both to meet the Duke of Vurthas. He is cousin to my wife Elenore," said Trevino.

"It is a pleasure to meet you, Your Grace. I've heard a lot about you over the years," said Saigai.

"It's my pleasure, Your Grace," said old Healer Goren.

"Good to meet you both. Archimage Saigai, you must be a water mage, by the look of all the water around the room," said the Duke.

"Yes, I am. I must always be prepared to protect the King," said Saigai.

"So, how are you, now that Marco is no longer here to help you?" asked the Duke.

"I'm making do. My brother Robert is taking care of all the judicial and foreign matters. I have the Duke of Abernathy helping me with the administration of the lands, and Horrel is here helping me with the administration of the merchants and the imports from the various kingdoms. Horrel has a great mind for commerce," said Trevino with a smile.

"It's good that you have your brother taking charge of all matters of the judiciary and foreign affairs. That is good to know, my friend, but are you aware there are rumors that you have a noble who is working with King Petro?" asked the Duke.

"Yes, that is true, but I do not know who he is. Nor do I have any evidence," said King Trevino.

"What about your Vanquishers?" asked the Duke of Vurthas.

"I've stationed each one of them in one of my four academies. My mages are holding strong and working for the people, as they should. But my loyal dukes have been dying from a mysterious disease, and the healers can't make it stop. I must demonstrate soon that I have a Regent to take charge of the kingdom, judiciary, merchants, farmers, and laborers," said King Trevino, drinking his tea.

"We need Soren back, and fast," said the Queen from the door.

"I'm sorry to interrupt darling, but I found out Gareth was meeting with you, and I had to say hello to my favorite cousin." Queen Elenore entered, regally as ever. Her dress made a shush sound as she walked, but her shoes made no sound on the marble floor.

She hugged her cousin, the Duke, after he bowed and gave her his respect. She looked just like the Hightower family. Her eyes were as dark blue as the Duke's, but her hair had turned completely white.

"You look beautiful, my Queen," said Duke Gareth Hightower.

"Ah, thank you. And where is my godson, and young Otto?" He'nico and Otto both stood, bowed, and the Queen hugged them.

"Come sit with us," said King Trevino, standing and holding his wife's hand.

"I'm so sorry for your loss," said the Duke of Vurthas.

"Thank you, cousin. I don't want to talk about Marco, it breaks my heart." The Queen sat, and then looked at her husband. "Have you asked him?" The Queen turned to look at her cousin Gareth with a sad smile.

"Not yet," said King Trevino.

"Your Highness?" asked the Duke.

"I'm happy you are in town and came to see me. I'm sorry I could not see you sooner. Things got in the way, but my friend, I need your help," said the King.

"Ask, and if it is in my power to do so, I will."

"I'd like you to join my brother Robert and his men to go find Soren and bring him home. I can't trust anyone but the two of you in this task," said King Trevino. The King coughed and his eyes watered. The Queen passed him a handkerchief and smiled.

Healer Goren spoke an incantation making the cough disappear, and he gave the King a glass of water.

"My King you need rest," said Healer Goren in hushed tones.

"I'm better, thank you Healer Goren," said Trevino.

"Darling!" The Queen's frown and sad face made her look older. Trevino patted Elenore's hand, and he looked back at the Duke of Vurthas.

"Neither Leer nor Joy can rule. They are both mages, and we fear for their lives. We have our most trusted men guarding them both. Will you go find Soren? Would you do this for me?" asked the Queen. The Duke smiled.

"Yes, I'll help you with this task. I'll take He'nico, Caleb, and Otto with me," said the Duke.

"I'll give you all the coin you need to get to the Pikes," said the King, almost out of breath.

"If one of your nobles is working for Petro, I must do this with as much discretion as possible. Hausman must stay and you can't tell him or anyone else you sent me. You don't know if Petro's spies have infiltrated his house. We must do this, letting no one in the court know," said the Duke of Vurthas.

"That's not possible. It was Horrel's idea to send you with Robert," said the King, between bouts of coughing and

Healer Goren murmured another incantation that again stopped the cough.

"I understand," said the Duke of Vurthas.

"Robert will leave in five days to go to West Franken. There, you will take command of a company of men to take with you up the mountain. Horrel suggested that you leave the guards behind and only take the men closest to you, but I disagreed," said the King.

"I'll contact Hausman and set everything up for the trip," said the Duke.

The men bid each other goodbye, and the Queen kissed her cousin and his sons. The Duke of Vurthas left the palace in a hurry. He had much to prepare and only five days to do it. His plans had changed. He was going to retrieve his godson himself.

"Father, there is more to the King's story," said He'nico once they reached their horseless carriage.

"Yes, I could feel it. It is obvious King Trevino is extremely sick. I'm afraid he may be about to lose control of his court," said the Duke.

"If all three of us are to go on this trip with you, what are we going to do with Ultima?" said Otto.

"On the one hand, we need her to help us infiltrate the King's court and help us find who killed Marco, but on the other, we will not be here to protect her. She must come with us. We can't leave her behind," said the Duke, as they traveled back to the manor.

◆◆◆

Ultima's mind was in turmoil. The attempt to assassinate her left her anxious. The very next day after she arrived at the manor, she found a piano in one of the two big ballrooms. Ever since then she had played for Akina. She played often and it helped her to relax. So, she and Akina practiced in the ballroom; Ultima played the piano and Akina danced. Ultima gave her instructions in the Palermo language and corrected Akina's dancing form when necessary.

"You need to raise your arms as you turn," said Ultima, and Akina did what she was told. When Ultima stopped playing, Akina dropped to the floor.

"I'm tired," said Akina with a giggle.

"Go drink some water. We've finished your dancing lesson for today." Ultima stood up and walked away from the piano, over to a small table where a pot of tea and accoutrements had been brought in and left by a serving girl.

"How did I do?" asked Akina.

"You did well. Akina love, are you happy here?" asked Ultima. The child sat at the small table and looked down at her shoes.

"Yes, I am. I love not having to take any more of the classes preparing me to be an Exotic. I love being able to give you all my love and not having to hide it. I love that I can use my magic out in the open. I love that Uncle Caleb is teaching me how to use my magic," said Akina from her chair.

"Good; that is a long list of things you love," said Ultima.

"Why are you asking me? Aren't you happy?" asked Akina.

"I'm happy; I don't have to work as an Exotic, but I'm bored to tears. I need something to do," said Ultima.

"Well, we can travel around the city, or we can ride the horses. Maybe we can work out in the garden." Akina went to hold Ultima's hand.

"You are such a good girl. I think I have the best daughter in all Tsestelago," said Ultima. Akina frowned and sniffed a little, considering a thought.

"Why do you think the Duke registered me as Lord Otto's daughter?" asked Akina.

"To make it easier to register me as his son's wife. It doesn't matter. You are Miss Hightower now and you will never have to think of the life Xawata had prepared for you. Let's go. You need to bathe, and I need a nap. I still—" Ultima didn't finish her sentence as Otto had entered the ballroom with resounding footsteps.

"No, she is Lady Akina now. I have registered her in Yakuta as Lady Akina Nívea Marie Georgina Hightower. She is my daughter and an arcane mage of nobility in the House of Vurthas. I need to talk to you," said Lord Otto, once he fully entered the room with the butler, Mr. Dobson, in tow.

"Akina, love, go take a bath and be ready to study your numbers. I'll be with you later," said Ultima.

"Yes Momma, excuse me, my Lord." Akina curtsied at Otto and left the hall in a run.

"My Lord—you changed her name?"

"I gave her Nívea after my mother, Marie after my grandmother, and Georgina after our King, both women being powerful mages, and a worthy King. She is a Hightower now. She is an arcane mage in the House of Vurthas. So, I gave to Akina what belongs to her by adoption," said Otto.

"Thank you, my Lord, what can I do for you?" said Ultima.

"Relax Ultima, all I need you to do is listen. Have you had your midday meal?" asked Otto, and Ultima nodded. "Mr. Dobson, bring me tea and something to eat, please," said Lord Otto.

"Yes, m' Lord." Mr. Dobson bowed briefly and left the hall.

"In five days, we will leave on a road trip, and you are to come with us. We will travel first by train and then by horse, so you must be prepared to rough it."

"Where will we be going?" Her back straight, hands on her lap, she maintained an appearance of being unmoved.

"Don't worry about where we'll be going. You just pack lightly and be ready to leave in five days." The butler came back with another servant who carried a tray of sandwiches and tea.

"What about Akina, will she be traveling with us as well?" asked Ultima.

"No, she will stay here. I've made arrangements for her to attend the Gayton Academy while we are gone," said Lord Otto.

"She has not been separated from my side since the moment she was born. That child has never even been to a school outside my reach," said Ultima.

"Akina is my daughter now. She is a mage, in need of training. Being brought up at Xawata's deprived her of magical training, and that must be corrected. She is an arcane mage in the House of Vurthas. All mages in the House of Vurthas serve King George and she will serve her new King as expected of a Vurthas. We will protect her. I'll make sure Caleb places several wards over her," said Otto.

"And my maid, will she be traveling with me?" asked Ultima.

"No, she will not be coming with us," said Otto, drinking his tea and eating his sandwiches.

"My Lord, I need to go and check on Akina. Will that be all?" asked Ultima. This man, her husband, made plans and took decisions with little regard for her or Akina. She and her daughter were vassals of King Trevino of Tsestelago, but now her loyalties were required to change, purely on his command. She was part of a family now that had different traditions, ones that she didn't know.

"Go, do whatever women fancy to do in the afternoons. And please don't be late for dinner. We have plenty to discuss later," said Lord Otto.

"One more thing, an old client of mine, Lady Michelle Polack, would like to visit me and spend some time talking with me. I'd love to—" Ultima wasn't given the opportunity to finish her sentence. Abruptly, Otto stood up, and Ultima followed his lead. He stepped closer to Ultima, as if to grab her, but held himself back.

"What? No! You are free. You will not receive any clients. You are not an Exotic any longer. What is wrong with you—asking such a thing?"

"The only thing she and I ever did was talk," said Ultima, taking a step back.

"No, I don't want any of your old clients to come visit you here," said Otto.

"Do you understand that most of my clients only ever listened to me sing, watched me dance, or just held conversations with me? I rarely had to have sex with any of my clients. Exotics are entertainers and academics first and foremost, besides being prostitutes," said Ultima.

"I don't care what you used to do. This home isn't your new brothel." He started to pace.

"Fine, what about going out, to town perhaps? I'd like to—" Once more Ultima couldn't finish her sentence.

"No, it's not safe for you. Someone tried to kill you. We are trying to keep you alive. Ultima, what are you thinking?" Ultima lifted her hand.

"Fine, fine, I don't want to argue!" Ultima took a deep breath and left the hall, upset.

Ultima wanted Akina to go to the Gayton Academy, but not this way. She wanted to be the one making the decision.

CHAPTER 13

A New Hightower

Ultima packed her bags for a one-month trip through the wilderness. Ultima had only ever once been to a manor outside the city, returning the same night. She did not know what she would need and what to pack, but she did her best with the help of Mariza. She had her riding clothes and boots and many serviceable dresses. Otto had given her no other information, other than to tell her she was to travel with him and his father. During dinner, the men talked about what provisions they were going to need and the best route to take, but they gave no specifics on personal items. And Ultima tried as she might to listen, but was at a loss when the men chose to speak in the ancient Yakutan language. She only knew the modern Yakutan.

"Ultima, you understand that we must leave in five days, and your maid isn't traveling with us?" asked the Duke.

"Yes, Your Grace. I understand. Akina will leave for the Gayton Academy tomorrow morning. Mariza will pack all my things, and I will be ready to go in time," said Ultima.

"Good," said the Duke. And the men continued talking among themselves, ignoring Ultima, which was fine by her. She was free to enjoy her meal and not have to fake interest in the conversations of men. From under her lashes, she watched Otto and wondered if he would ever come to her bed. They had been married for two months, and he hadn't been to visit her. Maybe he preferred the company of men. In the end, Ultima told herself she didn't care.

When dinner was over, the men went to smoke cigars and drink port, and Ultima went to the main parlor to sit quietly, sipping her tea. She wanted to run away. Life in the mansion was lonely. Akina was the only reason she had to not run away. Where to? It didn't matter; she wanted structure and a routine. She tried to establish her own routine in the manor, and had almost succeeded, when Otto told her she was to travel with them. Now with this trip, her life would be different again, and Ultima hated *different*. The men entered the parlor, and she took the opportunity to retire for the night.

"It is time for me to retire. Good night, Your Grace and my Lords." And she walked away, not giving a second glance at Otto, or any of them.

❖❖❖

"Brother, why are you being such a cold-hearted ass with your wife?" asked Caleb.

"What are you talking about? I'm sitting quietly here in the corner, drinking my whiskey. I haven't said a nasty word to the woman. Why are you calling me an ass?" Otto stood up and went to stand by the fireplace, and poked the fire.

"That is exactly why I call you an ass. You don't talk to her or even acknowledge her presence," said Caleb.

"I have an Exotic as a wife. I used to like bedding Exotics when I was a single man, but having one as a wife is something totally different. Now, I don't know if I made a mistake and if someone more respectable would have been better in my life."

"If you wanted someone respectable, then why did you go along with father's request when he asked you to marry her? You could have said no. Father asked me also, and as I remember, you volunteered," said Caleb.

"I thought it would be different," said Otto.

"Brother, you are definitely an ass. She is a beautiful woman and has acted with nothing but decorum," said He'nico.

"I don't hate her. In fact, I do like her a lot. I find her beautiful and smart. However, I thought it was going to be different. And now, I have a hard time every time I think of her servicing anyone. I have a wife that has bedded every rich man in this kingdom, and probably many in Alhambra and Palermo.

"How do you think I feel when I hear her talking about her *servicing* this man or that woman and wanting to see the people she used to *service*? No, don't say anything. I don't want to hear anything from either of you. You are happily married to the daughter of King Berlios of Palermo, my dear He'nico, and you, Caleb, are betrothed to the only daughter of the Earl of Spief. I want what you have, He'nico, and I'm afraid I will never have it with her. She still wants to see her clients. She still thinks she's an Exotic. Could I ever trust her to be faithful?" said Otto.

"It is good to know how you feel about me, *husband*. However, I must correct you, I'm a linguist, a dancer, a singer, an academist, and was so exclusive and expensive, only a few in the city could afford my time and even fewer could afford to bed me. I was a slave; I had to do what my master ordered me to do. You ask if I could be faithful? To whom? To what? I know respect and obedience. Hear me: I suggest that if I'm so repugnant to you, please give me a letter of divorce. It will not hurt my reputation or my feelings at all to be a divorced woman."

Ultima did not let anyone interrupt her; she was seething but delivered her words with a deliberate calm. "As long as I could take my daughter with me, I want nothing from you, Lord Otto."

Ultima had spoken from the doorway of the parlor while the men scrambled to stand, but they remained silent. She entered, walking directly to where she had been sitting earlier, passed by Otto without looking at the man, retrieved her fan from the small table near her chair, turned and walked out of the room with as much elegance and grace as she had when she first entered.

"I couldn't believe my ears, Otto Archer Fernand Milo. I heard the last of your conversation as I approached from the hallway, just before Ultima reached the door. I'm ashamed of you. I raised you to be a lord and a gentleman," said the Duke, and he too turned and left the parlor. The other two brothers followed their father out and left Otto alone with his whiskey.

♦♦♦

Ultima went to her room, and sat staring at the wall. She wanted to pack her bags and leave the manor. If she was really free, then she could just go. She didn't have to stay in the manor, and she didn't have to be with those men, but where would she go? She had nowhere to go, especially since Otto had registered Akina as his daughter, and anyway, she was his legal wife.

"What in hell does it mean to be a wife to this noble asshole?" said Ultima out loud, then growled in frustration. Ultima had enough of the Hightower family. They told her she was free, but Otto wouldn't let her talk to people or leave the walls of the manor, even just to go into town.

"You wouldn't be safe," Ultima lowered her voice an octave and mocked Otto, aping his voice and his mannerisms. She was free *dammit*, but she wasn't permitted to receive any visitors. Ultima understood she was no longer an Exotic, and she shouldn't provide services to anyone, but at least she could talk to some of her old clients. Ultima had many clients she considered acquaintances, friends even. She had clients with whom she could spend hours in interesting conversations, but Otto didn't want her talking to anyone from her old life. She might as well lock herself in a room. Half the aristocracy were her clients in one form or another.

❖❖❖

Morning came and Akina was outside waiting for her carriage. Ultima was standing by the door. She had to say goodbye to her Akina, but it hurt too much. Ultima gave birth to Akina when she was only nineteen. She remembered the day Akina came into the world. Xawata called a midwife, and the woman was with her for the ten hours it took her to birth the girl. When Akina was finally in her arms, she couldn't believe the child had her father's eye color, despite being a newborn. The babe was wide awake, and she didn't cry. Later, when Akina was a toddler, all in the house loved the little girl, but not Xawata.

"Keep Akina out of the kitchen and make her stay in your room," shouted Xawata. The rat-face man stepped near Akina and grabbed her little chin. "Come to think of it, she looks like a baby doll. This one will be a beauty." And Xawata released Akina's chin.

"I want her ready to be a prostitute by age thirteen, an Exotic by age eighteen, and get her full Exotic license by age twenty. You have work to do. I hope this time you stay fixed and do not come home with another bastard child," said Xawata as he left the room. The child stood with her head hung low, crying.

"Akina love, come to me, little one. I told you not to leave my side. What were you doing in the kitchen?" Akina walked to her mother with tiny steps, eyes glued to the floor. Ultima took the toddler by the hand, sat down herself, then lifted her daughter onto her lap, and combed her hair. Ultima loved her daughter.

"Ugly man, scary man," said little Akina.

"Don't worry about him. Now, I already told you, don't go wandering about. You stay with me. As long as you stay in my room, I promise no one will hurt you." Ultima played with her daughter a little, making the toddler smile.

Why had she disobeyed Xawata by not preventing the child? She didn't know. Once Ultima knew Akina was on her way, she loved her child. Back then, she didn't know the name of the child's father. Back then, she only knew how he looked, but she would never forget his face.

Now she knew the name of Akina's father, and he cared for the child.

Akina was grown, now, and about to leave her side.

"Akina, love!" called Ultima from the door. Young Akina turned around and saw her mother. She left her bags by the bottom step, and came running into Ultima's arms.

"Momma, do I have to go? I want to stay with you." Akina hugged Ultima. The girl was a little thing. She only reached Ultima's neck.

"Yes, you have to go. Lord Otto wants you trained as a mage, and so do I. If we are back by the end of term, I'll send for you for the winter festival, and you'll stay with me until the next term starts again in the spring. If it is up to me, I will not make you go back in the spring." Ultima kissed Akina and embraced her in a huge hug. The carriage pulled up, and the driver placed Akina's bags in the trunk.

"Momma, please, I don't want to go. Couldn't I have tutors? You said you would find mages you could service in exchange for their tutoring time. Now you don't have to do that, Lord Otto can pay for tutors. It would be no different than the tutoring I've had all these weeks," said Akina.

"Akina, come here!" commanded Lord Otto. The man had been behind Ultima the entire time.

"Yes, sir." Akina went and stood in front of Otto.

"You will be at the best school in Tsestelago, but for only a short time. You must learn to be a mage, and that will happen best by being with other mages your age. You will have fun in this school. You will make friends your own age, and before you know it, we will be back. Don't worry, the best magic school in the world is in Yakuta, and you will go there when we leave in a few months. Now, cheer up; you are not going to the gallows, young lady, just to school." And Otto gave little Akina a hug.

"Yes, sir," said Akina. She then turned back to her mother.

"I love you, Momma. I'll miss you every day," said Akina. Ultima smiled and gave her another hug, then kissed her daughter.

"I'll miss you more. I love you with all my heart, my Akina. Now go," said Ultima.

The girl turned and walked slowly to the carriage. When she entered the carriage, she was misty-eyed. As the vehicle pulled away, Akina looked back and waved at Ultima.

"You will see her again. We will be back before the term ends. Ultima, we need—" Ultima turned, looked at Otto, and left him mid-sentence. She said nothing as she walked around Otto without giving him a second glance. She entered the manor and went to her bedroom.

♦♦♦

Akina looked back as the horseless carriage drove away from the grand manor. She kept waving even when she could no longer see them. She had never been separated from her mother. She couldn't remember a time when she was more than a few floors away from her momma. Her life was her momma. Her earliest memory was of Ultima putting a pair of shoes on her for her first day of dance lessons when she was four years old. That was all the memory. Her momma in her most beautiful blue dress, having worked all night and waking early to take her to her first day of dance lessons.

Now, she was going away to school. Akina had had many teachers throughout her life, but she never had to leave her mother to get her lessons. The vehicle moved steadily, and it rocked side-to-side each time it took a turn. Akina started crying. *What will it be like not to have Momma with me?* she thought.

"Come on, Akina, you will see us again. Don't cry, little niece," said Caleb from the front seat.

"What are you doing here?" asked Akina, cleaning her tears with the backs of her hands.

"I'm taking you to your first day at school. Did you really think that we were going to let you go alone?" asked Caleb, looking back at her, his hazel eyes twinkling.

"I don't want to go. I want to stay with my momma and all of you. What's the point of having a big family now if I have to leave?" said Akina.

"You have nothing to be afraid of, young lady. You will be in one of the best academies of magic in the entire Kingdom of Tsestelago, but wait until you are in Yakuta. There, you will have the best time of your life," said Caleb.

"Why do I have to learn magic? I could be like Momma and not use my magic," said Akina.

"Listen, little one: you have a very special type of magic. You know—you are an arcane mage. We have been practicing your magic, you and I, but you need formal training. There is only one of us arcane mages for every five hundred elemental mages. And because you have a rare type of magic, we need to train you properly. It is important for you to know how to use your magic and gain your degrees of knowledge." Caleb could see he wasn't getting through the emotional turmoil. "Stop the vehicle," he said. The chauffeur stopped, and Caleb got out and climbed back in to sit in the back with Akina.

"Young lady, you are part of a unique family. We are the Hightowers of the House of Vurthas, from the Kingdom of Yakuta. Your father is a prince, and now you will be a princess. Your grandma is King George's sister, and she is so happy she has a granddaughter that she is making King George pronounce you a princess. You are her first granddaughter. She can't wait to meet you," said Caleb.

"Does she know I'm not really her granddaughter?" said Akina.

"Oh, but you are her granddaughter. You are the daughter of my brother, Otto," said Caleb proudly.

"I have no father. I asked mother, and all she said was that he was a handsome young man that danced with her at a party," said Akina.

"That handsome young man is my brother, Lord Otto, your father," said Caleb.

"If that's true, why didn't Momma tell me?" said Akina.

"I thought you knew," said Caleb.

"No, I didn't know. How do you know? Did Momma say anything to you?" said Akina.

"No, I know because it's part of my magic. I can tell when there are kin near me. And when I met you, I knew you were a true Hightower," said Caleb.

"So, I am—a Hightower," said Akina.

"That you are," said Caleb, and Akina smiled.

"What if the other children treat me differently? You know, if they find out I was training to be an Exotic?" said Akina.

"They don't need to know that do they? They will not know unless you tell them. And if for any reason they know, you can ignore them or just tell them you are well educated in languages, history and can sing and dance, and leave it at that. Just go to school and learn as much as possible. Your mother is forever bragging about how smart you are and how fast you can learn new things. Is she lying?" asked Caleb.

"I do learn really fast," said Akina.

"I know." He chuckled. "You have shown me when we practice our magic," said Caleb.

"What if they ask me about Yakuta? What will I tell them?" asked Akina.

"Tell them the truth. That you have lived here in Tsestelago with your mother your entire life, and now your father is here to take you and your mother to Yakuta in a few months' time. Ultima told us you know Yakutan," said Caleb.

"Yes, Momma taught me," said Akina.

"Try to make friends with Yakutan children if there are any," said Caleb.

"That's a great idea," said Akina.

"Don't be afraid of anything. I'm placing a few wards over you to protect you, but I noticed your mother had placed blessings upon you, and she didn't even know that she did them. It's sad that Xawata made your mother keep her magic a secret and didn't let her train in magic. Your mother is a special type of mage, too. She has many types of magic, the same as your grandfather, and they can control several things," said Caleb.

"Momma is a healer and a harmonizer, and she can levitate many things," said Akina.

"She can levitate many things, huh? That is good to know. I'm going to have a brief conversation with Ultima and see if she wants to practice her magic," said Caleb. They continued talking about the city and the things to expect in the school when the horseless carriage arrived at the Gayton Academy on the outskirts of Pailo.

The academy was an old abbey with many buildings built around the original abbey, and a magical wall surrounded it. The academy became so large that beyond the walls, a small town emerged with a tavern and inn, several shops, a market, and all the support staff and associated tourism.

"Here we are," said the chauffeur.

"And these decrepit old buildings are the academy?" said Lord Caleb stepping out of the vehicle. No one answered his question. He extended his hand to Akina, and he walked with her to the main entrance where a severe-looking woman with blond hair and small, blue eyes behind wire-rimmed glasses, was waiting for her at the door. A young redheaded woman was standing next to her.

"So, Miss Akina Hightower, this is the little girl—the daughter of an Exotic—the one that made us change our curriculum and make all sorts of concessions just for her? She doesn't look like much," said the woman.

"No, this is the Yakutan Princess: Lady Akina Nívea Marie Georgina Hightower, Arcane Mage in the Yakutan Ducal House of Vurthas. I'm her uncle, Prince Caleb Marino Hawk Jaren Hightower, Arcane Master Mage of the ninth degree and Lord in the Yakutan Ducal House of Vurthas. Her father is Prince Otto Archer Fernand Milo, Lightning Master Mage of the ninth degree and Lord in the Yakutan Ducal House of Vurthas. Here are all her documents and registry. And you are?" said Caleb, standing tall, passing a large envelope to the woman who stood more rigidly with every part of his introduction.

"I am Fire Master Mage of the ninth degree, fourth assistant Hall Lady of the Archimage Saigai, Tolafida Van Handac, and headmistress of this academy. The term started months ago. Why didn't your family send this child to the academy at the start of the school year?" asked the arrogant woman.

"That is my family's business. The child is here now. She has all her books and required uniforms," said Caleb.

"Huh, very well. Justa, take care of the child." And the woman turned and walked rapidly away.

"Hello, I'm a water master mage of the eighth degree, Camila Justa, the Assistant Headmistress of Gayton Academy. It is a pleasure to meet you, Prince Caleb," said the redheaded woman with a smile.

"Hello, Master Justa, have a good day," said Caleb.

"Come, Lady Akina, you are going to have fun in this school," said Master Mage Justa. Then Akina turned from the mage master and pulled Caleb's arm to whisper in his ear.

"I don't want to stay here," said Akina.

"Let your guardian angel from heaven protect you. Let the light of day brighten your path, and there be a guiding star during your nights. The Hightower leopards that fight with the rage of a thousand men will guard your way, and they will fight next to you. You now have the blessing of the Hightowers," said Caleb, and he moved his arms and fingers in deliberate shapes, speaking an incantation which made a ward shine all around Akina.

"I protected you, love. If you are ever in danger, call the leopards, and they will come. We will see you in less than four months," said Caleb. He gave Akina a hug.

"Now go. Hightowers face adversity head-on. I know you are strong and will forever make me proud, little Akina," said Caleb. Akina nodded, turned and walked toward the woman. Then at the last moment, she ran back and gave Caleb a hug.

"I'm going to miss you, Uncle Caleb," said Akina.

"I'm going to miss you too, Akina." Caleb stood looking at Akina, smiling from ear to ear.

Akina went to stand with Master Mage Justa.

Master Mage Justa took Akina by the hand and led her inside the main building. Akina turned around to take a last look at Caleb, who was still there looking at her as she left.

Akina took a deep breath and whispered, "I am a Hightower." And walked away bravely.

CHAPTER 14

Training Session

After Akina left for the Gayton Academy, a servant went to Ultima's room and asked her to meet He'nico, Otto, and Caleb at the back of the property, past the stables, in an hour and a half for a training session.
    Ultima changed to her workout clothing. Her teachers had trained her to do many things in the house of Xawata. Ultima dressed all in black. She wore tight-fitting pants and a black corset, and coat that provided additional support to her upper body. Ultima had a pair of leather gauntlets and wore leather riding boots. She was dressed comfortably for a training session on methods to fight on horseback, since she assumed that was what the men would be trying to teach her when they arranged the meeting near the stables.
    Ultima asked Mariza to go down to the stables with her, but when she arrived at the place where she was to meet them, she saw they had wooden weapons and even a bale of hay in a corner.

"My dear sister-in-law, since we are going to take you with us to a war zone, we thought we needed to give you some instruction on how to defend yourself," said He'nico.

"Mariza, darling, go to my room and bring me Jade and Jasper. You know where they are. Hurry, dearest," said Ultima. And Mariza left at a run back to the house.

"This woman wants her jewels in a training session! Father, it is best to leave her behind with Nehemiah's people. She is a soft little thing. She will run and get in the way at the first sight of trouble if we take her with us," said Otto.

"We can't leave her behind. You must train her," said the Duke from a balcony at the back at the house.

"Fine! Ultima, where we are going, we may encounter fighting. We may be close to a battlefield; we need you to be prepared. If you stay close to us, you won't need to worry as we will protect you and keep you away from the fight. However, just in case, we need you to know how to use a sword," said He'nico. Mariza came running with a long leather bag which she passed to Ultima. Ultima placed the bag on the ground next to her feet.

"Otto, let's show her with the training swords." He'nico and Otto picked up a pair of wooden swords, and they demonstrated some basics by moving the swords side-to-side gently to *show* Ultima. Then they repeated the demonstration but with lots of explanations; Ultima rolled her eyes. She couldn't believe these men. They didn't even bother to ask her if she knew any fighting. So, she let them play with the sticks.

"Did you listen to our instructions?" asked He'nico.

"Oh yes, intently!" said Ultima, with a sarcastic smile.

"Good, now, it's your turn. Come, take the wooden sword and try to hit the bale of hay. We have prepared some soft obstacles for you. Don't feel bad if you can't hit them to start," said Otto, in a condescending voice. Ultima was resting against a table with her arms crossed, looking at the men.

Ultima took her bag and walked with a sexy sway of her hips over to the weapons rack. She placed her bag on a table next to the weapons rack, opened the bag, and extracted a long rapier sword from its sheath. She walked back to the table with refreshments and without preamble, struck a watermelon they had on the table, cutting it right in two.

"Gentlemen, this—is Jade. I was taught how to fight using the fine arts of the Palermo short swords and additionally the arts of the Alhambran fighting style with the rapier and the long sword, and defense with sword and shield. Would any of you care to spar with me?" said Ultima, with a cheeky grin. Caleb walked in on their practice and was rubbing his hands, all giddy when he saw Ultima with a rapier in her hands.

"Oh me, me, me, me… I'll fight her," said Caleb raising his hand. Caleb jumped with enthusiasm.

"Please, let me fight her," said Caleb.

"Fine Caleb, you fight her first. This I want to see," said the Duke of Vurthas from the balcony.

Caleb selected a rapier, and Ultima, still holding her rapier in her right hand, picked up a dagger in her left hand. Otto called the fight, Caleb stood still. Apparently, he didn't want to start on the attack, so Ultima made the first strike and Caleb defended. She hit him hard and pushed him off balance. Caleb responded by hitting her rapier and Ultima countered with agility and guile borne from long hours of practice. Ultima moved left, then right; Caleb parried, but after a few minutes Ultima stepped back.

"He's not fighting me. His strikes have no power," said Ultima.

"Woman, a rapier is a thrust and slice type of weapon, and I don't have armor. Otto, she's a wildcat, this one. I don't want to be hurt by you, Ultima Hightower. Father, she's unpredictable. I thought it was going to be easy," said Caleb, looking at each person he addressed. The man stood a few feet away from Ultima.

"Come, I'll teach you how to fight with something you may not have seen yet," said He'nico, and he took a claymore from the weapons rack.

"Are you crazy? He'nico! You'll hack her into pieces with that thing," said Otto in anger.

"Then teach me how to counter an attack with a claymore," said Ultima, frowning slightly. This was something she could learn.

"I'm not going to fight her. She has no armor, and she obviously knows how to fight. I'm going to teach her how to counter a blow from one of these big boys. Caleb, come and help me," said He'nico.

Caleb took up a shield and a short sword and went to stand in front of He'nico. While He'nico talked, he moved with the claymore and Caleb countered.

"Ultima, if you see anyone come at you with one of these types of weapons, the best thing you can do is run. If you can't run, you must evade or find something to shield the strike. If you have a shield, then cover yourself but be ready for a strong hack. If you have armor and your opponent is strong, it will force you back. If you don't have a shield, but you are wearing heavy armor, it may dent your armor. A claymore can crack or bend your heavy armor, but it will not slash it. If you have light armor, then you're in trouble. The claymore can cut an arm right off your body," said He'nico.

"Take a shield and stand and cover yourself. I will hit the shield and I want you to expect power. I will hit you hard," said He'nico. Ultima stood with her shield up. She took a forward stand and expected a hit. He'nico swung hard and hit the shield, making a loud bang that hurt Ultima's ears. The power of the hack pushed her back, and she landed on her knees, but her shield stayed up.

"Excellent job!" said Caleb, crossing his arms. He'nico hit her three more times and Ultima took the power of the claymore well. After a few minutes, they rested.

"Let's work with short swords and shields," said He'nico.

"Ultima, you will get maximum power by stepping, lunging, or running forward while delivering your blows. Never, ever turn or show your back to your opponent," said Otto.

"If you find yourself almost touching your opponent, watch out for a fist, or a dagger, and you must wield your sword differently to accommodate the tight space. Remember, there are no pauses. There will be no teacher giving you a chance to rest. Things will continue at the same fast pace; you must draw on your reserves. Sometimes you will have the opportunity to withdraw safely, but generally, the one who retreats first gets hit," said Otto.

Ultima and Otto practiced with the short swords and the shield, and then Caleb jumped in to join the fray, he and Otto combining their tactics against her. They then stopped to teach her what to do when that happened.

"There are only a limited number of basic moves you can do with a sword. There is no magic to sword fighting. You can add magic power to swords, but there is a limit to what you can do to the action of fighting. In the end, fighting is like a game of chess. You win through strategy. The smarter fighter wins," said He'nico.

They took a few minutes to rest, and let Ultima stretch her arms. Ultima soon stood up, preparing to fight Otto. She took a shield and a short sword. They went and stood in the center of the fighting area; Otto brandished a short ax.

"You will encounter some warriors with axes," said Otto, and Caleb called the start of the fight. Otto swung the ax, letting it descend toward Ultima—she jumped to the side. They moved and Otto hit Ultima's shield, letting her feel the weapon's power. He hit several times. Ultima did the best she could with the weapons she had. She stopped the ax with her shield, but in a quick movement Otto swiped the shield out of her hold. He was about to strike at her chest when he stopped and threw the ax away.

"You must learn to fight with and against an ax," said Otto.

Winded and with sweat beading on her brow and face, Ultima walked to a nearby chair and sat.

"Well done, now rest. We do this again tomorrow," said the Duke from the balcony.

"No, we do this again now." Ultima threw the rag she had in her hands and stood up. And Otto turned his head, looked at Ultima, and smiled.

Ultima picked up a clean rag from the table, wiped her face, drank some water, and took her sword once more.

"I like the sword. Let's do this again, but this time no shield," said Ultima. The woman stood in front of Otto, and Caleb crossed his arms and stood aside.

"This I want to see. Watch out for her left hand. She has a powerful left," said Caleb.

"He is the best with that damn ax," said He'nico.

"No, we had enough fighting for one day. Trust me, you are going to be sore and in pain tomorrow," said Otto.

"One more bout," said Ultima, and she took a short sword and tossed it to Otto.

"Enough, neither of you have any armor and I don't want either getting hurt," said the Duke.

"How about letting her feel a group of soldiers surrounding her, no magic," said He'nico.

"I'll place a protective ward over them both. Let them use the rapiers," said Caleb.

"She's already tired, it will not be a fair fight," said Otto.

"I'll do it," said Ultima, placing the short sword back on the rack and taking up the rapier.

"Give her a partner. Otto, you fight with her, and we call the fight. In a war there will be more than two soldiers around her, and there will be a time when she will have to fight tired," said Caleb.

"Fine, but this will be the last fight for the day," said Otto. A group of five servants stepped in with swords, and they started fighting Otto and Ultima. Ultima fought hard, but their opponents were ganging up against her, at her back and surrounding her and Otto, until the pair were back-to-back.

"I'll cover your back," said Otto.

"And I'll cover yours," said Ultima. Otto reached back and held Ultima by the waist with his left arm.

"Let's dance. When you think to move, just tell me the direction and I'll do the same," said Otto. They fought the soldiers as partners. They moved left, right, parried and ducked until Otto disarmed and pushed out of play two of the five servants. Ultima hit the two servants she was fighting and even cut one of them, and Caleb called the man out of the fight. And still they fought until the Duke of Vurthas called the fight done.

"We won!" laughed Ultima.

"Well done, you must rest. We will train some more tomorrow. Caleb, I want you to enchant several shields to deflect spells. We don't know what we'll encounter. And boys, I want you to train Ultima on how to defend with a variety of weapons," said the Duke.

❖❖❖

Later, the duke and his sons were in the duke's study, planning the trip. "Were there any problems when you left the little one at her school?" asked Otto.

"No real issues. Akina was scared; she has never been separated from her mother, and that made her cry," said Caleb.

"She looks just like your mother. It's as though I'm looking at Nívea, but wearing a black wig," said the Duke.

"It's because she's Otto's daughter. She is one of us," said Caleb.

"That's impossible. Exotics can't have children," said Otto.

"She is ours. She has the spirit of the leopard running in her veins. That child is a Hightower. Ultima said she met you twelve years ago. Well, brother, you left her with your child," said Caleb.

"I knew she was a Hightower the moment I saw her. She is your mother's twin, still in the form of a child. I have a granddaughter," said the Duke, with a glint in his eye.

"Don't jump to conclusions. Exotics can't have children," said Otto.

"Xawata registered Akina as Ultima's daughter. And Ultima is like a momma bear with that child. You can't fight the fact," said Caleb.

"We all know slave masters damage Exotics to prevent them from bearing children," said Otto.

"Ultima certainly talks as though she gave birth to Akina," said Caleb, "but all I know for sure is that she is kin. I love that child."

CHAPTER 15

You Can Be More

They only had four days left to prepare for the impending travel that Ultima thought was going to be a few weeks up a mountain and back.

After training, Ultima rested. That evening the family had a quiet dinner together, during which Ultima kept to herself. She was starting to feel sore from the morning's training. Ultima had her dessert in her room, after which she settled with a book and read several chapters. A while later, Mariza came to her room and was helping her to ready for bed, when there was a knock on the door. Lord Otto entered her room dressed in his robe. Mariza was helping Ultima into her nightdress. She said nothing, just finished what she was doing, gave him a curtsy, and left the room.

Ultima gave him a cynical look. And she placed the cup of tea she was drinking on the table and capped the tea pot.

The man wore a robe opened at the top, revealing a broad chest. His pants had the top button open. He said nothing, just entered the room and walked to where Ultima was standing; she adopted her sexiest pose.

"Good evening, my Lord. Why are you here? If I recall, you said you wanted a respectable lady and not an Exotic as a wife. I supposed you would never have need of me. The first time we met, you didn't want me because I was a slave. And now that I'm free, I'm still not suitable," said Ultima.

"I didn't say you were not suitable," said Otto.

"No, I upset you. I can't help that I'm the most famous Exotic in all of Pailo," said Ultima, and she closed her robe so as not to show her best assets. She stood tall and gazed at the man whom she desired, above all else, to punch—the desire coming upon her like a heat wave hitting her square in the face. She could see in his eyes what he wanted.

"You misunderstood my words, and you were an Exotic," said Otto.

"I *am* an Exotic. My education will never go away."

"I have given you time to get used to the idea of freedom, to us, to me. Exotic was your trade. You don't have that trade anymore. You will not be an Exotic ever again," said the man.

"No trade, then what am I?" asked Ultima.

"Free, you are a Lady, free and without a trade until we have you trained as a mage," said Otto.

It had been two months since she married Otto and he had not visited her bedroom. Ultima knew it was bound to happen, but now she didn't want him in her room.

Lord Otto came to her side. He touched her face and her arms. He took her hand and pulled her gently toward the bed. Otto opened her robe, then her night dress buttons, and exposed her naked body. He traced the sides of her breasts, and his hands went to rest over her small waist. He took off her robe. Otto touched slowly. He raised her nightdress over her head and took it off. Ultima stayed in place, unyielding.

He didn't want an Exotic, so she would do nothing. All she knew was how to be an Exotic. His hands roamed all over her naked body. The man's dark-green eyes did not leave hers, but that only made her want to hit him. The same green eyes she loved.

"You are a beautiful woman. How old are you?"

"I'm thirty-one," she said.

"You look younger." Otto touched the round of her breast and moved his hand down the side of her waist.

Ultima couldn't take it any longer. She was an Exotic. Doing nothing was unnatural to her, so she took his hands and pushed them away from her. She took a step back and put on her robe.

"If I remember your words correctly, 'I have a wife that probably has bedded every rich man in this kingdom.' So, you don't want the spoils of another. And you said, 'I have the city of Pailo's most used woman alive.' Well, you said that I was an Exotic, and now you say I'm not an Exotic. What is it? Am I, or am I not? In truth, you didn't erase that trade from me: it is still in me, in my education, in my mind, and under the burn. In the back of your mind, I'm still an Exotic, and don't deny it. I will be nothing but an Exotic for you and all the people that know me in Pailo. And since I'm free, right at this very moment, this Exotic doesn't want to be touched by you," said Ultima, as she closed the side of her robe tightly and moved to stand behind her table in an unconscious, defensive way.

"Those were not my words exactly. You are putting words into my mouth that I never said and intentionally misinterpreted my meaning!" said Otto.

"Did I? How could those words be taken in any other context?" demanded Ultima.

"I will not lie to you. I wanted a lady from a respectable family, but—" said Otto, but Ultima interrupted.

"You knew from the start; I don't come from a noble family. So, I would never have been of sufficient quality for you? I am the best Exotic in the entire damn kingdom. I'm worth hundreds of gold coins, but I'm still not quality enough for you? What more education do you want? Oh yes, I'm not a noblewoman, so apparently I'll only ever be as good as a peasant," said Ultima.

"Ultima, you don't need any further education, and those words were not what I meant to say," said Otto, after taking a deep breath.

"Well, you said them. I know what I am. I'm an Exotic. I'm not a Lady. I don't know who my parents were—but remember, I never asked your father to buy me out of slavery. I was told to marry you. I was a slave when I married you. I did what I was told. I was a slave to your father, but not you! You are a free man. You could have said no. Why didn't you stand up to your father? If you hated the idea of having an Exotic as a wife, why did you say yes to this stupid idea? Why?" asked Ultima.

"I liked you from the first moment I saw you on the dance floor at the Grand Duke of Hausman's manor, so I kept quiet. And then when you reminded me of our time at the bachelor party, I knew you were the same woman I've been lusting over for the last twelve years. I thought maybe you could change, and it wouldn't be this hard, but I can't stop thinking that you have been in the arms of so many men," said Otto.

Ultima looked at the man, half believing his words, half wanting to hit him.

"You must be jesting. You married me because you liked me, and lusted over me? Many men like me, there are women that love me. There are men that love me and want me, there are many men and women that lust over me. So, you are the one that got to have the famous Exotic Ultima Skylar all to yourself. And now you regret your actions, because I'm *also* a prostitute? Otto, Exotics are high-end prostitutes. We serve men and women in sexual pleasures if asked and paid. I want to hit you, despite not being an aggressive woman. You are an asshole. You knew perfectly well who and what I was. What changed your mind?"

"I have my reasons. Hear me well, I'm not an unfair man, I want to give us a chance, but how do you think I feel when I hear you talk of wanting to see this or that client, or that you serviced this man or that woman? It makes me angry. I am outraged that you were a slave. I hate to think of other men or women touching you, and that you let them do so. How do you think it makes me feel as your husband?

"Ultima, you no longer have an owner. Now, you are free. I have you as much as you have me, and I want to give us a chance," said Otto.

"I don't want to *service* anyone. If you are referring to the other day when I asked to see Michelle—what I want is to talk to people. I need conversation and discourse; I like to entertain. I like to sing and dance for fun, but I can't do any of it because for you it is part of me being an Exotic. So, you're telling me that I don't have an owner? I'm a free woman?" asked Ultima, and Otto nodded.

"I may be your wife, but I don't know how to be a wife. That is the one thing I don't know how to do or be. All I know to be is an Exotic. I can't change my past Otto. I was a slave, and I did the job of my trade. You know what?—I don't understand how to be free. I don't know what you want from me.

"All I know is that I'm bored beyond belief. I used to have tasks. I had routines and a purpose. Yes, even as a slave I had purpose. Here, I have your type of freedom, but I've never felt so caged. I can't see anyone; I can't go anywhere." Ultima was almost shouting.

"Ultima, there was an attempt against your life. We are trying to keep you alive."

"You won't let me go to the stores; I don't even have my own coin. What do I have to do to earn coin with you? This isn't freedom."

"I'll settle an account for you when we return. That way you'll have coin of your own and being a wife for me isn't a job. You don't have to do anything for me but love me, and if you can't love me, then all I need is respect," said Otto.

"Otto, I don't know how to love. All I know is a trade. I know how to work. I know how to service people and obey my master. You are asking me to do nothing? I don't know how to do nothing. I've worked my entire life," said Ultima. This time her hands were clenched together, and she tried to relax them, but started rubbing her fingers.

"Why don't we start by learning to be friends? Can you be my friend?" asked Otto, extending a hand to her.

"I've never had a friend," said Ultima, her frown making her look older.

"What about Akina? Isn't she your friend?"

"Akina is my daughter and only family."

"I understand," said Otto, looking down.

"No, you don't understand. I lived a life without choice. I did what Xawata told me to do. Slaves in the house of Xawata didn't have friends. We lived to survive his anger and mood swings. We lived to work and stay alive. I lived to work and earn my gratuities. I held a high status at Xawata's, which helped to keep me distanced from his anger," said Ultima.

"So, you think things will be the same here?" asked Otto.

"I don't know what to expect. I am familiar with the greed of wealthy men and women, and I'm used to their deceptions. I'm waiting to see what your family's little secrets are, your deceptions and decadent desires."

"Decadent desires? Listen, darling, our family is not what you are used to or what you have been exposed to here in Tsestelago. We have honor. My father arranged for you to be my wife. I signed the marriage license, but I don't need your Exotic ways. If you expect us to be a bunch of ravaging savages, you will wait for eternity. We are a family rooted in faith, honor, and loyalty." Otto's anger rose to the surface.

"Well, debauchery, deceit, and decadence are what I know. Show me different and maybe my opinion will change. For now, all I have are my life experiences."

"Ultima, there is decency in this world. Well, at least in Yakuta there is," said Otto.

"I haven't been to Yakuta, all I know is what I've seen here in Tsestelago. My society made me an Exotic. I'm the best Exotic in the entire kingdom. I don't know what else to be," said Ultima.

"You can be more."

"What more? I have all the education coins can buy. What other skill would you have me learn?" she demanded.

"I don't want you to learn any other skill."

"How can I be *more* if not by gaining new skills?" asked Ultima, exasperated.

"You can be more by striving to be better than an Exotic," said Otto.

"Like what, a wife, a commoner, a peasant? What Otto? What do you want me to be?" asked Ultima in disgust.

"Kindhearted, loving, selfless, generous, merciful, things that come from the heart," said Otto.

"So, now I'm a heartless, bad person," said Ultima.

"No, I didn't say that at all," said Otto, passing his fingers through and over his hair, and moved closer to Ultima.

She walked away from him, over to the fireplace and picked up the poker. "Then, what did you say?"

"Now that you are free, you can work on you. Work on your person instead of your skills," said Otto.

"I'm angry with you. You don't even know me or how I feel. I don't owe you anything. I owe your father for buying me away from Xawata, but he gifted me my freedom by marrying me to you. Leave before I hit you and trust me, I will leave a nasty mark." With that, she raised the poker she held with both her hands, then brandished the rod as she had done with her rapier sword earlier.

He stepped back, with no illusions as to whether she would actually carry through with the threat. "I'll leave and no worries. I'll give you all the time you need. I'll only be back when you are ready for me. You will let me know when we can move on as a married couple," said Otto.

"Well, that's new—I have never before been given an option."

"You have one now, unless it is you who decides to deceive me," said Otto.

"Then what? You'll give me a letter of divorce?" said Ultima.

"I can't give you a divorce. Nobles marriages are 'until death do us part.' Unless I catch you in bed with another man, in which case I could make you a prostitute again. We are stuck with each other," said Otto.

"Lord Otto ... when I was an Exotic in Xawata's house, sex was business. The *only* time I shared my body willingly with anyone was with you at the bachelor party. I was never permitted to say I didn't want a client to touch me. If the client paid to touch me, the client had the right, and I had no say in the matter. Now, you are giving me options. I don't know how to deal with you. I don't know what it is to say 'no.' You are scaring me and angering me at the same time," said Ultima, still with poker in hand.

"I don't wish to scare you. How about I help you learn to say no when you don't want to be touched?"

"Fine, if that makes you happy, fine. If I'm free, then I want you to leave me," said Ultima.

"Have a good night." So saying, Lord Otto left her room, closing the door behind him. Ultima placed the poker back in the fireplace. She wanted to scream, but she didn't. It was bad enough she had to travel with a husband she didn't understand, but now he wanted to teach her things.

"Learn to say no," she said, in as deep a voice as she could muster, trying to mimic Otto. *Like a man would listen when a woman says no.* "'You can be more!' What kind of manure is that?" said Ultima out loud. *How could I be more?* thought Ultima.

She hurt no one on purpose. She gave all her love, and all she had to Akina. She kept to herself at Xawata's and obeyed him always. Ultima needed time to comprehend.

CHAPTER 16

The Train Ride

On the day of their departure, the Hightower brothers were up early. Ultima could hear the men giving orders outside her window. She got up and called for Mariza, and she broke her fast in her bedroom. After the night when she had gone back to the parlor and had interrupted Lord Otto's conversation with his brothers, Ultima had taken her meals in her room—but without Akina, her life was lonely. The men trained with her during the day. Caleb and He'nico were pleasant, but Otto was distant, and he rarely talked to her.

Besides being told they would be traveling near a battle zone, she knew little else. Even Mariza, with all the servants' gossip, couldn't help her; none of the servants spoke Yakutan.

"My Lady, do you know when you'll be coming back?" asked Mariza, while helping Ultima dress.

"No, I don't even know where we are going or why—simply that I have to go with them," said Ultima.

"The why is obvious. You need protection. Ever since that man tried to kill you, everyone in the manor has been told they must keep an eye on you. Plus, your husband wants his new wife by his side," said Mariza.

"No, that's not it. Lord Otto dislikes me and I have no regard for him. On our return, I'm going to talk to the duke and ask for a divorce. I can't go back to being an Exotic—Lord Otto erased my trade-tattoo—but I can always work as an artist," said Ultima, while pulling on her boots. Mariza looked alarmed, but said nothing. Ultima was ready to go. She took her coat, hat, and gloves and left her room.

When she reached the first floor, the duke and his sons were still giving orders to the staff, but when she arrived, they gathered their coats and hats, and they climbed into the carriage. They traveled to the train station. It was a quiet, short ride. Once there, Lord Caleb purchased their tickets. They were going to the city of West Franken and that was all Caleb told Ultima.

"Your Grace, when will we return?" asked Ultima.

"We will be back as soon as we find what we are looking for, and make arrangements for its return to the capital," said the Duke.

"Are you always this enigmatic?" asked Ultima with a smile.

"I have my reasons to keep certain secrets."

That was when the Grand Duke of Hausman appeared. He was there with the Earl of Portmore, and his second son, Lord Thomas, and another man.

"It is good seeing you, Gareth," said the Duke of Hausman.

"It is good seeing you too, Robert," the men greeted each other and hugged.

"I heard you bought Exotic Ultima Skylar from Xawata Faan. I thought you bought her as a mistress. Then I read in the newspapers that she married your son, Otto. Hello, Ultima, how are you?" said Lord Hausman.

"Hello, Your Grace, it is always a joy to see you." Ultima gave the Grand Duke a shy smile, and curtsied.

"No old man, Ultima isn't my mistress. The newspapers have reported truly. I arranged for her to marry my third son,

Otto. Thus, she is now a free woman," said the Duke of Vurthas.

"Ah, Otto, you are a lucky man. Ultima was the ruby on old Xawata's crown. Surely, she's not coming with us, is she?" asked Hausman.

"She is accompanying us, yes. I can't have her stay back at the house. Don't forget, she has stopped an attempted assassination on your life, Robert. And there was an attempted assassination on her own life at my mansion. Apparently, there's an assassin loose in the kingdom that wants to kill her next. No, she stays with us," said the Duke of Vurthas.

"Gareth, can she fight? We are going to a war zone. Leaving her here will be safer than taking her into the middle of a battle," said the Grand Duke.

"She can fight. I've seen her practice, but we will protect her. And who is this?" The Duke of Vurthas nodded at the Earl of Portmore.

"This is my soon-to-be son-in-law, Lord James Tanning, the Earl of Portmore," said the Duke of Hausman.

"Hello Lord Tanning, welcome to our expedition," said the Duke.

"Nice to meet you, Your Grace," said the Earl in a raspy voice, coughing and hacking, and he bowed his head to acknowledge the Duke.

"Are you sick, Lord Tanning?" asked He'nico.

"It's nothing but a cold," said the Earl, and he moved away to continue coughing.

"Hello gentlemen, I'm happy I made it in time," said Marshal Paul Donnelly.

"What are you doing here?" asked the Duke of Vurthas.

"I'm going with you. I requested permission from the King to go wherever Lady Hightower goes. Apparently, she was at the assassination of the Prince Regent and is part of the investigations of both the Grand Duke of Hausman's attempted assassination and Commander Baxter's murder. I can't let anything to happen to her," said Paul Donnelly.

"The King gave you permission to come with us?" asked Caleb.

"Yes, both he and the Duke of Horrel gave me permission to join this venture. I have my ticket. Shall we go?" said the Marshal.

❖❖❖

The group boarded the train. Once aboard, they separated and each found their private rooms. Ultima was to share hers with Otto. She was sure Lord Caleb did that on purpose. She wanted a cabin to herself. Being with Otto made her angry.

"I'll be in the dining car," said Otto, and he left her alone in the cabin. She sat on the cushioned bench looking out the train window and saw the surroundings go by as the train pulled out of the station. She had never been on a train. This was a first for her, and her mind went to her Akina. How was her daughter coping in the academy of mages? She already missed Akina. An hour passed and there was a knock on her door. She bid the person enter.

"Hello, Exotic Ultima. I see Lord Otto isn't here," said Lord Thomas.

"He is in the dining car, and I'm not an Exotic anymore," said Ultima, but the man entered the cabin without invitation.

"For those of us that have had you, you will be an Exotic forever, so it is good he isn't here," said Lord Thomas.

"Why?" Ultima could see the man was aroused. It was clear as day. He wore a tailored suit, but the bulk at his front told the tale.

"I want to talk to you alone," said Lord Thomas.

"I don't want to talk to you at all. Please leave." Ultima already guessed what was on his mind, and she wanted nothing to do with him.

"I'm going to talk plainly. I want to purchase an hour of your time. I know you are a free woman and can negotiate by yourself," said the Lord, sitting on the bench across Ultima.

"I'm sorry, Lord Thomas. I already told you. I'm no longer an Exotic." Ultima frowned and brought her hands to her lap.

"Exotics are Exotics for life my darling, I have heard rumors old Xawata increased your pain threshold before he died. If that's true, then it should be extraordinarily high now and I want to test it. I want to see every part of you one more time," said Lord Thomas, giving her a sly smile and moving toward Ultima, as if to sit next to her, just as Lord Otto entered the cabin.

"Lord Thomas, what are you doing here?" asked Otto, entering the cabin.

"I was looking for you. Father wants us to meet in the dining cabin at ten past six for dinner. We have much to discuss. I'll see you then." And Lord Thomas walked past Otto and left, sending a smile and a wink to Ultima.

"Please don't tell me Lord Thomas was one of your clients and he was here asking for services?" said Otto.

"I did nothing. Is our life going to be like this forever; you assuming every person who talks to me will be asking for services?" asked Ultima.

"It was obvious by the bulge in his pants," said Otto.

"I know how to deal with people I don't like. As an Exotic, I could never negotiate my time; Xawata did that. However, I learned how to redirect people to him or just rebuff people who I knew would not be worth my time," said Ultima.

"So that is supposed to make me feel better?" said Otto.

"Hear me well, my Lord, you are going to have to learn how to live with me and the people that know me. Akina and I are yours now. I know my place in this dynamic."

"It's as though we never had our conversation the other day. I don't own you. You are free," said Otto.

"Otto, you said you wanted a respectable wife. I know I am not respectable. I'm not of sufficient quality for you; I understand my place in our society. You must give me time to get used to being part of your family and my new free status. I'm still finding my place within this family," said Ultima.

"Ultima, I used the wrong words in that conversation with my brothers and later with you. Please, I know you may be angry with me, but all I ask from you is that you not bring shame to my family. Lord Thomas wasn't here for me, was he?" said Otto.

"Otto I'm not the type of woman given to bouts of anger. Why don't you go? You said I'm a free woman now, I want to take a nap," said Ultima.

"Fine, I'll go—take your nap," said Otto, leaving the cabin.

Ultima looked down and took a deep breath. She was supposed to be free, but that didn't matter. Her life was stained since her childhood. She stood and locked the door. She didn't want anyone else bothering her. She opened the bed, and lay down for a nap.

❖❖❖

At dinner time, Ultima changed into one of her most comfortable traveling dresses, but like all her dresses they were cut to reveal her Exotic-tattoo. She couldn't do anything about it. Lord Otto had not given her any coin to buy a new wardrobe, so she had to wear what she had.

When she entered the dining car, everyone in attendance turned to look at her. Her hair and eyes were of eye-catching colors; her hair was ebony, with eyes a crystalline blue, the color of a summer sky, with a sensual almond-shaped cast. Her complexion was the palest peach, soft and unblemished.

"Oh, here she is, my son's beautiful bride," said the Duke, when Ultima entered the car. Lord Otto was standing, watching from a corner. He hadn't gone to escort her from the cabin.

She entered alone, walked to where the men were sitting, and tilted her head in acknowledgment to the two dukes. "Your Graces." She couldn't curtsy. There was not enough space, and the car was moving sideways.

"Thank you, Your Grace, and good evening to all," she stepped lightly over to where the Duke of Vurthas had risen and held out a chair for her.

"Would you care for a drink before dinner?" asked the Duke.

"No, thank you," said Ultima. All the men were present, so they called the servant to take their orders for a meal. The night went on with the men talking about the status of the kingdoms and the negotiations between King Trevino and the Kingdom of Alhambra. Ultima answered a few questions the men had for her, and she ate her meal in relative peace. She could still feel the discontent, fear and anguish around the men. The two dukes were surrounded by auras of the darkest shades as they talked privately, while the other men talked among themselves with similar darkness surrounding them. All, except Lord Thomas, who kept looking at her with ghastly eyes. The man wanted her, and she knew it.

She stood up and went to sit alone by a window, away from the men, in a chair that overlooked the darkness of the night. When the desserts came, Ultima ate a piece of chocolate cake in silence, but after she finished eating, her husband Lord Otto came and sat next to her.

"You love to show your Exotic mark, don't you?" whispered Lord Otto.

"I don't have an Exotic mark anymore. You erased it, remember?" she whispered back at him.

"It doesn't matter. Everyone knows Exotics are the only ones tattooed on the left breast. Look at your dress! Showing your breasts for all to see where the mark once was," said Lord Otto.

"This is all I have to wear. You never gave me a budget to change my wardrobe before we left, nor would you permit me to leave the manor to go shopping for new clothes." She hissed in irritation. "If you wanted me to cover my mark, then you should have made it possible for me to do so." Otto raised his eyebrow and Ultima stood up.

"Well, Your Graces, it is time for me to retire," said Ultima in a soft voice.

"Good night, Ultima," said the Duke of Vurthas.

"You all have a good night," said Ultima, and she turned and left the dining car.

A few minutes after she reached her cabin, Lord Otto opened the door and entered.

"I'm sorry. I didn't think of giving you an account for your needs. I'll ensure you get what you need when we reach West Franken and later when we return to the capital. We will ride horseback up the mountains and it will be cold. You will need warm boots as well as a cloak. I didn't think of your needs as a woman, which is entirely my fault," said Otto, and he turned and left the cabin.

"What games is the man playing? One moment he is an ass and the next he is kind," said Ultima out loud. She unfolded the bed, changed clothing and went to sleep. She didn't know if Otto later came to bed with her or not. She had gone to bed by herself and woke in the morning by herself.

❖❖❖

Seven days of fast travel by express train, and they arrived at the city of West Franken. For the entire time they traveled, Ultima kept herself locked in her and Otto's cabin, only opening the door for Otto. Lord Thomas knocked on her door a few times, but on each occasion she stayed quiet and did not respond to the man's calls.

When the train approached the city nestled in a valley with mountains on either side, Ultima had to smile. *What have I been missing? This is beautiful,* she thought to herself. Again, she was alone in the cabin enjoying the view. Snow covered the mountains, but the valley was still showing signs of fall, and the city was full of life. There was a river flowing through the center of the city, with tall buildings dotted all around.

There was a knock at her door. "Ultima, open the door." It was Otto's voice. Ultima opened the door and let the man in the cabin.

"Why do you keep this door locked?" asked Otto.

"I want to feel safe. After the assassination attempt, I don't feel safe anywhere. The city is beautiful. How long are we going to stay here? Is this our destination?" asked Ultima.

"No, we will be here for about four or five days. We need to make several arrangements before starting our ride up the mountains. It will be another hour before we reach the station," said Otto, sitting on the bench in front of her and closing his eyes. Ultima stood quietly. Her Exotic training taught her to reserve her counsel, and to listen and observe. Otto fell asleep, and he snored, letting Ultima know the man had nothing else to tell her. So, they were going to travel up a mountain. She looked forward to that adventure as another first in her life. She had never journeyed up a mountain before.

A loud train whistle startled Otto and Ultima awake. She, too, had fallen asleep. They had reached the station, and Otto stood up and collected their belongings. When they stepped off the train, a servant took their bags. A black man as tall as a mountain was standing with two other tall, handsome black men, all of whom were waving at them. It was none other than the Duke of Franken. The man had a leg in a cast and was walking with crutches. He approached the Duke of Vurthas's group with a brilliant smile and the authority of a general.

"Hello Gareth, my friend. It's been ages since we last saw each other. How is Nívea doing?" said the Duke of Franken, hugging the Duke of Vurthas.

"My wife is as beautiful as ever, and not changed one bit since you last saw her. What happened to your leg?" asked the Duke of Vurthas.

"I fell off my horse and broke it in three places. The healer said my leg will be out of this cast in another month," said the tall black man.

"I see your sons are taking after their mother," said the Duke of Vurthas.

"Ha, ha, ha! Yes, Thank God, they are far better looking than their father. Robert Otarana! Well, well. The Grand Duke of Hausman, I never thought you would ever leave Pailo." And the men hugged each other as well.

"Well, we have business to attend to outside the city. You remember my youngest son, Thomas?" said Hausman, bringing his son forward with his hand on Lord Thomas's shoulder.

"Oh yes, he is well known for his victorious battle against the pirates of Shengara. You made Commander already, Thomas?" asked the tall man.

"Yes, Your Grace, I did. I am the Commander of the 5th Battalion of the Green Brigade," said Lord Thomas.

"I am proud of both my sons. My oldest is taking care of the Dukedom in Oliva City, and Thomas is a warrior in his own right and by his own strength. And this," he said, drawing Lord James forward, "is my soon-to-be son-in-law, Lord James Tanning, the Earl of Portmore."

"James, this is Nehemiah Stone, the Duke of Franken," said the Duke of Hausman.

"It is a pleasure to meet you, Your Grace," said the Earl after a bout of coughs.

"Nice to meet you too, Lord Tanning. I hope you are not sick," said the Duke of Franken. Lord Tanning shook his head and continued coughing.

"And this here is Marshal Paul Donnelly," said the Duke of Hausman.

"Hello Marshal Donnelly, welcome to West Franken," said the Duke of Franken.

"Thank you, Your Grace," and Marshal Donnelly gave a slight bow to the duke.

"Come, let's get you moving." And the Duke of Franken and his two sons started to show the way out of the busy station with its many platforms and frenetic activity. Trains were coming and going; many people were walking about, but all made way for the imposing duke and his sons. Many men bowed their heads, and the women would step aside and drop into curtsies. The people dressed differently than in the capital city and women wore lively colored dresses and had lovely, prominent hair pins.

They reached the street, and there they saw five horseless carriages waiting for them. Ultima was shown to a carriage which she shared with Otto and Caleb. They rode in complete silence. She looked out the window and marveled at the way people traveled on the river. They had large boats filled to the tops with merchandise. On the streets, people traveled on horses, carts, horseless carriages, on bicycles, and bicycle-pulled rickshaws, and yet others walked about. She noticed how they all seemed to miss each other at the last minute in the traffic. They left the city behind, and traveled through the outskirts of the city, up the side of one of the mountains she had seen earlier from the train.

Time flew by and the amazing views kept coming. The carriages continued up and around the mountain, switching back and forth as they climbed. Eventually, they reached a large set of gates. The manor's gates opened to a well-maintained lawn. They passed what looked like a small pond to one side of the road, and there, in a large, enclosed area on the other side of the road, were horses freely roaming.

Large pine trees partly obscured the view to the house, but there was a stone wall that ran alongside the path, leading the way to the house. Ultima realized this had to be the home of the Duke of Franken.

The carriage made a turn and left the pine trees behind, and they reached the front entrance of the property. It wasn't a manor at all; it was a castle. She had seen pictures of a few castles in books, but had only been inside the King's castle in Pailo. This one was the largest she had ever seen, aside from the King's own. The horseless carriage stopped, and the men stepped out first. Lord Otto offered Ultima his hand to help her step out.

"And what is Exotic Ultima Skylar doing here? Xawata would never let you out of his reach," said the Duke of Franken.

"I bought her from Xawata and now she is my son Otto's wife, Lady Ultima Leighton Hightower of House Vurthas," said the Duke.

"How did you get old Xawata to sell her to you?" asked Duke Nehemiah.

"That is a story for another day," said the Duke of Vurthas.

"Lady Ultima, welcome to the Shashmilone Castle. I'm Nehemiah Stone, the Duke of Franken. We met five years ago at the King's birthday ball," said the Duke of Franken, his bald, black head shining in the sunlight. He took Ultima's hand and raised it to his lips.

Ultima curtsied to the man, keeping her eyes low, and holding her cloak close to her chest. "Hello, Your Grace. I remember you and your lovely wife. You both were at the last theatrical play Xawata hosted last summer," said Ultima.

"My wife is a fan of yours. She loves to hear you sing," said the Duke of Franken.

"Thank you," said Ultima.

"Well, my friends, come inside, I have everything prepared for you," said the Duke of Franken.

The Duke of Franken entered the castle with the other men, and they disappeared into a large hall to the side of the entrance. Many servants were carrying their luggage. Mrs. Hardie, the housekeeper, escorted Ultima to a large room at the top of one of the towers. The room had rounded walls, and windows that opened to a mountainside view.

"My Lady, the duke sends word that you were not traveling with a maid, so I've taken the liberty to assign a maid who will care for you. Her name is Lila." The housekeeper ushered the young girl, Lila, into Ultima's room for the introduction.

"Thank you, Mrs. Hardie."

Mrs. Hardie left, and Ultima stayed alone in her room with Lila, who helped her change into a more comfortable dress.

"Lila, would you tell Mrs. Hardie I need her to call a seamstress and a cobbler. I need to see both right away. Please let them both know to be ready to provide me with serviceable clothing and boots for traveling horseback up the mountain. And this must be done fast, for I'm leaving in five or six days."

"Yes, my Lady." And Lila left the room in a hurry.

CHAPTER 17

Dinner and a Story

Later that afternoon, Ultima left her room for dinner and at the same time the Duchess of Franken was coming out of her room. Ultima had a shawl made of lace arranged over her breast to hide her breasts from the servants.

"That is Her Grace, Lady Hannah," whispered Lila, when Ultima was escorted from her room by the girl. Ultima curtsied when the duchess approached.

"Your Grace," said Ultima.

"Lady Ultima Skylar, the best performer in the whole Kingdom of Tsestelago. I hear Lord Otto Hightower married you. I say congratulations are in order. How long have you been married?" asked the older woman.

"Yes, Your Grace, thank you. We have been married for two and a half months," said Ultima. The duchess looked gorgeous in her red dress. Her flawless mocha skin made her seem enchanted, and the diamond necklace and earrings sparkled with every smile and tiny turn of the head.

"It is serendipitous for us to meet. I love to hear you sing. Whenever I was in the capital and Xawata put on plays or shows with you taking part, I always made a point to go attend. I'm a fan of yours," said the Duchess with a wide smile.

"Thank you, Your Grace," said Ultima.

"Let's go to dinner, the men must be waiting for us by now." The duchess's slim body didn't show she had given birth to three children. Her happy, deep-brown eyes made Ultima think of a fine chocolate. The women walked down the stairs to the dining room antechamber, where the men waited for them, talking among themselves, when the women entered.

"Hello, Gareth, it is so nice to see you. Robert, you look dashing, but why didn't you bring Lady Kaitlen?" said the Duchess.

"Hello Lady Hannah. You are ever so beautiful. My wife stayed home. This is not a visit for pleasure," said Robert Otarana.

And on, the men and the Duchess of Franken continued with their salutations and talking among themselves. After a few minutes of chatter, the duchess returned to Ultima's side.

"Well, Lady Ultima, I hear you requested the services of a seamstress and a cobbler. I had my housekeeper call the best in town," said Lady Hannah.

"Thank you, Your Grace. I appreciate your help greatly." Ultima held a glass of sherry in her hands, which she sipped a little, just as she was taught.

"Now, pardon my interest, but why didn't you better prepare for this trip?" asked the Duchess.

"I knew nothing of the destination, other than it was to be into the mountains. Until we arrived at the train station in Pailo, I had no idea we were coming to West Franken. They just told me I was to travel up the mountain. My father-in-law and husband gave me little time to prepare," said Ultima.

"Ha, men! They know nothing about women and our needs. I don't understand why they don't leave you here with us while they go gallivanting through the mountains." The duchess looked at Ultima and made no pretentions to hide her curiosity.

"My husband wants me with him," said Ultima, with a smile.

"Ah, newlyweds, I understand."

Dinner was called, and the Duke of Franken escorted Lady Hannah, and Otto offered Ultima his arm. They entered a grand dining room, where Ultima was seated next to the duchess. During dinner, the conversation continued.

"So, tell me Gareth, why did the King send you to bring back Soren? There are many others in the kingdom that he could have sent," said Duke Nehemiah.

"Trevino has his hands full and there is only a small group of people he trusts. Plus, after Marco's assassination, there was an attempt on Robert's life, and the assassination of the commander of the King's guards, Lord Baxter, during the annual fox hunt this year. All of which left Trevino unable to trust anyone," said the Duke of Vurthas.

"I was on the front lines eight weeks ago with Prince Soren. We were planning a counterattack. I only came back to bury my mother who died while I was up the mountain, and I haven't returned because of this broken leg. Then I received the order to organize supplies for the 102 Company to accompany you up the mountain," said Duke Nehemiah.

"I'm so sorry about your mother. We didn't know," said Hausman.

"Thank you, but we kept it to ourselves. We are private people. How is Trevino?" asked the Duke of Franken.

"Trevino is very sick and most distraught over Soren's disregard for his orders to return to the capital after Marco's death," said Hausman.

"It wasn't until very recently that we found out about Prince Marco's death. News and even supplies are taking extra-long to reach us," said the Duchess.

"Besides his physical health, something else is not adding up with Trevino. I'm not making treasonous allegations; he is giving strange orders and becoming aggressive, even toward his own guards. He even threatened to hang Commander Baxter if anything happened to Prince Leer or Princess Joy-Anna," said Hausman.

"I heard about Baxter's assassination from Lord Farlen. It was ingenious to commit a murder during the King's Fox Hunt. Baxter was the third son of Baron Teasdale," said the Duke of Franken.

"No, he was the second son of the Baron," said Hausman.

"And no one knows who did it?" asked Nehemiah, the Duke of Franken.

"No, I have my men following all the leads we have, but nothing. I have a theory. I think that bullet was meant for Lady Hightower and the commander was unfortunately in the way," said Marshal Donnelly.

"Do you think it was the same man that assassinated the Prince Regent?" asked Lord Hausman.

"I think so, I just don't have any evidence," said the Marshal.

"Is King Trevino still siding against Behui in the war between Behui and Alhambra?" asked the Duchess.

"It depends on who you ask. He was very much against Behui. He even helped the King of Alhambra, but King Victor hasn't accepted the help. And now Trevino is talking about sending ambassadors to Behui," said Hausman.

"What do you mean? King Trevino was definitely against Behui in the war," said the Duke of Franken.

"My brother is holding diplomatic conversations with King Petro of Behui, of a commercial nature. We placed an embargo on Behui at the start of the war, and now Trevino has rescinded that order," said the Duke of Hausman.

"I didn't know that; it makes no sense," said the Duke of Vurthas. "That will not bode well for Yakuta."

"I want Tsestelago to stay out of the foreign wars, but Trevino isn't listening to me or any of his advisors. He even wants to tear down the wall between us and Alhambra. I fear Trevino is being influenced by Horrel and his expansionist agenda," said Duke Hausman.

"Why do you believe Horrel is behind Trevino's decisions?" asked Duke Nehemiah.

"Horrel is making daily visits to the court. And he has audiences with Trevino on most of those visits. The Duke of Abernathy tries to help me keep the peace between all the dukes, but it isn't always easy. We need Soren to keep the nobles in their place," said Duke Hausman.

"Well, I'm going with you," said Duke Nehemiah, one fist striking his other palm.

"No, thank you, my friend. You are in no condition to travel with your broken leg. King Trevino sent us to take command of the 102 Company and to move rapidly into the mountains. Plus, we will need you to send a rescue party for us if things go sour. Also, you must send word to the King if we encounter any problems," said Hausman, touching his mustache as he talked.

"I'm sorry, Robert, but if you don't want my company, then you must at least take my healers. I'll send ten with you. What Trevino may not know is that the roads are dangerous in this part of the kingdom and with the war up the mountains people are desperate. We have highwaymen that don't care for anything but coin," said Nehemiah.

"I'm not one to disagree with you. Horrel wanted us to come here with the minimum of escort, and that was a little strange, seeing that Tsestelago is in the middle of a war," said the Duke of Vurthas.

"The Archimage Saigai suggested to my brother to make Horrel the Minister of State, and Trevino is considering it. I disagree completely, but my brother isn't listening to me at all lately," said the Duke of Hausman.

Dinner continued as expected. The men kept talking about their impending travels up the mountain, and the women chatted about trivialities. Dinner was over and the evening continued uneventfully, and when it was time to retire, Ultima said her good nights and left for her room.

❖❖❖

When Ultima reached her bedroom, she noticed that Otto's things were in her room. She took a deep, calming breath and began to undress. She didn't have the strength to deal with

Otto. Lila helped Ultima change into her nightdress, and left. Ultima walked over to the vanity and looked at herself in the mirror. She didn't look like the Exotic from Xawata's brothel. She looked tired. Ultima was supposed to be free, but freedom wasn't as she had expected. She combed her hair and went to bed. She would not wait up for Otto.

There was no need for any preparations for her husband. This was the first night in a real bed in several nights. She went to bed and soon fell asleep. Two hours later, someone opened her door and entered. Ultima woke and sat up in bed. Otto was undressing by the light of the fire, the only light in the room.

"Go back to sleep. I'll sleep on the floor if that makes you happy," said Otto.

"Why? The bed is large, and I don't care if you sleep here," she then lay back down to sleep, turning her back to him.

♦♦♦

Ultima woke a few hours later to find herself being held so tightly that she was being smothered by Otto. The man had moved from his side of the bed, and he had captured Ultima in his arms, as if she were a security blanket—or in this case, a security woman. Her face was pressed to his neck and his arms were holding her so close she could barely breath. Ultima needed to relieve herself. So, she freed herself and moved slowly out of bed, one limb at a time.

She was still trying to understand how Otto could sleep with a face stuck to his neck, and was almost out of his arms, when he stirred and grabbed her and pulled her back into a tight embrace. She'd had enough; she had to get up. So, she pushed the man hard, and Otto was startled awake.

"Are you well? What's happened?" asked Otto.

"Nothing, you were sleeping on top of me, and I needed to get up. Go back to sleep," said Ultima. She got up, and relieved herself. She stretched her back, drank a glass of water, and stayed watching Otto as he slept. He must have been overly warm; all the blankets were pushed off. The man had big feet. Ultima noticed his feet and his legs.

He sure is one handsome lightning mage, thought Ultima. Otto was sleeping on his stomach and the covers were covering him to a little above his knees. She could see the thin white and blue capillaries that marked his legs. Those were the telltale signs of a lightning mage. The red, blue, and white branching formations of capillaries that covered his legs, and which glowed when he used his magic, were beautiful. She removed the remaining covers, and saw the complete patterns—fine lines, mostly white, some red, and others looked blue, like very slender tree branches. He had gone to sleep naked. On his back were several scars, and more of the lightning markings, combining to make an intricate design that covered his shoulders.

Ultima had only serviced one lightning mage, and it was Otto as a young man at the bachelor party twelve years prior. His body hadn't looked the way it appeared now. She had never seen the naked body of a *master* lightning mage until this moment. Mages were rarely wealthy, and those who were wealthy hardly had time for Exotics. She wanted to touch Otto's skin. She wondered how his skin would feel to her fingertips.

She sat next to his leg and gently touched his lower leg, tracing a vein. His skin felt rough. He had hairy legs. She kept following his leg with her fingers until she reached his thigh and there she stopped. Otto stirred and moved to his side. And Ultima noticed he was starting to have an erection.

"If you are not planning to finish what you started, please stop and go to sleep," said Otto.

Ultima looked at the man. She had not had a man since the duke had bought her from Xawata. Sex was work for her, but through the years she learned to enjoy her trade. She had learned how to gain sexual gratification from several of her paying customers, and had had many clients who were also lovers. For the last two days, she had been feeling the loss of those pleasures. She was an Exotic, accustomed to a certain level of sexual dalliances. Her self-imposed celibacy would have to take a hiatus for one night.

"I need this," she said, as she continued to caress Otto, tracing the lightning-colored capillaries that so captivated her. Otto turned onto his back. With the softest touch, she traced the white color makings in the form of lightning he had on his shoulder and the connections they made to the lightning markings on his chest. It was obvious this aroused him further.

"You've had enough. Go to sleep," said Otto. He started to sit up and leave, but Ultima held on to his arm, then pushed him back down to lie on the bed, and straddled him.

"No, I haven't had enough. I want more," said Ultima. She removed her shift and took control, guiding him to her pleasure, slowly but emphatically. At some point, Otto reversed the situation and became thoroughly committed. Ultima decided she was blessed to find a man who knew his way around a woman, knowing what would please them both.

When it was over, she started to leave the bed to clean herself up, but this time Otto held her arm to stop her leaving.

"Thank you, you didn't have to do that," said Otto.

"That wasn't for you. It was for me. I wanted to touch you. I wanted sex. I guess that makes me less of a woman of quality," said Ultima as she sat up. Then Otto took her hand and pulled her back in the bed.

"No, it makes you my woman. You can have my full cooperation and enthusiasm whenever you have the need." And Otto kissed Ultima's head.

"Thank you," she said, a small smile playing around the corners of her mouth.

"Come into my arms, we need rest," said Otto, pulling Ultima even closer into his embrace. So, Ultima moved into Otto's arms, where she quickly fell asleep.

The next morning, Ultima woke to an empty bed. Otto was gone and Ultima felt sore but happy. She had sex, and it was good and afterward, she slept through the night. It had been a long time since she had had a night without nightmares or night sweats. She got up, went to the window, and looked out. The view was a majestic set of snow-covered mountains. Opening the windows, she inhaled deeply as the cold air rushed in, refreshing, and taking away all the warmth from the room. There in the distance she could see the town. The castle was high up, on the side of a mountain. There was a knock on her door. It was her maid, with a warm cup of tea and a bath to start her day. She sipped at the tea and hoped she would not regret having had sex with Otto.

CHAPTER 18

Wardrobe, Armor and a Lesson

For the following two days, Ultima spent her entire time with the duchess from early in the morning till late in the afternoon. And Otto didn't return to their room. She had no idea what they were up to, but the men stayed away from the castle for the two days. The duchess took it upon herself to help Ultima form a wardrobe suited to her imminent trip into the mountains. There was a whirlwind of activity. She needed to pull together a wardrobe from scratch and be ready to travel into the wilderness within five days. Another new thing in her life.

On the third day, the seamstress and cobbler arrived at the castle with their goods, and they were ready to make final adjustments. Ultima went to the room where the seamstress was set up for the final fitting, and where she would have to undress. Ultima wanted to empty the room of anyone other than herself and the seamstress, but the duchess was in a frenzy of movement, looking at fabrics and chatting away.

Instead, for privacy, Ultima went behind a screen to undress. The burned wife-tattoo on her arm did not hide the fact she was once a prostitute, and the burned wife mark on her left breast, over the mark of the Exotic, showed what she could never hide. She didn't want the servants to spread the rumors she was an Exotic, but her maid had already seen her naked. Otto had burned the wife mark, but he could never take away her history.

When she stepped out from behind the screen in her chemise, and went to stand in front of a large mirror. She noticed when the duchess saw her scars, both on her arms and breast and the tattoos that coiled up her arm illustrating her skill set. Ultima closed her eyes for a moment, lifted her chin and gave a genteel sniff.

"What is wrong?" said the Duchess.

"Aren't you upset I'm an Exotic?" asked Ultima.

"My darling, you were an Exotic when I listened to you sing so beautifully. I may not have known you personally, but I knew who you were. I don't visit the capital often, but every time I did, I would look out for your singing shows. Every duchess knows of Exotic Ultima Skylar, but it doesn't matter what others think. You are a well-educated woman with many skills and attributes, and Lord Otto is blessed to have you as his life partner," said Lady Hannah.

"Oh!" said Ultima.

"Look at my right arm. It's true, I have a wife-tattoo not a brand, but I don't have any wife-skill extensions to my mark," said the Duchess. "All the skills you have result in your tattoos covering both the length and circumference of your wrist, twice over. You are a gem and a beauty. And now you are free. That is a blessing—you must be happy," she said, with a soft smile.

"Thank you, Your Grace. I am happy I'm married to Lord Otto and not in the trade anymore." Ultima stood proud and stoic. She had nothing to be ashamed of or to be sad about. She had had a trade, it was in the past, and that was all there was to it.

"That is good, both for you and for young Otto. You are a beautiful and talented woman. He would be a fool if he's not proud to have such a well-educated woman by his side. And I'm glad you are free of your trade. Although, you are the best singer and dancer in Pailo, and probably the entire kingdom, and your fans will surely miss you," said Lady Hannah.

"I honestly don't care," said Ultima.

"Ha, ha, ha, good for you. Let's get you dressed and ready to go on this trip. You are going to need armor," said the Duchess.

"Armor, oh my, I totally forgot about armor. How will it go over these garments?"

"Don't worry, I gave instructions to the seamstress to make sure your new clothes would work under armor. If you are going to be near the battle, you will most likely end up fighting. According to my husband the enemy is using everything from simple firearms and magic, to swords, arrows, axes, trebuchets, and any handheld weapon they can find. Your father-in-law asked me to have you fitted with the best armor I could find. You need to be covered from head to toe. I will give you my best armor."

"But you are so tall, and I certainly cannot be described as tall."

"It no longer fits me—it hasn't in quite some time, but I never got rid of it. And now I think the only adjustments they will need to make are to fit new leather bindings."

"Thank you, Your Grace," said Ultima.

"I notice you keep trying to cover your arm and breast, don't worry about it for a single second within the walls of my home. If anyone treats any of my guests with anything less than the utmost respect, they know they will no longer be my employee. However, on the battlefield you'll want to keep those covered." And Lady Hannah helped choose the best clothing and boots for Ultima.

Relief poured out of Ultima with the duchess's reaction to her having been an Exotic. Lady Hannah's reaction was not what Ultima had expected.

When the seamstress had made the final corrections to Ultima's clothing, two servants entered the room with a set of armor. Her clothing was easy. She was going to wear pants, with a long over skirt and short coat, or a long coat to give her extra warmth. The duchess stood up ever so elegantly, placed her cup of tea on a tray, and arranged for her servants to place the armor on the table.

"Come. Try on those boots the cobbler made for you. Then you can try the padding the seamstress designed for you to go under the medium-weight armor. The padding is made in sections, to give you enough space for ventilation. You don't want to bake in this thing. The chest and back plates have slits to let air enter. The gauntlets are made of leather and metal, and the pauldrons are made of a light yet strong metal to cover not only your shoulder, but part of your breasts too. The lighter weight armor doesn't need padding so that one is done and waiting for you in your room," said Lady Hannah.

"The Boleños will probably use pistols and rifles. This armor will only get in my way. I need something lighter," said Ultima.

"A rifle can only shoot one bullet. After that, they will fight with swords and arrows. Boleños like to use cannons, but Nehemiah said they are not using them up in the mountains. This medium-weight armor can't stop bullets fired at a distance, but it will protect you from things like swords, mazes, and axes. If you are fired upon from a distance, with a smaller firearm such as a pistol, the armor will help you. Anything fired at close range will penetrate, but at least you will be protected from most other weapons," said the Duchess.

"Oh, that is good to know," said Ultima.

"I'll fit you with a lighter set of armor for traveling on the road. It will be enough to fight highwaymen if necessary. I still think it is lunacy for you to go along on this trip. However, if you must go, at least you will be well-prepared. Do you know how to fight?" asked the Duchess.

"My slave master gave me lessons on a style of hand fighting, and two special arts of sword fighting that I incorporated them both into my dancing. The sword fighting was done with padding and padded armor to start, and we were obliged to wear a special type of dress. One of my regular clients liked to spar with me or just watch me go through the different routines with the swords. Xawata, my owner, sold my time to clients from all over the world who visited the capital, and they had 'Exotic' requests from me, besides the usual," said Ultima.

"It sounds like your master spared no expense on your education," said the Duchess.

"He was greedy, lecherous, deceiving, and held his slaves with an iron fist, but he did have good taste in all mundane things and a great eye for details," said Ultima. The women continued talking and fitting the armor for Ultima. By the end of the fitting, Ultima had all she needed for the trip up the mountain. Afterward, they ate their midday meal and when they were done, a young man with very short black hair and almond-shaped eyes, entered the room and gave a perfunctory bow.

"Hello, Your Grace, my Lady Hightower!" said the man, in a slight Palermo accent.

"Hello, Koru, how are you?" asked Lady Hannah.

"I'm well. I'm here at the behest of your husband, my Lady. Apparently, Lady Hightower is a healer, and her husband asked the Duke of Franken if there was a healer in the region who could give her some training," said Koru.

"Well timed in that case. Please, Koru, meet Lady Hightower—Lady Hightower, this is Koru, one of our best healers despite his youth," said the duchess.

Koru dipped his head at Ultima, and said, "The Duke of Vurthas and his son want you trained on how to use your magic, my Lady Hightower," said Koru.

"Hello Koru, when do you want to start my training?" asked Ultima in excellent Palermo.

"You speak my language! Impressive, I haven't met anyone in West Franken who could speak in Palermo," said Koru in Palermo.

"It is one of the many languages I speak," said Ultima, returning to the local language.

"Well, my Lady Hightower, we can start now if you have the time," said Koru.

"You two train, I must talk to Cook about tonight's dinner. If you'll excuse me," said Lady Hannah, as she left the room.

"My Lady Hightower, what do you know about our magic?" asked Healer Koru.

"What little I know comes from books, and from healers that came to provide services and who I conned into teaching me some things," said Ultima.

"That is good—you have some basic understanding. We will see what you know and how I can expand on your existing knowledge. My aim is not to try to make you a master mage in just a few days. That is impossible. You would need many years of training to gain that level of mastery. For now, I want to make you comfortable in your skill so you could help others if no other healer is available. Does that make sense to you?" asked Koru.

"Yes, Master Healer. What are the things you wish to teach me?" asked Ultima.

"First, I'd like to teach you to use the basic elements at your disposal to gain access to energy which can guide or activate your magic. How have you used your magic?" asked Healer Koru.

"When I touch people who are hurting or sick, the first thing I notice is that they lose heat in the area of injury. So, I concentrate and use the heat from my own body and transfer it to whichever area in the other person's body where I feel the loss of heat. Then I use my magic to start the healing process once I have the heat problem under control," said Ultima.

"You are working by instinct, and you know how to detect the problem area. That is good, but, you don't want to use your own heat. That will debilitate you. We will work on your using the things around you to provide the person with heat and then start the healing." Koru smiled and he stood up. He reached around the door frame and picked up what she realized was a bucket full of water he'd brought with him.

"You see this water. We are going to use this water to help you patch people up. Come place your hands inside the bucket of water, they need to be completely wet." Ultima went over and placed her hands in the bucket.

"Now I want you to think of heat, then think of cold, and then, think of air. You must concentrate and use the material you have on your hands—in this case you have water—and you must use it to move heat from the air to the point where the person is losing heat. The heat is not coming from you. It's coming from the air, and going through the water, and then onto the person. The only thing you are doing is moving the energies around, giving them a pathway. You are the director of the flow of energy." Ultima tried to visualize what Koru was saying. The little man stood next to her, and he held her hand in the water.

"Lady Hightower, one thing you must know. For women, the strength of their healing magic changes at different times in the month. Women who are bearing a child are the strongest healers," said the man.

"That is good to know," said Ultima.

"It is imperative that you learn to use your magic. Tomorrow you must come to my shop. You need to be around the sick so you can practice," said Koru.

❖❖❖

The men returned to the castle and the group reunited. They had dinner, and later, Ultima was getting ready to go to sleep when Otto entered the room. This was the first night Otto came to their room after that first memorable night. Ultima was not yet in bed.

"I thought you might be asleep already," said Otto.

"I was about to go to sleep, but you don't have to go," said Ultima. She stood up, removed her robe, and slid under the covers. She didn't look at Otto; she just went to bed. Throughout the day, neither one made any attempt to talk to the other. And apparently Otto didn't want to talk about their night together, so Ultima had nothing to say.

Otto undressed, turned off the lights, and he too climbed into bed. Ultima was lying with her back to Otto, trying to fall asleep, but she felt she needed to say something, but nothing came to mind. Instead, she inhaled deeply and tried to relax, but she couldn't. She wanted to kiss Otto. Two nights earlier they had had sex, but they never kissed. This time she wanted to kiss Otto. She turned over, laid her hand on Otto's shoulder, and turned him to rest on his back. She touched his face and kissed him.

"The other night we didn't kiss," said Ultima.

Otto reached over and touched her face, and he kissed her back. "I want to touch you tonight, to caress you. Will you let me? This is the moment when you can say yes or no," said Otto.

"Yes, I want you!" said Ultima, and Otto took Ultima in his arms and kissed her, and Ultima made love this time.

❖❖❖

Once again, Ultima woke up to an empty bed. Otto's pillow held traces of his scent, and Ultima took it and breathed in deeply. He had a distinct scent, one she liked. They had shared their bodies again and this time it was Otto who took the lead, and the man was a generous lover. He had asked her if he could touch her. It was interesting, another first for her. She wanted him. After they made love, they soon fell asleep.

Ultima woke to a sore body once more, but she had to hurry. This was their last day at West Franken, and Healer Koru had asked her to go to his shop. She had to leave early in the morning to get to Healer Koru's shop in reasonable time. Ultima went to the city of West Franken with Lila, traveling by carriage. Master Koru's shop was in the center of the city, and it was a small place. It had a wooden sign that said, Koru's Healing Herbs.

When Ultima and Lila entered the shop, a little bell rang. "Bling, bling," and a powerful aroma of lavender and sandalwood permeated the entire shop. Farther into the shop Ultima could smell cinnamon, rosemary, and even mint. There were potted herbs and drying ones hanging from every rafter, and tables full of jars with ointments and lotions.

"Hello Lady Ultima, it is good to see you," said Koru from behind the counter.

"Hello Koru, you have a well-stocked store. I see you have a good supply of herbs," said Ultima.

"Are you an herbalist?" asked Koru.

"I know how to use a few herbs to prevent a woman getting with child, or to heal sexual illnesses, but nothing in great detail," said Ultima.

"I'll give you a lesson on how to use herbs to help heal cuts and infections. I'll also give you a small book to take with you. It will help you along the way. You came here to learn how to use your magic. I must go to visit a few of my patients. I'd like for you to come with me and watch me. I'll show you how to do things as I do them. Is that acceptable?" asked Healer Koru.

"Yes, that will be acceptable," said Ultima. So she spent the morning with Healer Koru, visiting his patients. In the afternoon, she had to return in a hurry to the castle. They were leaving the next day.

CHAPTER 19

On Our Way to War

On the morning they were going to leave, Otto woke her early. The night before, when he had gone to bed, he kissed her, and started to caress her breast as he held her in his arms, but Ultima said, "No, tonight we sleep."

"Yes, tonight we sleep," said Otto, and he turned over, giving her his back. She smiled and went to sleep.

She had gone to bed in her undergarment but had left her traveling clothes ready on a chair. When they woke, Otto and Ultima carried out their morning ablutions. Shortly after, Lila knocked on their door. Ultima was almost fully dressed with Otto's assistance, only needing to don her light armor and boots. The young servant had packed her medium-weight armor along with all her other travel clothing and had sent it all ahead to be packed on her horse. Lila entered, bringing them hot tea.

The men were all getting their horses ready before dawn, when Ultima reached the stables. During the day she saw little of Otto and when they did see each other, he didn't talk to her much, but at night he had become a passionate lover.

Ultima broke her fast with the men as they prepared to leave, but the men said nothing to the enigmatic beauty who would be traveling with them.

Otto helped Ultima mount her horse. The men mounted theirs, and the company began the trek to the site of battle. Scouts had to travel ahead up the mountain to ensure the paths were still open. The trip to find Prince Soren was sure to take at least two months. They had packed four days earlier, with great efficiency, ensuring they had their weapons and armor at the ready.

As the sun rose above the horizon, Ultima put on her hat and dark glasses.

"Good morning, Ultima. Is it not too early for dark glasses?" asked the Duke, pleasantly.

"Good morning, Your Grace. I'm not used to the early mornings. The light bothers my eyes and gives me terrible headaches if I don't wear my dark glasses." She readjusted herself on her saddle as they moved off to join the company of soldiers who would be escorting them. Otto had chosen a sturdy horse for Ultima, which he had loaded with her things at the back of her saddle. Her horse was a gentle giant.

"It sounds like Xawata had your life regimented," said Otto.

"My life has always been that way. I had a tight schedule of classes and chores in my childhood. When I started working, in my teens, I lived mostly indoors and only went outside during the hours of darkness. There was a period of my life that months would pass, and I never saw the sunlight. It's one of the dangers of my trade. We could get sick when we didn't see sunlight," said Ultima.

"It is good you are not in that trade anymore," said Otto, giving her a smile and then signaling to the soldiers to move on. He rode to the front of the group, leaving her riding near her father-in-law. Caleb had gone on ahead the day before with a group of five scouts. Two days before that, thirty of the one hundred men had gone ahead with Lord Thomas and Lord James, the Earl of Portmore.

The herbs and medicines the duke had brought with him were added to the healer's cart the Duke of Franken had given the group, along with food and other provisions. All had been assembled and were ready to leave when the group started to move out. They wanted to leave the town of West Franken well behind by dusk. As the day continued, Otto and He'nico traveled next to Ultima in sporadic moments, in between moving to the front of the group.

When the group left the castle, most of the men marched, some rode on horseback, and they passed through the outskirts of the city of West Franken. Ultima noticed she was the only female within the group. There were no female mages, warriors, or healers. At midday, Caleb reached them. He said he had found a great place to camp for the night.

Ultima rode all day, deep in thought, until the afternoon when Marshal Donnelly moved his horse next to hers.

"Lady Ultima how are you feeling?" asked the odious man.

"Hello Marshal Donnelly, I'm doing well, thank you. And you?" Ultima's dislike of the man grew with each interaction.

"I'm loving this. It isn't every day I get to go out into the field and babysit a lead in a murder investigation," said Marshal Donnelly.

"So, I'm a suspect?" asked Ultima turning in her saddle and looking at Marshal Donnelly.

"I never said *you* … were the suspect." And the marshal cantered on with a smile on his face. He appeared to be enjoying every minute of the ride.

"I don't know why we need to have that infuriating man with us," said Ultima to Caleb, who was riding next to her.

"We couldn't stop him. He is still investigating the deaths of Prince Marco and now Commander Baxter as well. Plus, the King himself ordered him to come with us," said Caleb.

"I'm so tired of this running around. I just want to live a quiet life," said Ultima, adjusting her hat to better cover her face from the sun.

"Soon, we will return from this trip and things will be less stressful, but life will never be simple as long as the King of Behui is waging war against his neighboring kingdoms," said Caleb.

"I want to be a fishermen's wife, or a seamstress, or a milliner. I can be a milliner, you know. I know how to make hats. Maybe that way I can live a quiet life in a town far away from war," said Ultima.

"My dear sister-in-law, you are a mage. We mages can wish all we want, but we are who we are, and for the likes of us there are responsibilities to the people. We can't just ignore the suffering," said Caleb.

"Caleb, that is easy for you to say, you had a wonderful life. I've been a slave all my life. I just want a little quiet and normality now that I'm free." Ultima spoke in quiet tones.

"What do you want in life?" asked Caleb.

"You are the first person who ever asked me that. Where to start?" She paused to think. "I want to live my life not being required to give explanations, nor to ask anyone permission to do anything. I want my daughter to be safe and to not have to worry for her future. I want to be loved for who I'm, and not for how I look or for what I can do."

"You have all of those things with us. I don't know about Otto, but within both our culture and our family, women are their own person. We don't require women to give us anything, other than respect to the family—but we ask that from our men as well. Your daughter has our name and is a Hightower in all senses of the word. She is cared for and protected. And while I don't know how Otto feels about you, you have already won over my father's heart," said Caleb.

"At the moment, as long as Akina is safe and happy, that is enough for me. She is my life," said Ultima.

"I don't want to be insensitive, and you can tell me to go pound sand, but ever since I met you, I wondered how you survived as a slave? How did you manage to become with child, and then to keep Akina with you and not let Xawata sell her?" asked Caleb.

"Hah, that is another question no one has ever asked me. I survived my entire life as a slave by being the best at everything I did, and keeping my daughter and myself away from the gossip and inner workings of the house," said Ultima.

"That must have been a lonely life," said Caleb.

"It was lonely, but I knew that as long as I was the best Exotic in Xawata's house, I would be treated with the trappings of status, and no one would mess with me or my daughter. I always had to be the best," said Ultima.

"How did you prevent Xawata from selling Akina or taking her away from you?" asked Caleb.

"I kept my daughter with me by signing a contract binding me to Xawata for life. An Exotic slave can gain her freedom at age forty, and leave the brothel if she wants, but my contract tied me to Xawata for all time. In exchange, he let me keep my daughter. I knew I would never learn what it is to be free, but I had to keep my daughter safe and I knew I had to work hard for that," said Ultima with a smile.

"Xawata held Akina as a slave and also blackmailed you with her? The man deserved to die a painful death," said Caleb.

"The moment she was born, he made her a slave. Xawata gave me status among the other slaves and even the servants, but he held Akina's safety over my head to ensure my compliance. Akina and I had no choices. Now, your brother gives me all these choices and I don't know what to do with them," said Ultima.

"You will get used to being free. It will take time," said Caleb.

"I'm working on it," said Ultima.

"When are you going to tell Otto that Akina is his daughter?" asked Caleb.

"What?" Ultima blanched. "How do you know that?"

"It is part of my magic. I know when a kinsman or woman is near, and Akina is a Hightower. Plus, all you need to do is look at her. She looks just like my mother, but with black hair," said Caleb.

"I don't know. I haven't found the right moment to tell him," said Ultima, looking forward.

"I say, do it soon." Caleb patted the neck of his horse.

"Do you know why Otto hates Exotics?" asked Ultima, looking away.

"That is an odd question to ask," said Caleb, appearing unready to answer.

"I need to know."

"My brother is an enigma, but I think I know the answer to your question. Not too long ago, he offered to pay for the services of an Exotic. Suddenly she jumped up and before Otto could say 'I'm sorry,' she had a dagger made of fire pointed at his throat. The fire burned his neck a little. She happened to be one of the Vanquishers of Alhambra, and the Marquis of Banefield ended up marrying her. She is one powerful fire mage. She almost decapitated him with fire. Ever since then, he doesn't go near Exotics." He chuckled lightly, "I'm not sure if he ever recovered from that moment," said Caleb, caressing his own beard.

"Oh wow, that must have been scary and funny to see at the same time," said Ultima.

"It was. My poor brother stayed well away from the woman after that," said Caleb.

"Otto is a man who doesn't talk much," said Ultima.

"Otto is a prince in Yakuta, as all my brothers and I are. We are nephews of our King. Otto is a diplomat, an ambassador for our King, and he's a master lightening mage of our kingdom. He has a lot of responsibilities. At the moment, our father has made him the pathfinder of this expedition. Give him time. I'm sorry to say this, but it is all I can think of to tell you about my brother at the moment. However, I suggest you talk to him and ask him directly," said Caleb.

"Wait, Otto is a prince?" asked Ultima in disbelief.

"We all are. Our uncle made us princes the moment we were born, at the request of our mother. She was born first and was supposed to be queen, but when her magic blossomed and she turned mage our uncle George had already been born, so they gave the kingdom to him. She often holds him to task over this." He winked, "Nah, they love each other very much and my mother and uncle are close friends and confidants."

"Why wasn't she made the Queen since she was older?" asked Ultima.

"Darling, mages can't rule. My mother is the senior master mage. She is the Archimage of Yakuta," said Caleb.

"For all the gods of Yavos, I'm married into the royal family of Yakuta!" said Ultima.

"Yes, you are," said Caleb, adjusting his butt on the saddle.

"I can't help my trade. I didn't ask your father to marry me to Otto," said Ultima.

"I know, darling, I know. And I don't see you as anything but a lady in our house. Talk to Otto, he is the one with the most education and wisdom of all of us," said Caleb.

"It is hard talking to him sometimes. He wants me to be more than an Exotic. And I don't understand what he means. It's hard for me to understand him most days," said Ultima.

"That is my brother Otto alright, just hang in there with him. Otto is a good man, and his heart is in the right place," said Caleb.

"I hope you're not just saying this because he's your brother," said Ultima.

"Well, he *is* one of my youngest brothers," said Caleb.

"Who is one of your youngest brothers?" asked Otto. He had slowly ridden his horse alongside Caleb and Ultima.

"You! I have a few other younger brothers, but we are talking about you. And I'm going to ride along so the two of you can talk a little," said Caleb, and he spurred his horse forward, toward the front of the group.

"What were you and Caleb talking about me?" asked Otto.

"Nothing, I was just curious about you. I know very little about you and your family," said Ultima.

"So, what do you want to know about me or my family?" asked Otto.

"What were you like as a child?" Ultima smiled, and it reached her eyes.

"I'm the third of eight siblings. So, I'm the middle child in this clan," said Otto.

"You must have had many fights with your older brothers?" said Ultima.

"No, on the contrary, I followed them around everywhere they went, like a puppy. Growing up, I idolized He'nico and Caleb. I wanted to be just like them. Father raised us to be close to each other," said Otto.

"How about sisters?"

"I have two sisters and they are spoiled by all of us in the family," said Otto.

"I bet," she said and chuckled a little. "Did you have many teachers or go to school?"

"We were taught by tutors mostly in the family's country manor. Mother and Father kept us away from court as much as they could help it, until we were old enough to understand the intrigues of the court. We are the nephews of King George, but we lived as much a normal life as Mother and Father could give us," said Otto.

"Did you go to a mages academy?" asked Ultima.

"Yes, we did, and we were expected to be the best in our class."

"And were you the best in your class?"

He smiled ruefully, "No, not at first, but my mother practiced with me during the weeks I was home from the academy. He'nico and Zeino, one of my younger brothers, helped me by taking me to the back of the property for target practice of my lightning magic, using old plates they had stolen from the kitchen. When Cook found us and told our mother, she made us work in the kitchen for months," said Otto.

"How about you? How was your childhood?" asked Otto.

"I don't remember my mother and all I remember of my father was him pulling me by the hand on the day he sold me to Xawata." Ultima was looking forward, her lips in a thin line.

"How old were you when Xawata bought you?"

"I was four years old," said Ultima, distracting herself by patting the head of her horse.

"You were really young. How was it growing up at Xawata's?" asked Otto.

"I don't remember much of my childhood. I blocked most of it. All I remember were lessons and chores."

"So, you never really had a family?" asked Otto.

"Not until I had Akina. The moment I gave birth to my child, eleven years ago, I came to have a family," said Ultima, smiling.

"What is the happiest moment in your life?" asked Otto.

"Easy, I have two. The day I gave birth to Akina and when you took my collar off my neck," said Ultima.

Otto looked at her with a smile. Ultima liked when Otto smiled. He looked very handsome when he smiled.

"What is your favorite food?" she asked, looking at him sideways, a little coyly.

"Deer roasted over a pit, well-seasoned, with potatoes and carrots on the side; that's the best. Now I'm hungry for button. I'm going to have some men go hunt for a deer. We'll talk later," said Otto, and he pushed his horse forward and left Ultima to ride alone.

❖❖❖

Weeks passed and the roads to the Pikes Mountains became colder, wetter, and snowier. They crossed the Valley of Warfield, then they entered the outskirts of the Mirrem Mountains. They had encountered no highway men along the way, which was good. The stench coming from the horses and the men who hadn't bathed in days made Ultima feel quite sick at first, but she became accustomed to it as the days passed.

After the first two weeks, she didn't even mind passing within three or four feet of a horse defecating as it walked along. Mud and slush covered half the horse, her boots, and most of her belongings, making her want to shout most days, but she contained herself.

"When are we going to return to civilization?" asked Ultima, exasperated.

"We don't know how long this will take. We need to find Soren," said Otto, who was riding next to her.

"I hate this form of travel. I hate mud and slush. I need a bath. Otto, I wasn't raised for this kind of life," said Ultima.

"As an Exotic, they trained you to tolerate discomfort. I guess you should use that training here."

"Yes, but in my training, it was to withstand discomfort for a limited amount of time. I knew it would last only minutes, an hour at most. This has been going on for days."

"I'm sorry. I can't do anything to make things better for you," said Otto, and he rode ahead. Ultima scratched her head, and she looked up to the sky.

"Lords of Yavos, I think I have lice. Why me? Freedom isn't what I had expected," said Ultima out loud.

"What did you expect freedom would be?" asked the Duke of Vurthas, riding up from behind.

"I'm sorry, Your Grace, I didn't notice you were near. I'm not feeling my best today. All this mud is getting to me. I think I even have mud between my braids," said Ultima.

"You are deflecting my question. What did you expect freedom would be?" repeated the Duke.

Ultima thought things through for a few seconds, then she looked at the duke and said, "Having the option to choose not to be in this mud."

"I am truly sorry. I took that from you. I was afraid someone would try to assassinate you while we were away, when we could do nothing to prevent it," said the Duke of Vurthas.

"And me traveling to a war front isn't dangerous enough?" said Ultima, and she let her horse sidle away.

CHAPTER 20

The Battle at Pikes Mountain

The Duke of Vurthas and his sons walked, ate, slept, and trained with their men. By the time they arrived at the outskirts of Pikes Mountain, three weeks after leaving the city of West Franken, they were soaked and covered with mud. The scouts found a suitable campsite near a small river with gently running waters that provided fresh food by catching some fish. The two dukes left a group of men in their rear to guard their retreat, and the rest of the group kept moving forward until, after one more day of travel, they found the front line of the war where the sides were engaged in battle.

Ultima and the rest of her companions could hear the battle a few miles away. The men shouted their desire to fight, and they galloped toward the sounds of war—to where the fire raged and smoke licked the clouds above. Ultima felt they had forgotten all about her. However, just as they arrived at the site, the Duke of Vurthas grabbed Ultima's horse's reins and she remained by his side.

Otto wheeled his horse around and rode up to the pair. He took Ultima by the arm, and tugged to ensure he had her attention. "Ultima, you listen to me. Listen! You must stay near me at all times. You must repeat this to yourself when in the heat of battle; you must tell this to yourself over and over." She was looking into the distance toward the fighting. Otto grabbed Ultima's chest armor and pulled her toward him, making her look at him.

"You must remember and repeat to yourself, 'I am not going to be captured. I will not end up as a slave. I survived many atrocities; this is going to be one more. Akina is waiting for me. If I want to see her again, I must fight.' You tell that to yourself. Do you hear me? Do not let them capture you, take as many of them as you can. Don't let them capture you alive—you fight to the end! Do you hear me, Ultima? You must fight! Do you understand? You must stay near me and fight," said Otto. His eyes were wide and his hand holding Ultima was clamped tightly on the armor. Ultima nodded and Otto pulled her closer, gave her a kiss, and let her armor go.

As the fight with the Boleños of the Kingdom of Boleña raged on, they had sent seventy of the one hundred men to wait outside the encampment of the forces of King Trevino.

"We will wait here," said the Duke. Otto and five soldiers stayed with the Duke of Vurthas and Ultima.

Ultima felt herself quiver from an overwhelming fear that hit her right in the center of her chest. It was as if all the memories of her life came to her at the same time in rapid succession, but with the memories, all the possible things that could go wrong also came rushing in. And then that inevitable thought: "*I'm going to die.*"

Just as she began to despair, Otto's words rattled through her mind. "*If I'm captured, I will not end up as a slave.*"

She hoped for any type of escape from this waking nightmare. Her hands shook and her breathing became shallow and fast. "I can't breathe," said Ultima, but no one could hear what she said. All the men with her were focused on the battle waging ahead of them. *Breathe, Ultima, but slowly. You must take one slow deep breath and then another or you will pass out.* She took a breath, held it in and counted, one, two, three, and exhaled.

You have survived many atrocities; this is going to be one more. Breathe girl, breathe, Akina is waiting for you. If you want to see her again, calm down and you must fight when the time comes. She took a deep breath. By now, sweat was covering her brow and a headache was taking over. The helmet felt heavier than before. She took her helmet off and a cold breeze hit her face. The cold air made her feel better.

Breathe, Ultima, breathe! You can do this. Smell the horse. He is alive under you and calm... Ultima lowered her head at first, then lifted her face to the sky, closed her eyes, and stretched her back. She needed air in her lungs. The sound of battle and the men's screams came like a whip hitting her hard. Battle and men dying ahead were in direct contrast to her desire to live and breathe.

Before they capture you, take as many of them as you can. Ultima took a few deep breaths and let them out through her mouth slowly.

"You don't let them capture you alive. You fight," said Ultima out loud, and she touched her face and her hair. She was alive.

At that moment she would do anything that could take her back to safety, even return to being an Exotic. *Breathe, Ultima, breathe. Akina is safe in her school, but she is waiting for you.* She opened her eyes and looked at the battlefield.

She put on her helmet again and continued to watch the battle from up in the hills. Her breathing calmed a little. She patted her horse on his neck and smelled her horse's mane.

"Horse, I'm on a horse. I'm safe now. The horse is calm." The horse moved his ears side-to-side and she smiled, but just then, a group of men came running out of the side bushes screaming with others on horseback. The attacking soldiers shot the only bullets they had left in their rifles, killing two of the five soldiers who had stayed with the Duke, Otto, and Ultima.

The horse whinnied and Ultima unsheathed Jade, her favorite sword and swung it against the man that was coming toward her. She maneuvered her horse left and right, avoiding any counterattack. Her horse became part of her weapons. It moved the warriors away from her. She fought hard, but a man grabbed her leg and pulled her off her horse. She landed on her side, but she held her sword tightly in her hand. He swung his sword directly over her, but she kicked his groin and rolled to her left. He hunched over; his sword fell to the side.

She kicked the man's knee, then stood up and ran to fight near to Otto and the Duke of Vurthas, who were also no longer on their horses. She moved left and right. The men came at her with force. She moved fast, right and left, never the same movements, but never still. The men hit her armor hard, but she stood up to it.

She hit another man on his side and then on his head, but he struck back with a spiked mace, hitting her chest plate with force. The weapon made a dent, but it didn't rupture the armor. The force pushed Ultima back, and she tripped over a dead body lying behind her. The man with the mace was about to hit her in her face.

"NO!" shouted Ultima, just as Otto appeared from behind him and cut off his head with his ax. Blood splattered all over Ultima's face. She blinked once, then twice more.

"Are you alright?" asked Otto, giving his hand to Ultima and helping her to stand.

"Yes," said Ultima, out of breath.

"Good, keep fighting," said Otto. Ultima's helmet covered the side of her cheeks. She wanted to take the thing off.

They continued to fight when a few more soldiers came at them from behind a bush. As the numbers dwindled, Ultima's strikes had less and less power. Once all the enemy men were dead, Otto went to Ultima. She took off her helmet, let it fall to the ground and followed it down, landing on her hands and knees, and vomited. Once finished, Otto helped her stand, and she took a few steps away. Otto gave her helmet back to her.

"You need to wash your mouth with this." Otto gave her a small flask. She took it and the liquid was whiskey. She rinsed her mouth and spat it out.

"Look at me. Take a deep breath. Look at me, Ultima," said Otto, holding Ultima by her chest plate. He gave her a kiss and a hug.

"Now, look at me; you fought by instinct. Next time, it will not be this easy. Next time you already know what to expect and your brain will over think it. You must forget this and think of Akina. I know you love her," said Otto. Ultima looked at Otto and she nodded.

Ultima was taking deep breaths and trying to listen to Otto, but when he mentioned Akina, her full attention snapped to him.

"Breathe and calm yourself. We must go." Otto let her go and went to look for his horse.

"Father are you ready to go?" asked Otto.

"Yes. Is Ultima ready? Can she fight?" said the Duke of Vurthas with a frown, looking at Ultima as she was putting on her helmet.

"I'm regretting bringing her here," said the Duke.

"She is here now. Let's get moving," said Otto.

Otto helped Ultima mount her horse. Caleb came galloping toward them from the group of men waiting.

"Father, are you alright? I found out they ambushed you," said Caleb.

"We are fine. Let's go, we must talk to the commander," said Otto.

So, the Duke of Vurthas, Otto, Caleb, and Ultima galloped on in search of whoever oversaw the fighting.

"I hope Soren is orchestrating the fight with his commanders from the rear," shouted Caleb. The seventy men they'd sent ahead were standing far away from the battle, waiting with the Duke of Hausman.

The snow was no longer white. Much blood, along with a torrential rain, covered everything and had turned the snow into slush and mud covering the land. The valley and mountainside were littered with destruction; weapons and dirt became the refuge and campsite for the soldiers from Tsestelago. The horses, hounds, and men lived together and fought together.

As the Duke of Vurthas and his sons approached, they encountered an old commander. A man Ultima didn't know.

"Are you friend or foe?" asked the Commander, pointing his sword at the Duke of Vurthas, just as the Grand Duke of Hausman arrived brandishing his colors.

"Where is Prince Soren? Where is my nephew?" asked Hausman.

"Your Grace, the last I saw of him; he was near the archers," said the Commander.

"How long have you been fighting?" asked Otto.

"The current battle has raged on and off for three days," said the Commander.

"Why didn't you send word you were on your way?" asked the Commander.

"We sent a messenger. Didn't you receive the message?" asked Hausman

"We have had no messages from the capital in months," said the Commander.

The banners of the red oak and black bear were the emblems of House Trevino, and could be seen for miles. What was once a peaceful mountainside was now the stage of a stalling war.

"What can we do?" asked Caleb.

"We need the soldiers to go around and give reinforcement to our left wedge. The Boleños are closing in on our wedge formation," said the Commander.

"He'nico, take the men and move them where the commander needs them; Caleb, Portmore, go find Prince Soren and give him protection," said Duke Hausman.

Ultima stood by the Duke of Vurthas and watched everything around her. She couldn't believe the destruction. It was devastation unlike any she had ever seen before.

When they arrived, Soren's men were being ripped apart by the Boleños' attack. The battle had been going on for an hour as He'nico's men advanced under cover, moving up the left side of the Boleños men. Soren's men were pushing out in a wedge formation, and the duke's fire mage's fire devoured the Boleños. A fresh line came up the right side, to the outer side of the V-shaped battle maneuver. The one hundred men that Lord Nehemiah had given of his own forces to help fetch the prince included twenty archers. The West Franken archers took up position, and they let arrows fly over the Boleños, decimating the advancing group. The Boleños kept moving forward from the right. Either they were utterly careless of death or drugged with hallucinogens and whiskey. An hour after the Duke of Vurthas's attack started, not far off in the center, Soren's flank was exposed, but the Duke of Vurthas and the Duke of Franken's men made a timely counterattack that restored the situation.

The air felt heavy and thick with a miasma of burned flesh and wet dog. The bugle call possessed the power to rise above the deafening sounds of battle. It gave the orders during battle, and it sounded with echoes as the grunt and shouts of men carried on the horrid tune of war.

Clouds of men closed in on the center of the Tsestelago forces, threatening to suffocate the men and Ultima's heart pounded faster.

"I must do something," said Ultima to herself. She stepped outside the tent where the men were planning their strategy. It took forever for them to decide.

Ultima left the suffocating tent, and stepped into the entrance to hell. The first thing she noticed was the pungent smell of gunpowder and dead, rotting flesh, from all the fallen men and horses, both friends and enemies. The cool wind that blew around her didn't help to get rid of the disgusting smell—it brought in additional horrors: smells of dust, smoke, and blood from the surrounding area. These aromas of war brought on feelings of anxiety, fear, and dread.

Will I be the next one to die?

BOOM! Something exploded ... too near; Ultima looked to her right.

She ventured farther, nearer to the trebuchet line. The screams and shouts from nearby soldiers grew louder.

BOOM! Fire, thunder and lightning, explosions, magic spells sounding close and afar.

BOOM! The trebuchet's fire and debris fell over Ultima.

She moved to stand a little away from the edge of the trebuchet, and she could hear soldiers singing a cadence—loudly—as they fought and hit man after man. As the cadence progressed, their voices gradually sounded less strong. Ultima couldn't take it anymore.

At that moment, Otto walked out of the tent, mounted his horse, and galloped away. Ultima didn't think. She saw Otto doing something, and she went after him. Ultima found her horse and followed. She didn't know why she followed Otto. It was a tug of compunction and a desire to do something, anything. She galloped toward the battle, unsheathed her sword, and fought. Ultima rode ahead with Otto, and swung her sword by his side. Otto noticed who his partner was.

"Ultima go back to camp," shouted Otto.

"No, I'll fight with you," said Ultima, swinging her sword next to Otto.

"Then stay near me," shouted Otto, swinging his ax.

"Soren, where are you?" shouted Otto.

"Soren, we have reinforcements," shouted a captain who had followed Otto and Ultima. A gust of air passed over, and the voices full of pain and associated desperate motions quickly changed from fear to determined warriors when the men saw Otto and Ultima fight together. The voices of the men around her hammered in Ultima's brain. Some begged and pleaded for their Prince to stop the fight, others shouted words of victory, but mercy or defeat were no longer an option.

Otto and the captain moved to the left, and Ultima moved with them. Then Otto cleared the fighting around a man with grime-covered silver armor with a black rose painted on the pauldrons.

"The Prince, protect the Prince," shouted the captain.

Ultima sat on her horse, swinging her sword as she had been taught. Her slave master, Xawata, had spared no expense in her education, and for that she was grateful. Even as the relief of her anger released with each decapitation of the enemy, seeing so many men dismembered replaced the feelings with an ever-growing dread and anxiety.

Then her voice persistently rose above and bellowed, "Fight! Fight and don't give up." Blood splattered her face and the smell of gunpowder filling the thick air made her want to puke. Snow fell over them.

The faces of the fighters were grim with the certainty of death and horror, but they forced themselves to fight. They waged their war and Otto fought on with a short ax that swung as easily as a clock's pendulum.

Then it rained, mixed with the snow. The fight continued, an occasional gunshot, arrows of fire flying above, swords, and magic spells.

Boom. Bam. Thump, and splat. Dirt, wet soil, and ash fell and slowed Ultima's movements. Squish, the horse stepped on the guts of dead men. The hillside they were on leveled out, and then it rose again into hilly terrain. Otto's horse slowly climbed higher and higher as Otto fought man after man, trying to stay close to the prince. All Ultima could think of was, *Stay close to Otto.*

A torrential rain poured down, making it hard to see as they fought, Ultima with her sword and Otto with his short ax. They reached Prince Soren, whose sword movements had slowed since they last saw him. After having shot the only bullet from the chamber of his rifle, all he had left was his sword.

Prince Soren and everyone around him could see Otto and Ultima fight as a duo on their horses, until an enemy unhorsed Ultima by pulling her leg. Otto jumped from his horse and went to her side. The man who had unhorsed Ultima was about to strike her with a two-handed sword as she was lying on the ground, when Otto threw a dagger at the man's head. Ultima stood up fast, and holding her sword, ran to Otto's side. They fought back-to-back, Ultima with her sword and Otto decapitated the enemy with his ax. She was shorter than Otto, but he held her by the waist with his left arm and swung his ax with his right arm. She stayed close to his back.

As long as my back touches his, he is standing and we are alive, thought Ultima to herself.

It was a beautiful, macabre dance of gore and guts. She pressed her back to his, and they danced. In every dance of her land, the man led, and she took her cue. She was the best dancer in the whole kingdom and fighting for her was just another dance. She used to be an Exotic. This was just another disgusting thing she had to do.

Ultima and Otto were given a reprieve when a timely counterattack was made by the men, galvanized by the Duke of Hausman, who literally hacked the Boleños to bits. Then Commander Rapino's bombardment came down. The intense and concentrated onslaught came from high above the mountain stopping the Boleños in their tracks, and the Boleños sounded the retreat. They broke formation, scattered, and ran in the opposite direction as falling shells made holes in the ground all around.

Ultima almost sighed, if she had had any breath left, when she heard the sound of the bugle and the Boleños men retreated.

She finally reached a point where she could rest a little. The enemy appeared to have retreated, but a few seconds later a group of Boleños came running toward them and again they were under enemy fire. Otto dropped to the ground and pulled Ultima down with him by her shoulder pauldron just as balls of fire flew over their heads, ricocheting off the trees several feet away from them. As she crawled from the ground to a nearby rock, a flush of blood rose to her head, sharpening her senses and speeding everything up. Ultima's vision moved into fast motion, and gave her the strength to continue fighting. When Otto stood up, she did too.

Ultima stood by Otto, wet from the mud and slush, but the rush of blood allowed her to forget about the foul taste of death in her mouth.

With the sound of the enemy retreating and victory becoming increasingly likely, the winning side fought as if they were invincible. Some succumbed to a frenzy and were on a rampage against anybody standing in their way, while others probably were spurred on by images of home and what they had left behind.

The Boleños left fires and smoke among the heaped-up bodies of their dead, but from the distance, the enemy's infernal trebuchets continued to fire powerful balls of fire over Soren's army. It was their attempt to help the last of the Boleños men escape, but that last bombardment did nothing to bring back the hundreds of lives of their dead.

The few enemy who were left alive near the Tsestelago camp were taken hostage, and the Boleños' line was pushed farther back. The Tsestelago forces had taken the Pikes back.

The mindboggling carnage covered the battlefield, but so too was the Tsestelago's bravery. Two armies fighting each other for territory, but it was clear who won. The dead of the winning and losing sides lay in large groups across the hillside valley. The toll on both nature and humanity was tremendous. Likely, it would take ages before the mountain and the valley would recover. The rubble and metal debris had taken the place of trees, plants and flowers.

The battle had ended, and it was good; Ultima had no more energy left in her. Her arms felt like lead and her head hurt. She could no longer hear what anyone was saying next to her. Her sword was too heavy, and her hands could barely grip the handle. She removed her helmet, and her hair released from the bindings to the side of her face. Small braids flapped out. As the rain slowed and stopped, she stood, like all the others around her, soaked through. Mud was smeared on her face where it was not covered by her helmet, but there was blood overlaying the mud.

"She is a woman. The warrior fighting next to you is a woman," said Prince Soren to Otto.

She had not taken three steps with Otto, when an arrow struck her side, entering the opening between the back and front plates of her armor. From whence came that arrow? She didn't know.

Worse than the arrow, was an ear-piercing blast that pushed her off balance, causing her to fall *splat* on her back. She fell onto the slush of melted snow and mud. She could feel her body start to lose heat and death came to caress her face in the form of water droplets as the rain once more started to fall. Droplets of water splattered over her, and she slowly lost consciousness. Suddenly, and without warning, a blast of heat, feeling like diabolical rage, was directed at Ultima. Otto stood in the way, screaming something to her as all went dark.

❖❖❖

After everything was over, Soren walked through the battlefield. Death and stench joined as brothers in the battle's aftermath. Everywhere Soren looked there were torn men with broken limbs. Others were alive but staggering, some creeped, all quivered. Dead faces looked up to the sky or at the man next to them. That odd look of fixed eyes staring, with a fog that conceals the color of the eyes. It rained again.

Soren found his squire at arms, Palao, underneath a dead horse. The young man of twenty had a crushed chest with blood frothing from his mouth and was gasping for air, opening and closing his mouth and resembling a fish out of water. Soren did the noble thing. He took a knife and cut Palao's throat. A quick death was preferable than the agony of asphyxiation.

Swallowing hard, Soren said a quick prayer to his personal patron of Yavos, The Lady of War, for the eternal soul of Palao. Closing his eyes and using an enemy's flag as a rag; Soren cleaned his knife.

A sharp pain and flash of angry energy made him shout thunderously, "AHHH, Damnation!" Soren bellowed to all the dead nearby as he stood up and kept walking through the battled, war-torn valley.

Squad after squad of men who had fought their way through the front line, lay dead with swords still clutched in their hands. All around, there were strange shouts of stubborn defiance mingled with the murmurs of petitions and stifled moans of men at the edge of death. Desperation overtook Soren.

"So many good men died today," said Jabert, Soren's first commander of his infantry. He had reached Soren's side, and they both said an ancient prayer. No words came from Soren after that, but a resolute look of pain in triumph. Victory seemed to be the only comfort.

❖❖❖

Later, in Soren's tent

"We need to give our men a decent send off. How are we looking?" asked Prince Soren of Commander Martiko.

"The number of bodies that lie under the winter sky are too numerous to count and have stained the snow red. The scavengers are getting bolder and the process of decomposition has already begun despite the cold. But without a single mark of identification, it is hard to tell who is who, the dead lie in their hundreds," said the Commander.

"I don't care which side they fought for, they died honorably, in battle at the behest of their rulers. And yet they lie there exposed to the wild animals and the snow. That's not acceptable," said the Prince.

"We don't have enough soldiers to provide a proper burial to this many men," said the Division Commander.

"They lie in every imaginable position, wherever they fell. We must do something," said Commander Martiko.

"Call your fire mages and set them on fire. Make a ceremony for the dead and give them all the blessings of warriors," suggested the Duke of Vurthas from the entrance of the tent. Prince Soren looked up at the duke's entrance and he smiled.

"Godfather, I couldn't believe it when I saw your colors in the distance. Thank you for your help," said Prince Soren.

"Always glad to help, although technically it was the Duke of Hausman—with Franken's men—who came to your assistance, since Yakuta is not in this war," said the Duke of Vurthas, as he walked toward Soren and gave the warrior prince a warm embrace. It had been many years since they had seen each other.

"Why are you here?" asked Soren.

"Your father sent me to get you. Why haven't you followed your father's orders to return to the capital?" said the Duke.

"Which orders? I haven't received any orders from father," said Soren with a frown.

"You do know your brother Marco died?" asked the Duke.

"What? No, I received no message. I didn't know. When did this happen? How?" said Soren, with obvious concern and sorrow on his face.

"Your brother's been dead for over five months now," said the Duke more gently.

"I received no message. Martiko you must find out why we haven't been receiving messages from the capital. Commander Takano, have the men reassemble and make an account of the provisions. I must return to Pailo at once." Prince Soren started collecting his things and placing them in a bag. "How is mother?" asked Soren.

"She is waiting for you," said the Duke of Hausman, now also entering the tent.

"Uncle, I swear, I didn't know. I would have returned the moment a message arrived," said Soren, walking to his uncle and giving the older man a hug.

"I know. Now let's talk about your return and who will take over command in your absence," said Duke Hausman.

"Major Larlan, I want all the wounded who can't return to battle, to be sent back to West Franken. I'm leaving as soon as I can secure my replacement," said Soren.

"That will not be a problem. My son, Thomas, can take charge of battle. And we will return as soon as the wounded can travel. We have several master healers with us," said the Duke of Hausman.

"We suffered many casualties, despite taking the Pikes back, but now we must keep it from the Boleños. Is Thomas up to the challenge?" asked Soren, turning his back and focusing on the large map spread out on the table.

"Ouch cousin, that one hurt. I'm only two months younger than you, and I went to the same military academy as you did. And don't forget, I have a few battles under my belt—granted nothing as big as today's fight," said Lord Thomas, smiling at his cousin despite his fighting words. Apparently, he had overheard Soren's last comment just as he entered the tent. Thomas was covered in dirt, blood, and grime from his head to his boots.

"I'm sorry Thomas, being here for all these months has made me cynical," said Soren. And the men hugged in a tight embrace, patting each other on the back.

Thomas and Soren were best friends and they counted on each other, even when their blood brothers were around. So, Soren was happy Thomas was there to take control of his army.

"Nah, don't worry too much. The King is sending General Heart up here as soon as he arrives from Palermo. I'll hold the Boleños back in their lands in the meantime," said Thomas, as he walked around the tent and went to stand next to his father.

"You win this war for us; I'll make you a general and a knight once I become King," said Soren.

"I'll hold you to that cousin," said Thomas, laughing.

CHAPTER 21

The Days After the Battle

The battle had been in the Pikes Mountain running north to south from Farhglen to Burhglen lands, in the contested lands of the northern parts of the Kingdom of Tsestelago that bordered the Kingdom of Boleña. The conflict traversed between the western side by the Burhglenen Road and the eastern Pikes Mountains.

Ultima woke surrounded by the sounds of moaning. She remembered images from the battle. Her mind still dwelled on the battlefield; smoke, fire, and copious amounts of blood surrounded her. Red covered the snow, and the shouts of many men still echoed in her ears.

However, now, lying on some type of makeshift bed, the rancid smell of mixed vomit, urine, shit, tobacco, sweaty men, alcohol, and kerosene made her want to gag. Her stomach revolted. She needed to get up and run away. She tried to sit, but a stabbing pain made her rethink that idea. The world turned and a gagging reflex made her dry heave with nothing left in her stomach.

"Oh, good—you're awake," said a young healer. "Get Lord Otto!" he shouted over his shoulder. "Your husband said to let him know the moment you awoke. He will be here soon to come get you. I'll be needing the bed to treat other wounded men," he said. Ultima looked around and as far as she could see, broken men lay on cots. Others lay on the bare ground, and still others sat leaning against one another. Amputees of one or more limbs, men missing everything but their heads. Tears fell. How could this world be so violent?

Short moments later, Otto entered the tent, and like an arrow went directly to where Ultima lay. Without a word to the healer man, he picked her up and took her away. Nor did the healer say a word to Otto. It was as though the man knew what was to happen. Otto quickly carried Ultima through the camp, and within a few minutes he'd taken her from the hospital tent all the way to where his father's men had established their encampment. Otto carried Ultima into his tent, and he lay her on a pallet of many furs.

"How do you feel?" asked Otto.

"My ears are ringing badly and my side is hurting. What happened?" asked Ultima.

"You were shot by an arrow. I took the arrow out and found a healer to give you aid. We don't know who shot you or how since you had on full armor and the enemy had already retreated. We don't even know from which direction the arrow came, but you are safe now. You must rest. We will be traveling in two days," said Otto.

"Is Prince Soren alive?" asked Ultima.

"Yes, he is fine, but there is something else," said Otto.

"What happened?" said Ultima.

"We think Caleb died in the battle. We can't find his body or any evidence of him," said Otto, looking down.

"No that can't be, but how and—where? I don't remember seeing him fighting near us," said Ultima.

"He was with a group of our men fighting a group of infantrymen who had mages with them. There were some Boleños lightning and fire mages," said Otto.

"Oh no! Caleb, was he alone?" asked Ultima.

"No, we lost him along with a few of our soldiers," said Otto.

"I'm so sorry, Otto," said Ultima. Otto closed his eyes briefly and when he looked at Ultima again, she could tell he was already grieving.

"I'll bring you something to eat; try to rest," and he left the tent.

Ultima couldn't believe the news. Caleb dead? He was her favorite of the brothers-in-law she'd met. She had to sit up. Prone on her back as she was, she would drown in her own tears if she let them fall. She could not hold back, she let her tears flow, and she tried to call on her own healing abilities as she laid her hands on her own wound.

❖❖❖

Otto brought food for Ultima, and helped her sit to eat and drank some ale he gave her. She wanted water, but Otto told her that the Boleños had contaminated their water, so she had to drink ale. The master healers from the West Franken contingent were doing all they could to clean the water and bring the men back to health. Sufficient at least to be in a position in which they could return to the fighting line, while any dismembered men would have to travel back to West Franken.

Ultima found the strength to slowly exit the tent on the second day after the battle, and she could see the bonfire on the field. An apple orchard near the site of the battle was destroyed, completely riddled with swords, arrows, axes, rifles and body parts. Flies buzzed over the dead and manure alike. Caked blood and mud made a revolting sight. Many trees had their trunks completely severed and lay broken, others had branches shattered by boulders which lay strewn about the ground, and arrows, too many to count, were embedded in the remaining trees. Ultima walked as though in a trance. She had received no training to prepare her for this experience.

Soldiers in the distance were collecting as many of the bodies and body parts as possible and a gag reflex brought what Ultima had eaten up to her mouth. They had to make several pyres with the bodies, as a single pyre would take too long to burn. Among the bodies they collected were the remains of Lord Caleb Hightower.

Later that day, the Duke of Vurthas had a special ceremony prepared for his son, in the tradition of Yakuta. The father and his two remaining sons, tightly wrapped Caleb's body in linens, and they carried out a ritual using herbs, water, and prayers for the spirit of the warrior. They burned his body in a separate, private pyre with his shield, his sword, and his armor. He was the son of a duke and a master mage.

Ultima stood with the Hightower family. She had painted her face, neck, and arms in the dark royal blue and yellow ocher colors, with the markings and symbols of the House of Vurthas. The men wore the side scarfs and long fur coats of the House of Vurthas. Ultima noticed they had polished the family and house crests on his armor and shield until they shined: a pair of leopards standing by a royal-blue castle etched on both Caleb's shield and on his pauldrons.

Ultima stared directly ahead when she noticed the Duke of Vurthas crying as Caleb's body was set aflame. Caleb was the arcane mage of the family. According to Otto, he was the only Master Arcane Mage of the Kingdom of Yakuta. The ceremony started and He'nico stood on the Duke of Vurthas's right side, Otto stood to He'nico's right, but the Duke made Ultima stand to his left, a place that by rights belonged to Nívea, his wife. A place representing the heart of the family. Unprompted, Ultima sang the song of the dead of the Yakutan people. Only women sang the song of the dead at a Yakutan funeral, so Ultima gave Caleb and his family that honor.

After the fire completely consumed Caleb's body, Ultima went and collected the ashes. She had a medium sized jar she had acquired from the healers, and she saved the ashes in the simple jar. As she walked back to the family's side, she said the prayer for the living and gave the jar to the eldest brother, He'nico.

"Thank you, but how do you know our traditions and that the women in the family collect the ashes of our warriors?" asked He'nico.

"I'm well educated, remember?" Ultima kissed He'nico's forehead, and went to stand by the Duke of Vurthas left side. When the old man turned and left, Otto took Ultima by the hand and the family left the site of the pyre to prepare their departure for the town of West Franken.

They walked back to the campsite in silence, and Ultima sat by the central fire, lost in her thoughts. The pyres of the dead raged on throughout the rest of the day and well into the night. The smell of burned skin and human hair made her want to cry. Abruptly, her thoughts were scattered.

"Well, well, well, well, well, and who do we have here— Exotic Ultima Skylar? What is my favorite Exotic doing in the middle of a battle?" Prince Soren stood behind Ultima. The man was taller than Otto. He didn't share his brother Marco's appearance at all. Marco had light, short hair, while Soren had long, dark-blond hair, worn in a braid down his back. Marco was clean shaven. Soren had a long, light-brown beard.

"Hello Prince Soren, it is good to see you alive," said Ultima, looking back at the man.

"It's been a long time since we last saw each other. Last time I saw you, I left you naked on a bed at Xawata's. You were impressive in the battlefield. Who taught you how to fight?"

"Hum, let me see. Master Magnamus Laria from Palermo taught me the finer arts of the Palermo short swords and Masters Marka Horroro and Tanita Okino from the old side of Pailo, they taught me weapons in general; Master Fabian Shihono from the city of Oliva taught me self-defense," said Ultima as she turned back to continue staring at the central fire. Prince Soren sat down next to her.

"Those are not classical skills for an Exotic," said Soren.

"No, they are not, but Xawata always had me learning new things," said Ultima.

"That he did. The man liked to keep you current. And I heard he increased your pain level before he died," said the Prince.

"Lord Thomas doesn't know how to keep out of other people's business," said Ultima.

"My cousin wants you badly. It is incredible that Lord Otto managed to marry the famous Exotic Ultima Skylar. I had been under the impression that was an impossibility," said Soren.

"We have a child together," was all Ultima said, by way of explanation.

"Another impossibility, Exotics can't have children," said the Prince.

"Things are not as impossible as you think. Excuse me, Your Highness," said Ultima. She stood up and walked away.

Ultima entered her tent and picked up her armor to clean it. She couldn't contain her tears. She rarely cried for herself, but here and now she had to cry.

❖❖❖

The three days later, the group had everything packed and ready to move for their trip back to West Franken. Otto saddled Ultima's horse for her. She traveled with most of her armor off and her head uncovered. Her injuries to her side were still raw, and she wanted the cool air on her head. It helped her heal faster. The healer that tended her didn't do a good job, in her opinion.

The group moved at a fast pace to start, and they carried their wounded in the healer's carts. Only those men who had lost limbs in the battle returned to West Franken. The healers did an outstanding job of bringing back to health those who had kept all body parts intact. Plus, many of the healthy soldiers the Duke of Franken organized into the West Franken company stayed with the main forces.

Otto traveled ahead with Marshal Donnelly, and Ultima traveled next to the Duke of Vurthas.

"How are you feeling today?" asked the Duke. His jovial demeanor no longer present. This was a man in mourning, who had lost his zest for life.

"I feel better than yesterday," said Ultima, and they rode quietly after.

❖❖❖

On the third day, while they were moving across a wide trail, Prince Soren, who had been staying close to Ultima throughout the journey so far, moved his horse alongside hers.

"Lady Hightower, how long have you been married to my cousin?" asked Soren.

"We have been married for almost five months," said Ultima, she kept looking forward.

"And you said you have a child together? You can't be with child so soon?" said the Prince.

"Yes, we have a grown child," said Ultima.

"You have a son?" asked Soren.

"We have a daughter," said Ultima, with a broad smile.

"So, she's Ottos child born out of wedlock?" asked the Prince.

"Prince Soren, my daughter is the joy of my life. Her life and happiness are my world. Do your questions have a reason or are you asking merely out of curiosity?" Ultima's brow furrowed.

"I'm just curious. I wanted to know how my cousin could have fathered a child when the last time he was here was twelve years ago," said Prince Soren.

"My Akina is eleven," said Ultima, and she made her horse canter on ahead. Prince Soren followed her and caught up.

"My apologies, I didn't mean to upset you. What I don't understand is how an Exotic can have a child." said the Prince.

"Could you change the subject, please? I have so much knowledge on so many subjects. If you are bored, I don't mind conversing with you," said Ultima.

"Fine, what do you know of the auctions of the Takapian racehorses, arranged by the Wallen family?" asked the Prince.

"The stallions or the geldings, because Sir Wallen rarely sells the mares in auction," said Ultima, and the Prince laughed. Ultima noticed Otto was looking at them, but he made no attempts to stop their conversation, so she kept talking.

❖❖❖

On the fourth day, they arrived at the small town of Lixtra, and they all needed rest.

Ultima's injuries were hurting her less, but she was happy she would have a real bed to sleep in. The soldiers were sleeping at a campsite on the outside of the town and the men accompanying the prince would be sleeping in the communal sleeping hall at the inn. Only the Dukes of Vurthas and Hausman, Ultima, and the prince were to have private bedrooms. Her small room had a bed and a chair, and nothing else. She cast a spell she had learned, in one of the books Roku gave her, to kill all the bedbugs, and then she cast a second spell to clean the pillows.

After dinner, the men stayed drinking. Otto had gone ahead with the scouts and wasn't expected to return until morning. She was used to the company of men, but after all the traveling, her body needed rest. So, Ultima went to her room soon after she finished eating her dinner.

Although she went to bed early, it was past midnight, and Ultima was still awake. Sometimes, fear overwhelmed her at night and sleep came in waves, but tonight, her sleep was disturbed by a knock at her door.

"I hope is not one of the drunken men," said Ultima to herself. She put on her robe and opened the door a crack.

"Hello, could we talk?" It was Prince Soren.

"Your Highness—could this not wait until morning?" asked Ultima.

"Please let me in," said the Prince. He wanted her and she could feel it. She hated her harmonizer gift and tonight she just wanted rest.

Ultima held the door tightly, but Soren pushed the door open and entered without permission. "Your Highness, what do you need? It is late and tomorrow we leave early." Ultima stepped back, almost to the wall. Prince Soren had the same blue eyes as his twin brother Marco, but Soren's hair was a lot darker than his brother's had been. Soren was a warrior, and his body was built for war.

"I know you were with my brother when he died. Was his death quick?" asked Soren.

"Yes! It was quick," said Ultima with a furrowed brow.

"Did he hurt you in any way?" asked Soren.

"No, he was dead before we could do anything. Why do you ask?" said Ultima.

"My brother and I were inseparable as children, but as we became men, we went our separate ways. But I loved him—I just want to make sure he didn't hurt you," said Soren.

"You need to leave Prince Soren. It is late and I need to rest," said Ultima, pointing at the door.

"Otto is out scouting; he will not be coming to your bed. I want you tonight. I'm going to make things plain and clear. You are free and capable of making your own choices. I can offer you a townhouse of your own in Kimira Square and a generous monthly budget. I don't care about your husband. It is obvious you don't care for him. You are a beautiful woman and I need beautiful tonight. The last time I had you was a year ago and I miss you."

"Thank you, Prince Soren, but I'm no longer an Exotic. You need to leave," said Ultima sidestepping toward the door.

"Please let me love you tonight. You are the most exquisite Exotic I have ever seen. I want you in my arms once again." Prince Soren took Ultima's hand, and he kissed her gently. Ultima pulled her hand from his.

"Hum, I have heard that from many others through the years," said Ultima.

"I meant my words. Please let me love you," said the Prince.

"I don't know love, Sir. You need to leave," said Ultima.

"And I don't know peace. Maybe we can find out together." He went and touched her arms, and then he kissed her. Ultima let him kiss her. After all, he was an old client. She had been an Exotic all her life. This was the first time she had been given an offer for her services, for herself. Was his offer enough for a night with her? It seemed excessive. Xawata charged fifty gold coins to lie with her for an hour and seventy-eight gold for two hours with her, but only one lay. A town house and a monthly budget for a one-time night sounded like a great deal. Sex was as normal to her as water and food. She kissed him back.

"I love the way you kiss. You look so beautiful. I can't believe you are a mother," said Prince Soren, trying to take Ultima's shift off, but then she remembered Akina.

"No, you must leave. Please, leave," said Ultima and she opened the door and stepped aside. Prince Soren said nothing else. He left with a wicked smile.

"Otto doesn't deserve you," said Soren, as he passed her.

"Good night, Prince Soren." And Ultima locked her door.

Early the next morning, she woke out of habit, but was tired. She was thankful for her bed, but she needed to sleep a bit longer. She didn't want to face the men so early in the morning. Thinking of the night before, when she had almost serviced Prince Soren, she wondered... what if he had stayed with her for the night? She would now have a townhouse and a budget, but what about Akina? Akina was registered as Otto's daughter. He would keep her.

It was morning. Ultima was happy she hadn't serviced the prince. It would have been a complication she didn't need. She and Otto had shared a bed, and she liked it. Ultima had used many of her Exotic skills on this trip for her own advantage, but she had not serviced anyone in bed. That part of her trade was a commodity she did not want to use. She was free, and she would not give Otto any excuse to trade her back into prostitution. She wanted Akina to have everything she could not give her otherwise. She wanted her to have a father and a family.

❖❖❖

All the men in the group were waiting for Ultima while they ate their morning meal. When she walked down, Prince Soren smiled, and Otto didn't even look at her. She walked to the table where the Duke of Vurthas was sitting, and joined him.

"Good morning," said Ultima. The men wished her good morning, and Prince Soren brought her a plate of porridge and a cup of coffee.

"Thank you, but I'm not hungry," said Ultima, giving a polite smile to the prince.

"Eat, we are not stopping until the evening meal," said Otto, pushing the plate toward Ultima.

"You stayed out late last night?" asked Marshal Donnelly of the Earl.

"Why do you say that?" asked the Earl, with food in his mouth.

"You look like you didn't sleep at all last night," said Marshal Donnelly. The earl's brown eyes were bloodshot.

"I couldn't sleep. So, I planned out the route. It's my turn to be the pathfinder. I'll be going out early with the scouts for the next five days. If we're planning to reach the next camp site before dusk, we need to leave now," said the Earl of Portmore in between chewing his food.

"Good, we will leave in thirty minutes. Everyone must hurry eating," said Otto, pushing the table as he stood up and he left the inn.

"Is he always this cheery in the mornings?" asked the Prince, pointing at Otto.

"He is usually not this happy. I have no idea which bug bit him this morning and made him this joyful. Excuse me, Prince Soren, Father, Ultima," said He'nico, and he too stood up and left.

After a few minutes, the rest of the men left, and Prince Soren was the only one left at the table with Ultima.

"Thank you for talking to me last night. I wish you were not married," said the Prince, he stood up and left.

CHAPTER 22

Unfaithful

They continued their travel southwest to West Franken through the Mountains of Mirrem. Ultima regretted not having had more to eat that morning. Otto had been true to his words; they did not stop that day other than to give the horses a few minutes rest and to answer the call of nature. Ultima's legs and back hurt.

Sitting on a saddle for an entire day with an injury to her side was exhausting. Ultima wanted to walk and even lay down for a few minutes, but that would not happen. She couldn't even use her healing magic on herself. She had no energy to spare for magic.

Seventy-three of the original one hundred soldiers who helped take the Pikes Mountains and wage a winning battle, were traveling back with them. There was an exchange of soldiers, and they traversed many miles of the Tsestelago countryside, on horseback or on foot. They came marching and countermarching in three separate platoons. The dull thud of marching feet, the metallic pinging of armor of the men on horseback, and of cups and utensils, made a cacophony of sound that calmed Ultima down. At the rear came the low rumble of all the supply carts and the healers' wagon that followed the procession.

Ultima rode along, watching the body of soldiers, relentlessly moving on, just to reach an advantageous point by the end of the day. Somewhere they could camp for the night that could be well-protected and, if feasible, provide the possibility of retreat should it become necessary. It was a cold countryside. It made a hellish living for those accustomed to warmer weather, as Ultima was. She found that the chill of the day entered through the legs and traveled all the way through to her bones.

Always, there was the added pressure of a possible second battle looming or a sneak attack from the Boleños. They were still in disputed lands, or so the Boleños called it. The fear was so present, the tension of impending interaction, that Prince Soren remained in the midst of those men on horseback, riding near Ultima the entire day. His presence made her uneasy.

Where was Otto? At the front of the group, leading. The unremitting plodding let her mind wander back to Akina in the capital. Ultima swayed from side-to-side, lost in thought and the rhythm of the march. Before she realized what was happening, her horse went down a sharp decline, into a hole in the ground and then up again, and Ultima fell off her horse.

Ultima shouted in surprise as she met the cold ground. Soren called the group to stop. It was midafternoon, and the group halted.

Soren jumped off his horse and went to pick up Ultima. Otto came galloping back, with his father close behind him.

"What happened?" Otto shouted as his horse slowed down. Prince Soren already had Ultima back on her feet by the time Otto arrived.

"Lady Ultima fell off her horse. We are stopping here for the night. Men, we will make camp. I want the scouts to go and search for a suitable area no more than thirty minutes from this location. I don't want any excuses. We are making camp near here," said Prince Soren.

"Prince Soren, the scouts have already found a suitable place to make camp three hours travel from here. We must keep moving," said the Earl.

"No, we will stop now. Lady Ultima hurt herself by falling and others are exhausted too," said Soren.

"We still have about three more hours of travel," said Otto in a stern voice.

"Don't you see? She is still injured and exceedingly tired, and so are the men and horses. The wounded and the horses need to have a longer rest. Wait a moment. Look at Ultima's horse. It threw a shoe. How can a warhorse lose a shoe like this?" said Soren.

"He stumbled in a hole," said He'nico.

"That is not a reason for a warhorse to lose a shoe so easily," said the Duke of Vurthas.

"We are stopping here. I think Ultima's horse is lame," said Soren, moving around Otto. Otto went to his father, the Duke of Vurthas.

"My wife can wait three more hours. She can ride with me," said Otto.

"We must keep going. I planned this route and our campsites based on our scouting reports. If we don't make it to the first site tonight, we'll never make it to the next resting site tomorrow," said the Earl of Portmore.

"Portmore, Otto, if you both don't stop talking now, I'll hit you both," said Prince Soren.

"Prince Soren is right, Ultima needs rest. We all need rest. We didn't stop for the midday meal. Three more hours of travel will take us traveling past dusk and not give us time to set up a proper camp," said He'nico.

"Am I going to have to change everything, just because of her?" whined the Earl.

"I suggest you stop talking, James," said Soren, who turned away and left the man mumbling to himself.

"Fine," said Otto. He too turned and left to tend his horse.

"Godfather, why is Otto such an ass with his wife? He seems as if he doesn't care for her well-being," asked Prince Soren.

"I don't know what is going on with him. I'll have a talk with him soon," said the Duke of Vurthas.

Ultima was listening to the exchange between the men. She knew the problem. She knew Otto wanted a woman of refinement, a woman of nobility, but to be such a callous and heartless man was a new low, even for him.

❖❖❖

Later that night, after they had established the main camp, Otto walked away from his immediate group and stood to the side of the healers' wagon to smoke his cigar.

"Otto, wait up. We need to talk. What is going on with you?" asked his brother He'nico when he caught up.

"What do you mean?"

The Duke of Vurthas joined them, having followed He'nico. "You seem not to care for anyone lately. Are you so saddened by Caleb's passing you've lost all compassion?" asked the Duke of Vurthas.

"I miss Caleb, but no," said Otto.

"Then what is it?" asked He'nico.

"Let me be, I'm not in the mood for talking," said Otto.

"Son, what is going on? You are not yourself," said the Duke.

"Talk to us," said He'nico. Otto looked from his father to his brother, and he rubbed his nose.

"She slept with Soren last night," said Otto.

"What? How do you know that? You were not at the inn last night," said the Duke.

"Yes, I do know, but I came back to the inn an hour past midnight and when I was walking to her room, I saw Soren step out. Father, you married me to an Exotic. She has a warrior spirit, and the heart of a true Lebarra woman, but she brings dishonor to our house," said Otto.

"Son, you know why I did what I did. We needed her out of Xawata's brothel to help us find Marco's killer," said the Duke.

"I know, father. I volunteered because I liked her. I let my lust rule my mind. The worst part is that I'm starting to love the woman, but now I'm a cuckolded man. And her lover is the Prince Regent of Tsestelago," said Otto.

"Otto, you are jumping to conclusions. You don't know whether she actually cheated on you," said He'nico.

"He came out of her room, and it was past midnight. And now she smells bad to me," said Otto with an angry look on his face.

"Otto, we all smell bad. We haven't had a proper bath in weeks," said He'nico.

"It may be my mind playing tricks on me but thinking of her and Soren together boils my blood. And you know it's part of my magic, I have a sensitive sense of smell. Now when I smell her, I am disgusted," said Otto.

"I'm so sorry, son. I should have thought about her as a prostitute first. I thought her Exotic training would make her different. I thought we could draw her out of the trade," said the Duke of Vurthas, looking down.

"Father let's forget this and deliver Soren back to his father. Once we get back to the capital, I'm going to return to Yakuta," said Otto.

"What about Ultima?" said He'nico.

"I don't know what I'm going to do about her. If I find her with Soren again, I will cast her out. I can revert her to prostitution again for cheating on me. One thing I know. I will not take a cheater with me to Yakuta. I detest having a woman who will not respect me, but I can't divorce her if I don't have proof. I just need proof now," said Otto.

"Son, I'm so sorry," said the Duke of Vurthas and the men walked away from the healers' wagon.

Ultima listened to the conversation from inside the healers' wagon. She had gone to find some herbs for the pain in her back that resulted from her fall from the horse. When she overheard the Vurthas men talking, her world turned.

Otto thought she had sex with Soren. And now the entire family thought that of her as well. Why did she let Soren in her room? She didn't let him in, he pushed her and let himself in. She didn't sleep with him.

Ultima stepped out of the wagon, and she walked to her pallet in a daze.

"Ultima, dinner is ready. Come, eat," said the Duke of Hausman as she walked toward her pallet.

"I'm not that hungry," said Ultima, not wanting to look at the man directly. She had done nothing of what Otto believed, but it embarrassed her nonetheless. Why? She was an Exotic. That was it. She wasn't supposed to be an Exotic anymore.

"You had little to eat at breakfast and only bread for the midday meal. You need to eat," said Otto, and he brought her a plate of food to their pallets.

"I feel nauseous," she was sitting on the ground and didn't want to look at him.

"Eat a little. I can't have you falling from your horse again tomorrow. We have a long way to go, and we can't keep stopping midway when you fall from your horse. Eat, you need your strength." Otto gave her the plate and a large tankard of ale.

"Thank you." Ultima took her food and ale and went to sit by the fire. Soren came over and sat next to her.

"This food is good, but I know of a tavern by the river Jern, on the outside of Pailo, that offers the best roast I have ever eaten. When we return to the capital, we should visit," said Soren.

"I must go, I don't feel well." Ultima smiled, she stood up, took her plate of food, and left Soren alone. She went to eat her food by her and Otto's pallets. She didn't feel like eating. Ultima had a knot in her stomach so tight, it made her want to gag, and it created a nasty pressure in her chest. Her earlier hunger had utterly disappeared, but she knew she had to eat. With each bite it hurt to swallow, and she felt it might come back up again, but she drank a little of her ale to wash it down.

Ultima ate her food, drank her ale, and cried a little, hiding her face from Otto. She placed her almost empty plate to the side. Ultima rummaged in her personal bag and found a clean towel and some soap, and went looking for water. There was snow on the ground, but little water to drink. She was determined; she needed to bathe. She couldn't control many things in her life, but she knew she smelled bad, and that was something she could control—her own smell. Ultima picked up her empty tankard of ale, stood up and looked around. Otto was sitting next to her smoking a cigar, and he watched her.

"Did you finished eating?" asked Otto, looking up at her.

"Yes, thank you—it was tasty." Ultima stood tall.

"You have a towel. What do you want to do? There is no stream and no creek," said Otto. From where Ultima stood in front of Otto she could see an area nearby with clean snow. She went and filled the tankard with snow. She walked past Otto and went to the fire pit. She found another empty tankard, and in a little time she had them both full of ice. She melted the snow and ice until she had two full tankards of warm water.

Ultima left the fire pit with her two full large tankards of warm water, and she walked back to their pallets.

"Will you come with me, please? I want to wash, but I don't want the men to see me. I need your help to watch out for others," said Ultima, looking directly at Otto. The man stood and took the tankards of water from her.

"Let's walk to the back of camp, I'll find a safe place away from the others," said Otto. They walked past the men, horses, and campfires until all they could see were the silhouettes of the men and fire in the distance. Ultima took the tankards from Otto, and she moved behind him.

"I'll be fast," said Ultima. She removed her shirt and pants. She took a rag and washed her neck, under her arms, and her private parts. She smelled bad to Otto and to herself as well, and she wanted to change that. While she was washing, she felt it. She looked around. It was as if the trees had eyes. She hurried. When she was done, she changed into a clean shirt and a pair of pants. It was a cold night, and it felt like it was going to snow. When Ultima was done, she walked back to where Otto was waiting for her.

"Let's hurry, I feel like there is someone watching us," said Ultima walking past Otto. Otto looked around, but all was dark.

She kept quiet, and so did Otto, all the way back to where the men had made camp for the night. When they reached their side of camp, Ultima sat. She lay on her side of the pallet and tried to go to sleep. There wasn't anything she could do. She hadn't slept with Soren, but Otto was convinced she did. Theirs was a strange type of marriage.

This wasn't fair, she thought. *Who said life was fair?* Otto had chosen his path. He had agreed to marry her, but there was something more. He said he was starting to love her. Why? How could he love her? She had done nothing worthy of love, but now he was angry and sure to send her back to being a slave. She cried again, but this time it was for herself.

❖❖❖

Ultima woke in the middle of the night from a nightmare. There was the same dream of her running through the hallways of the royal palace and a man chasing her. Once the man placed his hand on her, there was that voice that said:

Bitch, you will be dead in minutes. Sadly, I must kill you. You are such a beautiful woman.

And she awoke screaming, sitting up on her pallet. She looked out to the rest of the camp from her pallet. All was quiet. The roaring fire that had been near her and Otto, had dwindled to a few flames. The men on watch had kept the fire alive, but barely. It was snowing, covering everything, including the sleeping mounds, in a blanket of white, but the sky had a pink tinge to it. It would be dawn soon. Both her icy hands were on her face, as though they could keep in her waking scream. She turned and found Otto awake and looking at her.

"Nightmare?" asked Otto in a whisper.

"Yes," it was all she could say.

"Do you want to talk about it?" asked Otto, sitting down on his own pallet next to hers.

"It was Prince Marco's assassin chasing me and when he caught me, I woke," said Ultima.

"Do you have this type of nightmare often? I mean the assassin chasing you?" asked Otto.

"Yes, after the assassination I've been having dreams like these often, I can't sleep at all after I wake from them," said Ultima with her head hanging low.

"I'll place a spell around us. I'll use magic from my land. You will be fine. No one will hurt you. Come, lay back to sleep." Otto opened his arms and Ultima moved her pallet and went and laid next to Otto.

Ultima nestled in Otto's arms. He said a few words in ancient Yakutan and a few minutes later; she was asleep again.

In the morning, Ultima woke, and Otto was already packing his horse. She rose, rolled her pallet, carried out her morning ritual, and went to break her fast with the men. The cook made a porridge and a large pot of hot coffee. Ultima ate and went to saddle her horse.

"Let me help you with your saddle," said Soren. The man had appeared out of nowhere. He was standing behind her. Ultima jumped in surprise and dropped the saddle on her foot.

"Ah, you scared me," said Ultima.

"I'm sorry. I just wanted to help." The prince picked up the saddle from Ultima's foot and saddled her horse.

"Thank you, but I can saddle my own horse, when I'm not surprised," snapped Ultima.

"I'm sure you can, but why doesn't your husband help you?" asked Soren.

"Because she doesn't need my help. And when she needs it, she asks me," said Otto from behind Soren.

"Sometimes women don't ask for help, but they clearly need it, cousin," said Soren, and he left, leaving the pair alone.

"I swear, I didn't ask him for help. He came out of nowhere," said Ultima, packing her horse.

"I know. I saw him. I see your horse is already saddled. I hope you had plenty to eat. Today, again, we are not stopping until dusk," said Otto.

"Yes, I know. I don't want to argue this early. When I fell yesterday, I didn't do it on purpose. It was an accident," said Ultima.

"Fine, but you are traveling next to me today." And Otto went to get his horse.

He held her through the night, but now he was cold to her. Ultima couldn't understand the man. She had no desire or energy to deal with Otto's mood swings, but when she mounted her horse, Otto came and led her horse to where the Duke of Vurthas was waiting.

"Good morning!" said Ultima.

"Good morning," said both the Duke and He'nico. And they nudged their horses to start moving them along. The duke didn't say anything else. There was an obvious change in the way the Vurthas men were treating her.

Ultima rode with Otto and his father all morning and afternoon. The men's silence hurt, but Ultima was trained to keep to herself when silence was required. A few hours later they stopped to answer the call of nature and to give rest to the horses. They took the time to eat the midday meal, and soon after they were traveling again toward West Franken. However, the animosity between feelings and emotions was hurting Ultima.

"Otto, where are we going to stop for the night?" asked Ultima.

"I think there is a clearing, some miles up ahead," said Otto.

"Is there going to be water, a creek, or a stream?" Ultima tried to get the man talking.

"I don't know," said Otto.

"When did you send the scouts forward?" asked Ultima.

"Last night," said Otto. His horse moved a little ahead, and he said nothing else.

In all her Exotic career, she had never had a man with such a blank conversational repertoire when angry. Ultima looked down and sideways.

"He isn't much of a conversationalist," said Prince Soren. He had ridden his horse to catch up with Ultima. Her cheeks reddened and were hot; she was now the one that didn't want to talk.

"Soren, son, you know you must ride in the middle of the pack. We don't want anything happening to you," said the Duke of Vurthas.

"Godfather, I'm bored to pieces. Besides, I'm not a man who likes to hide," said Soren.

"Be that as it may, you are the Regent of Tsestelago, and we must protect you. So, get used to it, nephew," said the Duke of Hausman.

"Well, Lady Ultima, why don't you sing us a song? Maybe that way things will not be as boring on this journey," said Soren.

"Sorry, Your Highness, but no, I don't feel like singing." Ultima didn't know from where that defiance came. She had never said no to a request for a song, but she was tired of having men telling her what to do, making requests and expecting her to always obey.

Otto dropped back to where Ultima was riding.

"Hey Otto, why don't you tell your wife to sing for us," said Soren.

"If she doesn't want to sing, then she doesn't have to sing." And Otto took hold of Ultima's horse's bridle and urged it forward with him.

"Thank you, the truth was I didn't want to sing," said Ultima.

"You don't have to do anything you don't want to do," said Otto. She smiled, and she rode next to Otto for the rest of the day.

∙∙∙

A week later, they reached the Mirrem Mountains and as they ventured into the forest, they found themselves in an area marred by many damaged trees; every other tree had branches broken high up. It was as if a large group of giants had passed by the area. Ultima felt a presence. It felt like darkness; a presence that made her fearful. It started following them and was growing with every step they took. She had to say something.

"Your Grace, there is something totally wrong around us and it's moving ahead of us too," said Ultima.

"Yes, I can feel it," said the Duke of Vurthas.

"Gareth, you, and your sons are the mages in this group. What do you feel?" asked the Duke of Hausman.

"I don't know. I'm not a harmonizer or an arcane mage. Ultima, what do you think is going on here?" asked the Duke of Vurthas.

"Whatever it is, it has been following us for a while and it is concentrated in this part of the forest. Could we take another route? This place is evil." Ultima looked around and her hand went to rest on the pommel of her sword.

"This isn't the way we came," said Otto.

"This is a shortcut," said the Earl of Portmore.

"Who chose this path?" asked Marshal Donnelly.

"Our new pathfinder, the Earl of Portmore!" said Otto.

"I'm afraid this is the only way for us to take now. A different route would require us to retrace our passage for at least four hours, skirting the mountain on the other side. Going back would mean we would take a route where there is a ravine between us and the entrance to the Valley of Larley," said the Earl of Portmore.

"In future, I want to see the routes we are taking each morning before we get on our way. I don't care who's the pathfinder," said Soren, holding the set of knives that were encased on his chest's leather armor.

"Let's move through here fast," said Marshal Donnelly, pushing his horse forward and leaving the others behind.

CHAPTER 23

On the Way Back to West Franken

They rode faster through the afternoon, but they couldn't leave the eerie feeling in the forest behind. They reached an area where they made camp. The group quickly lit fires around the perimeter of the camp, and they also had a large central fire. He'nico positioned his fire mages at the outer corners of the camp, with large fire pits near them, while Otto placed his and Ultima's pallets close to the central fire pit. They tethered the horses to trees near the camp area and gave them food and water, and the healers' tent was set up in the inner circle of the camp.

Later that night, once the group had cooked their evening meal and had eaten, they tried to settle before bed, but there was unrest in the forest around them. The horses were whinnying and there was an icy wind blowing, but Ultima, and all the other mages, could feel a thickness in the air that made it difficult for them to breathe.

Preparing to sleep, Ultima stepped away from the camp to wash. Ever since Otto mentioned she smelled; she became self-conscious of her body. She tried to hurry. She could feel there was something wrong in the woods, so she didn't go too far away. However, on her way back, she heard a snort and a few grunts. She turned around to look behind her into the darkness. Trees stood close to each other like soldiers ready for battle, barring her way. And then she saw it. A small shadow moved in the distance. The shadow moved rapidly left, and then another moved right, and yet another came running straight at her. Ultima's ghost jumped out of her skin and she ran as fast as she could back to camp. As she reached camp, she found all men had their weapons drawn and at the ready.

"Otto! Shadows ... demons ... chasing," said Ultima, breathless. Otto was already moving lightning from one hand to the other, making a huge ball of lightning—as large as the entire group. His brother He'nico also transferred fire from one hand to another and all around him. The Duke of Vurthas held a large sphere of water in his hands. Each of the elemental mages had their particular magic ready in their hands, and Ultima wished she was an elemental mage.

"We know. I see them. Where were you? Come and stand between us," said Otto.

"Hurry, woman, do it now!" shouted He'nico. Ultima ran to her pallet, and took her sword from its scabbard, and then ran to stand between the brothers. Half the soldiers stood to attention around the camp looking fierce, the other half looked scared, when a cloud of black smoke slowly seeped in and settled over the campground.

Ultima used her harmonizer magic in an attempt to give a sense of calm to all around her, but it didn't work. A deafening, screeching sound of a million crows came from overhead, and a group of red wendigos fell from the trees above. Mouths full of teeth and nails long as talons came at them all in the camp. A wave of black and red banshees surrounded the camp. The wendigos came from everywhere. Fire, water, and stone magic combined to provide ammunition against the creatures from hell.

Ultima was tightly clutching her sword in her hands and was swinging it left and right, but she barely scratched the wendigos. Banshees ran toward them from the depths of the forest. Their screeching sounds made everyone cover their ears, for fear their eardrums would burst, which was the opportunity the wendigos took to strike the men. Otto moved toward Ultima and grabbed her to pull her away from the strike of a banshee.

She moved to stand back-to-back with Otto, nudged his back and shouted, "I'll guard your back!" and gave him a scared smile.

"And I'll guard yours!" said Otto, and thus they fought anything that came their way.

"Move to your left," screamed Ultima.

"Duck!" shouted Otto. As the demons continued to drop dead by their side. They had a synchronicity of movement.

He'nico, along with three other fire mages, used their gift to set wendigos and banshees alike on fire, making them die quickly or run away to escape the flames.

Soren had two short swords, moving them as if they were two large fans, and it surprised Ultima to see the Earl of Portmore fighting with a short ax and a shield. The man talked little, but he surely could fight for his life. The horses reared and were screaming. The wendigos killed a few of the horses, but many got loose and ran away.

They fought for what seemed like an eternity. Fire and lightning flew from one side of the camp to the other. Marshal Donnelly was firing his pistols at the creatures, and once out of bullets, he drew a long rapier sword and slashed his way through the demonic wendigos on his way to find his explosives. The sounds of Marshal Donnelly's guns and explosives—which he loved beyond measure—made an interesting counterpoise to the banshees' wails, making the battle even louder, if that were possible.

When Ultima had a moment to look, she noticed Marshal Donnelly was surrounded by many tiny, shiny, metallic bullet shells and much debris splattered all over the ground. Whereas the Earl of Portmore had an abundance of wendigo and banshee body parts laid waste around him. Clearly the Earl of Portmore was having fun with his ax and shield. The rest of the soldiers fought on bravely, with both swords and firearms. Ultima feared that her battle-induced blood rush would not be enough to get her through the fight.

Eventually, there were no more demons alive to fight. And after the smoke settled, and the creatures lay dead all around, calm settled. With the calm came the need to deal with the aftermath of battle. Some men were injured, and others had lost their lives. He'nico and Otto moved around the camp, ensuring all the banshees and wendigos were either gone or dead. When Ultima lowered her sword, she could barely move her arms. The fight had ended just in time. She was about to collapse, but just as she was about to give in to her fatigue, she noticed the Duke of Vurthas had received a grievous injury. The man had a wound to his shoulder. Ultima dropped her sword and ran to him.

"Otto cut his shirt off. I need to get to his skin," said Ultima. Otto complied, and she poured over the wound the water from the duke's own waterskin that he always carried with him.

She shouted to rally her strength, then whispered to herself "Please healing, come to my hands." Her eyes brightened and changed color to yellow, while a green light began to shine from her hands. She kept pressure over the wound with her hands and little by little the wound closed. As Ultima healed him, the Duke of Vurthas bellowed in pain, whereupon Prince Soren, the Duke of Hausman, and He'nico all came running over to find the Duke crying out in agony. The wound glowed as healing power spread over the skin. The Duke of Vurthas opened his eyes, and he and Ultima locked stares.

"I will not let you go," said Ultima. She leaned over him, her face covered in a sheen of sweat and contorted by the strain. She was doing everything Kuro had taught her. She knew how to bring healing to the man, but she still had no idea how much energy to give, nor how to disconnect. A young healer came to Ultima's side and sat next to her.

"My Lady, you are doing great, but would you let me finish?" The man placed his hands over Ultima's and took over the task.

"Thank you, Ultima," said the Duke, in a strained voice. Ultima let her hands drop, and she collapsed to the side. She smiled at the man.

"You—are welcome, Your Grace." Her eyes changed back to her blue color and her hands stop glowing. She rolled to the ground and lay on her side. Her energy exhausted. Prince Soren came to her, but she pushed him aside. Ultima tried to stand, but she stumbled, and Soren held her in his arms. Ultima pushed him away once again.

"No, thank you, I can walk on my own," said Ultima, and she tried to stand again, but could not move from the floor once more. Finally, Otto stepped in; he wrapped his arms around her from behind and held her by her waist and shoulders. She looked over her shoulder and saw it was Otto holding her. She held on to him and placed her head on his chest.

"Otto, I can't stand or walk, I need your help," said Ultima. He picked her up in his arms and carried her to their pallet. He sat her on their pallet and then noticed she had been hurt. Otto undid the ties of her shirt, carefully pulled it away from her shoulder and down her arm. It was only then that she felt the warm blood running down. Now that Otto had drawn her attention to it and removed her shirt from her arm, she saw the injury—just before Otto held a cloth to her arm in an attempt to staunch the bleeding.

"Ultima, you have your own injury that needs taking care of," said Otto. He stood up and left her, shouting for a healer to come and help. In a few minutes, a young healer came to help Ultima.

"How are you feeling?" asked Otto.

"Now that I've noticed the injury, the pain is almost unbearable," said Ultima. The young healer who had come running when Otto called looked over her wound.

"Your muscle was cut badly. It looks like it was done with a jagged edge," said the young healer.

"Can you help her?" asked Otto.

"I can, but I'm only an apprentice. She needs a senior healer." When the healer moved Ultima's arm, she almost fainted, but Otto held her.

"She also has wounds to the sides of her legs," said Otto to the healer.

They had fought without armor. The wendigos had caught them unprepared. Once the healer did what he could to her arm, he left some ointments and went to see where else he could help. Otto removed Ultima's clothing and he spread the ointment over her wounded arm and tended to the rest of her injuries.

He then went to see to his father, but he soon returned to Ultima's side a few minutes later. She appeared to be resting, so he just sat there and watched her. He was pouring some water over the back of his neck when Ultima talked, startling him.

"How is your father?"

"He will survive thanks to your ministrations. You gave him enough time for the healer to come find him. Thank you," said Otto.

"You are welcome. He is my father-in-law after all," said Ultima, closing her eyes again. A few minutes later she opened her eyes and Otto was sitting quietly, holding her hand, but with closed eyes.

"Do you think those things will come back tonight?" asked Ultima.

"I don't think so. After we fought them, the heaviness in the air dissipated. I think they are gone for the night. We will leave guards through the night. You rest," said Otto, and he lay down next to Ultima and held her in his arms.

"Otto, I'm scared," said Ultima.

"I'll not let anyone hurt you," said Otto. He closed his eyes and seemed to fall instantly asleep. Ultima too, fell asleep soon after, cocooned in Otto's arms.

❖❖❖

Ultima woke the next morning with a ray of sunshine hitting her squarely in the face. The wendigos and banshees had devastated the branches of the trees above them the night before. She woke alone and frozen to the core. Freezing rain had fallen and there were ice patches all over the ground. She got up and saw the havoc the wendigos and banshees had wreaked on the camp the night before, and the carcasses of the wendigos and banshees they had killed. It was a gruesome sight at any time, but especially first thing in the morning.

Ultima stepped away to carry out her morning ritual and as she was returning to camp, once again she had the feeling of someone watching her. She stopped and looked around, removing her dagger from its leather sheath, but all she could see were trees and shrubbery. Ultima returned to the campsite and walked around looking for the Hightower men. She found He'nico sharpening his sword.

"He'nico, we need to leave this place. For days, I've had this feeling as though there is someone watching us," said Ultima.

"We will leave soon. I don't like it here either. Otto was saying the same thing. There is a vibration of bad magic here," said He'nico.

"Did we lose any of our men last night?" asked Ultima.

"We lost a few, but not many. We must leave as soon as everything is packed. How are you feeling? Otto said you had an injury to your arm?" asked He'nico.

"I need a healer to finish mending my arm. I feel sore and tired, but I'll be fine. And I'm ready to leave, I have little to pack. How is your father?" asked Ultima.

"He is doing better than I was expecting. You saved his arm and his life. We are all thankful. I don't know what I would do without the old man. I'm not ready to lose him," said He'nico looking down at his sword.

"He's a strong and stubborn man," said Paul Donnelly from a short distance away.

"That he is," said He'nico with a smile.

"Do any of you know from whence those things came last night? It was as if they were waiting for us in ambush," said Paul.

"No, they were following us for a while before they attacked us. This trip hasn't been normal from the moment we left West Franken," said Ultima, and she left the men to find the Duke of Vurthas' tent. She wanted to see firsthand how her patient was doing. And she found him sitting on the edge of his pallet, trying to don his boots.

"What are you doing? You had a horrible wound to your shoulder last night." Ultima moved swiftly to his side and took the boot from his hand.

"I need to urinate and I'm not doing it here in any pot. I'm a man and there is nothing wrong with my legs," said the Duke.

"Fine, let me help you with the boots," said Ultima, and she helped the man put on his boots.

"You saved my arm and my life. Thank you," said old man Vurthas.

"You are welcome," said Ultima. After she finished helping him with his boots, she called for someone to help him stand and walk with him to the far end of camp and find a place to relieve himself. Ultima kept wandering around the camp and saw the men gathered by the fire distributing plates, and she remembered she was hungry.

Prince Soren, Otto, He'nico, the Earl of Portmore, Marshal Donnelly, and the Duke of Hausman were all together. Ultima joined the group and Cook gave her a plate of food. She sat quietly, slightly to the side of the group, to listen to what the men were planning.

"We can't return to West Franken, not after this ambush. We must take you to Pailo as soon as possible," said the Earl of Portmore.

"Why not? The faster we make it to West Franken, the faster we board the train to Pailo," said Otto.

"It took us two months to go from West Franken to the Pikes. The Duke of Vurthas needs expert healers. All the healers we have here are apprentices. He will lose that arm.

He needs a senior healer now. The town of Glauslag is only a week's travel from here. We must send the men ahead to West Franken, but we must go to Glauslag. We can catch the train to Pailo from there," said the Earl of Portmore, with his mouth full of food.

"The town isn't far from here. If we go to Glauslag, we can be in Pailo in another ten days if we don't linger in the town. Glauslag has a reliable passenger train twice per week; going there will save us a month and a half of travel through the Mirrem Mountains and Warfield Valley," said the Duke of Hausman.

"I know aside from the passenger train they also have a small carrier train traveling every day. We can catch that, we don't need anything fancy," said the Earl of Portmore, gargling with a drink in his mouth.

Yuck, that man Portmore is disgusting, the way he eats, thought Ultima.

"Cutting through that side of the Mirrem Mountains is perilous with an army. And Glauslag is surrounded by steep ravines," said Otto.

"Listen, all I'm saying is that we must travel to where we can find an expert healer fast and that we should separate from the rest of the soldiers who are slowing us down," said the Earl.

"What types of services are there in Glauslag? We need to get news from the capital, and we need to send news to the King that we found Soren," said the Duke of Hausman.

"Glauslag is a mining town. I think it also has a mill. They should have a communication office. I can ask when I enter and register at the Trades Office," said Paul Donnelly.

"Glauslag is a large town, but their entire focus is their mine. I know they have a strong wall surrounding the town," said Ultima.

"I think traveling through the valley will be easier on the Duke of Vurthas. He's only partially healed and we have several others who are wounded," said Marshal Donnelly.

"We are going to Glauslag. We must travel as fast as we can to Pailo," said Soren.

"How many men will we keep with us then? We can't send all of them to West Franken?" said Ultima, looking from one man to another.

"She's right, we need to keep a few of the men with us. The path is dangerous," said Otto.

"It's good our lady here is one who thinks. There might be Boleños in the way." Marshal Donnelly raised his voice a little as he'd moved a short distance from the group to smoke his cigarette.

"We can keep twenty men and the rest can go back to West Franken. I'll give the orders to the captain of the company. Finish eating, we are leaving in half an hour," said Soren, and he stood up and left.

❖❖❖

The group divided. The soldiers went on to West Franken and Ultima, the Hightowers, Hausman, Soren, the marshal, and the earl went on to Glauslag with twenty men. Ultima and the Duke of Vurthas went to ride in a cart. The healers were sent back to West Franken, leaving only Ultima to help the duke with his pain. After a few hours of traveling, the duke held Ultima's hand.

"Ultima, do you miss your old life?" asked the Duke.

"What do you mean? Living in Xawata's brothel?" She looked at the man. He nodded. He was sitting next to her, looking out to the scenery.

"What is there to miss? The fancy dresses, baths every day, sleeping in a warm bed, gourmet cooked meals, or not having a say about with whom I could talk, having to sleep with anyone even if the person disgusted me, the golden collar, having my daughter's virginity sold at twelve. No, I don't miss it at all. Why are you asking?" Ultima had an idea why he was posing the question, but she wanted to hear him say it.

"After living your entire life in luxury, I wondered if you wanted to return to a life of privilege," said the Duke.

"Ha, do you think I had a life of privilege? I was a slave. I lived in a gilded cage. I had everything anyone could ever want, but I lacked the one thing a soul needs, freedom, and the best thing in life, love."

"At least you had Akina," said the Duke.

"Yes, Akina was my family, but she was a slave just like me. Xawata stole our humanity. He made her a slave the moment I gave birth to my Akina. We were *things*, not people for Xawata. I wanted so badly to find an escape for her from that brothel. And now she is free. I'd rather be here, in danger, under the rain, in the mud, with your family, than back in the brothel where my daughter was being forced into prostitution," said Ultima with a big smile.

"So, the life of the Exotic is not for you anymore?" said the Duke. Ultima didn't look at the man.

"You took me out of slavery and I'm ever so grateful. I'll forever have the education. No one alive can take my education away from me, but I am free," said Ultima.

"You have that forever, but your old life was comfortable," said the Duke.

"If you are asking if I enjoyed being an Exotic. All I can say is that I had no comparison to balance my preferences at the time. I lived a limited life. I did what they trained me to do. I was the best in the industry, and because they raised me to believe what I was doing was correct, I didn't know any better. I expected nothing more, but now I have more. All I knew was that I wanted something different for my daughter. Xawata had sold Akina's virginity. Xawata was waiting for her to turn twelve and a half, to give her to the man that bought her."

"What? She is a child of twelve who still plays with dolls," said the Duke.

"She is the primary reason I'm so happy I'm out of the brothel," said Ultima.

"That is good to know. I'm happy I got you both out. For a while I was worried I had made a mistake," said the Duke of Vurthas.

"I like my life. Otto is a good man. I don't know how to deal with him some days. I had my share of horrible men in my life. So, I know how to deal with horrible, but Otto is unusual," said Ultima with a smile.

"I raised my sons to be gentlemen," said the Duke.

"That he is," said Ultima.

"When I first saw Akina with you, I couldn't believe it. She is like my wife's twin, but in a child form. And she has the exact color eyes as those of my wife and Otto's. Is she really your child?"

She chuckled, "Yes, she is. I gave birth to her a little over eleven years ago," said Ultima.

"I thought Exotics couldn't have children," said the Duke.

"Xawata had me *fixed,* so I would not have any children when I was about twelve, but it didn't work. I'm a healer and harmonizer. Twelve years ago, I serviced a man I liked. I ended up with child. I kept my child secret until it was too late to terminate the pregnancy. Xawata had no choice but to let me have her. As you discovered, he had her registered as my daughter, but with no father," said Ultima.

"Do you know who the father is?" asked the Duke.

"Yes, I do," said Ultima.

"Who is he?" asked the Duke.

"He was a young man who won me at a game of cards at the Duke of Greenwood's bachelor party," said Ultima.

"Well, he can't come and claim her, she is ours now," said the Duke.

"Your Grace, the young man was Otto," said Ultima, with a smile.

He smiled back. "So, Caleb was right all along," said the Duke.

"What do you mean?" asked Ultima.

"Caleb told us that Akina was a Hightower. The only way she could be a Hightower was if Otto was the one that got you with child when he was in Tsestelago twelve years ago," said the Duke.

"Yes, she is Otto's," said Ultima.

"Wait until my wife sees her. She will not let you take her away from us. Akina is our eldest grandchild, you know. He'nico's boys are seven and four," said the Duke.

"I like that my Akina has a family and a father, and that she will grow up to have choices. I like she will have the right to train to be a mage and not have to be an Exotic. That alone is incentive enough for me to not want to be an Exotic. Why are you asking me all these questions? Are you planning to return me to a brothel? I need to know," said Ultima, giving the man a worried look.

"Otto believes you serviced Prince Soren, and that is grounds for him to make you a prostitute," said the Duke. Ultima took a deep breath, and she looked down at her hands and then at the old man.

"I haven't done such a thing. After you married me to Otto, I have serviced no one. I've only been with Otto since we married. Why is he believing I serviced the prince?" asked Ultima.

"Back at the town of Lixtra, Otto went to your room at the inn just past midnight, and he saw Soren step out of your room," said the Duke. Ultima looked at the duke and then at her hands. It was best to tell him the truth. The man was an elenchus he would know if she lied to him, anyway.

"Yes, he came to my room, and he pushed himself inside, but nothing happened. He did ask for services, but I refused. I didn't service him. I swear on Akina's life," said Ultima.

"I believe you, but it's not me you need to convince. It's your husband," said the Duke.

"Well, it's good to know what he believes. So, this is the reason he's been such an ass since I fell from the horse," said Ultima. And the duke smiled.

"Yes, he's sour," said the Duke, with a chuckle.

❖❖❖

While cutting through the mountains, they reached a narrow path where they had to dismount and walk the horses along a ledge. The Duke of Hausman's horse tripped and fell down the ravine and would have took the duke with him if it hadn't been for He'nico who grabbed the duke and pulled him back up onto the ledge, thus saving his life. The Earl of Portmore, who had been following behind the duke, said the horse tripped on a loose rock.

On another occasion, a snake bit Soren, and Ultima had to give him healing. Then Marshal Donnelly lost his cigarettes, and his world ended two days into the trek through the mountains.

Two days before they arrived in Glauslag, the Duke of Hausman sent a messenger ahead to the Marquis of Muneer to let him know that he and the prince would require accommodation in his home for the night. After having had the conversation with her father-in-law, Ultima needed to talk to Soren. They traveled swiftly during the mornings and slowed down in the afternoons. So, for the last two days of travel, Ultima rode her horse all the way to Bertha Abbey, the residence of the Marquis of Muneer.

Ultima rode her horse past Otto and He'nico and went to ride near Soren's. She used her harmonizer magic. She needed his attention.

"Prince Soren how are you feeling today?" asked Ultima.

"I'm doing well."

"I hope your snake bite wound isn't infected," said Ultima.

"No, it's not. You did a good job with your healing," said Soren.

"Thank you. How long until we reach the town?" asked Ultima.

"We will be there in another day," said Soren.

"That is good to know. I hope there will be a senior healer there whose services can be retained," said Ultima.

"I don't mean to be rude, but you never start a conversation with me. Is there something wrong?" said Prince Soren.

"I apologize, if I've bothered you," said Ultima.

"No, you're not bothering me. So, are you going to let me take you to dinner once we reach Pailo?" said the Prince.

"No, I'm for Otto and Otto alone. I just needed to talk to you and remind you, I'm only an amateur healer. What I did for you and the duke was just a patchwork. When we get to the town, he needs immediate attention from a senior healer and you should also let a healer see your snake bite. I, too, need the services of a healer myself," said Ultima.

"If I had not seen it with my own eyes—I can scarcely still believe you are a healer. That is another impossibility. Mages are *not* Exotics," said the Prince.

"When we reach the town, there must be expert healers there. I hope you arrange for our group to get the services we need right away."

"We all are going straight to the healers. Don't worry, I know," said Soren.

"Well, this healer mage, who used to be an Exotic and is now a married-mother, must return to her family." And with that done, Ultima moved her horse back to where Otto and He'nico were riding.

CHAPTER 24

Otto or Soren

They reached Bertha Abbey, the seat of the Marquis of Muneer, late in the afternoon. When they arrived, the servants took the Duke of Vurthas to a room where a healer was called for him. Another was called for Ultima and for any other person who needed help, so they could receive the care they needed and make them comfortable for the night. The rest of the group met with the marquis and marchioness, and they paid their respects to one another. It was interesting to see the way the marchioness behaved when Ultima appeared and was introduced as Lady Hightower. The woman's surprised face was comical to Ultima. In the case of the Muneers, the marchioness had been one of Ultima's clients.

"Exotic Ultima, you—a Lady in the House of Vurthas of Yakuta—how did that happen?" asked the Marchioness as the women were walking up to the rooms.

"Hello Samila, it is great to see you. I am no longer an Exotic since I married Otto, almost five months ago," said Ultima.

"Exotics don't marry, they can never leave the trade," said Samila, holding Ultima by the arm and stopping her mid-stairs.

"Otto and I have a daughter together, which allowed him to get me out of the trade," said Ultima, and she continued ascending the stairs. Lady Samila showed Ultima her room.

"A daughter? I didn't know you had a child. She must still be a babe," said the blond-haired Marchioness.

"No, she is quite grown. Xawata and I kept it a secret," said Ultima.

"I was counting the days until my next visit to the capital to see you, and now, here you are. I will give you the ruby and diamond necklace you liked so much the last time we saw each other, just let me visit your room for an hour. I want you for an hour. Will you give me an hour one last time?" asked Lady Samila, holding the doorknob and caressing Ultima's face.

Ultima held Samila's hand, brought her wrist to her lips and softly kissed it, then released the marchioness's hand and said, "I'm not a thing for sale anymore. I'm a free person and I only want Otto and my family." Ultima turned and entered her room and closed her door.

Once Ultima was in her room, she realized she had a bathroom. She removed her armor and her clothing. All her dirty clothing was taken to be washed by a maid who had been in the room waiting. Ultima was able to take a proper bath before dinner. The healer came to her room and provided her care, and he gave her some salves for her cuts. Ultima kept thinking about Samila's reaction. She knew similar reactions like the Marchioness of Muneer were to be expected from her old clients, but Ultima worried what would happen in the case of her more aggressive clients. She had a few old clients who were quite belligerent, so it was only a matter of time before she would have to deal with them.

Dinner was interesting. The marquis acted like a peacock in heat, and his wife kept looking for Ultima's attention.

After dinner, Ultima avoided the marchioness by sitting next to Otto and listening to the plans for the next day.

The marquis gave them news that there had been an attempted assassination of Queen Elenore. Once Soren heard the news of his own mother in danger, his desire to reach the capital intensified. They sent word ahead of their party, to King Trevino, that his brother the Duke of Hausman had found Soren and was returning with him. They heard too that King Trevino had fallen ill, and he wanted to send a squadron of soldiers to bring Prince Soren back in a hurry, but they were in the remote mining town of Glauslag, and it was easier and faster for them to travel back directly alone.

The marchioness had been accommodating to everyone in the group. It wasn't every day that the Prince Regent and the Grand Duke of Hausman visited the marquis and his family. Once the men began to drink their ports and smoke their cigars, Ultima knew it was time to retire for the night. They were going to travel back to the capital city the next morning. The Marquis of Muneer had been gracious and had given them shelter for the night, and he provided what they needed for the Duke of Vurthas. Ultima went upstairs, on the way to her room, the marchioness encountered her at the top of the stairs.

"Are you sure you will not accept my diamonds? I can offer you my pearls as well. Please, give me one more night," begged the marchioness, holding Ultima's hand.

"I'm a free woman. I'm no longer an Exotic and I want to stay free. I'm a Lady in the House of Vurthas and a mother with a child. I have a husband who loves me, and whom I love," lied Ultima. The marchioness smiled at Ultima and released her hand.

"Good night my lovely Ultima," said the Marchioness.

"Good night, Samila," said Ultima. She opened the door to her room and entered, locking it behind her.

Ultima's room wasn't large, but there were floor-to-ceiling windows, which she opened to let some fresh air into the room.

Ultima removed her clothing, put on a shift, and donned a robe that Samila had given her in preparation for bed. Ultima needed sleep. She went to get her bed ready, fluffing the pillows and pulling back the cover when the healer came to attend to her wounds. He took most of the pain away, but she still felt tender where the injury was still mending. She was taking off her robe when there was a knock at her door.

"I hope it isn't Samila," muttered Ultima to herself as she put her robe back on and walked to the door.

She opened the door, but it was Soren, and his foot prevented her from closing the door.

"Your Highness, you should not be here," said Ultima, trying to close the door.

"Please let me in," Soren begged.

"Could it not wait until morning?" asked Ultima.

"I needed to see you, to touch you one more time. I love the way you moved and how you looked when we made love," said Prince Soren with a smile.

"Please stop this, I can't see you. And we never made love. You had sex, and I had no choice," said Ultima.

"Please talk to me. Give me one night. I want you one more time, for old times' sake," said the Prince. Ultima closed the door a bit and hid her body behind the door.

"No, I can't. You must go, Otto will be here soon," said Ultima, holding on to the door and closing it a little more, but the prince kept his foot jammed in the door.

"This will be the last time I could see you and where we could be alone before we reach Pailo," said Prince Soren.

"I'm sorry, I've already told you many times. I can't do this with you. I'm not an Exotic. I'm a free woman and I want to stay this way. Otto will be here at any minute, and I want you to let me be," said Ultima.

"Otto is out with the men and knowing him, he will not return to the manor. Besides, you don't even like that fool of a husband of yours," said Prince Soren.

"How do you know how I feel about my husband? We are married and I don't want to go back to being a prostitute if he catches me being unfaithful. If nothing else, I owe him and the Duke of Vurthas respect," said Ultima.

"You owe him nothing. Your husband has done nothing for you but ignore you. I want you and I can give you all the gold and jewels in the world."

"Otto loves me. He saved my life back at the battlefield. I enjoy being free. On the other hand, you ..."

"Otto doesn't love you," said Soren.

"Well, I love him," said Ultima. *Do I?*

"Please go! With you, I'd still be an Exotic no matter the riches. I'm a free woman with Otto and I like who I'm becoming. I love my daughter and I want to keep her free as well," said Ultima.

"Ultima, I'm the heir to the throne. Since my brother's death, I have no choice about whom to marry. I must ensure there is no doubt in the line of succession. I must marry someone who can give me an heir of impeccable lineage from within the nobility. Leer and Joy-Anna are mages, and they are also too young. You know I need an heir of my own, but you will be my only love. I can promise you that."

Somehow, Prince Soren had pushed the door open again and she felt him touch the side of her face and her lips with his thumb.

"No! That's not what I want. Good night, Prince Soren." And Ultima pushed the man, took his hand from the door, and closed and locked the door to her room. She walked to her window. The room was chilly, but she needed the window open. She needed to have air in the room. Her body overheated in the few minutes Soren was at the door. Five minutes later there was another knock. She went to open the door, ready to tell the prince to go away, but when she unlocked and opened it, she found Lord Otto on the other side. He pushed her aside and let himself in.

"Why do you find the need to lock the door against me? I need to talk to you," said Otto.

"Could it wait until tomorrow—please?" asked Ultima, closing the door, and rubbing the back of her neck and the side of her body where her injury was niggling. Her tired body needed rest and she needed to refresh her mind with sleep.

"Prince Soren was at your door a few minutes ago. What did he want? I know he came to your room; and don't lie to me. I saw him," said Otto, irritated.

"He wanted to talk. And he never entered my room. Please go, Otto, I don't have the energy to deal with you tonight." Ultima started to walk past him, but Otto grabbed her arm.

"And what did he want?"

"He wanted to talk, but I sent him away," said Ultima, rubbing her forehead.

"You sent him away, why? I know you two are lovers. I'm not stupid," said Otto.

"Lovers? I have no lover!" Ultima took a deep breath. "Otto, you need to leave me be. I've had enough of you. I'm tired and we have a long way to go," Ultima pulled her arm from Otto.

"Ultima, I don't understand you. You went out of your way to talk with the prince today. He is most attentive with you and now you tell me you sent him away," said Otto harshly.

Ultima walked to the window again, and she took another deep breath. She looked out to the darkened garden and closed the window. "Please Otto, I'm exhausted. I haven't done anything. I'm your wife and I've not done anything to bring shame on you or the family. I sent him away," said Ultima.

"Explain. I need to know why you sent him away," said Otto. It took Ultima a few seconds to respond, but she then turned and faced Otto.

"I sent him away because you saved my life and I like the way you hold me when I'm scared. I'm learning how to be free, and I'm no longer in the Exotic trade, and I'm delighted about it. Because you are my husband. And even though you may be distant to me on some days, you have decency, and you give me choices. Moreover, I want to honor your father, and I want more in life than I ever had before. Because I love Akina, and I want her to stay free. So, there you go, I want to live a life free of all the hate that once surrounded me as an Exotic," said Ultima. Otto stepped back, as though her string of words had a physical impact.

"I'm sorry if I've been a terrible man. To be completely honest, I want a family. I want a child of my own. I want what my brother He'nico has with his wife. A marriage based on love. There is no love between us, and we can't even have children. So, where does that leave us?" said Otto.

"Why do you think we can't have children?" asked Ultima, looking up at him.

"Everyone knows Exotics can't have children," said Otto.

"Otto, you know I gave birth to Akina? Right?" asked Ultima.

"I know you said you are Akina's mother, but I have no idea how that happened. Knowing Xawata's reputation, I felt certain he would have had you fixed. Exotics can't be mothers after all," said Otto.

"I already told you I birthed Akina. And you make too many assumptions. You know little about me. You don't ask or want to know anything about me. And apart from that conversation we had at Pailo, you don't talk with me. You talk at me. I feel you don't listen when I talk. I've had enough tonight. And I'm not having an affair with the prince. I have *never* been unfaithful to you. I want to rest. If you are staying, please, drop this conversation or leave," said Ultima.

"All this time, I've been trying to show you that there are men who are decent and not depraved." Otto looked at her, turned around, and quietly left the room.

He wanted to show me he wasn't depraved? Huh! Well, he didn't act depraved, but she didn't feel loved. She felt wanted, but not loved. She would need to tell him to work on those traits next. Ultima looked at the door and wondered if she was ever going to have a more caring conversation with the man.

Once Otto left the room, Ultima walked back to her windows and looked outside again. She finished preparing her bed the way she liked it, turned off the lanterns and candles, and went to sleep despite the cold.

Ultima had a restless night. She woke herself with a scream from a nightmare. Her nighttime terror came to her as it did when she least expected it. A shadowed man approached her from behind, and despite running away he always caught her and she would wake just as he began to stab her. When she was living at Xawata's brothel, those nightly horrors kept her awake for hours. Now, she was just as scared, but on this night, Otto was with her. He too woke and found her sitting up in bed.

"What is it? Are you alright?" asked Otto.

"It was a nightmare," said Ultima, rubbing her eyes and then looking at Otto.

"Is this the same dream you've been having during the last few months? Do you want to talk about them?" asked Otto.

"You have your own room, why are you here? When did you crawl into my bed?" asked Ultima, and then continued without letting him answer, "I'm surprised you remember those dreams. I didn't think you'd remember anything of what I've told you."

"I like to sleep next to you. I came to your bed an hour after our conversation. Yes, I remember your nightmares. You know, we have shared a tent and a bed many times before, I just leave before you wake. Some nights when you have had nightmares, I've used my magic to calm you.

"… I think that answers all your questions, but if I've missed one, let me know," said Otto. Ultima smiled.

"Yes, you've answered all my questions," said Ultima.

"Your arms are cold. Come!" And Otto placed his arms around Ultima and held her close to his chest.

"I don't remember you sleeping this close to me, other than the few times at the Duke of Franken's castle. We did sleep next to each other when out in the open on pallets," said Ultima.

"Where do you think I slept in the train? Where do you think I slept all the nights we traveled to and from the Pikes

Mountains? I used my magic to keep your mind calm and help you sleep," said Otto.

"I never knew that side of your lightning magic, or is it something else?"

"Like my father, I have the magic of the land. I used it to help you sleep," said Otto. She turned to face him and placed her head against his neck, as Otto rubbed her back.

"You said you wanted to show me you are not depraved, but in that case why were you nice at night and so distant during the day?" asked Ultima.

He gave a soft chuckle, "I'm not a gentle man. I do care about you, but I also want to give you space. I wasn't kidding when I said I would only be near you when you ask me to return to you. I want you to learn to make your own choices."

She looked up at him and caught him looking down at her. She liked the way he held her in his arms. From the moment they met, Otto had given her little attention during the day. The family showed her respect. She liked respect.

"Otto, back in Pailo you questioned if I could be faithful to you. Well, I am. Since we married, I haven't shared my body with anyone but you," said Ultima.

Otto nodded, and he kept rubbing her arms, warming, and caressing.

"It is hard for me to see you as only mine," said Otto.

"And it's hard for me to see you liking only me. I don't know how it feels to be loved by a man," said Ultima.

"It is a weird feeling," said Otto, and he kissed the top of her head.

This time it was Ultima who took his face gently and kissed him. Her kiss deepened, and he kissed her back. Otto's hands moved slowly to her shoulders, then to her neck and lower.

They began to undress one another, gently and unhurriedly, as they continued kissing and touching one another. He moved her closer to him.

"I want you, but this is the moment to tell me to stop and I will leave," said Otto, looking directly into Ultima's blue eyes.

"I want you too, Otto. Please love me tonight." He smiled and kissed her, this time with more passion and she kissed him back. They were lost in their kisses, and caresses, unfettered and moving freely as the mood took them.

"I know you are sore from your injury, and I don't want to hurt you," said Otto. Ultima took him by the hand and pulled him closer to her side of the bed where she sat up facing Otto, and took off her shift, lifting it over her head.

"There are a few things you could do without hurting me. I'll let you know if I'm in pain," said Ultima.

And so they continued, each finding pleasure in the other. Early on, Otto showed the utmost concern for Ultima's injuries, but she re-assured him he was not hurting her, and they both found nirvana in each other's arms.

Ultima had found another high of ecstasy that she'd missed since they'd left West Franken. When Ultima descended from heaven, her lover kissed and caressed her, and gently rocked her. Then it had been his turn, and he watched her face throughout.

Replete, they collapsed together, he gently holding her.

"I love the way you smell. Even when we were in the mountains, you had a scent of lavender about you," said Otto.

"I remembered you said I stank. Up in the mountains," said Ultima, looking up at him.

"I never said that to you."

"I overheard a conversation between you and your family."

"Ah … that's when you became obsessed with washing. That was the reason, because you eavesdropped on my conversation?"

"I didn't do it on purpose. I was in the wrong place at the right time. And yes, I didn't want you to be repulsed by me," said Ultima. He gathered Ultima into his embrace and fell asleep.

Ultima was wide awake. She had enjoyed the act of sex with many men when she had been an Exotic. This was different ... she was married and this was her husband. She had been married to Otto for almost five months and at the start she thought the man hated her. However, now, here, he was gentle and she began to change her thinking.

Ultima wanted more in life than being an Exotic, and now she was a nobleman's wife and a warrior, but she still wanted more. No one had ever asked her what she wanted in life. Fate threw her onto this path, and she went along. Had she been asked, she would most likely have chosen this path anyway—this path was good for her; she had a family. It was a crazy family, but it was hers.

For now, she was safe. For tonight, she found pleasure in the arms of her husband. Was he just like all the other men? She didn't think so. He was different. He gave her space and choices.

She was married to Lord Otto Hightower, she mused. He held her in his arms whenever she was scared, hurt, or in pain. Otto fought by her side in battles and saved her life many times. He noticed she had nightmares and apparently even calmed them. They shared their bodies, and she liked it. They had sex twice at West Franken. She liked it then, but it had been difficult for them to move past their differences. Ultima didn't want to shame his family. Although, they already thought she had an affair with Soren. However, tonight, they had talked, and she told him she hadn't. He seemed to believe her. She felt relaxed and happy, even though she didn't know how to love.

"Try to sleep, my beautiful Ultima," whispered Otto, in his sleep, and she fell asleep nestled in his arms a few minutes later.

The next morning, soon after dawn, Ultima woke wrapped next to Otto. They had finally found a common ground for their marriage, and it was more than sex. He had spent the entire night with her, and apparently, she had stayed in his arms. She wanted to use the commode, and she was thirsty. Enough to make her want to get up and drink a gallon of water, but first, she needed to leave her bed without waking the man who shared it. She slowly moved away, and Otto stirred, turning over to lie on his back. Ultima left the bed feeling dizzy and tired. She went to the bathroom and cleaned herself. Her room had a small bathroom in good working order, so she bathed and changed into a clean nightdress.

When Ultima returned from the bathroom, Otto was still sleeping. She stayed quiet, lit a lantern, and sat next to the fireplace. Ultima took her knitting out of her personal bag and continued working on a pair of socks she was making for Akina. She carried those needles everywhere.

She wondered how her Akina was doing. Was she coping in her new situation? It must be overwhelming for her daughter to have been birthed in slavery, but now free and in the bosom of her biological father's family. She stayed there until she was tired again, and quite cold as the fire had all but gone out. She lived with the constant expectation that someone might enter her room via the window. She checked and made sure the window was locked. Then she returned to bed, lay down next to her husband, and fell asleep again soon after.

The morning arrived and Ultima woke alone in her bed. *Where is Otto?* wondered Ultima. He was gone, and she still needed to pack the few things she had. She rolled out of her bed and began her morning ritual. By the time a maid came to her door, she had finished braiding her hair and was already dressed. It was easy to get dressed now that she wore pants, a shirt, and no corset.

"My Lady, Prince Soren is eating breakfast, and he asks if you would join him," said the maid.

"Could you bring my breakfast up to my room and please tell the prince I said thank you for the invitation, but no thank you. I'm still getting ready to leave." Ultima sat by a dresser, undid her braid, combed her hair, and braided it again.

CHAPTER 25

Are We Riding Horses to Pailo?

It was early morning, and the train station was full of people. The group had left Bertha Abbey, the Marquis of Muneer's home, and together they rode in one large group. The Duke of Hausman talked with the Duke of Vurthas. As always, the Earl of Portmore sat on his horse quietly, keeping no particular company. The man said little, which Ultima found most distressing. He had magic, but no one ever saw him use it.

Ultima couldn't tell what type of magic it was. *Could he be a therion? No, he can't control animals. I've never seen him even remotely interested in any animals,* Ultima thought to herself. She thought he could be a shifter, but Ultima's harmonizer magic couldn't let her see past his outer shell.

Otto had been serious all morning, and He'nico was buying the train tickets and making the arrangements for traveling. Prince Soren was as always ever so intimidating, but not to Ultima. After all, he used to be her client; to Ultima, he was attentive and caring. Besides, her Exotic training made her look beyond the intimidating exterior of men.

"You look rested this morning," said Soren, standing behind Ultima.

"Thank you!" Ultima turned her head to look over her shoulder at the prince. "I feel well today. Excuse me, Your Highness," said Ultima, and she went to stand next to the Duke of Vurthas.

"What is taking so long? If we catch the morning train, we will be in Pailo by midnight, seven days from today," said the Duke of Hausman.

"There are many people milling about here. I wonder if there's an issue with the train," said Soren. Prince Soren had followed Ultima and now spoke with the two dukes.

Just then, the Earl of Portmore approached the group with a stressed look on his face. "I'm sorry I'm the one that has to give you the bad news, but we are going to have to travel by road," said the Earl, apparently out of breath.

"Why? What happened?" asked the Duke of Hausman.

"The trains are not running. There is a problem with the trains coming from Pailo. They said it will take a few days to fix the line," said the Earl of Portmore.

"We must use road-carriages, but not the big ones. They would make the ride through the winding roads that much longer. We need to travel light and fast," said the Duke of Hausman.

"This is going to be a nuisance. We don't have enough guards or mages to help us on the journey. Plus, traveling by road will take us another four weeks to go via West Franken like we'd intended. I thought this was going to be faster," said Otto.

"Robert, maybe you should stay here another day. Gareth may benefit from an extra day of healing. Perhaps in another day the problems with the trains will be solved," said the Marquis of Muneer, who was waiting with them.

"No. What I heard of the problem concerned the tracks themselves, and no trains will be coming this way for a few days," said the Earl of Portmore.

"Thank you, my friend. You and Samila have been great hosts, but we must make it to Pailo posthaste. When we left, Trevino had already become unwell, so Soren must reach the capital and take up command of the court and kingdom," said the Duke of Hausman.

❖❖❖

He'nico, Otto, and the Earl of Portmore went to find horses and carts to travel down to the city of West Franken, as intended. The group left early in the morning, and they planned to reach the village of Cirlick.

Ultima rode next to the Duke of Vurthas.

"What? Are you making sure the old man is comfortable? Huh, Ultima?" said the Duke.

"Well, an ax to the shoulder isn't anything to be taken lightly. That wendigo could have taken your entire arm off," said Ultima.

"I know. I thank you. You saved my arm. I can move it. The healers back in Glauslag also did an outstanding job," said the old man.

"Hey, Ultima, how is father?" asked He'nico.

"He can move his arm so he thinks he can take on the world," said Ultima.

"Will the two of you stop it! I'm right here. You can ask me, He'nico Benicio," said the Duke of Vurthas.

"Oh, I'm in trouble now. He used two of my names," said He'nico, riding away laughing. Ultima laughed, feeling more comfortable with her healer skills.

"This is stupid. We should have gone directly to West Franken instead of taking this detour to Glauslag," said Marshal Donnelly.

"Well, what is done is done, let's keep going," said Otto, as he brought his horse alongside that of his wife. Ultima noticed Otto looking at her, as he let his horse ride next to hers.

"What?" asked Ultima. Otto smiled at her but said nothing. She smiled back at him.

"You snore," said Otto.

"Do I? I'll ask to see if there is a cure for it. Once we get to the next town, I'll contact a healer," said Ultima, in a sassy voice.

"No, don't. I like it when you snore. It is more of a quiet whistle," he said.

"Oh, like that's better," said Ultima. Otto laughed and rode ahead a little. They went on for a few hours more until they stopped for the night. They didn't make it to the village of Cirlick, so they had to make camp. Soren, the Earl of Portmore, and Otto went with three more men to look for wood and the rest stayed behind setting up camp. Ultima had been in a cheerful mood all day. She felt relaxed and happy. Maybe after the conversation the previous night with Otto, things would be different. She already thought of these men as her family.

Akina had been her only family for the last eleven years, but now she was part of this clan of men. Maybe she could learn to live free, maybe she could be more than property, maybe. That night they had time to pitch their tents and make a proper camp. She went to help He'nico cook the food when she saw Otto return with Soren. They were carrying many pieces of wood, but Otto looked aggravated.

What happened? she wondered.

Otto left the wood by the side of the central fire and went to his tent. The food was soon cooked, and they all came together by the center fire, all except Otto. So, Ultima plated up a portion of food and took it to their tent. Otto had to eat. There was something wrong, and she was going to find out what was making Otto so upset. Ultima entered the tent and found Otto looking for something in his bag.

"Are you alright?" asked Ultima.

"Yes, why are you asking?" Otto kept looking in his bag.

"You seem upset. What happened out in the woods?" asked Ultima.

"Soren can be exhausting at times," said Otto and he sat on the ground looking up at Ultima.

"People can get on our nerves. Do you want to talk about it?" asked Ultima.

"No!"

"Fine—here, eat! You need to eat and rest. We have a long road ahead of us tomorrow," said Ultima. Otto ate his food and drank from the flask of whiskey he brought from the capital. Ultima sat a small distance away, ate her own food and watched him eat. Once she was done eating, she placed her plate aside.

"I want to hold you in my arms," said Otto, placing his plate aside and cleaning his hands on a towel.

"That I can do," said Ultima.

"Would you take off your armor?" he asked. So, Ultima removed all her armor, including her boots, but stayed in her pants and shirt as she sat back down in front of Otto. He reclined against his saddle, upon some furs that made their pallet for the night and Ultima lay next to him with her head on his chest. Slowly he began to unbutton Ultima's shirt and reached under to caress her skin.

"I like the way your skin feels to my touch." Otto continued stroking her skin, from her neck, down to her breasts. Ultima enjoyed the attention and changed her position slightly to enhance their contact and began to reciprocate. She looked up at him and smiled.

Despite his great efforts, Ultima's mind was far too busy and she knew that on this occasion, all would be for him. She didn't mind. It would be fun anyway, and she felt he needed it. She decided to play along; there would be no harm in letting him believe she, too, was fulfilled. She made sure that when he was done, he found her out of breath, just as he was. She had an arm over her head, covering her eyes and a smile on her face.

"Otto, I think you just let everyone in the camp know we just had sex. You do know that don't you?" said Ultima, still with her arm over her eyes and not wanting to look directly at Otto.

"I let Soren know I do lie with my wife," said Otto, still breathing heavily.

"So, this was about Soren? I don't understand. What do you mean? Why let him know you lie with me? What did he say to you?" asked Ultima, sitting up and readjusting her pants.

"He wanted me to let him sleep with you. He said since I don't sleep with you, he figured I wanted to sell you," said Otto, hitting the ground next to him.

"Otto, I can't believe it. Why would he say something like that?" said Ultima.

"For him, an Exotic is in the trade for life. You are not property. No one will touch you. Do you hear me? No one will touch you but me. I always wanted someone I could trust with my life, and I found you. You are my wife, my warrior soulmate. He is crazy if he thinks I will let him touch you. I don't share my wife. I will forever care for you and Akina. I will never share you." He kissed Ultima as she lay back on the pallet. Otto lay on his back and closed his eyes.

For Soren, she was nothing more than an Exotic. She knew he felt that way by the way he treated her, but what about the others? Otto would never sell her. She wasn't just an Exotic to him. Ultima was more than his wife. She was his warrior soulmate. She liked that title. In any case, she needed to rest, she was exhausted. Sleep, she needed rest. Lately, she tired so easily.

♦♦♦

Morning came and Ultima woke with a pain in her side and back. She must have not moved the entire night. She woke alone. Otto wasn't in the tent with her. When she stepped out of her tent, the men treated her like they always did, and she gave little thought to anything. Although Prince Soren was distant. The Earl of Portmore was hacking a lung. It was incomprehensible how a man so young could have so many ailments. At any time and for no apparent reason, he'd have bouts of coughing that ended up with him losing his breath mid-sentence. Conversely, Marshal Donnelly was placidly smoking his morning cigarette and saddling his horse, while He'nico and others were breaking down tents and preparing to leave camp, but where was Otto?

She had to hurry. She went a little away from camp and did her morning ritual. Once again, this morning, she had a feeling that someone was watching her on her way back to camp. The last time she had the feeling was when they were attacked by the wendigos, but here it was again. She hurried back to camp. They were ready to move, but when they mounted their horses, Ultima noticed something different. It was a presence in the forest.

"We need to leave this forest and find a road. This place is making me uneasy. I feel someone is watching us," said Ultima to the Duke of Hausman, Otto, and the Duke of Vurthas who were waiting for the others.

"I know what you are saying; I feel the same way. It's like the woods have eyes. Come, let me help you pack your horse," said Otto.

"We will pass Cirlick and arrive at a village called Kartory next—that one we will surely reach. It is a river port village, growing fast and soon will become a town if their population keeps growing," said the Duke of Hausman.

They mounted and moved off. They traveled all day until late in the afternoon when they reached the village of Kartory. The village was quite large; they even had a tavern and an inn. The group found accommodations for the night, split between tavern and inn. It was a picturesque little village, and they had a market that was still open. Ultima wanted to visit the market, and Otto agreed to take her. Soren and Marshal Donnelly came along.

There were tables with vendors of fruits, vegetables, fish of different kinds. There was a stall that had pots and pans, and many stalls with trinkets. Ultima walked along the many stalls, admiring it all.

"I can give you all you ever wanted and more. All you need to do is come with me and ask," said Soren, startling Ultima. He was standing behind her.

"What? Oh, Prince Soren, well, thank you, but I already have all I ever wanted," said Ultima and she moved past him. Ultima could see that Otto was watching them talk, but he stayed away. Soren came back to her side and passed her a piece of fruit.

"Otto is a prince because he is the nephew of the King of Yakuta, and will only ever be a Lord, the third son of a duke. He will never inherit anything. I can give you a title if that's what you want."

"This little game needs to stop. I don't want a title. I am happy with the title I have now, and I don't want another," said Ultima.

"Really, what title is that?" Prince Soren's voice dripped with sarcasm.

"I'm Mother to my Akina and a Lady in the honorable Ducal House of Vurthas, the best titles any woman could ever have. Excuse me, Prince Soren." With that, Ultima walked away from Soren toward Otto.

"What did he want?" asked Otto, walking next to Ultima, away from the market and back to the inn.

"Nothing of import, he wanted to give me a title," said Ultima.

"And what did you say?" asked Otto.

"I told him I already have a title that I like. I'm Akina's mother, and I'm also Lady Ultima Hightower of the Ducal House of Vurthas." And they both laughed.

"I think we must leave for Yakuta as soon as we reach Pailo. I was thinking of staying until Akina finished the school year, but there will be war between Alhambra and Behui which will make traveling difficult," said Otto.

"This is the furthest I've ever been from Pailo in my entire life," said Ultima.

"I think you will love traveling around the world," said Otto, holding Ultima's hand and giving it a kiss.

"I think Akina, will love traveling as well," said Ultima.

"There are many things we need to prepare before we leave, but we must find Marco's assassin first," said Otto.

"I can still hear the assassin's voice, telling me he would get me," said Ultima.

"We will not let him get—"

Otto never finished his sentence, as a group of men ambushed the couple. A man grabbed Ultima from behind and gagged her. Several other men hit Otto over the head, placed a rag over his nose and mouth, and Otto fell to the ground. The men dragged Otto and Ultima over to a nearby carriage, threw them onto the back of the carriage, and left in a hurry. Ultima heard Soren shouting as he gave chase, until his voice faded into the distance.

CHAPTER 26

Captives

The ropes around Ultima's wrists were cutting the circulation to her hands. Her fingers hurt every time she tried to move them. The leader of the group had attached her hands via a rope to his horse's saddle, forcing her to walk behind. She had been walking for hours and now, with every step, her legs began to buckle and she stumbled repeatedly.

The Boleños stopped, and she gave a silent thanks to the Lord of the Sky. Ultima looked around for Otto. The leader holding her rope jumped off his horse, unbound her from the hook of the saddle, and pulled her over to the nearest trees. He tied her to one of the trees and left to provide water for his horse. She could see many prisoners attached to a long rope in a line, but she was the only one that was being held by the leader.

The Boleño men were a filthy bunch. Not by what they were saying, for Ultima couldn't understand their language, but the smell and look of the men reminded her of a pack of wild animals. The leader's blond hair was cut short to the sides, but he kept it long on the top and at the back of his head, which he held back in one long braid that reached to his waist. His face was painted with royal-blue stripes that crossed his face, and he had caked blood and mud covering his brown leather armor.

The leader stepped away and talked to some of his men, and a few minutes later he walked back to Ultima. His beefy hands untied Ultima from the tree, pulled her to the side, and gave her a skin of water. He made a gesture indicating she should drink. Boleña was a strange language. One that Ultima had never heard of nor even remotely studied its origins. Boleña was a secluded kingdom with secretive folk who kept to themselves. They had no interactions with any of the people of the Kingdom of Tsestelago, where there were only rumors about them and their barbaric ways.

Ultima noticed none of the men had trade-tattoos. They had tattoos on their exposed skin, on their bodies, but no trade-tattoos around their right arms. There was no way for Ultima to know what trade any of the Boleños had, or even if they had any form of cast or organization. Ultima tried to look for Otto again. She knew they had captured him too, but she couldn't see him anywhere. The man who held her, and appeared to be the leader, pulled her via the rope away from the others. When they stopped, the man pointed at a bush and said a word. Ultima looked around. She couldn't understand what he wanted.

The man, exasperated, unbuttoned his pants. Ultima opened her eyes wide and moved back a step or two. She hadn't expected she would have to do the job of a street walker, minus the payment. However, what he did was pee. After he was done, he pointed at her and then at the bush.

"You want me to pee? Oh, that I can do." Ultima went around the bush, and she peed. The man eased some of the rope for her to move freely. She thanked the Lord of the Sky the man wasn't one of those perverts who liked to watch women urinate. When Ultima was done, the man led her back toward the group of Boleños. They were just approaching the main group of soldiers when Ultima saw Otto.

"OTTO, DID THEY GET ANYONE ELSE?" shouted Ultima.

"NO, I JUST SEE US TWO," Otto called back, and a Boleño soldier hit Otto in his stomach and shouted something at him.

The leader pulled Ultima back to his horse, and he reattached the rope to his saddle horn. He mounted his horse which side-stepped—unexpectedly to Ultima—causing her to fall. The horse almost stepped on her with his hind legs. Ultima screamed as she tried to stand. She barely got to her legs when the leader shouted, looked up to the sky, and pulled Ultima up onto his horse in one clean pull. The man was pure muscle. She rode with him. They continued for a few more hours until they encountered a larger encampment of Boleños. A large company of military men.

When their captors approached the Boleños encampment, the entire group was surrounded by warriors. A subset of young warriors dressed in light-brown leather took control of the prisoners, including Otto, leading the long line to an empty section of the camp. Just before Ultima was pulled off the horse, she saw the line of prisoners being transferred to metal shackles and attached to a distant tree, with burlaps put over their heads. The leader jumped off his horse and pulled Ultima after him. She too was placed in metal shackles, but he tied her to a nearby tree at the edge of the encampment. Ultima was glad he let her be and did not cover her head. He then went to help the men set up for the night.

The Boleños made a fire. Some of the men from the group who had taken Ultima and Otto captive returned to the camp carrying two deer and they quickly went to the task of dressing the animal, cutting it, and setting it over the fire.

There is going to be button on the soldiers' menu tonight. I hope they feed us, thought Ultima.

And to Ultima's happiness, they took some food and gave it to the prisoners. Ultima had expected not to be fed, but they brought her food too. Having food in her tummy was a good thing. Night came and with it the cold. The warrior had tied her far away from the fire and her freezing feet began to feel numb. Ultima wore only half her armor. She didn't have on her gauntlets, liner gloves, or pauldrons, which left her upper body extra cold.

Although the metal of the chains was getting colder with the night and her shivering body couldn't get comfortable, a young soldier came and released her hands, while another pointed a spear at her. It didn't matter; she was in no position to fight. She couldn't move her fingers or her hands, and her fingers had become swollen and itchy from the earlier ropes. The young man gave her water to drink, and a blanket, and then replaced the thick metal cuffs around her wrists. She was still bound, but the cuffs did not constrict her blood as the ropes had done. The chain was now loose enough to let her lie on the ground to sleep.

❖❖❖

A soft pinky-orange light woke Ultima. A magnificent array of colors surrounded her, and she had to look away as the light became brighter. The light always bothered her eyes, but she had neither her dark glasses nor her helmet. She feared not having either to impede the light would cause an intolerable headache.

Ultima tried to accustom her eyes to the light, but the light caused a sharp pain that made her grimace and eventually the pain in her head became unbearable. So, she loosened her chest armor and reached underneath, to her inner clothing from which she tore a section to make a covering for her eyes. She needed something, anything. As the morning passed, she began to heal her own eyes and head, but with no food in her stomach her energy remained low, and she didn't know how to access energy from anything else but water. Ultima could see both through and over the piece of cloth.

Dawn merged into mid-morning, and thirst parched her lips. No one came with food, or even any water. Until, at last, a young girl who couldn't have been older than sixteen arrived. Ultima saw her approach through the makeshift bandana she wore over her eyes. The girl had so many bangles on both arms they could have been used as gauntlets. The girl arrived bringing gifts. She gave Ultima a piece of bread and a cup of tea.

"Oh, thank you," said Ultima. She ate her bread and drank her tea eagerly. The tea was cold, but Ultima didn't care, her hunger took over her food pickiness and she was truly thankful. The young teen sat next to her and talked in her native language.

"I'm sorry, darling, but I can't understand what you're saying," said Ultima. "Can you speak Yakutan?" asked Ultima, in perfect Yakutan, but the teen only smiled and tilted her head. Her red hair looked like fire with the brightness of the morning sun. It was mostly in small braids, close to her head, but here and there, loose strands escaped the braids, curling this way and that.

"How about Behuian? Can you speak Behuian or Parshtishi?" asked Ultima, each of the languages spoken with a perfect accent. The girl continued smiling amiably.

"Palermian perhaps, maybe you can speak Palermian? Or how about Catalagac, the language of Alhambra?" asked Ultima, trying to sit straighter on the hard ground. The young girl touched Ultima's eye covering and gestured with her hands: *Why?*

"You don't understand any of those languages, great. The light hurts my eyes, and the covering helps with the pain. It shades my eyes a little from the brightness." Ultima gestured with her hands, pointing first at the light and then at her own eyes, and the young girl smiled again. She then took Ultima's right arm and tried to lift her sleeve, but Ultima pulled her arm away.

"No," Ultima shook her head, but as if they knew she would refuse, immediately two men came from the far side of a nearby tent and pointed swords at her. The young girl took Ultima's right arm and then her left one, said a few words, then shook her head and pointed at Ultima's arms.

The girl touched the burn mark on Ultima's right arm, and gave a quick nod.

"I'm a married woman." Ultima didn't gesture or look at the men. The teen let go of Ultima's arms, stood up, and took the men with her.

Ultima then leaned back against the tree and brought her knees to her chest, whereupon she rested her head. How was she going to escape these people? As the day grew warmer, the ever-brightening light became a burden. Her neck and shoulder were tired from trying to shade her face with her hands. To make matters worse, the air was still cold and there was snow on the ground, reflecting the light back up to her eyes from below. Her body wavered between shaking with cold to breaking out in a sweat.

❖❖❖

An hour after the girl left, a soldier came and took her from the tree. They walked through the encampment, passing by a series of little tents and a central fire pit. There was a wagon full of what looked like weapons and another wagon that may have been for the healers. Eventually arriving at the biggest tent she had seen.

They entered the large tent, and it was much darker than the daylight outside, for which Ultima was thankful. She removed the bandage from her eyes, and once she adjusted to the light, she noticed there were many warriors standing around a table. At the center stood a man with a red tribal tattoo around his neck, and he looked like the leader. They were a dirty bunch. The Boleños leadership dressed in black leather armor that sported many knife attachments. The men had their heads shaved along both sides, and like the leader of the group who captured her and Otto, they braided the remaining hair that grew along the central line of their scalps in a single long braid that hung down their backs.

The man with the red tattoo around his neck approached Ultima and stopped in front of her. He removed the cloth eye covering from around her neck, and then he took one of her braids in his hands. She looked at him and waited.

"Pretty ... I'm the commander of the Boleños, Aa'hono Bara Tamina. Who are you?" said the man with a heavy

Catalagac accent. Aa'hono then stepped back and sat on his chair.

"My name is Ultima," said Ultima.

"That doesn't answer my question. I asked who you are, not your name," said the man.

"I'm Lady Hightower. A woman from the capital city of Pailo," said Ultima.

"That isn't what your tattoos say. Now, let's try this again. Who are you?" said Commander Aa'hono.

"My tattoo says, I'm Lady Hightower. I'm a married woman to the third son in the Yakutan Ducal House of Vurthas," said Ultima.

"Hum, your people brand their wives. Interesting," said one of the women in a sarcastic tone. Then the men talked in their language and Ultima looked from one to another.

"Why did you go out of your way to kidnap me and my husband?" asked Ultima.

"Your husband? Huh—I saw you and your—husband, fight in the Bincara style. How did you both learn how to fight in our sacred style?"

"What are you talking about? My husband and I fought next to each other, but I don't know any Bincara style," said Ultima.

"She is lying. Let me ask her some questions. I know how to make women tell the truth," said an older woman in a heavy Catalagac accent.

"NO!" said Commander Aa'hono, and he lifted a finger. She bowed and took a step back.

"I'm not lying to you. I don't know what you are talking about," said Ultima.

At that moment, a tall and equally dirty man was pushing Otto into the tent. Otto stood next to Ultima.

"Man, these people stink!" said Otto in Yakutan, looking at Ultima.

"Who are you?" asked Commander Aa'hono. Otto looked from one man to the next. Otto had a black eye, and his hair was a mess.

"I'm the third son of the Duke of Vurthas of Yakuta, Prince Otto Archer Fernand Milo Hightower. One of the Lords of the Ducal House of Vurthas and nephew to King George of Yakuta."

"Finally, someone that knows how to answer questions," said Aa'hono.

"What kind of lord has a warrior partner for his wife?" asked a man from somewhere near the side of the tent, and others in the large tent grumbled agreement.

"Quiet!" said the Commander. And everyone in the tent quieted down.

"Our women are warriors, just like our men. Our mages are fighters regardless of gender," said Otto, standing tall.

"Our women are warriors too, just like our men, but our wives are not our fighting partners. It makes us weak and unreliable. Who taught you our sacred style of fighting?" asked Commander Aa'hono.

"I don't know what you are talking about. What sacred style of fighting?" asked Otto, looking from one man to the other.

"We saw you fight back-to-back. That is our sacred way of fighting," said a man standing to the right of Commander Aa'hono.

"My wife and I fight close together and sometimes we fight back-to-back, but only because it was easier for us when surrounded. No one taught us that, we just did it to protect each other's back," said Otto.

"Please let us go, we have nothing to do with your war. My husband is not from the Kingdom of Tsestelago. We were caught in the middle of the battle. We were looking for someone and we had to defend ourselves," said Ultima.

"Why do you have a burn mark over your trade-tattoo?" asked another man.

"They burned my wife mark over my trade-tattoo," said Ultima, not wanting to enter into any details.

"They burn wife marks like one would brand cattle. And they call us barbaric," said the man standing to the right of Commander Aa'hono.

"Marjon, my friend, don't be harsh. We each have our own eccentricities," said Commander Aa'hono.

"And what was your trade?" asked the Commander.

"I was a singer," said Ultima.

"What are you going to do with these two now that you know how they learned our fighting style?" asked a man at the back of the tent.

"You could let us go. We were on our way to the capital of Pailo and from there in a few more days my wife and I were leaving Tsestelago to Yakuta," said Otto.

"You forget we are at war," said Marjon. The man was as beefy as Commander Aa'hono.

"At the moment, my people are not at war with yours. My uncle, King George, has no quarrel with the Boleños. In fact, your people could benefit from commerce with Yakuta," said Otto.

"You talk for your King?" asked Commander Aa'hono with a smirk.

"I'm a diplomat from the Kingdom of Yakuta. I'm prepared to talk for my King in matters of commerce," said Otto.

"Take them away. I must think about this before I make a decision," said Commander Aa'hono. So two guards stepped forward and took Otto and Ultima away. They ended up being tied together to a tree near the horses.

"Otto, what do you think will happen to us?"

"I don't know. They might let us go, or they could kill us. They may take us as prisoners to their capital, and they can make us slaves. There is a plethora of things they can do with us," said Otto.

"Oh great, you are cheery," said Ultima.

"Hell, what you want me to say? I don't know," said Otto off-hand.

"Couldn't you be optimistic? Maybe be a little positive?" Ultima couldn't believe the man could be so nonchalant about the situation.

"Fine, I'm positive we are captive. I'm positive we are separated from the family. I'm positive that tonight we will not sleep together and make love. I'm also positive there will not be any cake for dessert," said Otto.

"If it wasn't for my hands being tied, I would hit you," said Ultima.

"Come on, you must admit it was a little funny?" said Otto, giving his wife a little smile.

"It wasn't funny," she said, trying to pout, but breaking into a smile.

"You look as though you're in pain," said Otto.

"My back hurts and I'm tired. I can't seem to ease my back," said Ultima, trying to sit up straight.

"You are afraid, I know," said Otto.

"Otto, I'm afraid they will turn me into a prostitute again," said Ultima with her eyes closed.

"Listen, these people don't have trades and I don't think they know the intricacies of prostitute trade work," said Otto.

"That doesn't matter. They can still make me a sex slave and slaves are slaves anywhere in the world," said Ultima, her voice cracked and her hands had begun shaking.

"I'm still a mage and before they turn you into a slave, I'll burn this place to hell," said Otto.

"Do you really mean it?" asked Ultima.

"Yes, I mean it." Otto looked toward the big tent. "It's cold. Could these people hurry up and make-up their minds?"

CHAPTER 27

The Boleños

Otto and Ultima had had nothing to eat after they broke their fast with a watery and cold tea and a piece of bread in the morning. It was late in the evening when a pair of guards came and took them back to the big tent. Commander Aa'hono and his men were there, and this time the young girl who had *interviewed* Ultima in the morning was in the tent as well.

"Lord Otto, we considered the matter, and I liked the idea of having commerce with Yakuta, but my father the Zar would not want any of your people on our land," said the Commander.

"I'm sure we can come to an agreement," said Otto.

"I'll let you go, but I know your wife is an Exotic. I have never had an Exotic. She stays with me. Take Lord Otto away," said the Commander.

"NO, NO, LET MY WIFE GO. ULTIMA! NO—" Otto struggled with the guards holding them, but one man hit him in the gut, face, and head, rendering Otto unconscious. And the guards took Otto away.

"No please! I'm not an Exotic. I'm a free woman. I'm married to Otto. I don't want to do this." Ultima pulled on the chains that bound her, but the guard hit her face and drew blood from her lip.

She was taken to a nearby smaller tent and pushed inside. Three men walked into the tent. When she saw what the tall man had in his hands, she stepped back.

"NO, I'm a free woman," cried Ultima. Then two men held her, while the other placed a collar around her neck and locked it. It was an iron slave collar. Ultima felt as though a freezing hand had been placed around her neck. Her body numbed, and she sighed profoundly, a prelude of sorrow. The men pushed her to her knees and left. A few minutes later three very tall women entered the tent. They removed her armor and left her shivering in only her inner clothing. Ultima knew what was coming next. Her hands were still shackled to chains and her head hurt so much she thought it would explode.

The women walked in and out of the tent, bringing towels and linens, and they brought her food and mead. They forced her to eat. They then brought buckets of water and made Ultima wash thoroughly. They appeared to know what was expected of a prostitute. Perhaps they were prostitutes themselves.

Ultima did everything they forced her to do, and when they dressed her in a clean shift and painted her face, Ultima sat and cried. Here she was again, forced back into the trade she thought she had left behind forever. The woman shouted at Ultima in their language, and after cleaned her face with a rag. They pointed at her burned mark on her breast, and shouted some more, but Ultima didn't care. The women couldn't make Ultima stop crying. She kept pushing the women's hands away and making them angry with her reluctance to get ready.

The women left the tent. And Ultima fell to her knees, looking like she was going to the gallows. She laid her head on a pallet of furs.

I refuse to return to being an Exotic. I am a free woman. No man owns me. Tonight, I am going to be raped because I am not going to do anything willingly. I don't have any god, but if there is one out there listening, I need help. I don't want to be touched by that disgusting man. Please spare me that torture, I am no longer in the trade. I've been a good woman to Otto and a good mother to Akina. I have nothing to trade. Please, help me. Ultima prayed, and tears rolled down the side of her face. Her nose was runny and her heart pounded furiously in her chest. She tried to calm herself, taking a deep breath and then another, her hands trembled, but she sat up straight. She cleaned her nose and eyes and kept on breathing deeply. An hour passed and the dirty man, Aa'hono, entered the tent.

"Exotic! That is your trade, according to your breast. The women told me you refused to cooperate when they prepared you," said Commander Aa'hono. He took his armor off and then his shirt, showing a chest full of scars.

"I'm for my husband and only for him. I'm a Lady, and no longer an Exotic," said Ultima while sitting on the raised pallet made of furs. Her body was visible through the sheer shift, so she talked, covering her breast with her arms.

"Stand and let me see you," said the man in a gruff voice. Ultima shook her head.

"STAND—DO IT NOW," shouted the man. Ultima jumped where she sat, and lowered her head. She then lowered her arms to her sides, but she didn't stand for the man.

"How about if I sing for you? If you have a lute, I can play as I sing. Come sit, relax!" said Ultima in a soft voice. She raised her head and arms and gave him a gentle smile.

The man stood there looking at her for a minute, but then went to sit next to her.

"You don't know any of our songs," said the man touching her braids.

"I know many songs in Catalaga." Ultima began singing a nursery song in Catalaga. The commander sat and continued touching her braids and then her face as Ultima sang. A few minutes later she stood and went to a stump of wood that served as a table, and took a plate of fruit that was left there. Ultima finished the song and began another, passing fruit to the man, first to his hand and then to his lips.

She fed him fruits, and he reclined on his pallet of furs as Ultima watched the man eat. Ultima let him touch her arms and her breast. She was breathing hard, her eyes shining and full of tears, but she didn't cry. The man touched her face and then pulled her face toward himself and kissed her. Ultima closed her eyes. Her ears rung with a high-pitched sound and her hands turned cold. The last time she was that nervous when pleasing a man was when she was a teen, but this time she was like a hammock in a windstorm. When he was opening her shift sideways to expose her body, there was a blast.

BOOM! And then another, BOOM!

The commander pushed Ultima aside, jumped from the pallet, took his sword, and left the tent. Ultima stood up quickly and went to look outside the tent. There was a firefight, fire and lightning exploding in every direction. Men were running and there was no one guarding the tent. She went back into the tent and tried to find her armor but found nothing other than a short sword. She took the sword and closed her eyes and said a prayer to the invisible god that had helped her that night.

BOOM! Another blast and then an arrow with fire hit the tent where she stood. Ultima went to the entrance, looked around, and found mayhem outside. She left running. Fire balls flying over her head, and then she saw men with the Otarana colors and the Yakutan House of Vurthas' crest.

"OTTO!" shouted Ultima as she ran and evaded fighting men. "OTTO, WHERE ARE YOU?" shouted Ultima as she ran through the men fighting. When she saw Otto, he looked like a berserker, lightning shooting from his fingers at people all around him, she shouted his name. "OTTO!" His face was contorted in rage. He was levitating off the ground and lightning surrounded him, until he saw Ultima running toward him. He dropped back down and ran to her.

"Are you hurt? Did that Boleño, son of a whore touch you?" asked Otto.

"No," Ultima managed to say, just as a pair of Boleños jumped up and attacked them. Otto threw a bolt of lightning at the pair, and they lay back down, dead.

"Why didn't you use this magic in the war?" asked Ultima.

"Snow, water, and you ... We'll talk later."

Otto took Ultima by the hand, and they left running. Eventually they found Soren, the Earl of Portmore, and the Dukes of Hausman and of Vurthas fighting a group of men. The Duke of Vurthas was using his water magic when Otto and Ultima arrived. They joined the fight. The few Boleños who were alive and fighting were being overwhelmed by magic.

Once the fight was over, the men gathered together near the Duke of Hausman and the Earl of Portmore.

The Earl of Portmore was detaining one of the female warriors at sword point. The woman was lying on the ground, bleeding to death.

"Don't worry. You will be dead in minutes. You are one beautiful woman, though," said the Earl of Portmore.

Ultima jumped, and looked at the Earl of Portmore with fear. Those were the same words the assassin had said to her; that was the same voice. The earl wasn't coughing, gagging, or gargling his words. He sounded loud and clear.

"My Lord Vurthas!" shouted Ultima at the duke. "It's him! He is Prince Marco's assassin," said Ultima, pointing at the Earl of Portmore. The Earl of Portmore was standing in a direct line to Prince Soren. He took a knife and threw it at the prince, but Otto jumped in the way and took the knife for Soren.

"NOOOOOO!" wailed Ultima, as she ran to Otto's side.

The Duke of Vurthas raised his sword against the earl.

"Stop! There is no place for you to hide," said Paul Donnelly, stepping in front of the Duke of Vurthas.

"Get out of my way. I have him," said the Duke of Vurthas.

"We must take him alive," said the Marshal.

"You have me nothing. I killed Prince Marco and both your sons and there is nothing you can do to me." So saying, the earl transformed into a wolf and took off running. The Duke of Vurthas created a ball of water and engulfed the head of the wolf; at the same moment Ultima raised her hands and shouted in her grief.

"Stop running."

The wolf levitated and was brought closer to them.

"Stop, we need to capture him alive," shouted Marshal Donnelly.

The Duke of Vurthas didn't listen; his face was filled with the hatred of a father looking for revenge. The wolf form of the earl jerked and contorted, but after a few minutes he stopped moving. His head hung languidly to the side, and his body fell to the ground when Ultima dropped her hands and turned her attention to Otto.

He was still alive, but with a knife to his chest. His breathing shallow, eyes closed, blood pouring out of the wound, he touched Ultima's right arm where her burn mark was.

"We need a healer. Now!" shouted Soren.

"Tear open his shirt. I need his skin exposed," Ultima told Soren. The prince's eyes opened wide. He looked askance at the woman who was in a frenzy, but his gaze turned to amazement when her eyes turned yellow and then red, her hands shone green and yellow, and he did what Ultima asked.

"Father, give me water. I need water now," screamed Ultima at the Duke of Vurthas. The duke formed a small ball of water and placed it over Ultima's hands. She closed her eyes tight and shouted: "AAAAAAHHH, healing, NOOOWWWW!"

Magic had never come to her in such a manner. Her hands glowed bright yellow. She moved her hands over the wound, left and right, up and down, just as Koru had taught her, and she hovered over the wound, now making her hands shine bright green. Soren sat on the opposite side of Otto, but the Duke of Hausman pulled Soren away, giving Ultima plenty of space to work.

"We are not done fighting. We must ensure there are no more Boleños around," said the Duke of Hausman.

"I'll stay protecting my son and Ultima. He'nico, you make sure there are no other worthless Boleños alive in this camp," said the Duke of Vurthas.

Ultima pulled out the knife in one fast movement, and kept working her magic without rest or hesitation.

❖❖❖

The next morning, Ultima woke inside a tent to a hand touching her arm. There were no healers among the group, so not only had Ultima pulled the knife from Otto's chest and given him the immediate first aid he needed to stay alive, but she had to call on all her healing abilities to repair as much of the wound as she was able and to lessen his pain. It took her three hours of constant work to keep Otto alive. Several times during those three hours she had fallen, exhausted, but on each occasion her father-in-law supplied her water to drink, as well as sugary treats and many pieces of button to keep up her energy. He'nico stayed vigilant throughout, bringing her everything she requested. Finally, she had collapsed and fallen asleep next to Otto. The others transferred them into one of the Boleños' tents that had not been burned down by the fires, leaving a lantern in case either awoke during the night.

Sometime after midnight Ultima roused herself long enough to see that some color had returned to Otto's face and his breathing had become more relaxed. Ultima lowered her head again and placed her arm over his belly, just to make sure he was alive. She told herself she wanted to notice if his breathing changed, and once more she fell asleep next to him. An hour after dawn, Ultima woke to Otto touching her arm.

"How are you feeling?" asked Ultima.

"I don't know. I feel like a horse sat on my chest, but also like a ball of snow has melted over my body. It's a weird feeling," said Otto.

"I had to do things I have never done before. Don't ask me what I did, I just followed Koru's instructions."

"I know about Koru," said Otto.

"He taught me a lot." Ultima smiled and touched Otto's chest. Her fingers started to sparkle again.

"You are not fully healed. I just stopped you from bleeding to death, and I think I'm preventing your wound from getting infected. But you will need a master healer," said Ultima.

"Did the commander get to … you know … hurt you last night?" asked Otto.

"No, thank the Lady of the Lake, the fighting started before he could do anything. I sang for him and was trying to use my harmonizer magic to make him fall asleep, but I'm happy the fighting started when it did. He wasn't falling for my tactics," said Ultima.

"Is that a collar around your neck?" asked Otto.

"Yes," and Ultima's smile left her face. "It's okay, I'm used to wearing a collar. I've been a slave all my life." Ultima touched the collar and buried her face in Otto's side, and she cried.

"I want that thing gone. You are not a slave. You are not property. You are free," said Otto.

"I don't know why I'm crying so much lately. I never cry," said Ultima.

"Women cry, men cry, that is part of life," said Otto.

Ultima got up and looked out the tent. "He's awake," said Ultima, and He'nico entered the tent in a hurry.

"Hey, little brother, it's good to see you awake. You have one stubborn wife," said He'nico, and Otto smiled. The Duke of Vurthas walked in next.

"Son, I'm glad you are awake. I'm overjoyed I married you to a healer," said the Duke, giving Ultima a huge smile.

"Did you get that son of a bitch who tried to kill Soren?" asked Otto, his voice barely audible.

"You better believe it. Between Father and your wife, they drowned that waste of skin," said He'nico.

"He'nico, please take that collar off her neck. Do it now, brother. My wife is a Hightower warrior and a powerful mage. She is a free woman," said Otto, pointing at the lead collar Ultima wore around her neck.

"Will do," said He'nico.

"She also needs clothing," said Otto. Ultima had not noticed she was only wearing the sheer shift from the night before.

"I'll get her a pair of pants and a shirt," said He'nico.

"Urt," Otto made a hurt sound and flinched.

"That's it. You all need to go. He needs rest," said Ultima. So the duke and He'nico smiled in acquiescence and left. Later, some food was brought to the tent for the couple. She tried to feed Otto some broth, but he wouldn't eat, and he fell asleep soon after. A while later, He'nico appeared with clothing for Ultima.

❖❖❖

"Uncle, Godfather, I know Otto is still injured, but we should leave this place now. I know how those Boleños behave; I've been fighting them long enough. They are like a pack of Gargon wolves. When they are hurt, they scatter, but they come back with reinforcements," said Soren to the two dukes.

"We are now farther north. The nearest loyal town is Flora, four days away. But if we ride hard, we can make the town in three days," said Soren.

"Are you sure Flora is the closet town from here? Do they have elemental mages?" asked He'nico.

"We send mages to Flora who have been trained in the capital to protect the town, and they have a wall around the town," said the Duke of Hausman.

"No, Otto can't be moved. Not like this, I don't know what else to do. I'm afraid he could die," said Ultima, who had approached the men and caught the end of their planning.

"Ultima, they will return with many more men than we have, and he will surely die," said Soren.

"That is enough. I agree with Soren. We leave in an hour. He'nico see if there is a cart or something we can use to move your brother. We must put as much distance between us and the Boleños," said the Duke of Vurthas.

"Yes, father," said He'nico.

"And He'nico, have the men find as much water as we can carry. No one is touching my boy," said the Duke of Vurthas.

"Lord Hightower, you will answer for the death of the Earl of Portmore," said Paul Donnelly, pointing a finger at the Duke of Vurthas. "He was a member of the Tsestelago peerage. You don't know whether he was the assassin or not. Just because that woman said he was the one, you all jumped to get him. Due process should have been followed, with the earl appearing in front of a judge and the King,"

"Listen Marshal Donnelly, I'm the Prince Regent now, and I can pardon whomever I want. Lord Hightower, I pardon you for killing the man who tried to kill me and I pardon any and all other of your perceived transgressions—and I have the Duke of Hausman as my witness. There, let's go," said Prince Soren, and he pushed Paul Donnelly away.

The marshal said nothing else, but his red face and shaking hands told a tale of a man barely containing his temper. Ultima left and ran to the tent where Otto was lying. A few minutes later, He'nico appeared with a soldier. They lifted Otto and carried him to a cart.

❖❖❖

They had rounded up as many horses as they could find that had returned to the camp for their journey, enabling them to switch horses throughout the day. They did not take any rests, but for a few minutes to answer the call of nature. The small group traveled as fast as they could move. The injured men in the cart did not complain or moan, other than occasionally in their sleep.

Ultima rode in the cart with the injured men. She eased their pain where she was able, but that was all she could do for them. She was tired and her own body was losing heat fast. The day became overcast with darkened cloud-cover, and freezing rain followed. It was good that the cart had a tarpaulin, so at least the men stayed dry. All around turned into mud and slush, and the group traveled in a single file. They traveled for four days before they reached the town of Flora late in the night. The Duke of Hausman had sent word to the Earl of Polion in Flora, who fortunately was in residence.

The Earl of Polion woke the mayor of the town and let him know the Prince Regent would be arriving soon. The mayor woke all the townsfolk and guard, and arranged for them be on a higher level of alert for a possible attack from the Boleños. The town mages took positions in the wall towers, and once Prince Soren and his friends arrived in Flora, the gates in the wall were closed completely for the night.

CHAPTER 28

When Men Talk, Women Roll Their Eyes

It was late at night when they arrived at the Earl of Polion's home, and two servants carried Otto to a room on the second floor of the castle. The castle was an old structure, with rooms added on every decade or so, whenever there was a new owner. The earl had been one of Ultima's clients. Although he preferred the company of men, he liked to hear Ultima sing, and he loved to dance with her. Nevertheless, the earl had a wife, and they had three children as society expected of him, but he also had a lover in the capital of Pailo. His wife, too, had a lover of her own. Ultima knew all the dirty little secrets of many of the peerage.

Otto's room didn't have a bathroom, but what it lacked in space was made up for by a large balcony that overlooked the town below. The countess gave Ultima a room of her own, but she stayed in Otto's bedroom. Ultima made sure Otto was comfortable. She lay next to him and fell asleep soon after.

The next morning, Ultima woke to the sound of her stomach grumbling. She sat up and looked at Otto; he was still asleep. Ultima was more than hungry. She had been using her magic nonstop to reduce Otto's pain and her body needed nourishment. She stood up, and the world turned. She had to wait a few moments until her head stopped spinning. Ultima then dressed and opened the door. There was no one in the hallway, not even the floor servant. Ultima walked out and descended the stairs, at the bottom of which she found herself in a large receiving hall. To the right side there was a set of double doors that opened to a spacious dining room.

Upon entering the dining room, she found Prince Soren sitting alone at a round table, apparently lost in thought as he didn't seem to notice her approach. He was eating what appeared to be porridge, and bread and cheese, with a cup of something hot. As she got closer, it smelled like coffee and Ultima's stomach made a loud noise. Soren looked up in the direction of the sound.

"It appears I'm not the only one hungry this morning," said Prince Soren.

Ultima gave him a curtsy. "Good morning, Prince Soren, I didn't mean to interrupt your meal," said Ultima, and she turned to leave.

"Ultima, stop!" said Soren. Ultima stopped and looked back at the prince.

"Come sit and have a cup of coffee. Wait a moment, those animals put a collar on you," said Soren when he took a good look at Ultima.

"Otto told He'nico to take it off me," said Ultima. Soren said nothing about it further, but his irritation was evident by the rough way he called for the servant to bring food for Ultima.

"I'm really hungry," said Ultima.

"It is customary to wait and break one's fast with the lord of the castle, but I couldn't wait. And technically, I outrank him, so I arranged some food for myself, and now for you. Eat, we will not be in trouble. I doubt Barney would mind us eating without him," said Soren.

A servant appeared with food and coffee, and Ultima ate with gusto.

"How is Otto?" asked Soren.

"He still needs a healer," said Ultima, between sips of coffee and mouthfuls of food.

"I'll make sure he gets one today. I wanted to ask you how you knew that the Earl of Portmore was my twin brother's assassin? He has been with us all this time," Soren sat back and crossed his arms.

"Until the night of the fight, he hid his true voice. The entire time he was around me, he always sounded hoarse, with a raspy voice. Either he was coughing, whining, or not talking at all. It wasn't until after the battle with the Boleños at their camp that I heard his true voice. He was looking at the dying woman whom he held at sword point on the ground, and he said the same threatening words to her that he had said to me when he killed your brother. His voice was clear, and I recognized him. I knew it was him. It was the identical voice, timbre and choice of words as the man who killed your brother," said Ultima. By then, the Duke of Hausman had entered and joined them at the table, followed shortly after by the Duke of Vurthas who sat next to Ultima.

"We all knew he was a warrior by his skill with the sword. He must have had the warrior-tattoo and the shifter's extension. His status as a nobleman kept anyone from seeing his tattoo. Now we will never know since he died in his wolf form," said Soren.

"Noblemen don't have trade-tattoos, but he inherited the title when his father and both his older brothers died. He must have had a trade; he probably never expected to be earl," said the Duke of Hausman.

"I'm glad cousin Nancy isn't marrying him," said Prince Soren.

"Let's introduce her to my son, Zeino. Maybe they'll like each other. What say you, Robert?" said the Duke of Vurthas.

"Let's give her some time to mourn this creep. I think she really loved him," said Robert, the Duke of Hausman.

"She is better off this way," said Soren.

"How's Otto?" asked the Duke of Hausman.

"I just left his room. He is better than yesterday. Prince Soren, Otto wants to talk to you when you have a chance," said the Duke of Vurthas. As though drawn by the conversation, He'nico entered the dining hall a few minutes after his father.

"I'll be up in a few minutes," said Soren.

"If he is awake, I must bring him something to eat. He hasn't eaten anything in almost three days," said Ultima.

"Ultima before you take food to Otto, let's find the smith and see if he has pliers to cut that collar from your neck. Otto will be upset with me if I don't take that off you soon." He'nico smiled and winked at Ultima.

❖❖❖

Once He'nico arranged to cut the collar from Ultima's neck, she told the servants to bring porridge, some bread, and tea up to Otto's room. Ultima reached Otto's room just as he was trying to stand up. She ran to his side.

"What are you doing? You are barely healed," said Ultima.

"I need to use the chamber pot," said Otto. She helped him sit back down and brought over the chamber pot for him. Once done, when Otto was struggling back into bed, a servant entered with Otto's breakfast, and he finished helping him lie back down.

"Fine, you finished your call of nature. Now you need to eat something," said Ultima, bringing the porridge to his bedside.

"I'm not hungry," said Otto.

"Not acceptable. You must eat, even if it's a little. You have had nothing in your stomach for three days. Open your mouth, you must eat." Ultima used her magic to relax Otto. He said nothing but looked at her and opened his mouth. She fed him and he had just eaten enough to make her happy, when there was a knock at the door.

"Enter," said Ultima; it was Soren. He entered the room and stood by Otto's bed.

"Cousin, you look better than I had been told, but with such a wonderful healer I guess it was to be expected. I must thank you for saving my life."

"You are the future King of Tsestelago and a life worth saving," said Otto.

"Your father said you wanted to see me. What can I do for you?" asked Soren.

"I'll leave the two of you alone to talk. I'll be waiting outside." Ultima didn't wait for a response from Otto. She stood up, placed the plate of food on the table near the bed, and left, closing the door behind her.

She reclined by the wall of the hallway and waited. What would Otto want to talk about with Soren? The answer to that question could be anything, and it was best for her not to wonder. If Otto wanted to share with her, he would, but she tried to tell herself that she cared little one way or the other. Only a few minutes passed and Soren came out of the room.

"Ultima come here; Otto needs you," said Soren from the door. "I'll see you later, cousin. I sent for a healer to treat you at the behest of your wife. I think she is a better healer than she thinks, but who am I to know. I'm not a mage," said Soren, and he stepped out of the room and walked away.

Ultima entered the room, then opened the curtains and the windows to let some fresh air into the room. Otto fell asleep as soon as the cool air started to circulate around the room. Ultima lay down next to Otto and fell asleep in a few minutes.

❖❖❖

It was late in the afternoon when Ultima woke with a frozen nose. She got up and closed the windows.

"Thank you, I'm freezing. Only you kept me warm," said Otto.

"Why didn't you wake me?" asked Ultima.

"I like to watch you sleep."

"And you'd rather freeze?"

Otto smiled in reply.

"I'm leaving for Yakuta as soon as we return to Pailo if I'm strong enough to make the trip. And I need to know what you want." asked Otto.

"What do you mean?" Ultima looked at Otto and then at her hands.

"I need to know if you have feelings for Soren. When I asked him, he denied having an affair with you. I know you said you've never been unfaithful, and I want to believe you. But, Ultima, if we are to make this work you must tell me the truth. I must know if you love him," said Otto.

"I've already told you, no. I've never been unfaithful. And that is the truth."

"Do you want to be with me? I need to know," said Otto.

"Why are you asking all these questions?" asked Ultima.

"Ultima, I need you to be with me because you want to be, not because my father forced your hand," said Otto.

"I know you don't want me because I'm a tainted woman. And since you don't want me, I'll take Akina and leave," said Ultima. She turned and started to leave the room.

"NO! Wait. That's not what I said. I never said I didn't want you. You and Akina are mine. But I need to know what you want. I *want* to know what *you* want, and if you don't want me, then what is the point?" said Otto.

"I only know I want my Akina, I want to be free, and I want to be loved," said Ultima. She lit the candles and the lantern in the room and left.

❖❖❖

Ultima went to the room they provided for her and took a bath. The countess had lent Ultima a dress to wear for dinner that evening, and she wore it with a sash in the Vurthas colors to give it an accent. It was an interesting gathering. The Grand Duke of Hausman and Prince Soren were the highest-ranking nobles in the castle as the brother and the son of the King, respectively. The Earl of Polion and his wife did all they could to be gracious hosts.

Dinner went well, and they all enjoyed the company of the earl and his wife, but Ultima stayed mostly to herself.

She had been thinking on the conversation she had had with Otto Earlier. Did he really mean it when he asked her what she wanted? No one had ever asked her what she wanted. Ultima always did what others told her to do. Xawata had been her master from her childhood, and then her father-in-law had married her to his son, giving her no real choice in the matter. Refusal would have meant both she and Akina would have remained Exotic slaves. However, Otto gave her a choice twelve years ago when he let her choose whether or not to service him. And now he asked her to choose again. She could choose to stay or to go.

Choices in life were a new thing for her. Xawata let her choose her wardrobe and the colors to decorate her room. He let her choose how to teach Akina and he gave her control of the everyday workings of her own servants, but that was not having control of her own life. That was a mirage. Today, she needed to choose wisely. She needed to talk to Otto.

After dinner, Ultima excused herself under the guise of going to care for her husband. There was much she needed to say to Otto. The man needed to explain her options. She needed to understand.

Ultima walked up to the second floor and encountered a healer giving magical treatment to Otto. Otto appeared to be sleeping. She called a servant and had him light the fire in the fireplace, and then waited for the healer to finish his ministrations.

"Lady Hightower, I hear you were the healer who removed the knife from his chest," said the healer. The short mage was an old man who wore his pants with the waist reaching all the way up to the middle of his chest. He used suspenders to keep them up and he smelled of lavender.

"I tried my best," said Ultima.

"I know some nobles don't permit their daughters to get magical training. There ought to be a law against that type of nonsense. All mages regardless of status need mage training," said the old man, placing his vials of potions in his bag with trembling, aged hands.

"You are a powerful healer. I'm done here. He needs rest. His chest is completely mended," said the old man.

"How do you know he is fine?" asked Ultima.

"Girly, I am the best in the kingdom, better even than Healer Joe Goren himself," said the old man, his chest puffed out with pride.

"That is good to know," said Otto, giving his wife a smile.

"Bah, you two younglings have a good night. And you, young man, you are an exceptionally lucky Yakutan, having a healer for a wife. That knife almost pierced your right lung. And it came but a sliver from your kidney. It did damage your liver, but your wife patched that well enough for me to finish the job. You can eat, walk, and do most things, but avoid sword training or using your magic for a few weeks. You need to regain your energy reserves," said the old man, walking to the door.

"Thank you, Healer Senmonka," said Ultima. She followed him to the door and locked it after him.

It was good Otto was awake and in good spirits. She needed to talk to Otto tonight, and the man was going to answer. Ultima walked toward him, but before she reached Otto he was already sitting up, leaning against the headrest of the bed. On his chest, the stab wound was covered by a bandage and she stared at it, as though mesmerized.

"Thank you for lighting the fire. Healer Senmonka kept this room icy, like the Pikes Mountains. This room needs to warm up fast," said Otto.

"You are welcome," said Ultima.

"How was the dinner? You've returned early," said Otto.

"It was jovial." Ultima noticed the dark circles under Otto's eyes that she had seen earlier were no longer there.

"Why are you up here so early? I already ate. I don't need you to feed me, really. I feel better." Otto frowned and tried to reach her arm, but Ultima pulled her hand away.

"I need to ask you some questions and they can't wait." Ultima crossed her arms, looking down and away from Otto.

"Ask."

"I need to know … what … what you meant when you said earlier, 'If you don't want me, what is the point?'" asked Ultima.

Otto took a deep breath. "Simple, I don't want to be with someone who hates me. *I want* to be wanted. Ultima, I want to be respected and loved. I know you don't need me. You have so many skills you can do anything you wish, now that you are free. But do you want me?" asked Otto.

"I thought you wanted a respectable woman?" said Ultima. She turned and sat on the bed next to Otto, facing him.

"I want a woman who respects me and loves me. By fighting alongside us in the battle of the Pikes Mountain, you have brought honor to me and my family. You didn't sleep with Soren when he asked you to return to your old trade. You make me happy in bed, and I find I like to smell you and watch you sleep. I wanted children, but I can live without them. At least we have Akina. If you want me, I want you," said Otto, reaching for her hand again. This time Ultima let him hold her.

"Otto, let me tell you a little secret about me. You know I'm a harmonizer and healer mage. The day I found out I was a mage was the day Xawata sent for a midwife-witch to damage me internally. It was the day after Xawata had sold my virginity and he didn't want me getting with child.

"I was lying on my bed. She had my legs tied to my bed posts. The woman came at me with a pair of long, thin silver scissors and a long needle. I was so scared looking at the woman from my bed. She had made me drink a potion to make me sleepy, but it didn't work. She spoke an incantation that made me bleed. I was twelve and so scared. The woman sat by my feet, and I sang a lullaby that came into my mind. She barely got the instrument in me, when the woman fell into a waking-sleep type of state. Whatever she did made me bleed a little, but it did not injure my womb. The instrument barely entered me. I didn't feel any pain.

"When I stopped singing, the woman mostly woke, but still in some form of trance, she removed her instruments, cleaned them, placed them back into her bag, and then stood by my side. When Xawata's housewife entered the room to check in on me, she found me covered in blood, but awake and the witch standing next to me. The housewife asked if she was done, and I said yes, and the witch just left. She said nothing, so, I said nothing.

"That was when I realized I was a mage. After that moment, I prevented children, until the time I discovered I was with child with Akina. I kept my pregnancy quiet until I couldn't keep it a secret any longer, and Xawata had to let me have her. After Akina was born, I didn't want my insides damaged. So, I paid the next healer with the jewels I had been given as gratuities. The woman didn't hurt me and since then I've prevented children with all the means at my disposal," said Ultima.

"So, you can have children?" asked Otto.

"Yes, I can. I'm not damaged. The only thing stopping me from getting with child, was me," said Ultima.

"Would you consider having one with me?"

"Yes," said Ultima and Otto reached for Ultima and kissed her.

"I will hold you to that, as a promise," said Otto.

"That is fine," laughed Ultima, her smile bright.

"Don't laugh, I mean it," said Otto

"Why do you want children so badly?" asked Ultima.

"I come from a large family. I want a large family with the woman I love," said Otto.

"You what?" asked Ultima.

"I want a large family with you," said Otto.

"No, what you said before," said Ultima.

"That I love you? Are you surprised?" asked Otto.

"Yes, no one has ever loved me, aside from my daughter."

"You had best get used to the feeling. I love hard and my family loves freely," said Otto. And he talked about his brothers, and Ultima talked about her skills, and afterward they fell asleep in each other's arms.

❖❖❖

Ultima woke in the middle of the night with Otto caressing her nipples. The room was warm, and the only light was from the fire in the fireplace.

"What are you doing?"

"I'm trying to wake you," said Otto.

"You are supposed to have little energy," said Ultima, turning in Otto's arms to face him.

"I'm a lightning mage. How many times do I need to remind you, I draw energy from the air and the electrical waves of living things," said Otto, flipping a nipple up and down until it got perky.

"But, I've seen, you don't use your magic often," said Ultima.

"I don't use my gift near water or snow. It can easily kill anyone stepping in water nearby, even the people I don't intend on killing. I don't like to hurt people who don't deserve to die."

Otto then suckled Ultima's nipple. "When you give birth, will you let me taste your milk?" asked Otto, kissing the hollow of Ultima's neck.

"Yes!" Ultima traced Otto's nose with one finger, and they began a session of lovemaking.

♦♦♦

In the morning, Ultima woke alone.

Where's Otto? she thought. The man was never around in the mornings. The bed covers were all in knots. Otto and she had made love. For the first time in her life, it wasn't just sex. She made love with Otto the previous night and now she felt good about herself. All her life, her body had been used to provide sexual satisfaction to others. Her body wasn't really hers. It was the property of Xawata. He sold her and her skills. She was an object.

When she met Otto, her life changed. In her society, the only escape for prostitutes was the entrapment of marriage, often loveless—and almost never for Exotics—but for her it became freedom. As a slave, she made a few minor choices, but her master made her pay dearly for those, but now her body was her own. Her life was her own. And the previous night she had *chosen* to share her body with Otto, and she liked it. Ultima needed to learn to accept the changes. She had shared her body with a man she wanted. And he said he loved her. What did it mean to be loved? Ultima was going to find out. It would be different, now that she knew how Otto felt.

A little while later, Ultima descended the stairs and went to the dining hall. She had taken a bath earlier and was wearing a clean pair of pants the countess had given her. Ultima had lost all her armor, and both Jasper and Jade, her personal weapons. She had nothing, but she had her family. Interesting; she had her family.

When she entered the dining hall, she saw Otto already sitting and waiting for his meal. Soren, He'nico, and the Duke of Vurthas were also at the table. She wondered how Otto was going to behave toward her in front of his family. They had shared a bed many times before, but she felt much had changed this time.

The night before he specifically said he loved her—Ultima—not the Exotic, but Ultima. The previous day, Soren had confirmed to Otto what she had already told him, that she had never serviced Soren since being his wife. Otto said he wanted her to stay with him, but men were fickle beings and she expected little from Otto when surrounded by other men. She didn't know how men behaved when they loved.

When Otto saw her at the entrance, he stood up and walked slowly toward her.

"Come, I want you to sit next to me," said Otto to Ultima in hushed tones. He took her hand, and they walked together to the dining table. The Duke of Vurthas smiled at his son and daughter-in-law. Paul Donnelly entered the dining hall at that moment and sat with the group as well.

"Lady Ultima, did you sleep well last night?" asked Soren.

"Yes, and you?" Ultima saw a wicked grin on Soren's face.

"I couldn't sleep a wink, with all this ruckus I heard from the room next to mine. The noise went on and on until late last night," said Soren.

"Cousin, you are being an ass," said Otto.

"Otto, whatever that healer gave you, I want some of it. You went from a man almost dead to a savage lover," said Soren.

"Enough, you are making Ultima uncomfortable," said the Duke of Vurthas, drinking his tea.

"I didn't hear a thing, but then again, my room is on the third floor," said Marshal Donnelly, between sips of his coffee.

"Anyway, now that Otto is feeling better, we must get moving," said He'nico.

"Could we please travel by train? I'd give anything to travel by train," said Marshal Donnelly, lighting up a cigarette and continuing to drink his morning coffee.

"We can't take the trains. They are not working," said Ultima.

"That was what the Lord of Portmore said, remember," said Otto.

"Did any of you check if he was telling us the truth? That man was shifty, and he could have lied about the trains," said Ultima.

"No, we never actually checked on the truth about the trains," said He'nico.

"Damnation to hell, if that rat James Tanning lied to us about the train and had us traveling by road, I'm going to piss on his grave. And there's no way I'm going to continue giving him the honor of calling him the Earl of Portmore. I wonder what else he may have lied about and what other shit he might have done," said Otto.

"Hell, this is an easy fix. We go and ask the communication mages about the trains. If we are leaving by train from here, we can make it in seven days. These trains make many stops. Or we can take a train down to West Franken and take a fast connection to the capital from there.

I see Lord Otto is up and about. So, this will be an easier venture for us," said the Marshal.

"I'm with you. I don't want to ride on a horse unless I absolutely have to after this injury," said Otto.

"Have any of you given some thought to the assassin? If James Tanning was the assassin, someone must have paid him to do the job," said He'nico.

"I've been thinking about that as well," said the Duke of Vurthas.

"If we want to discover who the mastermind is behind my brother's assassination, we must reach Pailo," said Soren.

"No, there is another problem; Trevino's health is frail, and yet, my brother is stronger than me. I think there is either magic or foul play, but I can't prove it," said the Duke of Hausman.

"I say we should take Healer Senmonka with us. I have a feeling Healer Goren is not giving the King the best treatment," said Ultima.

"That man raised Otto from the dead and made him a bucking stallion. I'm taking him with us to the capital and making him my personal healer," said Soren.

"Are you ever going to stop?" Otto raised his voice.

"Nope, I'm jealous," said Soren, laughing his head off and drinking his coffee.

And the group continued talking about the impending travel back to the capital and laughing with intermittent jokes. Ultima wanted to believe all would be well, but she had a bad feeling about the entire plan of returning to the capital. There was something not right. She couldn't pinpoint what was making her feel apprehensive, but she kept her thoughts to herself and simply listened.

CHAPTER 29

Evil in His Home

The train rocked from side-to-side as it made its way back to Pailo.

"Your Grace, when we reach the capital, I have to report the death of the Earl of Portmore, and the circumstances behind his death. So, I will need to visit your manor in two days at most to get a declaration from you. You must expect a lawsuit from the family of the earl. Also, since the Duke of Horrel, at the request of the King, was the one that sent me with you to follow Lady Ultima, I must report to the duke. I'm getting a headache just thinking of the paperwork I must do," said Marshal Donnelly.

"We have many threads to follow up once we reach the capital. All investigations will be up to you, me, and Ultima. The person who hired the earl to kill the prince will now double his efforts in coming after us, since we killed his operative," said the Duke of Vurthas.

"Father, I don't like the idea of using Ultima as bait," said Otto, holding Ultima's hand.

"I understand son, but you know we must find the real killer. As long as you and I are near her, she will be fine. The house already has the wards that Caleb added, and He'nico will join us in ten days. Soren gave us those ten days to get as much information as we can gather before he arrives. We must do this fast," said the Duke.

"I still don't like this; I have a bad feeling about this plan. We should have stayed in West Franken for an extra day," said Ultima. Otto held Ultima's hand, and he gave it a squeeze.

"After we left Flora and spent those wretched six days on that cargo train to West Franken, I wasn't looking forward to any more time traveling. Three days in West Franken was enough time to rest. We need to get this plan under way," said the Duke of Vurthas.

"We will not let anything happen to you. I'll light up the city if I have to," said Otto.

"We will arrive in Pailo in about an hour. Gentlemen and Lady, I hope this plan works. I have serious doubts regarding your ideas of who the culprit is in all this, but I'll go along with you for now," said Marshal Donnelly.

They all stood and left the dining car, each going to their cabin. Otto and Ultima reached their cabin, where he turned to her and held her in his arms.

"I still think you should have stayed behind with He'nico," said Otto.

"You know I was the one that was present when Prince Marco died. Marshal Donnelly will need me to give a report to say that the earl was the killer," said Ultima.

"I know," said Otto.

They arrived at the busy train station, reaching the station at the worst time of day. When they stepped down onto the platform, Otto called for a porter to help them with their bags. There was no one waiting for the Duke of Vurthas, Otto, and Ultima as no one was supposed to know of their arrival. They collected their belongings, walked with haste through the crowd, hailed a horseless carriage for hire, and left for the manor.

When they arrived at the manor, Mr. Dobson and Mrs. Taneda hurried to greet them at the door.

"Your Grace, it is good to have you home, but we are afraid we have bad news for you," said the butler.

"I haven't even crossed the threshold of my door, but instead I'm received with bad news," said the Duke.

"Your Grace, we tried to send you a message, but you didn't leave us an address to send you any correspondence," said Mrs. Taneda.

"Come to my study, we can talk there," said the Duke.

"Oh no, Your Grace, it is best for us to give you the news here," said Mr. Dobson.

"Talk man, what is it," said the Duke, exasperated.

"The manor was ransacked, and your study was almost entirely destroyed. We don't know what the thieves were looking for, but when we entered the room in the morning everything was in disarray and destroyed, books, the desk, even the chairs," said Mrs. Taneda. As the butler and housewife were talking, the duke, Otto, and Ultima went to see how bad it really was. Arriving in the study, the duke was astonished to see that it looked like a tornado had passed through it. The servants had obviously tried to clean, but there was still so much destruction.

"When did this happen?" asked the Duke.

"About a week after you left, Your Grace," said Mr. Dobson.

"What else did they destroy?" asked Otto.

"Lady Ultima's room, and the Duke's room were also destroyed. We don't know how it happened. We went to bed one night and when we woke the next morning, we found destruction," said Mr. Dobson.

"No one heard anything, but when we looked around the property all we found were dog tracks. We called the marshal. The deputy came and said it must have been a rogue shifter mage. But we don't know any shifter mages that may be in dispute with Your Grace and felt sure you would have mentioned it before you left, if it were so," said Mr. Dobson.

"Call the Marshal's Office again, tell them I'm in residence. I also want to set a pack of Gargon wolves to guard the property," said the Duke of Vurthas.

"Father, Gargon wolves! Isn't that a little excessive? They train those wolves to kill. Once their trainers let them loose on the property, it doesn't matter who they find, they will kill until their masters recall them," said Otto.

"I've lost one son already, I won't lose you or Ultima," said the Duke.

"What if He'nico arrives unannounced?" asked Otto.

"We will post warning signs all around the perimeter of the property. Otto, I'll protect my family with everything at my disposal." He turned and left the room.

Ultima went to her room. Her bed was destroyed, and the furniture was useless.

"Mariza, take your mistress's things to my bedroom," said Otto, standing behind Ultima.

"What were they looking for in my room?" asked Ultima.

"I don't know. My room is fine, so you will not stay here." Otto took Ultima by the hand and led her from the room.

Later that evening, they had an early dinner, after which the Duke of Vurthas went to bed, so Otto and Ultima followed suit.

"Otto, do you think it will take us long to find information about who hired the earl?" asked Ultima.

"I don't know; everything is obscure these days." He shrugged, and got undressed and climbed into bed. Ultima changed into a nightgown and went to bed with Otto. She lay on her side, but Otto pulled her into his arms.

"I need you next to me, to know I can protect you. Please, would you stay in my arms?"

"Yes, but if I get hot, I'm moving away," said Ultima.

"Deal," and Otto closed his eyes and went to sleep.

❖❖❖

The next day Ultima dressed early and went to the Gayton Academy to visit Akina. She had to see her child. She had missed her terribly. Ultima had passed by the old Jarney Abbey buildings many times before, which now formed the Gayton Academy, but she had never been inside the walls of the school. Ultima found herself in the office of water master mage of the eighth order, Camila Justa, the assistant headmistress of the Gayton Academy. She was waiting to see Akina.

When she first arrived at the academy, a servant met her at the entrance and escorted her to Master Mage Justa's office. The place was old and had many wards and spells of protection. Ultima could feel them, she could almost see them in some corners. As she walked around the academy, Ultima noticed that the designation of each building was named after a class of magic: arcane, mental, elemental, healing. When she entered the main building called the Kigledan building, there were offices full of floating papers and ringing bells, with people casting spells to keep things moving. There were mages trying to keep birds in line while they adjusted mail inside a round mail holder tied to their legs. A mage made a broom sweep paper from the floor while she wrote a letter. Ultima saw into one of the offices where a little elf woman sat by her desk, making her spoon stir her tea while she read her mail. Ultima had never seen so much magic freely showcased and accepted.

Her Akina was a strong arcane mage, and she had an affinity to perform charms. Ultima wondered how the young girl was doing in her new school.

She waited and waited, but sitting still for so long, she got bored. There were a pair of little dice with eight faces on top of the desk, so Ultima levitated the dice. Magic was suffused throughout that school. She knew it would be easy for her to levitate the small dice, so she focused and started to play.

She concentrated and lifted them from the table, made them roll and bounce. She moved them from side-to-side as if tossing them in a game of catch. Ultima was having so much fun with the dice until a hand swiped the dice mid-air.

"You are a mage, and yet I don't know you," said the woman. Ultima stood up and looked at the woman directly.

"I'm not registered," said Ultima.

"I'm Master Mage Camila Justa, the Assistant Headmistress of Gayton Academy," said the slim and serious-looking redheaded woman.

"I'm Lady Ultima Hightower."

"Rogue mages are against the law," said Master Mage Justa.

"I had no choice. I was a slave, and my owner kept my magic a secret. He treated to kill me and later my daughter if I made my magic known."

"You are Lady Akina Hightower's mother, and you were a slave?" said the woman and Ultima raised the sleeve of her right arm and showed the mark burned into her skin.

"You were a courtesan, but with all those added skills?" asked the woman.

"Needless to say, my master made much coin from me." Just then Akina entered the office and when she saw Ultima she ran to her mother's arms.

"Momma, it's so good to see you. I missed you terribly every day. How is Father? How is Grandpa Gareth and Uncle Caleb? Wait until I tell you what happened." Akina was her exuberant self.

"Before you leave, we will talk again, Lady Hightower," said Camila and she stepped out of the office.

"Momma, you look tired. When did you come back from your trip?" asked Akina, sitting down on a chair opposite her mother's.

"We have been in town for less than a day, but I had to come and see you. You look happy," said Ultima.

"It's a hard school. I've been learning a lot of things," said Akina.

"Have you made any friends?" asked Ultima, reaching for Akina's hands.

"I have three: Leer, Joy-Anna, and Cascade. They are more trouble than they're worth, but they saved my life two or three times," said Akina, smiling.

"What? Saved your life? What kind of school is this that would risk my daughter's life?" Ultima raised her voice and stood up. That was when Master Mage Camila entered the office again.

"Why would a student need to save my daughter's life?" demanded Ultima.

"Calm down, Lady Hightower, the students play a game that teaches them to be battlemages. Their lives are never in danger. As they learn to use their magic, they rely on their skills and those of their partners. As they go through the obstacles, they gain knowledge. At the end of the year if they completed the game and gained all the skills for the level, they get to move up to a higher level in the game. The higher in the game they move, the higher their level or order of magic. I'm a level eight water master mage. I was told your husband is a level nine lightning master mage," said Camila.

"Momma, I must finish the school year, so I can fight through the level and be a level one arcane mage," said Akina.

"Great! I see you like your magic training," said Ultima.

"Yes, Momma! I like it a lot, much better than my Exotic training." Akina was all smiles.

"Akina, now you've seen your mother, you must return to class," said Camila.

"Yes, Master Mage Justa. I love you, Momma. When can I see you again?" asked Akina.

"I'll come see you in a few days," said Ultima.

"Good, I'll see you soon. I love you, Momma. Tell Uncle Caleb I'm learning to be a good arcane mage, just like he is." Akina gave Ultima a hug and skipped out of the room with her mother's voice trailing after her.

"I love you, Akina of my heart."

"Akina was an Exotic student?" Camila asked, one eyebrow shot up.

"I was the Exotic slave Ultima Leighton Skylar. My slave master was forcing me to train Akina as an Exotic. He was doing to her what he had done to me, depriving her of magical training and of her childhood. When her grandfather came and got us out of the trade, he gave her the opportunity to learn magic. Me, I'm learning from books, and from mages who are willing to teach me things here and there." Ultima talked, looking down at her hands.

"Lady Hightower, you are welcome to come and train with our healers anytime you like. As for your telekinesis, you will need a special teacher for that one," said Master Mage Camila.

"How do you know of my healing magic?" asked Ultima.

The headmistress laughed, "That is part of my magic. Come, let me give you a tour of the school," said Camila.

❖❖❖

Three days later, the Duke of Vurthas was breaking his fast when Otto and Ultima came down.

"Good morning," said Ultima from the door. They entered and Otto pulled out the chair for her to sit.

"Good morning. How are you?" asked the Duke.

"I'm so tired from this trip. I think I need to sleep for a week to recover," said Ultima. A servant came and served her some fruit, a portion of eggs, pastries, and coffee.

"It was eventful," said the Duke, lowering the newspaper he had been reading. The servants came and served Otto his ham, eggs, toasts, potatoes, and some coffee; his usual morning choices.

"I found the shields that Caleb enchanted to reflect magic. It was a good thing the thieves didn't know the value of those shields," said Otto.

"I still don't know what they were looking for in my room. Nothing is missing," said Ultima.

"I'm still taking inventory of my study," said the Duke.

"Father, we need to have an audience with King Trevino in the next two days, at most. And we must send word to

King George of the things that are happening here. This can't be delayed," said Otto.

"Son, we must be patient. If Soren arrives and we haven't caught the leader of the assassins, what do you think will happen? They will hire another assassin to go after Soren. We still don't know why Soren never received his messages at the battlefront. Someone is trying to usurp the throne and we must find out not only who it is, but we must also find the evidence to prove it," said the Duke, and he took a long sip from his coffee.

"I think we need to let everyone know we're back in town. The lead assassin, who wanted me killed, may send someone else to try again. If I serve as bait, we can then catch him, but could we please make sure we have the Gargon wolves patrolling the house first," said Ultima.

"Listen to this, here in the morning paper, it says that a new tax is going to be implemented on all goods imported from Alhambra, making the *New Start Treaty* with Alhambra and Yakuta null and void," said the Duke of Vurthas.

"That can't be. We signed that treaty in good faith only a year ago," said Otto.

"I'll send a message to King George this morning and another to King Trevino. There has to be a reason Trevino had rescinded the treaty," said the Duke.

"What is this *New Start Treaty* you are talking about?" asked Ultima.

"Essentially, the treaty said that Tsestelago would help Alhambra during their war by not increasing taxes on goods imported from Alhambra, and Yakuta would do the same. In exchange, Alhambra was to provide the black powder Trevino needed for his weapons, giving a twenty-five percent discount on the cost," said Otto.

"It is insanity to back away from such an advantageous treaty. There has to be something wrong going on," said the Duke of Vurthas.

"Father, this sounds like the machinations of that maniac, Jadro, from Alhambra," said Otto.

"We all know Jadro and pray he is not instigating the turmoil here in Tsestelago. I will need to let Trevino know about our plans for trying to figure out who the mastermind is behind Marco's assassination, now that we know that the Earl of Portmore was the man who actually carried out the assassination," said the Duke of Vurthas.

"There is too much at stake in the kingdom. Soren has given us only ten days to find as much information as we can gather. And the brunt of the information gathering task belongs to Marshal Donnelly. But now we have the ransacking of our home to add to our problems," said Otto.

"Who could have done such a thing? And what were they looking for in the manor? It makes no sense," said Ultima, between listening and eating her meal.

"I don't know. I must go and tend to some business. Are you going to retrieve Akina from the academy?" asked the Duke.

"No, she will stay there until we go home. Father, I'm taking my family to Yakuta. We are leaving Tsestelago in the next few weeks. I'm sorry, Father, but I've had enough of Tsestelago. If you stay here, I'll send Zeino or Pelatano to support you," said Otto.

"As soon as we help find the lead assassin, I'll be leaving as well. I miss your mother. Anyway, I'll see you both later," said the Duke of Vurthas and he stood up and left Otto and Ultima alone.

"Are you assuming you'll be taking me and Akina with you to Yakuta?" asked Ultima, once the duke had gone from the room.

"Ultima, you are a free woman; you can stay if that is what you desire. But Akina is registered as my daughter and I'm taking my daughter with me," said Otto, with a smile.

"You are a horrible man. You know Akina is mine," said Ultima.

"Well, I guess you'll be coming along with us." And with that, Otto stood up, gave Ultima the sexiest of smiles and bent down to kiss her.

"I love you, Ultima Hightower. I must go to town. I have some business to attend to. Don't wait for me to eat the noon meal; I'm not sure if I'll be back for midday. I'll see you later," said Otto, and he left the parlor.

CHAPTER 30

Mage Training

After breaking her fast, Ultima went to change into a traveling dress. She wanted to be presentable, but with clothing that was both practical and that would not be a problem if soiled.

Picking up her coat, reticule, and gloves, she gave instructions to the housekeeper, "Mrs. Taneda, I'm going to the Gayton Academy. I'll be visiting Akina, and I also arranged to have some healer lessons for myself. If Lord Otto arrives before I do and he asks where I am, please advise him where I went," said Ultima.

"I will, my Lady. Should we expect you for the midday meal?" asked the housewife.

"Yes, I will try to return by late morning. And please call a seamstress? I need some new dresses," said Ultima. She called for a carriage and left the manor soon after, going straight to Gayton Academy. Water Master Mage Justa had said she could have magic lessons starting that week and that a mage expert in telekinesis would work with her as well. She had some training for her healing magic, but she had used her telekinesis magic by instinct. For years, she had looked for books on telekinesis, but had not found any books on the subject.

Ultima was looking forward to her lessons and meeting mages who could help her control her magic. Ultima's eagerness made her sick to her stomach. She needed to get started to calm her nerves. The carriage rocked and bumped its way across town. As she traveled the streets of Pailo, she had never noticed how far from the inner city the academy was located.

When Ultima finally arrived, Master Telekinetic Jericho was waiting for her at the entrance of the abbey's main gate. Assistant Headmistress Justa had assigned him as an instructor for Ultima when she last visited the academy.

"Hello Lady Hightower, it is good to see you again," said Master Jericho.

"As Mistress Justa said last time we saw each other, I'll be your instructor, but we will have a student come and give us a hand later today," said the man. He had a patch over his left eye. Master Jericho couldn't have been older than forty, but he looked battle worn. He stood upright, with his hands behind his back.

"Hello, Master Jericho, it is good to see you. How are you today?" asked Ultima.

"I'm well, thank you." He gave Ultima a slight bow, and he showed the way with his right hand, from which, Ultima noticed, the man lacked two fingers. "If you care to walk this way, Lady Hightower. We have much to go over, and we only have a little under two hours to spare for you this morning. I'll be lending you a book to read. It will provide some information on your magic," said the mage.

"Thank you, I appreciate anything you can do for me," said Ultima.

"I trust you understand, you can never reach any degrees of magic. At least not in any academies in Tsestelago. We don't have the facilities to evaluate you, but we will train you in the basics and intermediate levels," said Master Jericho.

"Why can't I get a mage degree?" asked Ultima.

"The way the mages get their degrees within mage orders is by learning the skills throughout the year. At the start of the year, we place each student in a group of four members where they work as a team all year. At the end of the year, they enter an arena of obstacles. They must use what they've learned throughout the year to get to the end of the course as a team. If one team member fails, the entire team fails, and they must repeat the year. There is no way for us to make a team of four adults," said Master Jericho.

"Surely there must be a way to get four adults in need of training," said Ultima.

"You don't understand. The teams are composed of one elemental mage, one mental mage, one arcane mage, and one healer mage. We have very few arcane mages, so in the absence of arcane mages, we are allowing two elemental mages, one mental and a healer," said Jericho.

"Now I understand," said Ultima.

"In your case, I hear you are a healer, and you also have mental qualities. That is so rare that we encounter this maybe once in a hundred thousand mages. I have never met someone with those abilities in my entire adult life, until you," said Master Jericho.

"Will you believe my father-in-law is one also? He is both an elenchus and a master water mage," said Ultima.

"Now that type of combination is more common. To have an elemental mage with a mental combination," said Master Jericho as they were walking through the hallways of the abbey.

"He and his sons are impressive with their elemental master magic," said Ultima.

"I bet they are. May I confirm, Lady Akina Hightower's birth father is a mage?" asked Master Jericho.

"Yes, I did just say the Hightowers are all mages. Why are you asking?" asked Ultima.

"Just an observation. She has a fantastic affinity for magic. You must be proud of your daughter. She has been doing very well for having missed the first few months of the academic year," said Master Jericho. They continued walking, out from the building, across a path alongside a well-kept lawn and on toward a tall and imposing house.

"She knows how to study," said Ultima. They reached the structure, smaller than a manor but much larger than a house.

"This is where we are going to train. This is Letcher's house," said the master telekinetic as they entered the building. Once inside, they first encountered a set of stairs directly ahead of them, with a hallway to the right of it. There was a large room to the immediate left, and another large room to the right of the stairs, both rooms with barn doors.

"Please, we are going to the room on our left," said Master Jericho, waving Ultima forward. When Ultima entered the room, there were tables against every wall, full of large and small objects of different materials. There were small wooden boxes, tiny wooden horses, porcelain dolls, silver spoons, large crystal vases, bricks, marbles, feathers, pens, long rulers, metal sticks, a cane against a wall, umbrellas inside a trash bin, coins in a tin box, teacups, tea plates, and many other objects. There were chairs and toy trucks of varying sizes and colors, dolls and stuffed animals, and things in disarray across the floor of the room.

Ultima saw the room, and immediately wanted to pick things up and organize the items by material or by color. It all seemed chaotic to her. She didn't know where to stand. There were so many random things on the floor. She looked at Master Jericho with a frown. What was this all about? How was this mess going to help her with her telekinesis?

"Lady Ultima, your first lesson in telekinesis is going to be to control your power. I need to know the extent and limitations of your magic. I need to know from where you draw your energy. So, consider this a test," said Master Jericho.

"I'm ready," said Ultima.

"There are many things in this room. Part of our magic is being able to find things that are lost. It isn't always easy, and it requires a lot of practice, but I want you to try. In this room, there is an ashtray made of pure onyx. I want you to try to find it. When you find it, I want you to tell me where it is. If you're ready, I need you to take a deep breath, close your eyes, and let your magic flow," said Master Jericho. Ultima took a deep breath and did what she was told. She closed her eyes and tried hard to let her magic flow. She felt her magic come to her, but she couldn't do what he was asking.

"I can't do it," said Ultima.

"That is fine. Don't be discouraged. Now, look around the room and find the royal-blue umbrella. Do you see it?" asked the mage.

"Yes, it's in the trash bin," said Ultima.

"Good, I want you to lift it and make it come to your hand," said the Mage Jericho. Ultima smiled. That she could do, she had levitated things before, and the umbrella wasn't a large object. She took a deep breath, pointed at the umbrella, and the umbrella lifted from the bin, evaded the few objects in its way, and she caught it in her hands. She had a big smile when she was done.

"Nicely done. And you could evade the objects in its way. Now, let's see how heavy an object you can levitate. Do you see the bucket of bricks on the floor?" asked Master Jericho, and Ultima nodded.

"I want you to make them come to my hand this time," said Master Jericho.

"This is new. I have always made the objects come to me, never go someplace else," said Ultima.

"Well, just give it a try," said Master Jericho. Ultima again took a deep breath, looked at the bucket of bricks. She pointed with her right hand, and the bucket slowly lifted from the ground. The bucket levitated and moved an inch at a time toward Master Jericho until it reached the man's hand. Ultima's brow was beaded with sweat, and her cheeks were flushed with the effort. She had held her breath most of the time while levitating the bricks.

Out of breath, Ultima leaned over, resting her hands on her knees, and said, "Oh, I feel nauseous." She huffed and puffed a bit more, still bent over and now closed her eyes. "How did I do?"

"That was a great first try. However, to progress, first, you must breathe while doing your magic. Second, you must never use your body's energy to fuel your magic. And third, you must always maintain awareness of your surroundings. Look behind you," said Master Jericho.

"Gasp!" When Ultima looked behind her, there was a rapier pointing at her.

"All the time you were using your energy doing your magic, I had a rapier pointing at your back. Our magic is dangerous and we can be lethal in a battle, but we must know how to use our magic well. Now relax and take a drink of water. Here, I have a glass of water for you; take several deep breaths which will help with your nausea," said the mage.

Ultima and Master Jericho trained for the two hours Jericho had promised. After two hours passed, Akina entered.

"Hello Momma, I'm so happy you're taking lessons with Master Jericho.

"Oh, Akina love, what are you doing here? Is she the one that will come and help us?" asked Ultima to master Jericho.

"I thought you would like to see her. I'll leave you here. I have a class of second years to teach. I'll see you tomorrow, Lady Ultima." And Master Jericho turned and left the room.

"I am here to escort you back to the entrance of the academy, and I want to introduce you to my friends." Akina had arrived with three young people in tow: a girl with blond hair and a young boy who looked exactly like Prince Marco, and the third was a boy as happy as the sunshine in a meadow, with black hair and dark, slanted eyes.

"Mother, these are Leer and Joy-Anna, Prince and Princess of Tsestelago. And that is my dear friend Lord Cascade from Ambria. He has black hair just like you and me. We four are a team here at the academy. I am the arcane mage of the team," said Akina.

"It is a joy to make your acquaintance, young ones," said Ultima.

"Lovely to meet you, Lady Hightower," said Prince Leer.

"Akina talks about you all the time," said Joy-Anna.

"She said Master Tanita Okino trained you how to use weapons. My father had me trained by Master Okino as well," said Cascade.

"Mother, you must read the book Master Jericho lent you, and you must practice every day. Knowing Master Jericho, he will expect you to read a page or two of the book tonight before you come back here again tomorrow at the same time," said Akina.

"Akina, Leer, before I go. I need your assurances that the teacher mages and senior mages are not trying to make you do things against the crown," said Ultima.

"The teachers keep us away from the general population of mages," said Leer as they walked through the academy's buildings.

"Leer and Joy-Anna, you both are the future archimages of the kingdom, you need to be watchful. We believe there has been a breaking between the leaders in the Kingdom and I want you to be careful," said Ultima.

"Yes, Lady Ultima, after our father's assassination we have been staying alert. And we have guards protecting us," said Leer. Giving a hug and a kiss to her daughter when they reached the front door, Ultima smiled and said her goodbye to the others

"We must go, Momma. I'll see you tomorrow." And Akina and her friends left running.

❖❖❖

Ultima arrived home, and was stepping out of her carriage, just as Otto returned from his business meetings.

"Ultima, where have you been? You didn't say you would be going out," said Otto when he saw her.

"Hello, I have news. I went to visit Akina the other day. When the assistant headmistress of the Gayton Academy found out I'm a mage, but have never had lessons, she said I should get lessons at the academy. I went for my first lesson today." Ultima said it with a smile spreading from ear to ear.

"That's wonderful news. How did you do in your lesson?" asked Otto.

"I did as well as could be expected. I loved my lesson," said Ultima, as she entered the manor, passing her gloves to Dobson. Book in hand, she entered the parlor, followed by Otto.

"Ultima, why didn't you tell me you were going to get lessons before going to the academy this morning?" asked Otto. Ultima sat down and paused for a moment to give it some thought.

"I didn't tell you because before we left for the mountain, you wouldn't let me leave the manor. I was a hostage in this place. I wanted to have the lessons so badly that I couldn't bear for you to tell me I wasn't permitted to go. In the event you said 'no,' I would have gone against your will, which in turn would have brought strife between us," said Ultima.

"I understand, but next time, talk to me. I know we were overprotective with you before we left for the mountains, but there was an attempted assassination against you, and we were worried about you. The assassin is dead now, so I'm glad about your lessons." Otto gave Ultima a kiss and took her hand. "Come, let's have our midday meal, but first, tell me, how is Akina?" asked Otto.

"She loves the academy. And she keeps asking for Caleb. I don't have the heart to tell her what happened," said Ultima.

"Don't tell her while she's in school. It will only make her sad. We'll tell her together when she's home with us," said Otto, as a servant brought them their tea and meal.

❖❖❖

The next day, Ultima, Lord Otto, and the Duke of Vurthas were in the parlor eating their midday meal. They were talking about all they had discovered while visiting in town. Apparently, the King had been bedridden for weeks, and the Queen was kept away from the King to prevent him from being exposed to further illness she might carry with her.

The King's sister had been sent as an emissary to Behui, and the Marquis of Lorlay, the oldest son of the Duke of Hausman, was made to deal with the fishermen's guild. They were most disturbed by events, and they told Ultima that almost all the treaties with Yakuta had been rescinded.

"You don't know the worst part," said Otto.

"Oh, this gets worse?" asked Ultima.

"Archimage Saigai is now the interim regent. He isn't even a member of the royal family," said Otto.

"I'm concerned that our messages may not get through with everything I've heard, but we have got to try to contact Soren. He must return to Pailo, now, and Hausman will have to take control of the House of Dukes. Soren must take charge of the kingdom without delay," said the Duke of Vurthas.

"I sent word to Marshal Donnelly that we have to change the timeline. He will not have his ten days," said Otto. They had not finished talking when a servant entered the parlor and announced that Marshal Paul Donnelly was at the manor.

"I'll receive him in the study. He is surely here to talk about the Earl of Portmore. He did say the family may file a lawsuit, and he was going to update us on the matter," said the Duke of Vurthas.

"Father, Soren gave you a pardon with the Duke of Hausman as witness," said Otto.

"That will only count if Soren comes to the capital and makes it official with the city clerks," said the Duke. Ultima stayed silent, absorbing everything the men said. She didn't feel like talking that afternoon.

"Ultima, you need to come with us. He may have questions for you if this visit is in regard to the Earl of Portmore," said the Duke of Vurthas.

The three of them walked to the study, and there they found Marshal Donnelly in his customary long, brown coat, under which he wore his tailored suit.

"Hello, Donnelly, how are you?" asked the Duke of Vurthas. Marshal Donnelly gave the duke a slight bow.

"Hello, Your Grace. I hope you are doing well. I heard there was a disturbance in your home. Someone came and ransacked your manor while we were up Pikes Mountain. I have my best men investigating the case. However, there are very few leads since none of your servants saw anything, and they can't even say if there was anything stolen," said Donnelly.

"I'm distressed over this event. They destroyed my study, my room, and Ultima's room," said the Duke.

"Do you know if they stole anything?" asked Donnelly.

"I still haven't gone through my entire study. As you see, it is still a mess," said the Duke.

"I see... well keep my office informed if you become aware of anything missing. In the meantime, I'm here for three reasons. The first is to tell you that, as expected, the family of the Earl of Portmore has pressed charges against you. So, it is my duty to let you know you are in litigation, and you will need the services of a lawyer. Second, I'm here to get an official account of what happened to the earl from you and Lady Ultima," said the Marshal.

"And the third reason is?" asked Otto.

"My deputies have a theory that the messages are not getting through to the front lines because the communication mages are not sending the messages. My men think the mages have some sort of issue with the King, or there is a traitor within the mage community trying to overthrow the royal line. They think it is all connected to the assassination of Prince Marco," said Donnelly.

"It makes sense," said Otto.

"You are all mages. I need one of you to infiltrate the mage society and find out if there is any foul play within the group. Mages are a tight community. They keep to themselves, and there is no way for my men to infiltrate that group," said Marshal Donnelly.

"I don't know how we can do that, but we will try," said Otto.

❖❖❖

The following day, Ultima woke, tired and feeling quite nauseous. They had been in Pailo for over two weeks, and things were getting more complicated as the days went by and more information was found and confounded them. She went to the academy every day for magic lessons. Ultima spent two hours with Master Jericho and two hours with Master Verity practicing her healing magic.

Ultima was getting better as time passed, and she visited with Akina every day. It was comforting to know she could help her family if there were ever the need again, like when they were in the mountains. Healing was a lot more than calling energy to an affected area. It was a work of love and compassion.

She woke before Otto, sat on her side of the bed, and vertigo swept over her. She had to wait a few seconds until her world stopped spinning. Then she took a step away from her bed and ran to the toilet. Ultima vomited what little she had in her stomach. She had not been feeling well for days. Ultima cleaned herself and went back to the room.

Her body felt tired and lethargic, but she sat to read the book Master Jericho had lent her. The book was on the fireplace mantlepiece, so she used her magic to make the book levitate toward her. Ultima was getting better at moving objects around.

She tried to read, but she couldn't concentrate. Her mind dwelled on her sick stomach and the way she had been feeling lately. Ultima had to stop making excuses for herself. She needed to see a healer. She couldn't keep feeling sick every morning and throughout the day.

CHAPTER 31

The Return to the Trade

Ultima sent word to her mage instructors that she couldn't take her lessons that day, so she had the entire morning to herself. The night before she had told Mariza to call for a healer. They had been back at the manor for two weeks, and for the entire time, they worked to get the manor back to its original state of beauty. Now Ultima needed to take care of her own problem. When she and Otto had first left the manor for the mountains, their interactions had been on bad terms, but their relationship blossomed. Now her courses were late, for over three months, and she was never late.

The healer arrived mid-morning, and Lady Ultima met with her in the front parlor. The woman entered the parlor with a large bag in her hand. Ultima thought she had the biggest gray eyes she'd ever seen on anyone. She wore a long dress, with a thick black belt over her protruding, very pregnant, belly, and she wore a wig with bangs. She looked odd with the wig.

"Hello Lady Hightower, I'm Healer Belem," said the woman.

"Hello Healer Belem, thank you for making an exception and seeing me so quickly with such short notice," said Ultima.

"My Lady Hightower, let's take care of your illness. Where does it hurt? Do you have a wound or are you ill?"

"I don't have an illness or a wound. I have another problem. I think I'm with child and I need you to confirm my suspicions," said Ultima.

"And this was the emergency? A pregnancy is hardly anything of urgency, unless—are you planning to get rid of it? In that case, the sooner we do the procedure the better."

"I just need to know. I'm older, and I've contracted sexual diseases before and I've heard that once a woman has had those, a child can be born sickly," said Ultima.

"Oh, you used to be a prostitute?" asked the healer.

"No, I used to be an Exotic," said Ultima.

"Exotics can't have children," she responded by habit.

"I was never damaged."

"*This* I need to see. Where can we go for me to check on you?" asked Healer Belem.

"Let's go to my bedroom."

♦♦♦

"If I hadn't seen it, I would not have believed it. You are with child," said Healer Belem.

"That is splendid news," said Ultima.

"Oh, I'm sure it is for you. You are about four months pregnant. We saw the signs of life and since you are a healer, I showed you what to do, so you could show your husband if you wish. Now, what do you want me to do? If by any chance you think to terminate your pregnancy, I am obliged to tell you it will be dangerous now. It will cause great pain for you, and you may even lose your life. The child is too big, but if that is what you want, it would be best to do this as soon as possible," said the healer.

"No, this is my choice. I want my child," said Ultima.

"If you change your mind, just call for me, but you can't wait too long. I will not terminate the child beyond this week. You would lose your life," said the healer.

"I understand. I already have a daughter," said Ultima, getting dressed.

The healer left, and Ultima, delighted with the news, couldn't wait to share it with Otto. A child was on the way. She decided she would tell Otto that night when they were alone in their room. Ultima had made her decision, and she knew he would welcome her choice. Once she had the news confirmed that morning, she had been giddy and happy.

※※※

Later that day, Otto, Ultima, and the Duke of Vurthas were having their midday meal together. They were having their coffee, when Marshal Donnelly was announced. He had come to the manor that day to see both the Duke of Vurthas and Lord Otto.

Ultima remained in the parlor while the men left to meet Marshal Donnelly in the study. Although she had a book in her hands, she tried to read to no avail. Her mind dwelled on the news she had for Otto. She was preoccupied with all the ramifications. Why did she let it happen?

What would Otto say? Would he be happy? He said he wanted to get her with child, but was he being truthful with her ... with himself? Ultima started thinking that he had been talking in jest. He couldn't be serious.

Mrs. Taneda disrupted her reverie when she came running to the parlor.

"Lady Ultima, please come, you must come. The marshal is arresting the Duke and Lord Otto, and he wants to see you too," said Mrs. Taneda with an anxious look on her face.

"What? No!" Ultima ran through the halls of the manor. Her book lay, forgotten.

"What is going on, Marshal Donnelly? What are you doing?" asked Ultima. Only then did she see the Duke of Horrel standing with a guard alongside the marshal. Otto and the Duke of Vurthas were being arrested, taken away in an official carriage used by the marshals for common criminals.

"Lady Ultima, you will be taken back to The Kasaka Brothel, formerly known as Xawata's Brothel. The Duke of Horrel has formally filed a lawsuit against the Duke of Vurthas for your sale, and he has won the case. You belong to him. Your marriage has been annulled. He is here to take you back to the brothel," said Marshal Donnelly.

"Oh, she is no Lady. She is the Exotic Ultima Skylar," said the Duke of Horrel.

"What will happen to the Duke of Vurthas and my husband?" asked Ultima.

"He's not your husband," shouted the Duke of Horrel.

"The Duke of Vurthas has been charged with forgery of a business contract, theft, and the tampering of a trade-tattoo. You husband has been charged with tampering with the trade-tattoo of a slave and …" Marshal Donnelly couldn't finish his sentence.

"Enough explanation. She is a slave. Where is her collar?" asked the Duke of Horrel of the servant he had brought with him. The servant came forward and gave him a golden collar with a ruby encrusted in it. Ultima took a step back.

"No, I'm a married woman. I'm carrying my husband's child. I can't be a slave," said Ultima.

"You are a liar. Exotics cannot be mothers. Xawata had you damaged internally when you were young," said the Duke of Horrel.

"No, he didn't, how did you think I had my first daughter with Lord Otto?" demanded Ultima.

"Ah, the child, Akina, I can't legally touch the child. Lord Otto recognized the child as his daughter, and Xawata did have her registered as your daughter," said Horrel.

"Mr. Dobson, Mrs. Taneda, please make sure to send a message to Lord He'nico about everything that has happened here as soon as possible," said Ultima.

"Lady Ultima, I'm sure the servants know to send a message to Lord He'nico and to the Duke of Hausman at the inn in Norval, today," said the Marshal, giving her a stilted smile. A servant held Ultima still, as the Duke of Horrel placed the cold collar around her neck.

He lifted her hair, placed the collar and secured it. The cold touch of metal on her skin was like receiving a slap to her face.

"Don't pack any of my things or send them to the brothel. He must provide me with everything anew," said Ultima to the servants with the arrogance all Exotics had.

"Lady Ultima, what about little Lady Akina?" asked the housekeeper, Mrs. Taneda.

"Lady Akina is a Hightower. Her custody will now fall to Lord He'nico until Lord Otto is released from jail," said Ultima.

"Let's go, Ultima," said the Duke of Horrel. Ultima didn't look at the Duke of Horrel. He grabbed Ultima by the arm and pulled her out of the manor as if she were a rag doll. The servants looked on and Ultima's eyes watered, but she didn't cry.

She rode in a carriage with the Duke of Horrel, and the man placed his odious hand on her leg.

"Don't touch me," said Ultima, pushing his hand off her.

"I'll touch you if and whenever I want to, you are my property," said the Duke, holding tightly onto her leg, no doubt leaving bruises there as was his wont.

"I'm a Lady in the Yakutan Ducal House of Vurthas and neither you nor anyone else can change that fact," said Ultima.

"A judge ruled in my favor, and now you are mine. I had to send a few men to the Vurthas manor to find the contract Xawata signed selling you. After looking everywhere, they found it, but not your old golden collar. I thought you would have saved it. I wanted it back. It was worth over ten gold coins and I wanted you to wear it again," said Horrel.

"So, you were the one behind the ransacking of the manor," said Ultima.

"I said I would get you back. I'll be calling a healer to get rid of this child. You will not damage your body" said Horrel.

"I will be out of your brothel in no time," said Ultima.

"We will see about that. You will have your new tattoo first thing in the morning," said the Duke. The ride to the brothel was the longest ride through the city she had ever had. The city streets looked dirty. She realized her dire situation. Her neck and her head hurt. The tension in the back of her neck made her want to scream. How could she be a slave in a brothel once more? Otto said she was a free woman. Otto said she didn't have to do anything she didn't want to do, but now she was going back to a life of sexual servitude.

When they reached the brothel, a servant opened the door, Horrel had Ultima by her wrist, and pulled her through the door. Mr. Lovewell, the butler, wasn't at the door. It was a beefy man in a butler's suit. Horrel had made many changes. The front gallery of the brothel had been redesigned to look more masculine. Horrel walked through the brothel like a man who knew his property well, until he reached Ultima's old working room. When they reached the room, Horrel opened the door and pushed Ultima inside.

"Here, *love*, this is your old room. Your workspace is ready for you. You will have two clients tonight. And don't worry about what to wear. I have ordered a few items for your work tonight. It's nothing extravagant," said Horrel.

"You changed things," said Ultima. The room had less furniture, and the paintings … where were the paintings?

"Xawata had this place looking like a museum. This is a whorehouse," said Horrel, as he turned to leave.

"Wait! What about my private room? I need my private room," said Ultima.

"Oh yes, I almost forgot about that. Orrun come here! I know you have been waiting for your mistress," shouted Horrel, and the servant Orrun entered the room. He had a black eye, and cast his eyes down to the floor.

"Take your mistress to her private room. Call a seamstress and a cobbler. She is going to need new everything. After all, she is an Exotic. And do things right this time if you don't want me to kick your other eye," said Horrel. And the man left the room.

"Orrun, darling Orrun, what happened? Let me heal you." Ultima went running over to the servant's side. She called energy to her hands and placed her hands on Orrun's face.

"Thank you, sweetheart. I can feel that you can use your healing magic well now," said Orrun, as Ultima healed his eye.

"Yes, you know Xawata gave me zero training, but I learned how to use it when I went to live with the Hightowers."

"It is so good to see you," said Orrun.

"What happened to this place?" asked Ultima. Orrun made a sound of hush with a finger to his lips, and he shook his head.

"Come, let's take you to your room," said Orrun. They walked through the hallways in silence. However, Orrun didn't take Ultima to her old room. Instead, he took Ultima to one of the rooms that had belonged to a second-class Exotic. When Ultima entered the room, she saw they had decorated it in a pale blue, and it had white rugs. It was a small room, but clean.

"This is all wrong. What in the world has this man done to the place?" asked Ultima.

"When you left, Horrel was enraged. He took it out on the staff. It was horrible. He made serious changes. Now, we offer the services from Exotics through to street walkers," said Orrun.

"What? Brothels are not meant to offer the services of street walkers. They are called street walkers for a reason. They only deal with sex. Is this man out of his mind?" said Ultima.

"He said that by offering their services through the brothel, we offer them protection from predators and violence. However, once they enter the doors of the brothel, they can't leave. And they are treated poorly, even worse than the rest of us," said Orrun.

"Who treats the staff poorly?" asked Ultima.

"Horrel hired slave masters who control everything. Most of the teachers were released, and the Exotic students are being taught through fear. If you thought Xawata was bad, this man is evil," said Orrun.

"Oh, my goodness, that is horrible. What happened to my position; who took over as the top Exotic?" asked Ultima. She went to look out the window, which overlooked the back alley.

"Jamila became the top Exotic of the Brothel after you left, and she has already tried to commit suicide. Horrel has two to three clients for her every night. Some nights she even has four clients, and he makes her work five days a week. Some nights after her last client, he goes into her room and spends the night with her. She is glad you are returning," said Orrun. Ultima was rummaging in the closet.

"I'm so sorry for Jamila, but I can't stay. I must leave this place." Ultima turned and faced Orrun.

"It is impossible to leave. Mr. Al at the front door will not let you out, and there is a bully just like Mr. Al at every exit of the house," said Orrun.

"There's got to be a way for me to leave. Orrun, I'm with child and Horrel wants to destroy it," said Ultima.

"You can't be with child. Xawata had you fixed again after you had Akina. I escorted the midwife-healer to your room the day he had it done," said Orrun.

"I used my magic on the midwife doing the procedure and paid her with my jewels so she would not hurt me after I birthed Akina. The woman never touched me, and afterward I used every trick in the book to prevent myself from getting with child," said Ultima.

"And what changed?" asked Orrun.

"When I got married, I no longer cared to prevent it," said Ultima with a smile.

"Honey, you have one big problem. There is no way to escape. Many of the girls have tried and they have each ended up with broken ribs and black eyes, but I'll help you if you want to try. You are my favorite Exotic for a reason," said Orrun.

"I'm sorry you didn't get your freedom when Xawata died," said Ultima.

"Darling, I'm an old diva. I have no place in this society but in this old brothel. My place is here, taking care of my pretty girls and serving the occasional man who requires my attention. You on the other hand were educated for something great. I always knew you could be more, and now I see a noble lady standing before me," said Orrun.

"Thank you," Ultima sat on the bed and bent her head.

"Come, let's get you ready. You have two clients tonight and Horrel will take it out on all of us if you are not at your best. I know if someone can charm a client it is you," said Orrun.

"Fine, bring me all the clothes I have at my disposal. I will also need new make-up and body lotions. Please tell me we have top-of-the-line products and that Horrel didn't get cheap with Exotics' necessities?" said Ultima.

"He is providing all Jamila is requesting. At least in that area he has not made any cuts. The man charges excessive amounts of coin for his Exotics," said Orrun.

"Sometimes is best to dance alone, other times is good to have one good friend," Amparo Feal

CHAPTER 32

Old Clients

Ultima took a few minutes to walk around the brothel and like Orrun had said, there were bouncers on every exit door of the house. There were slave masters in charge of slaves, and a new housekeeper in charge of the servants. A feeling of dread and hate permeated the entire house. It was as if fear had tentacles that had been attached to every slave and servant of the house. Ultima could feel the sadness. The slave masters treated her well enough, but with disdain. After all, she was the Exotic who had previously got away.

Ultima walked through the house until she reached the classrooms. The laughter that once brought some joy to Ultima was no longer there. She looked in on the Exotic class, but there were only two Exotic students—one was missing. There used to be four with Akina. Horrel must have shifted her into prostitution before allowing her to finish her Exotic training, or maybe he had sold her. Ultima didn't want to keep thinking of the possibilities.

She needed to return to her room. If the Duke of Horrel made her service two clients that night, she would need a nap. She had become used to going to sleep early at night and waking with the dawn. So, she went to her room, locked her door, and tried to sleep for at least an hour.

When it was time to get ready, she only found one dress that fit: a simple, long, form-fitting black dress, but no shoes were available in her size. She only had the shoes she had on when she arrived at the brothel, which were not suitable to wear with the dress. So she decided to go barefoot under her dress. Two servants came to help her get ready. They assisted in bathing her, then gave her a back and neck massage with oils. The servants removed all her body hair, arranged her hair in elaborate braids piled on her head, and painted her face with make-up.

Ultima couldn't fight the servants helping her. Among the servants was a slave master supervising her preparation. Once she was ready, Orrun escorted her to her working room and there she waited for her first client. Ultima couldn't think of a way to escape. How could she avoid having sex with a man who wanted her? Had paid for her? She needed to be smart about her dealings.

"Ultima, darling, your first client requested you sing for him tonight. He also wants to dance with you. So, there will be a mage providing music for you to dance with your client. He also wants sexual services from you. I'm sorry, darling," said Orrun, as he opened the door to the bedroom for Ultima to enter.

"At what time will the client be here, and who is he?" asked Ultima.

"It's one of your regulars, the Earl of Furlong. He is already here waiting for you," said Orrun.

"Send him up, I'm ready for him," said Ultima. The man was in his thirties. He was an arrogant man who thought he was the best there was in bed, when in reality he didn't last long. Ultima always found she had to fake having a good time with him on each of his visits. When she was a slave, he paid Xawata enough to ensure Ultima gave him a good time—so she did what he paid her to do. However, despite wearing a collar around her neck, she knew she was a free woman now, and she did not want to do any of that. She needed to play her cards right.

The contemptuous man entered the room. Ultima didn't have her signature mask on. She was *not* an Exotic, so she didn't see the point of playing any games. She was sitting by the small dining table at the far end of the large room. He took a few steps inside, and Ultima did not say a word.

"Exotic Ultima, it is good to have you back where you belong," said the Earl.

"Hello Johannes, how are you doing as of late? It is good to see you. My husband, Lord Otto Hightower, and I would love to have you and your wife at a ball in celebration of our wedding. We didn't have time to throw a party before we had to travel to the country. The Duke of Vurthas is hosting the party in our honor in another week," said Ultima. The man was taken aback. Ultima never spoke to him with such liberties. She stood up and walked over to stand near him, but she didn't curtsy.

"Your father-in-law announced your marriage in every newspaper in the capital, and none in our circles believed it. Then you disappeared from the roster here at Xawata's and there were no explanations. So, what are you doing here again?" asked the Earl.

"The Duke of Horrel has sued my father-in-law, the Duke of Vurthas. The duke bought my contract from Xawata and gave me my freedom. Horrel is suing my husband. I have no idea why. We are married and our marriage is completely legal. But in the meantime, the court has required me to stay here until they settle it all. I have no idea why the Duke of Horrel thinks to have me take clients when I'm still married." And Ultima showed the wife mark on her arm to the earl.

"I paid good coin to hear you sing, to dance with you and a decent lay, and now you're telling me I won't get anything?" asked the Earl.

"Oh, for old times' sake! I'll sing and I'll dance with you, but I certainly can't lie with you. I'm a Lady in the Yakutan Ducal House of Vurthas after all," said Ultima.

Without waiting for his response, she turned away from him and went to sit near the fireplace. She picked up a lute and sang his favorite song. She sang several more songs for him, and they danced, and talked for a while. He only had an hour of her time, so she used her harmonizer magic to get him talking more until a servant entered the room and told him his time was up and he needed to leave.

"Well, I hope your stay here is brief," said the Earl.

"I think the Duke of Horrel is making a mistake making a married woman work as an Exotic, but that is something the trade officials need to deal with him about directly," said Ultima.

"Yes, you are right on that one. Goodbye, dear Ultima."

"It was good to see you, Johannes." And the Earl of Furlong left. One was done and the second client was still to come. Orrun entered the room.

"That was incredible, the way you handled that man. I was watching the entire time. You haven't lost your charm," said Orrun.

"So, who is my second client?" asked Ultima.

"That I don't know. Horrel kept that one to himself. I think the person wants some anonymity, but I found out that once there was word on the street you were back in the house, this one particular client paid handsomely for two hours with you," said Orrun.

"Oh no, two hours! I need to know who it is, or at least what is it I'm supposed to be doing. Orrun, please go and try to find out. Please," said Ultima.

"Fine sweetheart, I'll try, but I cannot promise anything," said Orrun, and he left the room, leaving Ultima in the bathroom. She wet a towel and placed it on the back of her neck, and tried to relax a little. Who would be the second client? If it was an aggressive person, then her chances of manipulating the person would be less likely to succeed. She had to find a way to avoid servicing anyone.

An agonizing hour passed and then another until Orrun opened the door and Ultima jumped.

"Orrun, you almost killed me. Do you know who my next client is?" asked Ultima, but Orrun appeared to be struck dumb, when Samila stepped around him and entered the room with an arrogant air to her movements. The woman had a red fan in her hands, and her black dress made her look smaller than she was. When Ultima saw Samila enter the room, she almost fainted, but somehow, she kept smiling.

"Ultima, where is your mask? I loved your distinctive Exotic mask," said Samila.

"Exotics wear the masks, I'm not an Exotic," said Ultima with disdain.

"The marchioness has two hours. She has paid to hear you sing, dance, and to lie with you," said Orrun. He turned and left the room. Ultima stayed standing by the dining table, and Samila gave Ultima a wicked smile.

"Lord Otto didn't wait long to discard you. You didn't want my jewels when you were free, and now you are back at being a slave with a collar," said Samila. Her words hurt.

"Otto didn't discard me. The Duke of Horrel had him arrested and is holding me hostage. He claims my marriage is annulled, but he has given Otto no chance to defend himself," said Ultima.

"Well, you have a collar and are in the brothel, what is more evidence than that?" said Samila. Ultima showed Samila her arm.

"Samila, I haven't been rebranded as an Exotic. I know you paid handsomely for me, but please don't make me do this. I'm not property. I'm not an Exotic anymore," said Ultima.

"Darling, you will always be an Exotic. Look at all the skills around your burn mark. You are a special member of this society, an irreplaceable trade, one that we can't go without." Samila raised her hand and touched Ultima's face. Her hands caressed her neck to her shoulders, down Ultima's arms.

Ultima turned pale and her hands cold, and a rush of nausea came to her. Samila drew Ultima by the neck toward her and gave her a soft kiss. Ultima had been nauseous all day. She tried to stay unmoved, but her desire to regurgitate won out. Ultima pushed Samila away and ran to the bathroom.

Ultima was on her hand and knees, giving the toilet pot a deposit. Samila entered the bathroom and kneeled next to Ultima, holding her hair back. Ultima had been hungover many times and sick on occasions too, but this time she was regurgitating for no reason other than being with child.

Samila reached for a towel, wet it, and placed it over Ultima's neck. She helped Ultima stand, then left her alone in the bathroom. When Ultima looked at herself in the mirror, she saw a woman in distress. Her make-up was flawless, but her eyes showed her true emotions. Ultima had always been strong but compliant. This time she was going to rise. Ultima walked out of the bathroom and found Samila leaning against the bedpost.

"Are you sick? Did Lord Otto provide you proper meals? In all the years I've known you, you have never been sick," said Samila.

"No, I'm not sick, and Otto fed me well," said Ultima.

"So, what's happening to you today?" asked Samila.

"I'm with child. Otto and I are expecting our second child," said Ultima with a smile.

"Second child? Exotics can't have children and you claim to have two with Lord Otto," said Samila with a frown.

"I already told you, in your home. Otto and I have a child, which is how he got me out of the trade. I was never damaged. Our daughter Akina is eleven and in the Gayton Academy."

"And how can that be?" asked Samila.

"Xawata kept her a secret. And I kept the identity of her father to myself. She was the child of a Yakutan lord," said Ultima.

"I don't believe you," said Samila. So, Ultima approached Samila and took Samila's hand. She placed it over her own abdomen with her own hands over the top—Ultima's hands glowed green. Samila's eyes opened wide.

"You are a healer mage?" asked Samila.

"Yes, I am," smiled Ultima.

"I can feel a pulse coming from your body," said Samila.

"That is the life of my little one," said Ultima.

Samila pulled her hands away, and Ultima gave her a gentle smile. Ultima raised her right hand and pointed her fingers at her brush that was on the dresser. The brush slowly levitated, and as the object flew through the air, Samila stepped back. She kept her eyes on the brush as though it might bite her, and her face turned pale. When the brush reached Ultima's hand, she fixed her hair a little and let her hair back.

"Xawata kept many things about me a secret," smiled Ultima.

Fear was written all over Samila's face, followed swiftly by a sorrowful look.

"You know Horrel will force you to rid yourself of your child," said Samila, looking down.

"I know, he already told me a healer will come tomorrow to remove my child," said Ultima, and Samila's head snapped up.

"I have two children and they are the love of my heart. He is depriving you of that choice. You need to leave this place," said Samila.

"It is near impossible for me to get away from here. There are guards on every floor and at every door. I'm hoping Otto will get out of jail and find a way to get me out of here before anything happens to me and our child," said Ultima.

"Call for hard liquor and lots of it," said Samila.

"What?" asked Ultima.

"Trust me, call for a lot of hard liquor," said Samila. Ultima frowned at the woman. Samila never used to drink, but she called Orrun and asked for a decanter of whiskey.

"Samila, what are you doing? You never drink anything but a little wine," said Ultima.

"I'm your last client for the night?"

"Yes, but what—" Ultima couldn't finish her sentence.

"Sing, Ultima, I need you to sing loudly." Ultima sang two songs and Samila picked up the whiskey and poured some of it over her clothing. She took a sip and then another.

"Sing loudly, Ultima, then sing some more," said Samila, and she made noise all around the room. She dropped chairs to the floor, giggled loudly, and throughout, she kept sipping her drink.

When it was time for Samila to go. She took her dress off, stepped on it and messed it up, tousled her own hair and smudged her make-up. She got dressed again, but not completely.

"Get naked, Ultima, and make your dress look disheveled. Do the same as I did. I'm not fully drunk, but this must do."

"What are you doing?" asked Ultima.

"Do as I say, please," said Samila. Ultima got naked and made a mess of her dress, make-up, and her hair.

"Call the hallway bouncer. You must have the hallway bouncer carry me to my carriage, that way it will open a way for you to get to the first floor. From there, use your magic or something to get past the bouncer at the front door. Once you get out, run as fast as you can and I'll reach you two blocks from here," said Samila.

"Why are you helping me?" asked Ultima.

"First, because I'm a mother, and second, because I love you," said Samila, touching Ultima's cheek.

"Time is almost up; call the bouncer," said Samila and she made a mess of the bed and went to recline on the sofa. Ultima went to the door and called for the hallway bouncer.

"Hello, whatever your name is. I need help. Lady Samila is drunk and can't walk to her carriage. Could you be a dear and carry her?" said Ultima.

"That's not my job, whore. My job is to keep you whores safe. Call the man servant Orrun to carry her."

"Oh, so you are the one I must thank. You are doing an outstanding job." Ultima let her magic pour out of her. Her words came out with sugar and spice. "This place has never been this calm; I have no fear, unlike when Xawata owned it.

Sadly, Orrun is hurt and can't carry her. Lady Samila is one of the most renowned and respected clients. She only came here to see me, since I'm back. I am sure our boss will appreciate it greatly if a strong and handsome gentleman such as yourself helps her." Ultima used more of her harmonizer magic, and this time she gave her most charming smile.

The man walked toward Ultima. He entered the room and found Samila sprawled on the sofa with her dress and hair all a mess. Ultima walked over to Samila and kissed her.

"It was an interesting night, Samila," said Ultima. And the man picked up Samila in his arms. When the man turned to face the door, Orrun came in with a sling under his arm. Of course, he had overheard Ultima's comment and played along.

"Thank you for your help, I couldn't have carried her," said Orrun, and the bouncer left with Samila giggling.

"My darling, Ultima, I heard everything through the hidden room. This is your chance, go, run. I love you," said Orrun.

"I love you too." And Ultima left running barefoot out the door of the room, not making a sound through the hallways. She descended to the first floor and saw Al, the beefy bouncer in the butler suit. He stood holding the front door open for a new client entering, and for the bouncer taking Samila out. Ultima hid behind an ostentatious statue in the corner, the only redeeming feature was that it was so large it afforded her a good hiding place.

As always, the client was shown into the parlor to the right of the entranceway, but Al remained with the door opened, waiting for the other man to return. Ultima used her magic and caused the client in the parlor to fall from the chair he had been sitting on. She managed this by making the chair legs break. There was no water for her to use, so she had to draw on a lot of her own energy, but she didn't care. She needed to leave the brothel. The client shouted out and Al, the bouncer, left the door unattended. Ultima saw her chance.

Move, Ultima, move! She thought. She could barely walk, much less run. Her legs moved slowly. She had used too much of her own energy to break the chair. She stumbled along, holding onto anything she could find for support.

Run, Ultima, move faster.

Ultima could hear the garbled conversation between the client, who was still intermittently howling in pain, and the bouncer. She heard a grunt from the bouncer and figured he must have just picked the client up in his arms.

Walk faster, Ultima. Run if you value the life of your unborn child. She hobbled along the long hallway. Ultima could see the bouncer inside the parlor begin to turn just as she reached the door and stepped outside.

Move faster! Otto always said he used the energy from the air and vibrations from people around him to power his magic. She wished she knew how to do the same. Using her own energy always left her exhausted. One, two, three steps down, she could do this. She looked over her shoulder, and the bouncer with the fallen client in his arms was walking into the hallway that Ultima had just left. *Go down the steps, Ultima*, she admonished herself, thinking her legs might give way when she tried to bend her knees and lower herself to the first step.

Outside, the bouncer from the second floor, who had taken Samila to the carriage, was now beginning to turn from the carriage back to the front of the house. Samila's and Ultima's eyes locked.

Ultima stumbled.

Samila grabbed the man by his neck and pulled him in for an embrace, hugging him tightly, and thanked him profusely for helping her to her carriage. She even tried to give him a gratuity. Ultima almost fell down the steps, but she managed to reach the last step without disaster. She moved to the right, walking faster, until she reached the corner of the block, where she turned right again.

Ultima walked as fast as she could, when a carriage stopped next to her.

"Hurry, get in!" said Samila. Ultima entered the carriage and collapsed. She was out of breath, and she shook from head to toe. Her head hurt and the cold of the night seeped in, all the way to her bones.

"I don't know where to go," said Ultima. She was rubbing her cold arms. With ringing ears, she could barely hear what Samila said to her. Samila took Ultima in her arms and enveloped her inside her coat, rubbing heat back into her arms.

"You stay with me," said Samila. They rode in Samila's carriage, sitting close, next to each other. Ultima's dress was a mess, and having no shoes on, the hem of her dress was filthy and wet, having dragged through the mud and grime of the streets of Pailo.

"Samila, my dress is muddy."

"I don't care. You are out of the brothel," said the Marchioness.

"Thank you for your help, Samila," said Ultima.

"You are welcome, darling. I'm taking you to my townhouse," said Samila. They reached 9th Avenue, where Samila's townhouse in Pailo was located.

"I'm nauseous and tired all the time. It wasn't this bad with Akina," said Ultima.

"I was nauseous my entire pregnancy with my first. You will be fine. I need to go to sleep. I'm drunk," Samila said, as the doorman opened the front door and they entered Samila's townhouse. The housekeeper was waiting at the door.

"This is Mrs. Liares. She has been my housekeeper for over a decade," said Samila.

"Hello Mrs. Liares," said Ultima.

"This is Lady Skylar, a trusted friend of many years," said Samila.

"Hello my Lady," said Mrs. Liares.

"Show my friend Lady Skylar a room. I don't want anyone in this house talking about my friend to anyone if they value their employment with me. I'm going to sleep now. I don't want to be disturbed early. I don't care if it is my husband, don't wake me. Please take care of Lady

Skylar." Samila gave Mrs. Liares her instructions as she removed her hat, cloak, and gloves. Turning to Ultima, she said, "We'll talk in the morning, love. I know I'm going to pay for this when I wake." And she left for her room.

CHAPTER 33

When Persecuted, We Run

Ultima woke late the next morning. She had had a bad dream, but she couldn't remember what it was about. Lately, she couldn't remember her dreams; in a way it was good. She didn't want to deal with the craziness of dreams and the depression nightmares would bring. She opened her eyes and for a moment, she couldn't remember where she was. In a flash, the entirety of the day prior came rushing back. She recalled being taken captive and managing to escape on the same day. She needed to message He'nico. Marshal Donnelly was a traitor. How could he come to the house and arrest Otto and the duke? This was happening too fast.

    Ultima got up and put on a robe and slippers that had been given to her by the housekeeper. After carrying out her morning routine, she went downstairs. She had no clothing other than the skimpy dress she had been wearing the previous night. The house was quiet, but she found a parlor where Samila was sitting, drinking her morning coffee, with the curtains closed.

"Good morning, Samila," said Ultima, entering the parlor. She went and sat next to Samila.

"Good morning darling, come in and break your fast. And please don't talk loudly, I'm hungover and it is all the fault of that damn Duke of Horrel. I hate liquor."

"You saved my life and the life of my child last night," said Ultima.

"Don't mention it. You are a free woman. The Hightowers set you free," said Samila.

"Tell that to the Duke of Horrel," said Ultima, drinking the cup of coffee that a maid had served her.

"The Duke of Horrel has made a claim for you and apparently, he has won the lawsuit. You need to fight on the grounds that you are a married woman with two children. Whether Xawata sold you or not, you were officially married and out of that union there is a child of a Yakutan lord. You need to let the trade officials know all these facts," Samila drank her coffee and rubbed her head.

"I need to find a way to contact the duke's man of business. I just don't know how I'm going to go about doing it," said Ultima.

"Darling, all I know is that it will not be long before Horrel will come knocking at my door looking for you. We need to hide you someplace safe. My head hurts so much. OH, MY STARS! We forgot about your collar," said Samila, pointing at Ultima's golden collar.

"What?" Ultima frowned.

"Your collar will give you up as a slave. A golden collar will give you up as an Exotic slave. A golden collar with an encrusted ruby will definitely give you away. You can't step outside with that thing around your neck. How many Exotics with golden collars, with a ruby embedded, do you think there are in the kingdom!" said Samila.

"I can't take this much longer." Ultima stood up and tried to leave, but Samila went after her.

"Listen, we need to get Lord Otto out of prison. He has only been there for what, a day? He is a lord, I'm surprised he wasn't out yesterday and tearing that brothel down trying to get you back," said Samila. She opened a curtain in her parlor and let a little light in. Her painted red nails made her skin look ever paler in the morning light.

"A little light will be good for both of us. Honey, let's eat and later we'll go and change. I'm a much taller woman than you, but besides my pants, almost everything else should fit you. I'll have one of the maids fix the hem of one of my dresses. You need clothing and I need something to do," said Samila.

"I'll go to the manor, get a few of my old things and try to travel to West Franken. I'll try to hide with the Duke of Franken. They were kind to me," said Ultima.

"Are you crazy? Horrel will send men to wait for you at the manor. You can't return to that place."

"I must go and get some of my things. I can't travel with nothing," said Ultima.

"Wait, I'll go with you. You can't be seen in the streets with that collar. We need to find a way to hide it from view," said Samila.

✦✦✦

Once the women finished eating, a maid came and hemmed one of Samila's dresses and adjusted where necessary. It was a dark, navy-blue dress that made Ultima look elegant. Samila placed a scarf around Ultima's neck and topped the outfit with a hat, hiding as much of Ultima's hair as possible. They took Samila's carriage and went to the Duke of Vurthas's manor. As they approached the entrance to the manor, Samila noticed the men standing guard at the gate.

"Do you see them? I told you that bastard Horrel would send guards to wait for you at the manor," said Samila, pointing at two beefy men guarding the entrance to the manor.

"What am I going to do? What if they send guards to your house to look for me? I'll be back at the brothel by the end of the day. I'm in so much trouble," said Ultima.

"We covered your collar, and you have a new dress and shoes. Let's take you to the train station. Forget everything and go to West Franken. I can't take you to Glauslag. There are no trains leaving until the end of the week," said Samila.

They traveled to the Silver Gradient Train Station. Samila left the carriage to buy a ticket for Ultima to West Franken to avoid Ultima's exposure, while Ultima waited in the carriage. It was best to stay hidden until it was time to board the train. When it was time to leave, Ultima reached for Samila.

"Samila, you have been more than a friend. Thank you for all you have done for me and my child," said Ultima and she took Samila's face with one hand and kissed Samila softly.

"If your child is a girl, will you give 'Samila' as one of her names? I realize that may anger Otto, but I will forever know that at one time you loved me," said Samila with a smile. Ultima chuckled.

"Samila, I was a slave. Slaves don't know love. I was made to give you my body, but I did enjoy our conversations. And once I knew you loved me, I looked forward to your visits. If I have a girl, I will give her your name, because you loved me when no one else did." And Ultima left the carriage in a run.

It was midday, and the streets and stores of Pailo were full of people and vehicles moving in every direction. The coolness of the day contrasted with the bitter coldness of the Pikes Mountains, but people dressed to keep warm, which was good because it justified the scarf Ultima kept firmly in place around her neck. She ran across the street, and walked rapidly along the length of the station to reach its entrance. She had a few minutes to reach her train. The platforms were full of people, some carrying large bags, others carrying nothing at all, just like her. She only had a small reticule.

Ultima reached platform seven and there she waited. The light of the day bothered her eyes, but there was little she could do. The train door opened, and the train attendant stepped out.

"ALL ABOARD," called the attendant. Ultima boarded the train.

"Let me see your ticket and your right arm," said the attendant. Ultima showed her ticket and showed him her right and left arms, showing her Lady Hightower tattoo.

"You can board, my Lady," said the man. Ultima took a deep breath, and she walked past him, entering the corridor of the train and found her cabin. Entering, she locked the door and felt relief flood her from head to toe ... until there was a knock on her door. Ultima opened the door, and a guard pushed her backward. He stepped inside and grabbed her by the neck. A second guard stepped into the cabin and handcuffed her.

"We found the escaped Exotic. Duke Horrel will be happy to get his property back," said the guard.

A third guard stepped behind Ultima, but said, "First, we are arresting her. The Duke of Horrel will have to wait to get his slave back, just like any other slave owner."

The men exited the train, pulling Ultima by the arm. Ultima's world turned.

"I'm dizzy," said Ultima to one of the guards.

"Keep moving, Exotic, like our boss said, we have to take you directly to Tsuyoi Edo Castle," said the guard.

"I am married to a lord. I am free," said Ultima.

"That is not my business. You're on our list of escaped slaves, so we're arresting you," said the guard.

The people in the train station moved aside to make way for the guards and their captive. Slaves, by their nature were peasants, and were often caught trying to leave the city by train, but Ultima was dressed like a Lady, not a peasant.

•••

It was past midday by the time the guards had arrested Ultima and were transporting her to Tsuyoi Edo Castle. In the city of Pailo there were two castles, the royal castle where the King lived, and the notorious Tsuyoi Edo, where all manner of legal events took place and where the city's dungeons were located.

Tsuyoi Edo was an enormous structure made of large white stones, having several towers and a beautifully shaped roof. Its walls were punctuated by tall, stained-glass windows. The guards took Ultima through a side entrance and down a series of hallways, ending up in an office of the department of the Slave-Trade division. The guard forced her to keep moving and made her walk past a crowded room. The room had many rows of benches, all of which were occupied by people who were escaped and re-captured slaves. However, Ultima could see by the way they acted and dressed that none were Exotics.

Ultima looked around. They all wore collars, but she was the only one with a golden collar. The people looked weary, feeble, and some even emaciated. There were children with sticks for arms, but distended bellies.

Oh no, poor babies, those bellies must be full of parasites, thought Ultima.

Cold sweat trickled down her spine. The place smelled of men and women who hadn't bathed in months, of dirty swaddling clothes, of urine and feces. Decay and despair lingered and its brother, hopelessness, jointly reigning supreme in that room of desolation. Every man, woman, and child sat next to one another, but alone, with eyes cast down at the floor. No one had any fight in them, and Ultima's eyes watered. She understood their plight. They all wanted freedom. The one thing the Duke of Vurthas had given her. The thing that Otto's burned mark gave her, and may soon be taken away. Her heart hurt. Slavery was a horrible thing. Warm tears fell and her heart squeezed in her chest. The guard pushed her into a small room containing one chair, a small table, and no windows. The dark room cradled Ultima, allowing her to shed silent tears.

A few minutes later a jiggling of keys was heard outside, and someone opened the door. It was the same guard who had placed her in the room. He entered and took her by the arm. "Exotic Ultima Skylar, it's your turn," said the man.

The man didn't give her time to stand or walk unaided, just dragged her, pulling her from the room. He smirked when he saw she was struggling to stand, and when she did finally manage it, he grabbed her by her neck and pushed her forward.

"Runaway slaves are the worst kind of trash," said the guard.

Ultima and the guard walked through a long hallway, and he pushed her into a larger room with a long table. There at the table, a rotund, bald man, and a thin, tired woman were waiting. The officials didn't look up at Ultima when she entered. They stayed glued to their chairs behind the large table, with books opened in front of them and acting dismissive. The guard stood behind Ultima, still holding her by her neck. There was a chair in front of them.

"Take the cuffs from her wrists. I need to see her trade-tattoos. If those have been drawn over, I will be able to tell," said the thin woman.

"Remove her top, I must see her left breast. Her Exotic-tattoo must be there," said the rotund man perusing through his books.

The guard removed the cuffs, and he tore her right sleeve, but Ultima unbuttoned the top of her bodice, not wanting the man to destroy her dress as he had her sleeve.

"I'm Mrs. Klyne, sit there and let me see your arm," said the woman. The guard pushed Ultima forward to sit on the chair. Ultima showed her right and left arms to the woman.

"So, you were definitely married, and to a lord. For all the Lords of Yavos, Claude look at all these added skills! It's impossible for one person to have this many skills. Claude she was married to a Lord in a Yakutan Ducal house and a Jonellen priest officiated the wedding. This is outside our jurisdiction," said Mrs. Klyne.

"Let me look at the Exotic skills books. She must be registered here," said Claude.

"Hers is an official Yakutan marriage. According to the registry it was done on consulate land, and registered in both kingdoms," said Mrs. Klyne.

"This will be a problem. The contract has been disputed and our legal system has given ownership of the slave to the Duke of Horrel," said Claude, the rotund official.

"However, when she got married, that wasn't the case. According to the records, none of this evidence was taken into consideration when the case went before the judge for litigation," said the official, Mrs. Klyne.

"We're not judges. We don't interpret the law; we follow the law. According to the ruling, she is an Exotic and a slave, and she belongs to the Duke of Horrel. We are here to return her to her master," said Claude.

"Look at her breast. Her Exotic mark was burned over," said the woman.

"WHAT? That can't be. Let me see." When the official named Claude saw the burn mark, he rubbed his eyes. "For all the Lords of Yavos, it is burned. She can't go back to being an Exotic," said the rotund man.

"There is something else. I'm carrying my husband's heir. He is a prince in the royal family of Yakuta. My father-in-law is married to the sister of King George of Yakuta and is cousin to Queen Elenore," said Ultima.

Both man and woman dropped their pencils and looked at each other and then at Ultima.

"Exotics can't be mothers," said the man.

"We have an eleven-year-old daughter. Lord Otto is her father, and we are expecting our second child. May I approach your side of the table to prove I am with child?" Upon their assent, Ultima walked around the table and approached Mrs. Klyne. "Give me your hand," said Ultima. The woman furrowed her brow and did what she was asked to do.

Ultima brought her hands over the woman's against her lower belly and made her hands light up.

"There is a pulse in her," said the woman.

"That is the life of my child," said Ultima. The woman pulled her hand back and rubbed the palm of her hands.

"And she is a healer mage," said the man.

"I'm not going to touch this one. If you want to proceed, it will be on your conscience. I will not sign the release papers. You know this will come back to haunt us," said Mrs. Klyne.

"We have an order to return this woman to her master, but she is a mage. Mages are never slaves here, nor in Yakuta. My next question is, how did she end up as an Exotic and a slave?" said Claude, pulling the hairs of one of his eyebrows.

"What are we going to do? She's not a slave according to the treaties. She is a married woman and a mage," said Mrs. Klyne. Ultima's heart was beating faster and faster. Maybe they were going to let her go.

"This will not fare well. The Duke of Horrel won the lawsuit, but we can't give her to him. She is a mage," said Claude. And Ultima levitated one of the pencils and made it come to her hand.

"Look at that, she is definitely a mage, with child, and the duke from Yakuta can counter sue," said Mrs. Klyne.

"I'm not going to deal with mages, send her to the dungeon. We need to contact the Yakutan consulate and the mages academy on this one. We are dealing with the Yakutan royal family and if the duke is King George's brother-in-law and cousin to the Queen, he should never have been in the dungeon in the first place. We have a mountain of paperwork to do. Why is the duke in the dungeon?" said Claude.

"Guard, take Lady Hightower to the dungeon, until we can figure this out," said Mrs. Klyne. And the guard stepped forward, cuffed Ultima and walked her out of the room.

Ultima was scared. *The dungeon!* She had never been to a dungeon. She had never been to many places, but since marrying Otto, she had been exposed to many new things.

The guard had been listening. He stopped manhandling and pushing Ultima. He was now guiding her down the stairs. Her eyes needed to adjust to the change in light. Torches illuminated their path as the stairs turned into a spiral. They reached a hall where there was a table, and three guards stopped their path.

"Who's this? A golden collar? Is this an Exotic slave dressed like a Lady in the dungeons?" asked one of the guards.

"Don't be fooled by the golden collar. Apparently, she is a mage and the wife of the Yakutan Lord we are holding," said the guard who brought Ultima.

"Should we room them together?" said a pimple-faced guard in the room.

"We don't have an empty cell. We might as well. This way we will keep her safe from the others," said the oldest of the guards.

"Fine, let's go, Lady Hightower." The young guard with a face full of pimples took Ultima by the arm and walked her through a door to the left and down a series of steps. A musty smell hit Ultima like a whip, and it got stronger as they walked lower. They reached a landing where she could see a large room full of individual cells separated by metal bars. Each cell had a hole in the ground, a bucket of water with a ladle, a pallet with a blanket, and some had cups. All the cells had people in them, standing, sitting, or sleeping. The hall was lit only by torches in each corner.

The men moved Ultima through the hall until she stood in front of the cell where Otto was lying asleep. One of the guards took a set of keys, chose the right key, and set the key in the lock. Otto woke and looked around. When he saw Ultima, he jumped up and went to stand by the entrance.

"Ultima are you hurt?" asked Otto.

"Step back," shouted the pimple-faced guard. Otto stepped back, and the guard removed Ultima's handcuffs. The guard opened the door, led Ultima in, and locked the door behind her. Otto embraced Ultima and kissed her head.

"Horrel said he won a lawsuit, and you were his slave. Did he hurt you? What is it with you and collars?" said Otto, holding her collar in his hand.

"He took me to his brothel, but I managed to escape before anything could happen to me," said Ultima.

"I've been worried for you all this time," said Otto.

"Where is your father?" asked Ultima.

"I'm here. Did you call He'nico? Donnelly was a traitor. He got us jailed and has done nothing to get us out," said the Duke of Vurthas from the cell next to Otto's.

"I haven't seen Donnelly. Horrel made it impossible for me to do anything. What made a difference was that we were legally married in a Yakutan-owned property, and a Jonellen priest officiated our marriage. The officials could not send me back to Horrel. Also, when the officials found out I was a mage, things changed completely. Apparently, mages can't be slaves. And when I told them you are the brother-in-law of the King of Yakuta, there was a big commotion," said Ultima.

"I let them know who I was the moment I arrived here, but they arrested us anyway, and threw us in the dungeon regardless of our status. They didn't even let me call my man of business. I hope the servants had enough sense to call my lawyers," said the Duke of Vurthas.

Ultima's stomach made a sound.

"I hope they bring us food today. I'm so sorry you have to be here. I'm so sorry I'm not taking better care of you," said Otto.

"I understand. I must sit, I'm dizzy. It has been a trying day," said Ultima and she sat on the only place that had a modicum of cleanliness about it, the pallet. Otto sat next to her.

"What I'm most surprised about is that they didn't send you back to Horrel and sent you here instead," said Otto.

"The fact I'm a mage made them upset, and you gave me a gift that played a role in avoiding being returned to Horrel," said Ultima.

"What gift?" said Otto.

"Otto, I'm with child," said Ultima.

"What?" Otto stood up and looked at Ultima, and then he went to the entrance of the cell.

"Are you sure? A child, you, me, ours, a son?" asked Otto.

"Yes, I'm sure, and I don't know if the little one is a son or a daughter."

"I need to get you out of here. We can't be in here. This is no place for a woman with child," said Otto.

"Well, congratulations are in order. I have a new grandchild on the way. With Akina and this one, it makes four grandbabies," said the Duke of Vurthas.

"Father, we must get out of here NOW." Otto's hands lit up with lightning.

"Otto, calm down! We need to plan how we are going to do this the right way. We are mages and between all of us there must be a way to escape this place," said Ultima.

"I'm giving my lawyer one more day to get me out. If I'm not out by tomorrow, we are leaving. As a member of the Yakutan royal family we have some entitlements, but I'm afraid if we escape, we will have to leave Tsestelago and never be able to return unless Soren pardons us. We need Soren," said the Duke.

❖❖❖

The night was bitterly cold, but Ultima and Otto slept close to each other. They woke to the sound of jiggling keys. Two guards were walking down the stairs and along the hallway toward their cells. The guards unlocked the doors and let them out. The other guard released the Duke from his cell.

"Come with us," said a guard. They took their coats and left with the guards. Ultima held Otto's hand, and they walked out into the hall and up the stairs to the landing, but the guards didn't stop there. They continued up the stairs until they reached the first floor, where they were led through a series of hallways to a large room, and were left to wait there. Ultima noticed the room had four simple, wooden chairs and a large table, and behind the table there were three wood-and-leather chairs.

The Hightowers stayed quiet. There was nothing to say. They had nothing to comment. Ultima kept close to Otto, but would have rather been anywhere else than in that room.

Moments later, the door opened and there was Mr. John Sheldon, the Duke of Vurthas's lawyer.

"I'm sorry Your Grace, but it took me all this time to get a release. I had to request an injunction, and a counter lawsuit to contest the allegations the Duke of Horrel raised against you. The man never sent me any documents stating he was suing you, which in fact helped me get enough leverage to acquire your release," said the lawyer.

"How did Horrel manage to get a judge to rule against another duke without a defense present?" asked the Duke.

"I don't know. Things are getting bad around here," said the lawyer.

"Why did he come after me?" asked Otto.

"He is a vindictive man. You married Lady Ultima and he wanted her back. In your case, it was a little easier to get you out of this place. You only married the woman. Your father gave her to you in marriage and you accepted in all honesty. Your father, however, bought Lady Ultima from Xawata, his business partner, without Horrel's knowledge which has incensed him. Lady Ultima is still being contested as a slave. However, I found out from one of the trade officials that she is a mage and with child and those are excellent attributes. Moreover, she is bound to you by the laws and traditions of the royal Yakutan family. So, I managed to get her out of the dungeon on grounds of her being a mage and thus entitled to her freedom," said Mr. Sheldon.

"I'm so glad to see you," said Ultima.

"Thank you, my Lady. Anyway, Your Grace, that isn't the bad part," said Mr. Sheldon.

"Oh, there is more?" said the Duke.

"You have a charge of treason against you. The King ordered you to go find Prince Soren, and you returned to the capital without the prince. I'm arguing you can't be charged with treason since you are not a citizen of Tsestelago and you were merely doing a favor for the King, and not carrying out an order from him," said Mr. Sheldon.

"Who is pressing those charges?" asked Ultima.

"Of all people, it's the Duke of Abernathy. He is the one pushing this charge against you," said Mr. Sheldon, passing some papers to the duke to read.

"That is odd. How is it that the Duke of Abernathy is making those charges and not the Interim Regent or the Duke of Horrel?" asked Otto.

"I don't know, but I'll have my people investigate this further. In the meantime, you must present yourselves to the interim regent, who, I'm sorry to tell you, is the Archimage Saigai," said Mr. Sheldon.

"Yes, we know the archimage is the interim regent."

"This is getting worse by the minute," said Ultima.

"We need Prince Soren here now," said Otto.

"Let's get you out of this place. Your audience in front of the interim regent is set for tomorrow," said Mr. Sheldon. Ultima took one step and then another next to Otto, but her legs felt like jelly. Her hands and body shook to the core.

"This has all the signs of fraud," said Ultima.

"I think fraud is just the start. All I know is that I need a drink!" said Otto.

CHAPTER 34

Wrong Assumptions

On the ride to the manor, Ultima said nothing. For a while she looked out the window of the carriage onto the busy street, then fell asleep. The last forty-eight hours had been among the worst in her life, and yet, she still fell asleep. When the carriage approached the entrance to the manor, Ultima woke. She saw the bully men standing by the side of the road, but the carriage with the Vurthas's Ducal seal drove past them and onto the property. They couldn't do a thing.

Otto, Ultima, and the Duke of Vurthas arrived at the manor and entered through the front doors where Mr. Dobson and Mrs. Taneda waited excitedly, with no decorum, but much enthusiasm. They went on and on with a litany of congratulations for the trio to have won their freedom, but especially for the duke. Ultima stepped into the entrance hall where Mariza reached her in a run. Crying and laughing a little, the young girl clung to her hand. Ultima went to Otto's and her room, and she gave instructions to have all her things brought up to her from her original room.

"All your things are in your room. We never packed any of them. We left everything exactly as you left it. We knew you would be back," said Mariza, drying her tears.

"I want to take a bath and get out of this clothing," said Ultima. Mariza helped her get a bath going, and not long after, Ultima was in the tub relaxing. Mariza returned with some tea and helped her finish bathing.

Ultima was still drinking her tea when Otto entered their room with an enormous set of pliers.

"Ultima, where—oh there you are," said Otto.

"I'm right here, but what are you doing with those pliers?" asked Ultima, placing her cup on the table.

"You will not be wearing that collar a minute longer than it will take me to cut it off," said Otto.

A manservant followed Otto into the room, despite Ultima only wearing her cotton robe. Clearly this was so important to Otto, that he didn't care for the impropriety. Otto and the servant maneuvered the large pliers, and they cut the golden collar from her neck.

"You will never have a collar as long as I live. You are my wife and a free woman," said Otto.

"Thank you, but you need a bath. You smell," said Ultima, after he finished cutting off her collar.

"You're welcome," said Otto.

"I'm sorry, honey, but you smell bad," said Ultima, stepping back from Otto.

"I was in prison for over two days, and I stepped on horse manure looking for these pliers." Otto kissed Ultima.

"Oh, I recognize the smell. It was the aroma I woke up to for the last seven-plus weeks as we traveled up and down the Pikes Mountain," said Ultima. Otto gave the pieces of the golden collar to the servant and went to take a bath.

Ultima combed her hair and anointed her skin with lotion and perfume while she waited for Otto to finish his bath, but she couldn't wait. She was too tired, so she went to bed to take a nap. When she woke up, it was time to get ready for dinner. Otto had not bothered her during her nap, and for that, she was grateful.

During dinner, they finally got together to talk about what would happen the next day.

"I'm afraid I'll be forced to return to the brothel," said Ultima.

"Over my dead body. You are my wife and carrying my child, the son of a Yakutan prince. Even if I have to smuggle you out of Tsestelago, you will not be going back to that brothel," said Otto.

"Son, hopefully, we will not get to those extremes," said the Duke.

"Did you really forge the contract between you and Xawata?" asked Ultima.

"No, the contract was legal. I sent a copy of the contract to Xawata's lawyers two days after he signed it, but that was the day he died. However, that wasn't my fault, nor my concern. I had the contract registered, and the signature was witnessed by my dear friend the Marquis of Carlton," said the Duke of Vurthas.

"The Duke of Horrel wanted me back badly," said Ultima.

"We must not underestimate Horrel," said the Duke of Vurthas.

"Father, why do you think the Duke of Abernathy is the one pressing charges against us for returning without Soren?" asked Otto.

"I don't know, Abernathy keeps to himself, and he is a loner. He is in the inner counsel of the King, so this will be interesting tomorrow. Especially as the interim regent is Archimage Saigai. I don't know what games this man is playing, but we must wait until tomorrow to hear what he has to say," said the Duke of Vurthas.

The trio finished eating, and they all went to bed early, although each in his or her own time. Ultima went up first and was in her room waiting for Otto —there was something on her mind she needed to speak about with him. When Otto entered the room, she was sitting on a chair by the fireplace with a book.

"You are still awake. I thought you'd be asleep by now," said Otto.

"I need to talk to you," said Ultima.

"What about?" Otto came into the room and began to undress.

"I was thinking that maybe the archimage may have something to do with the messages not getting through to Soren," said Ultima.

"That is a good assumption, but why?" said Otto.

"Think about it. Saigai is a mage, the interim regent, but he's not a member of the royal family. He may have orchestrated all of this with the communication mages to retain his position," said Ultima.

"That sounds about right, but we can't know until we've talked to him. We'll have to see what happens tomorrow," said Otto. They both climbed into bed, whereupon Otto kissed Ultima and fell asleep.

They were all so tired after having spent two nights in captivity.

❖❖❖

Their audience in front of the interim regent, the Archimage Saigai, was scheduled for an hour past the noon meal. They were to go to the King's receiving room at The Tsuyoi Edo Castle. The Assembly of Dukes were in session even though the Grand Duke of Hausman wasn't there presiding. The Duke of Abernathy had taken over the post in the absence of the Duke of Hausman.

"Hello Gareth, I heard you had been called to see the interim regent." Ambassador Bellamy Glasberg of the Kingdom of Yakuta was waiting for the duke outside the receiving room.

"Hello Bellamy, great to see you here. What happened? Since when can an archimage become an interim regent? And the Duke of Horrel as Minister of Interior?" asked the Duke of Vurthas.

"Yes, and the Duke of Abernathy is now heading the ouse of Dukes. King Trevino is on his deathbed, and there is no heir to put on the throne. Neither Soren, nor Robert are here to take charge. I'm here to ensure I get you and your sons out of Tsestelago alive. Saigai started cutting ties with Yakuta little by little, but he's picking up speed," said Ambassador Bellamy.

"This is not possible," said Otto.

"Oh, it is happening," said the Ambassador.

"My Lords, let's go; we are being called," said Mr. Sheldon.

The Duke of Vurthas, Lord Otto, Ultima, and the other two men entered the receiving hall, where the thin, gray-haired Archimage Saigai was sitting on the King's throne; the Duke of Horrel standing by his side.

There were guards at each corner of the hall and along the walls. Ultima noticed large basins of water to the side of each guard. A steward held open the book of the day's dealings, and the scribes were at their tables writing down all the proceedings. When they reached the front of the hall, Mr. Sheldon stepped forward, and they all waited for the archimage to start first.

"My dear Duke of Horrel, who do we have here?" asked the Archimage Saigai.

"The Duke of Vurthas is finally here, but he appears to be missing some of his companions. Oh, look, he brought back my runaway slave. You found my Exotic," said the Duke of Horrel.

"Ultima is my wife," said Otto. However, the archimage lifted his hand to stop the argument progressing any further.

"Lord Hightower, I was in the room when King Trevino gave you an order to bring back Prince Soren. What happened? I don't see the prince. You returned with only three companions from the group of nine who set out with you. What happened to the others?"

"I am friend to the King, from another kingdom, not one of his subjects to be given orders. Nevertheless, I will answer. We encountered many obstacles along our path," said the Duke of Vurthas.

"That doesn't tell me anything. What happened with the others?" asked Saigai.

"Lord Thomas elected to remain at the battle front at Pikes Mountain, and …" the Duke faltered, finding it difficult to continue.

"Did you find Prince Soren?" asked Horrel.

"Yes, we found the Prince," said the Duke.

"And what happened? Where is he?" Saigai moved forward on his chair.

"He returned with us," said the Duke.

"Where is he then? And the others, the Duke of Hausman and the Earl of Portmore?" asked Saigai, sitting back in the chair and beginning to enjoy the duke's discomfort.

"The King's brother will be traveling back in a few days, but we lost the Earl of Portmore," said the Duke of Vurthas.

"What? Why? What happened to the earl?" asked Horrel.

"He was Prince Marco's assassin, and in the fight to capture him, he lost his life," said the Duke.

"Lies, an Earl can't be an assassin," said Saigai.

"He confessed to the crime," said Otto.

"And where is Soren?" asked Horrel.

"He is on his way," said Otto.

The inquisition was disrupted by raised voices just outside the doors to the King's receiving room, which then swung open without ceremony.

"No, he is here," said Soren from the door. He was accompanied by the Duke of Hausman, He'nico, Mr. Donnelly, and a group of six other men.

"I've just come from the House of Dukes where they recognized me as the son of King Trevino and heir to the throne of Tsestelago. Will you be so kind as to step down from my father's throne?" said Soren, walking briskly to the front of the hall.

"Your father was the one who appointed me as an interim regent," said Saigai.

"And the law of the land appoints me Regent of the Kingdom." Soren took a step closer to Saigai, but the old man stood up from the throne, raised his hands and summoned a ward, which he pushed in a wave, away from himself and the throne. The guards at the corners of the room pulled out short staffs from behind their backs, and the other guards along the walls drew swords and pointed them at the group inside the hall.

"You are not worthy to rule. I've seen this family destroy this kingdom for years. Why can't a mage be King? Prince Leer is as capable as anyone else, but no, he is a mage. So, the law gives the throne to you. Marco was incompetent, but you are by far the worst in the Otarana family. I had Marco killed, and you will never be King. So, either you will announce for all to hear that you'll step down, or none of you will leave this room alive," said the Archimage Saigai.

"You need to stop. There are three master mages inside this circle you've created, and we are a dangerous trio," said the Duke of Vurthas.

"Really! I am the Archimage of the Kingdom. What makes you think I should be afraid of you?" asked Saigai. He raised his hands and created a wall of water between him and all three Lords of Vurthas.

The Duke of Vurthas moved his hands in a partial circular motion and drew some water from the basins in the room's corners. He hurled it at the guards with the staffs, but the guards blocked the water with their magic. He then began to undercut the wall of water the archimage had created. Soren and the Duke of Hausman drew their swords, but there was nothing they could do against magic. Instead they fought the guards who held swords and appeared to be non-magical.

Just as the battle began in earnest, Akina, Leer, Joy-Anna, and Cascade entered the hall by a pre-arranged signal, crouching low as they entered and going relatively unnoticed to the back of the room to use their magic.

They wore no armor, but made each strike count, relying—as mages do—on their magic. Soren used the room to his advantage. One mage, near to Soren, tried to strangle him using the curtains, but Otto threw a knife at the mage's head, straight between his eyes. The six other men who arrived with Soren and Hausman also fought the guards.

While Otto kept the mages and their magical spells focused on himself, Soren and the Duke of Hausman fought to keep the guards away from Otto. Mr. Donnelly used his pistols, aiming to hit each guard squarely in the head.

All the while Horrel hid behind the throne, but he fired one shot and then another, hitting his targets in the head or chest. Ultima crouched low and tried to stay out of the way. She had no sword or weapon, and her magic was primarily passive.

Akina created protection wards around her father and grandfather.

"Akina, make a ward around our uncle," said Leer. He could do simple charms and used his fire magic on the guards. He tried to help He'nico with his magic and then evaded retaliation by hiding behind a column.

The mages dressed as guards fought Otto's lightning with lightning of their own, and He'nico's fire with water. Otto could easily electrocute the mages if they were wet, but if there was too much water, he would kill everyone, friend and foe alike. The battle raged on, destroying everything in the room, tables, chairs, and all the beautiful decorations and artifacts that had been on display around the room.

Horrel shot several of the men who had accompanied Soren, and hit Donnelly in the leg, but Otto pitched lightning at Horrel. It hit the wretched man's chest, sending him flying against the wall, and He'nico lit him on fire.

Horrel shouted as he continued to burn alive, trying to find one of the basins of water. He ran toward the wall of water, but Ultima levitated him, whereupon Horrel became a floating human torch.

"That is for all the evil you've done, you demon from hell," shouted Ultima.

Ultima spotted the chairs and tables being broken near the guards. So, she levitated pieces behind the mages and used them to strike the mages on their heads. Soren's men fought the guards, evaded spells, and they all benefited from the shields Caleb had enchanted before he died.

The Duke of Vurthas was still fighting the archimage. The archimage pulled water from the basins near him and made a large ball, which he then shaped into a wave and cast it over the group, but the Duke of Vurthas repelled the wave, making it hang stationary in the middle of the room.

"Ultima, pour a basin of water over Saigai," shouted Otto. Ultima looked around. There was a basin behind Saigai, which she levitated above the man, and poured it over his head. Otto's hands glowed with lightning. He raised his arms and shouted at Saigai, "Argh, go to hell."

Lightning struck the archimage's head. The old man had a ward protecting him, but the force of the lightning strike thrust him back and sent him to his knees. The water wall disappeared.

"He'nico light him up," shouted his father. He'nico pushed away the mage he had been fighting and lit him on fire. He then focused on the archimage, and hurled fire balls at the man. Otto lifted his hands once more, with lightning pulsing through them, and he lowered it down on Saigai again. The combined magic sent the old archimage flying back, hitting the wall with a thud and falling hard onto the floor.

Soren ran over to where Saigai was lying, and held his sword on the archimage's neck.

"Tell your men to stop," said Soren.

"STOP FIGHTING!" shouted Saigai. And all the fighting stopped.

"You arranged to kill my brother, now you die," said Soren.

"NO! Don't kill him," shouted Mr. Donnelly, but Soren stuck his sword through Saigai's neck. He never let Saigai talk or ask for mercy. He gave him no chance to beg. Saigai had gloated when he confessed to orchestrating the assassination of Prince Marco, and that was all Soren needed.

Leer and Joy-Anna ran to stand by their uncle. Both children appeared scared, but said nothing. They looked from their uncle to Archimage Saigai.

Soren removed his sword from the man's throat and cleaned it on Saigai's coat. He walked over to where the rest of his friends were standing.

"Leer, Joy-Anna, what are you doing here?" asked Soren, but he was hugging both children as he spoke.

"We found out what happened to Lady Hightower, and we came to help. We are going to be your archimages, Uncle. Our place is by your side when you take your throne," said Leer.

"Your grandfather is still alive. And you still have a long way to go before you can take your place as the Kingdom's Archimages." And Soren hugged the children again. Soren stood up and led the children away from Saigai's body.

"You don't believe in giving people a fair trial. Huh, Prince Soren?" asked Mr. Donnelly.

"He confessed and then tried to kill me. I do admit I have a lot to learn," Soren went to his father's throne and sat.

"This is one uncomfortable chair. I don't know why anyone wants to kill to sit on this thing. It needs a cushion," said Soren, and he stood up, shaking his head.

"Excuse me, Your Highness, I need to sit down," said the Marshal, pointing to his wounded leg. There were no unbroken chairs left, so he simply dropped to the floor. "I needed to interrogate him," said Mr. Donnelly. "He couldn't have been the only one behind all of this."

"Why do you say that?" asked Soren.

"He's not that smart," said Mr. Donnelly, considering all who had been supporting him. The marshal lit up a cigarette and continued. "Think about it. He was too eager to fight us. His motive to kill Prince Marco was childish and easily manipulated. He was placed there as a decoy to distract from the actual person making the decisions. The Duke of Horrel is also dead. We have no one to interrogate," said Mr. Donnelly.

"Did you really think it would be this easy to get your throne back, Prince Soren?" asked Ultima.

"Do you think that was easy? Woman—a fight is never easy; our lives are always in danger when bullets, swords, and magic are involved," said Soren.

"Godson, you must listen to what Donnelly and Ultima are saying. You must be careful," said the Duke of Vurthas. Soren took a deep breath, and started to pace a little around the room.

"I'm a commander of troops. I'm a warrior. I was never trained to be King. Marco was the one prepared from birth to rule. This is all new to me," said Soren, looking at his uncle and his godfather.

"You need to take a minute, think what you are going to do, and then decide," said the Duke of Hausman.

"Godfather, I don't know who to trust," said Prince Soren.

"You trust those who earn your trust. And you must take your time to give that trust to people. For now, you have your Uncle Robert and your cousins who have fought by your side," said the Duke of Vurthas.

Ultima was listening but focused on healing Mr. Donnelly's gunshot wound to his leg.

"Mother, we needed to talk to you. We found out the mages were siding with Archimage Saigai. They were forcing us, and all the other students, to side with the archimage," said Akina.

"They were controlling the messages around the nation; Saigai only releasing to the kingdom what he wanted the people to know," said Leer.

"We had to escape from the academy to let you all know," said Leer.

"I knew it had to be Saigai," said Ultima.

"Godfather, what if this goes deeper?" asked Soren.

"That's why I needed Saigai alive, to interrogate him," said Donnelly.

"My gold is on Horrel," said He'nico.

"Let's go to the King's residence. I want to see my brother," said the Duke of Hausman, and all in the group left with them.

"He'nico, would you please take the children back to the academy. Leer, Joy-Anna, Akina and Cascade, thank you for the information, I'll be sure to investigate the matter," said Soren. He'nico nodded.

"Come Akina, you make me a proud uncle. The power of the twin leopards flow within you. You will be a powerful mage, young lady. My boys are going to love meeting you." said He'nico, taking Akina by the hand. Ultima walked with the children out the door.

CHAPTER 35

The Prince, Queen, and King

When Ultima and her companions entered the castle, servants were rushing about, each bowing to Soren as they passed. The castle steward and butler stammered their words as they talked. All of which gave Ultima a bad feeling. The last time Ultima had been inside the royal residence was the night Prince Marco had died. She didn't want to remember that night. On that occasion, Ultima had been brought up to the prince's chambers through the servants' entrance, accompanied by guards the entire time. She had never been left alone on that occasion. Although at other times, she had been allowed to wander in the public parts of the castle—at a few of the parties the King and Queen hosted, and when other clients had requested from Xawata her services. She remembered the lavishness of the palace.

This time she entered through the family entrance, toward one side of the castle. This entrance was reserved for the family and their close friends. She was shocked to see the simplicity of the foyer and entrance compared to the main entrance. The entrance to the Hightowers' manor was grander than the family entrance to the royal residence. There was a marble table right by the entryway and an exquisitely carved armoire to the left. There was a parlor to the left, just beyond the armoire, and another to the right.

They approached a grand set of stairs that rose up directly ahead at the end of the foyer, which led up to the second floor. There, the large hallway opened out to a set of spacious rooms. The servants led them through to a room that appeared to be a library, with several tables and chairs. And there they waited. The Duke of Housman walked in and ordered a servant to bring drinks. Marshal Donnelly walked around, holding his hands behind his back and his head held high. The marshal stopped next to Otto, where they stood waiting and listening. The Duke of Abernathy was already waiting in the room.

"Prince Soren, Robert, it is wonderful to see you both," said the Duke of Abernathy.

"Horatio, where is my mother? Please would you tell her we have arrived," said Soren to the steward. The Duke of Hausman lit up a cigarette before addressing the Duke of Abernathy, "Hello Noah my friend, what are you doing here?"

"I visit every day to give accounts to your mother. She trusts only a few people," said the Duke of Abernathy.

"My mother never used to be paranoid," said Soren.

"Things changed while you were away. I'm afraid the kingdom needs a strong hand," said the Duke of Abernathy.

"While it's true that Marco was supposed to be King, not me, I am not weak," said Soren.

"Nephew, you are the direct heir, the one in line for the throne. We will train you to be King. You are already an excellent leader," said the Duke of Hausman.

"Gareth," began the Duke of Abernathy, "About the charge of treason laid against you, the Duke of Horrel and Archimage Saigai wanted to send you directly to the gallows, without trial, the moment you returned from the front line. The inquiry was the only way I had to keep you alive long enough for your ambassador to step in and get you out of the country," said the Duke. His light-brown hair neatly combed, and his tailored suit made him look very attractive in Ultima's eyes.

"That inquiry had us all questioning your motives," said the Duke of Vurthas.

"Horrel and the archimage made many changes while you were gone. I took control of the House of Dukes at the request of the queen, in the hope to keep some semblance of order," said Abernathy.

While the dukes talked, Queen Elenore entered, walking slowly with the help of two maids. When Ultima saw the Queen, she gasped. The queen's eyes had sunk in her skull, and dark circles surrounded them. Her skin was bleached of color, making her appear ghostly white, and her once lustrous, shiny hair was now dull and hung limply. The old woman appeared to have lost thirty pounds, at least.

"Mother, what ails you? Oh mother, has the healer seen you?" asked Soren, helping his mother sit down.

"Soren, I can die happy now. Healer Goren comes every other day, but I have the same ailment your father has. And Healer Goren says he can do nothing for us," said the Queen, touching Soren's face.

"Bring Healer Senmonka. Where's Healer Senmonka? Uncle, look at her, this can't be," said Soren.

"Senmonka accompanied us the castle but he had to stop to get some ingredients for his medicines. He is on his way here as we speak," said the Duke of Hausman. As if hearing his name, Healer Senmonka was ushered into the room, with his pants raised almost to his chest and his white hair combed over to the side. When he saw the Queen, his hands shook, but he bowed deeply.

"You brought Otto back from the dead. In my book, you are the best healer in the world. The Queen needs the best. Look her over and tell me what you think," said Soren. Healer Senmonka nodded but said nothing. He wet his hands with some water he carried in his healer's bag, then the old healer closed his eyes, murmured a few words in an ancient language, and called for his healing. He moved his hands, first spanning to the left and then back to the right, his hands shining green and yellow as he moved them. Still, not saying anything, he moved his hands up to her head and back down the length of the queen, to her feet. Ultima watched everything Healer Senmonka was doing. After only a few minutes he lowered his hands and looked up.

"She has been slowly poisoned. I need to get the poison out of her. Since I don't know which poison she's been given, I must cleanse her body slowly," said Healer Senmonka.

"Who could be poisoning her, and how?" asked Soren.

"It could be through her food, water, or maybe she's been given a daily dose of something," said Healer Senmonka.

"Mother, have you been drinking something out of the ordinary?" asked Soren.

"No, I only drink the medicine Healer Goren left me, which was to help prevent me from getting ill like your father." The Queen shook her head as she smiled at her son, even through her pain.

"Your Highness, I need to see that medicine," said Healer Senmonka.

"Sani, go get my medicine. You know where it is," said the Queen to her maid.

"Yes, Your Highness," said one of the maids who had helped the queen enter the study. She quickly curtsied and left running. While the maid went to get the medicine, the others talked quietly, discussing aspects of the trip back to the capital. The maid, Sani, came back quickly with a small vial in her hand, which she handed over to Healer Senmonka. The healer took the vial and opened it. He cautiously smelled and tasted the contents, and then cupped the vial in his hands, which glowed yellow, and the vial glowed blue.

"Prince Soren, My Queen, this isn't medicine. This is definitely poison," said Healer Senmonka. His eyes had turned bright blue from their normal brown.

"The King has been taking the same medicine for months," said Queen Elenore.

"I'll make an antidote for you, but I don't know whether it's too late to help the King. If he's been taking the poison for so long, the antidote may be too late," said Healer Senmonka.

"Please, do whatever you can for them," said Soren. Healer Senmonka's eyes reverted to their original brown color, and he started looking for things in his bag.

"Nephew, we took care of Horrel and Saigai, but Goren is another problem entirely," said the Duke of Hausman.

"Or Goren could be the third part to this group of men trying to destroy this kingdom. Men of this type—cowards—rarely work alone," said the Duke of Vurthas.

"What are you going to do about Healer Goren? Are you going to kill him too? You must remember, if you kill him, I have no one to interrogate," said Marshal Paul Donnelly.

"You are right, Marshal. I want Healer Goren arrested for attempted assassination of the King and my mother, the Queen," said Soren.

"Just do me a big favor? Could you please avoid killing him after the arrest? We need to interrogate him and find out who is behind all of this. My gold is on Horrel, but we can't be too sure," said Marshal Donnelly.

"I won't kill him ... for now. However, you must make sure you get as much information as you can, as fast as you can. I swear to you, if my father dies, I will not make any promises," said Prince Soren.

And the marshal went to arrest Healer Goren.

❖❖❖

The ride back to the Hightowers' manor had been fast. Ultima wanted to stop at the academy to see Akina, but she knew the others wanted to go home and rest. It had been both an eventful and an impactful day. Horrel was dead, and with his death there rose the possibility of freedom for the brothel slaves ... maybe. It all depended on who held the financial loans of the business. *There were so many good people in that place,* reflected Ultima. She wanted to do something for Orrun, but she knew that before anything could happen to free the slaves of Tsestelago, the laws of the land had to be changed. And for the laws to change, they needed a new King. Maybe Soren would be that King who brought change to the land. He was unlike any other at court, that was certain.

❖❖❖

After dinner, the Hightowers gathered and enjoyed time in each other's company.

"Father, are we still leaving in a week?" asked He'nico, sipping his whiskey.

"No, we'll be leaving in three days. I spoke with Mr. Sheldon and Ambassador Glasberg after our little pow-wow with the archimage. I have no desire to remain in this kingdom any longer than I need to. I miss your mother and we must be in Yakuta before the summer," said the Duke.

"How will we be traveling back home this time? Are we crossing Alhambra by land?" asked He'nico.

"No, we will be taking a train from here to the port of Harra, on the far side of Tsestelago, and from there we will cross the sea of Ohms. En route we'll pass by the Isles of Schor although we'll not be stopping, and finally we should arrive back in Yakuta at Port Fallula," said the Duke.

"Father, you're sure you don't mind the rough seas at this time of year? We *are* in the middle of winter," said Otto.

"By the time we sail from Harra, it will be early spring. It will take us another three weeks by ship before we reach the Isles of Schor. Besides, I'll ensure we go from port to port on the Alhambran coast if that makes you happy," said the Duke.

"It sounds like a good idea," said He'nico.

"I agree, I don't want us to travel by land across Alhambra," said Otto.

"I would like to reach Yakuta in less than two months, but if we hop from port to port, it will take us about three months," said the Duke.

They all agreed, no traveling port to port—they wanted to spend as little time traveling as possible.

Later that night, Ultima and Otto were in bed holding each other. He held his hand against her belly, moving his finger gently over her skin.

"Our task here is done. Father and He'nico will leave in two days, and we will be leaving for Yakuta with them," said Otto.

"We can't leave so soon. Akina needs to finish the school year. She loves the school, and her teacher said she is doing very well. She can reach her first level ahead of time and with all the other children in her class," said Ultima.

"I'm glad she likes the magic training, but she will continue in the best mage academy in the world. The Warwick Academy in Namina, the capital city of the Kingdom of Yakuta."

"Really? Is it that good a school?" asked Ultima.

"All the royal family mages and the Hightower mages have graduated from Warwick. My mother is the Archimage of Yakuta, thus she oversees all the academies," said Otto.

"Will they accept Akina into the school?" asked Ultima.

"My mother will make sure she gets accepted. I graduated from Warwick with top honors, my daughter will graduate from Warwick as well," said Otto.

"Otto, how did you know Akina was your child?" said Ultima.

"All you have to do is look at her, she looks just like my mother. Plus, Caleb told me she's my daughter and my father told me, you told him, when we were in jail," said Otto.

"Are there no secrets between you?" asked Ultima, playfully.

"My mother is the only one who can keep a secret in this family," said Otto. They fell asleep, only to wake early the next morning to go see Akina at the academy. They waited two weeks for Akina to finish the school year, then left Tsestelago for a new adventure awaiting them.

CHAPTER 36

The Dead Sing

"Master appointed Jadro to turn the kingdoms to his dark pleasure, and Jadro has worked for years to fulfill his purpose. So far, Behui is under our master's rule, Alhambra will fall at any moment. Jadro gave us our instructions—to destabilize the Kingdom of Tsestelago. He told us to ensure Prince Soren dies, but here he is, very much alive," said one of eight hooded men, speaking from the shadows. The man shouted his words and slammed his hand on the table in front of him.

The eight hooded figures all surrounded a dimly lit table, each one had his right hand resting on the grip of his sword. The large table and eight chairs were dust free, but none of the figures were seated.

"This has been the worst debacle ever. We lost four of our best colleagues," said a second dark figure from the shadows.

"Portmore was our best assassin," agreed another.

"It is ironic. Portmore was killed by the Exotic Ultima Skylar—his next assigned target. What I want to know is how could an Exotic get married?" asked one of the figures.

"It is a loophole in the law," said Lola, the free Exotic from Xawata's brothel.

"We must close that loophole. What do you think, my Lord?"

"Our first priority is to kill Prince Soren. Jadro wants the last and only heir of Trevino from the Kingdom of Tsestelago to die. It will be much easier to usurp the existing royal line that way and place one of our own on the throne. We almost succeeded, but stupid Archimage Saigai fucked it up with his ego," said the man from the shadows.

The room was an abandoned train car storage facility. Old train cars lay in every direction and there were pieces of machinery lining the wall. They had converted the warehouse into a den of iniquity. The leader wore his hood in such a way that the others present could not see his face. Each one of the men and women in attendance had been carefully selected and groomed for their own unique roles and tasks to assist in carrying out the master plan to destroy the Kingdom of Tsestelago. The leader turned and scrutinized each of his people once more, but all that could be seen around the table were pairs of golden eyes under each hood.

"I say we kill Prince Leer next. He is a child of only eleven and it will be easier to get to him," said Lola.

"We have our assigned targets. We must kill the King's brother first. Jadro wants the child, Leer, alive," said the man from the shadows.

"Will Jadro ever come to Tsestelago? We need help eliminating the Vanquishers in our land. We can't touch them yet. They are all too well-trained, in full capacity of their talents," said a man with a black beard and a baritone voice.

"One step at a time. For now, I plan to call my favorite demon and see if it can help us kill as many mages as we can who are not already on our side," said the leader.

"Our tasks have become more difficult now that we no longer have Horrel and Saigai at court," said a woman in a dark gray hood.

"Be that as it may, you must all carry out your tasks. We cannot tolerate any more failures. The King's brother, his sons, daughter, and Prince Soren must all die. I'm happy Xawata Faan is dead. That sniveling rat kept increasing the fee of the lovelies I liked to fuck. I love greed, but not when it's applied against me."

"Lola, you did your job well, and the official ruling for Xawata was death by misadventure, from an overdose," said the man with the black beard.

"We lost Portmore, Horrel, Saigai, and Healer Goren is in jail. Those losses will not be easily replaced," said another female voice.

"Leave that to me. I have others in line for recruitment. That is all for now. You must all go and do your tasks. Soon, Soren will trust me, and Tsestelago will be in our master's hands. Jadro and I will select the next King, and the mages in the entire region will either be dead or serve our master. Go!" And all eight of the hooded figures left one at a time, through a side door.

The leader from the deepest shadows remained, and all his demons emerged from the shadows.

"Noah, darling, these useless people can't get simple things done. Jadro will be most displeased when he hears of Horrel and Portmore's deaths at the hands of an Exotic," said the tall, slim, masculine demon. Its white, curved horns shone with what little light was in the room.

"Greyleg, you know as well as I that an Exotic is one of our master's pawns. Leave the details of the control of Tsestelago to me," said the leader.

"Fine, but know I'm here to help you. All you have to do is ask and I'll do my thing," said the grotesque demon, as he licked his black fingers and long, curved claws. Noah touched Greyleg's face and smiled. Then he knocked back the last of his drink, slammed the glass on the table, and he too left the room.

It was almost dawn when the dark figure of Noah stepped out, onto the street, from the meeting with the dark brotherhood. Each man and woman owed him their lives and thus their loyalty. He ruminated over all his hard work in the kingdom that was lost in just a matter of hours. Saigai couldn't keep his mouth shut, and the Earl of Portmore wasn't as good an assassin as his mother said he was. He needed to start an alternative plan. And this time he needed to move faster if he wanted to obtain control of Tsestelago by the time Jadro finalized his control over the Kingdom of Alhambra. He needed to start again with Soren, but all in its due time. All four Vanquishers were active and fully trained in Tsestelago, so maybe the next step was to kill at least one vanquisher.

His favorite demon, Greyleg, wanted to help, but the demon had no sense of the proper way of doing things. It would leave a destructive swathe of carnage in the wake of its kills, but he needed his targets to be eliminated elegantly, making them appear like accidents. Failing *stealth*, at least it needed to be done without the world knowing it was demons doing the killing. The still-hooded Noah walked to the cemetery and found his family's mausoleum. His favorite place to rest when he was upset.

The other figures in his team were not aware of his favorite home, and he liked it that way. Noah walked through the cemetery and found the mausoleum. He looked around before opening the door and entering. Once inside, he spoke the incantation and the lid of the stone sarcophagus slid open. There was a set of winding stairs leading down.

The man shifted his weapon to his left hand and traced a spell in the air with his right. The weapon became smoke, which then spread across the wall, whereupon a painting of the weapon appeared on the wall. There were half a dozen drawings of weapons on both sides of the walls as he descended the stairs. Once he reached the bottom, the lid at the top closed and four torches lit up along the stairwell. At the bottom, the stairs ended in a dungeon where there was a casket, displaying the Duke of Abernathy's Crest on the top, in the room's corner. Noah removed his hood, opened the lid of the casket, entered, and lay down.

"Soon, Soren will trust me, just as Marco did," said Noah, the Duke of Abernathy and he closed his eyes, sure to slumber for a few hours.

Ingram Content Group UK Ltd.
Milton Keynes UK
UKHW011816250423
420711UK00003B/94